HUNTING LION

Part 3 of The Pride of Lions

ANTOINETTE GEORGE

This series of books is dedicated to my late father.

History always fascinated him and I believe that's where my love of the subject comes from. He always encouraged me to read anything and everything, just as he did, and he was a fount of knowledge on all sorts of random subjects.

I'm not sure what he would have made of all my books, but he was always supportive of everything I tried to do and I like to think they would have amused him no end.

It's many years since he passed, but I still love and miss him a lot.

The Granville Legacy: Set Two

THE PRIDE OF LIONS

Nicholas de Bresancourt was an aristocratic but penniless refugee of the bloody French Revolution from which he'd escaped as a four-year-old orphan, thanks to Francis Granville and his friends. Nicky had lost everything: family, estate and fortune, and grew up hating those responsible in France for ending countless innocent lives on the guillotine and then Bonaparte, whose megalomania had put his country through so much further upheaval and war. With no other means to support himself or earn a living, and his pride refusing to allow him to accept the charity of his wealthy adoptive family, Nicky has joined the British army, keen to serve and help end the interminable war in Europe.

With Francis as a mentor, Nicky has matured into a charismatic, capable man and a clever fighter, as well as a lover of many women. He is also trilingual, thanks to growing up and being educated at an English school with a Spanish step-mother and French step-father. He is therefore ideal material to work undercover and put his talents to use on behalf of his adopted country. First, as an agent liaising with the

Spanish rebels and guerrillas as the British endeavoured to drive the French out of Spain during the Peninsular War, and then as a full-blown spy for an anonymous Whitehall Department and Wellington, on the trail of a dangerous and ruthless French agent operating in both Spain and France: a man with a long-standing, personal vendetta against The Shadow, the man he suspected had caused the death of his father.

PART 3: HUNTING LION

France 1814

Still saddled with a wife he despises for her treachery, but besotted with the little daughter he discovers he has fathered, and now a rich man due to his unexpected inheritance, Nicky has returned to France to try and reclaim his long lost family estates and restore his former, but now ruined family home in Valenciennes. The French monarchy has been restored, Bonaparte is in exile in Elba and there seems to be peace at last in Europe.

However, Nicky has suddenly left Valenciennes and disappeared. Lord Ashcroft is at the bottom of it, as the intrepid Bella discovers and, fed up with fretting and fuming in London, she sets off in search of her errant spouse, accompanied by Jack Vallance, a young groom with an unfortunate background but some very useful talents.

From Valenciennes to Paris, and thence down to Nice, while Bonaparte's supporters secretly plot his return to France, Bella has doggedly tracked her husband. Now aware of what he's up to and the danger Frederick Bernheim presents to him, her family, and her country, not to mention herself and Jack, Bella inadvertently finds herself caught up in a desperate situation where her life, and Nicky's, are at stake and there is only Jack to help.

Historical Landscape

Dear Readers,

If you're following the continuing saga of the life and times of Francis Granville, I hope you're going to enjoy this sequel story about Nicholas de Bresancourt, Duke of Valenciennes, adopted son of Edouard and Carlotta de Mornay. The twisting and turning plot is full of even more adventure and drama, love, passion, steam, fascinating characters (some new and some familiar) and of course, a really evil villain! And lions.... Rawwwwr!

But it's also based on what I think is a fascinating period of history, both English and European. If you aren't very familiar with this era, its revolutions and wars, or it's been too long since you were at school (!), I thought I'd give you a brief overview which will help put the events in the story into perspective. There are a couple of maps here as well (in case your geography is also a bit hazy) to help you understand what was going on in Spain while the British army was there, and then back to southern England and northern France where of course the main characters have their roots.

Historical enemies down the centuries, probably since William the Conqueror invaded England back in 1066, and the English controlled part of France during the Hundred Years War in the Middle Ages...

during the 1700s, Britain and France were yet again involved in significant wars both in Europe and far from their shores. From the beginning of the century in 1704 when John Churchill, Duke of Marlborough, (the ancestor of Winston Churchill), resoundingly defeated the forces of French King Louis XIV and his allies at Blenheim, the old rivalry continued unabated. Both nations vied with each other for supremacy as they sought to either influence who ruled the various countries of Europe, or colonise new territories around the globe, in North America, Africa and the Far East, seeking both power and influence as well as new trading opportunities.

By this time, Great Britain, or more specifically the all-powerful British East India Company, controlled large areas of the Indian sub-continent as it expanded its commercial interests across south-east Asia. Army units fought various wars in alliance with local rulers until eventually, the decisive battle between the British and the French at Wandiwash in 1760 cleared the way for Britain to become the main European power in India and it became a springboard for further expansion of trade and influence throughout that part of the world, all the way down to Australia where the first convicts landed from a small fleet of British ships in Botany Bay in 1788. A penal colony was subsequently set up near there and thus began the colonisation of Australia by the British (who incidentally just beat the French to it; they landed in Botany Bay 6 days before the French expedition arrived.)

Although a British commanded army continued to have a significant presence in India after 1760 and be involved in local battles well into the 19th century, the focus of the British and French animosity turned west and both countries became embroiled in the American Revolutionary War from 1775-83.

France's help was a major contribution towards the United States' eventual victory and resulting independence. However, as a cost of participation in the war, France accumulated over 1 billion *livres* in debt, which significantly strained the nation's finances. The French government's failure to control spending compounded many other growing social problems and led to serious unrest in the nation which eventually culminated in the Revolution in 1789.

Thereafter, while Britain came to terms with the loss of its American colonies, France was in turmoil and descending into anarchy.

At the start of 1791, the other monarchies in Europe became concerned at the serious Revolution happening on their doorsteps and they considered whether they should intervene: either in support of King Louis XVI, to prevent the spread of revolutionary fervour across the continent to their own countries, or to take advantage of the chaos in France to expand their own borders. By 1792, France found itself at war with its neighbours and after a series of small victories, a series of defeats followed and this downturn allowed the radical Jacobins to rise to power and impose the Reign of Terror. This inevitably led to Louis XVI and Marie Antoinette, along with large swathes of the French aristocracy and upper classes, meeting a grisly end on the guillotine. Tens of thousands were either executed or murdered across France in under a year during this most bloody period of French history.

From 1794, the war situation turned again and improved dramatically for the French. A hitherto unknown officer from Corsica, one Napoleon Bonaparte, had been rapidly rising through the ranks. Appointed Brigadier General in 1793 at the age of only 24, he began his first full campaign in Italy in April 1796. Within a year, French armies under Bonaparte were overwhelming their enemies and one by one the European states sued for peace.

By the start of 1800, Britain was becoming ever more alone in its successful resistance to Bonaparte. Its maritime supremacy was of growing importance as a series of naval victories secured control of the Mediterranean while it endeavoured to blockade France by sea. There was a brief peace and break in hostilities in 1802, but inevitably it didn't last.

Bonaparte's star continued to rise, he was an extremely capable military general and his victories made him increasingly popular in France where he continued to consolidate his own political power. In 1804, he was crowned Emperor Napoleon I as his armies continued their conquest of Europe. However, at sea, Britain reigned supreme and Nelson's famous victory at Trafalgar in 1805 decimated the French and allied Spanish navies and prevented a potential invasion of England itself.

Fuming and frustrated by the old enemy across the Channel and hoping to isolate and weaken Britain economically, as she was trying to do to France through her naval blockade, in 1806 in retaliation, Bonaparte introduced and tried to enforce his 'Continental System'. This was a large-scale embargo on British trade, and even the post, which forbade the import of British goods into any European countries allied with or dependent upon France. But it was ineffectual as smuggling became rife and trade simply continued through Portugal, Spain and Russia, much to his irritation. As a result, Bonaparte launched an invasion of Portugal, the only remaining British ally in continental Europe. After occupying Lisbon in November 1807, he seized the opportunity to turn against his former ally, deposed the reigning Spanish royal family and declared his brother King of Spain in 1808. The Spanish and Portuguese revolted, and Britain supported them, and so began the Peninsular War.

Bonaparte did well when he was in direct charge, but problems and losses followed his departure from Spain to re-focus his attention on subjugating and controlling central and eastern Europe, leaving his Marshals to run the campaign. He severely underestimated how much manpower would be needed, and the effort in Spain was a drain on that as well as money and prestige, and ultimately failed. Especially once an able British commander, Sir Arthur Wellesley, was put in total charge of the British army, supported by the Portuguese and Spanish rebels and ruthless guerrillas. Wellesley had recently arrived after a victorious tour of duty in India. His success in the Peninsular War saw him elevated to become Duke of Wellington and eventually the two opposing military leaders faced each other at the epic Battle of Waterloo in 1815. After that, Europe enjoyed nearly a century of relative peace and prosperity.

Against this background, England in 1812 was itself experiencing a difficult year.

The war against Bonaparte and the French seemed never-ending and was a constant drain on the country's finances. In particular, action in the Peninsula was at a critical point as Wellington's fortunes continued to ebb and flow in his efforts to push the French out of Spain and back into France. In Europe, meanwhile, Napoleon's ego had made him cast his eyes east and the French were now marching on Russia. There seemed to be no stopping his megalomania. On the domestic front, the Government continuously watched public feeling, wary of radicals who sought social change and in May, to the shock of the country, the Prime Minister, Spencer Perceval, was assassinated in Parliament, in the lobby of the House of Commons. And if all that wasn't enough, tensions with the new United States caused an outbreak of hostilities between the two nations in June, known as the War of 1812 (which actually lasted until early 1815) with Britain subsequently having to defend its colonies in Canada from American incursion.

And the middle of 1812 is where Pride of Lions starts. So read on and find out what Nicky, Francis and their eccentric family and friends get up to as their tale continues some 20 years on from where Behind the Shadow finished in 1792…

Apologies for the boring history lesson, I trust it hasn't sent you to sleep! But I hope you move on and enjoy the fiction story now as much as I enjoyed writing it. And if by chance you are interested in little historical anecdotes related to events in my books, keep an eye on the blog on my website where I occasionally write further musings: https://antoinettegeorge.com/blog/

Antoinette…

Channel Coasts of England & France,
1790-1816

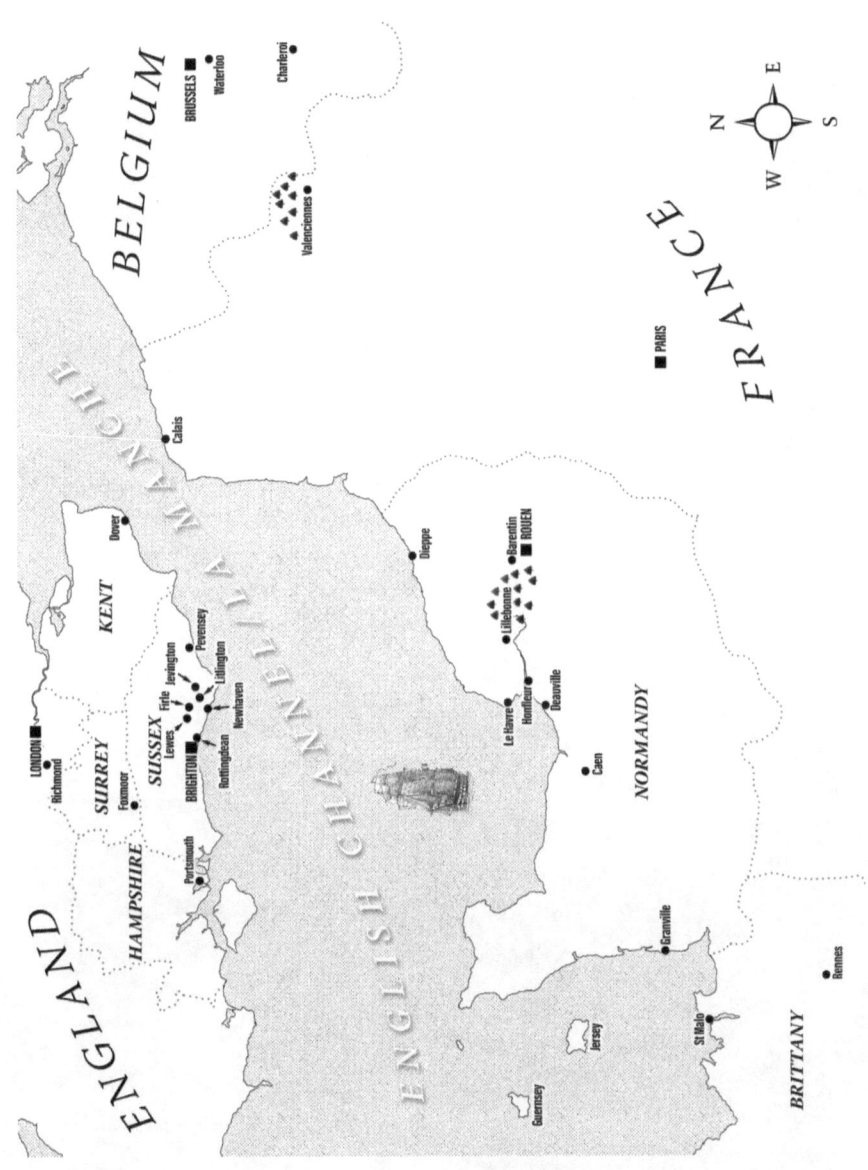

BELGIUM

BRUSSELS ■
Waterloo ●
Charleroi ●

Valenciennes ▲

FRANCE

PARIS ■

N
E
W
S

LA MANCHE

Calais ●

KENT

Dover ●

Dieppe ●

Barentin ● ROUEN ■
Lillebonne ▲

SUSSEX
Pevensey ●
Jevington ●
Firle ● ●
Lewes ●
Newhaven ●
Rottingdean ●
BRIGHTON ■
Litlington ●

Le Havre ● ● Honfleur
Deauville ●

SURREY
Richmond ●

LONDON ■

Foxmer ●

HAMPSHIRE

Portsmouth ●

ENGLISH CHANNEL

NORMANDY

Caen ●

Granville ●

Rennes ●

BRITTANY

Jersey

St Malo ●

Guernsey

ENGLAND

Southern France, Spain & Portugal with the Main Battle Sites of the Peninsular War

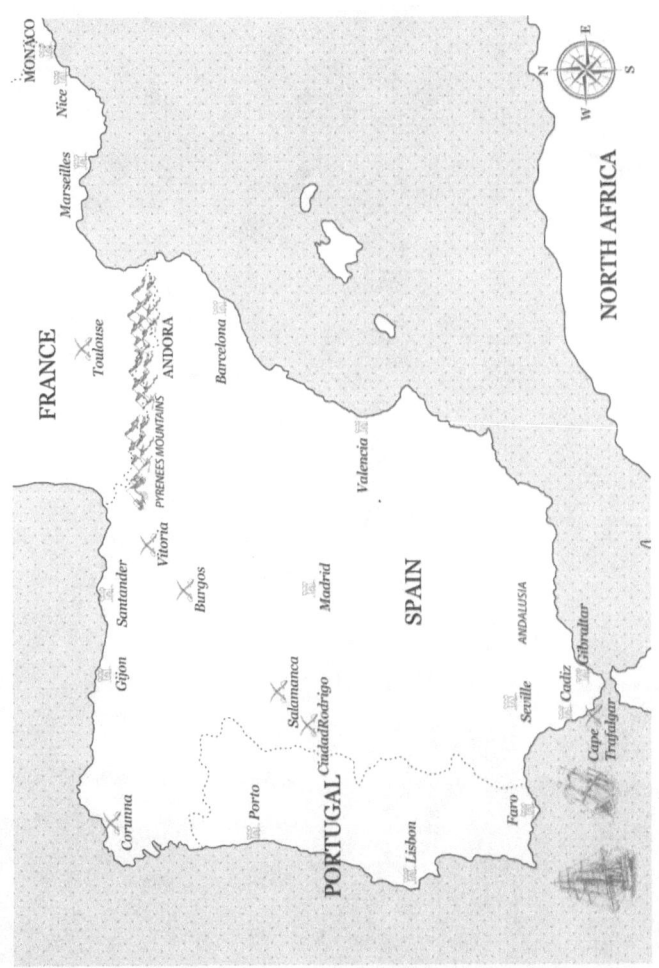

Chapter One

Frederick Bernheim was almost salivating. Although outwardly he appeared urbane, cosmopolitan, charming and appropriately restrained, as befitting the manners of a refined Gentleman, inwardly, his senses were on fire. The woman sitting opposite him was stunning. Although she appeared cool, aristocratic, ladylike and reserved in her elegant and obviously expensive cream evening gown, he sensed she had hidden depths. Her neck-hugging, single string of exquisite pearls with matching earrings and bracelets exuded class, but their understated diamond clasps set off the intense spark in her green eyes. He meant to discover more about those depths. A great deal more.

His dinner companion's arrival at the hotel bar was a sumptuous distraction, but Bernheim's mind was elsewhere. Whilst other guests relaxed with their aperitifs to watch the sun go down over a superlative view of the beautiful *Baie des Anges*, Bay of Angels, his thoughts drifted to what was transpiring at his villa, up in the hills…

He'd been more than surprised to discover none other than Nicholas de Bresancourt, the man behind his untimely departure from Spain, his empty-handed and wounded departure, as he'd reminded himself angrily, had turned up here in Nice. He'd thought the man dead, back in his villa outside Madrid, along with the whore, Carmelita. However, when his faithful manservant, Mustapha, who kept a discreet eye on all interesting movements to and from Nice, essential activity in his line of work, had reported the arrival of a tall, golden-haired man, late one night in a privately hired carriage from Paris, his curiosity had been aroused.

Mustapha, a Turk, former guard to the Ottoman Sultan himself and part of his personal retinue, was mute, having had his tongue ripped out for talking to one of the women of the seraglio, usually guarded by eunuchs. He'd been glad to escape from Constantinople with his life. Devoted to Frederick Bernheim, who had picked him up in Naples a decade previously when he was virtually destitute and seeking employment, the giant normally kept watch over his master's house in Paris, when he wasn't accompanying and guarding him on his travels or any particular missions. He'd been with him in Madrid but had left in advance of his Master's departure with his golden hoard to return to Paris to check the house wasn't being watched, ensuring Bernheim himself could return in safety; also to relay some confidential messages to other contacts in the French capital, before awaiting further instructions. But of course, all those plans had gone awry. After a recuperative and safe sojourn in Venice from where he could watch events in France and Bonaparte's downfall, His Master had taken up residence in his villa outside Nice. The devoted Mustapha had accompanied him… but had since been tasked once again with relaying confidential messages to and from Paris. Which, ironically, was why he happened to be at Bernheim's old home when the 'charity collectors' called and had departed a few days later to return to the *Côte d'Azur*.

Mustapha had soon run the golden-haired man to earth in one of the cheap lodging houses at the back of the town. Bernheim had watched quietly in the shadows, recognising de Bresancourt instantly when he'd arrived back there one evening. It was too much of a coincidence to find de Bresancourt in Nice, just when Bernheim had been plotting an escape from Elba for Bonaparte, on behalf of a group of wealthy individuals, all of whom wanted to see war in Europe resumed and the Bourbons thrown out again, either for their own commercial or political benefit. They were a mix of armaments suppliers and bankers in the main, apart from a couple of wealthy radical zealots.

Two of the armaments suppliers owned or had interests in munitions factories across Europe, so the more countries who were again drawn into conflict, the richer they became. It mattered not to them which side they supplied. As for Bernheim, he had no interest whether war recommenced or not, nor whether Bonaparte or the Bourbons ruled France, but the gold he was being paid to facilitate the former Emperor's return to French soil, was considerable, more than considerable, and that interested him over and above anything else. His plan involved laying the ground for another coup and seeing Napoleon safely ensconced in Paris once again with his old faithful soldiers guarding him. Bernheim had no intention of losing out a second time, especially to de Bresancourt, even if this amount of gold didn't come near to what he'd lost in Madrid. However, it was still a small fortune and that was what mattered.

Nicholas de Bresancourt. The French *Duc de Valenciennes*, yet also a man with close connections to Wellington, obviously one of his agents…AND with knowledge of The Shadow…which must mean all those involved with the mysterious and inconvenient death of his father, including the consequent loss of his fortune. Which had changed the course of his own life. De Bresancourt owed him in more ways than one.

De Bresancourt was therefore now enjoying his hospitality in the cellars up at his villa. Before long, he would know what the man had discovered about his dealings with the pro-Bonapartist group, as well as information about The Shadow and the woman who had killed his father. Maybe even information about the treasure his father had sought from both de Bresancourt's father and The Shadow.

Bernheim smiled a self-satisfied, malicious smile as he thought about that, casually sipping his champagne, looking for all the world as if he was merely contemplating and enjoying the beautiful sunset over the tranquil, blue waters of the Bay of Angels.

So far, beating and whipping, starvation and other physical torture from Mustapha, no mean exponent of the art, had produced few, if any, results. However, now the Chinaman had arrived from Paris with his little box of needles, Bernheim trusted he'd shortly have the information he sought. In the meantime, this little diversion here at the hotel with the enigmatic and exciting woman he'd accidentally discovered, would keep him occupied. He always needed the release of sex when one of his missions or plots was coming to fruition and the restless excitement of anticipated success bubbled through his veins, seeking an outlet. The woman had arrived like a ripe peach on his plate, at exactly the right time. And a peach she certainly was, with her long lustrous hair, her soft, creamy skin and alluring scent, tantalising his vision and senses in anticipation of devouring her. Between her discovery and that of de Bresancourt, it seemed Fate was most definitely conspiring in his favour.

Chapter Two

They discussed art, music, commerce and politics. While Bernheim found her both extremely intelligent and very well informed on all topics they touched upon, Bella's mind was racing as to how to turn the conversation to his current activities there in Nice. Apparently, idle queries about his views on the current regime in Paris and the state of French foreign affairs would elicit little comment from Bernheim and, although he seemed well informed about investments and foreign trading opportunities, he gave little away. Now in charge of Elizabeth Granville's not inconsiderable business and investment portfolio, Bella decided she knew far more than he did about the subject, but didn't push. After all, that wasn't the information she was after.

"So, *Chère Madame*, My Lady," Bernheim leaned back in his chair, sipping from his coffee. "You are most surprisingly well informed on a wide variety of subjects. It has been such a delight sharing dinner with you." He paused for a while to finish the fragrant brew and then he leaned forward and studied her face intently. "However…you have said so little about your personal 'interests' and 'affairs', or even your name. I don't suppose you would care to enlighten me?"

Bella fanned herself calmly and looked back into Bernheim's obsidian eyes, considering her words carefully. "Well, *Chevalier*," she began, "as I said, my husband has interests overseas and spends most of his time away, so I have developed my own little business interests in London to keep me occupied."

"Really? A Lady with her own business interests. Most unusual. And what sort of little business interests are they, if I may be so bold?"

Bella continued to fan herself slowly. "I suppose one could say I am in the entertainment business," she mused.

"Entertainment?" Bernheim obviously wasn't expecting that. "You mean singing, dancing, the theatre?"

"Oh, no, *Chevalier*," Bella leaned forward and her fan tapped Bernheim playfully on the hand. "Much too commonplace and there's little money to be made in that sort of enterprise, at least not at the level which interests me." She looked at him consideringly, "I have expensive tastes which I like to indulge." Her fan idly touched on her necklace of large, perfectly matched pearls. The intimation was she'd bought them for herself; Bernheim wasn't to know they lived in the sixth drawer down of the late Dowager's jewellery chest. Below the diamond drawer and then the sets of rubies, sapphires, emeralds and amethysts. The pearl drawer contained ropes of them, in all sizes and lengths with accompanying earrings, bracelets and brooches. "Actually, I am in the gambling business" Bella said softly.

"Gambling?" Bernheim's eyebrows rose. "Now that IS fascinating," he lisped.

"Mmmmm, isn't it now?" Bella replied slowly and archly. "I own two gaming houses as a matter of fact. Even though I say it myself, they are currently the toast of London, absolute gold mines." She sat back and smiled at him like a cat.

"TWO gaming houses? *Chère Madame*, I am seriously impressed! And you are so very young?" He was no stranger to flattering women but in this case he thought he was right as he looked at her beautiful, flawless peachy skin, not a blemish or wrinkle in sight. He concluded she was still in her twenties, mid-twenties, he finally decided.

"Well, why have one when you can have two, or three or four?" Bella mused coquettishly as she regarded him over her fan. "Anyway, age is no barrier to being successful in business. If I were a man, you wouldn't think it so odd" she said slightly tartly.

"Perhaps, no, obviously not, My Lady..." said Bernheim expectantly as he hovered over her title once more.

"Ah, I can see you are determined to have my name," Bella smiled at him seductively, her womanly wiles working overtime. "Well, *Chevalier*, since you are SUCH a charming and gentlemanly Gentleman, SUCH an intelligent man for a change and I have enjoyed SUCH a pleasant evening, I think I may tell you." Bernheim looked at her, completely riveted and strung out.

"You may call me *Lionesse*. That is how I am known in my saloons, *Le Lion d'Or* and *La Lionesse d'Or*." Bella paused for effect as Bernheim looked surprised at the nickname. "Of course, I always appear incognito there. I wear a lion's mask to keep myself anonymous and my life private, but down here in Nice, this little backwater," she shrugged her Gallic shrug, "I don't have to worry about irritating matters like that. Actually, if truth be known," she added conversationally as she leaned towards him, "one of the reasons I came over to Paris, then on down here, was to see if it would be worth opening more of my saloons in France, especially here, to get in before anyone else does. The place is apparently becoming more and more popular and Gentlemen are always looking for upmarket entertainment on quiet evenings...and the social scene here is very quiet and I am exceedingly upmarket..." Another seductive smile as she leaned forward, her voluptuous bosom and cleavage more exposed in the low-cut gown she'd chosen deliberately. The dress was artful, seeming plain, elegant and conservative on appearance, but when the wearer moved or bent, it became a study of enticement if one had the appropriate assets.

"*Lionesse*?" Bernheim murmured. "That is a very interesting nickname. What made you choose that and the names of your little enterprises?"

"Wouldn't you like to know!" Bella purred quietly and flirtatiously, tapping him with her fan again and looking deep into his eyes.

Bernheim leaned forward to whisper at her, "I would like to know very much, *Lionesse*."

"It's because I claw people who get in my way, or don't pay their debts," she mouthed slowly and curled her long, elegant fingers with their beautifully buffed and manicured nails into claws. "Rawr-rrrrrrrr," she purred as she carefully drew one clawed fingernail down the side of Bernheim's face and then sat back to survey his reaction. It had been a serially inappropriate thing to do and she wouldn't have dreamed of behaving like that in London, but then this wasn't London and the situation she was in was surreal.

Bernheim's body hardened immediately as his black eyes glowed. He knew she had depths, and what depths! *Madame*, how wonder-fully…feral," he whispered. "Do you scratch and claw people often?" he enquired.

"Oh, now and then, when the fancy takes me," Bella replied airily before saying slowly and maliciously darkly in a soft voice, now full of implied viciousness, "or when I need to teach somebody a lesson. I particularly enjoy that. No one cheats, crosses or owes me and gets away with it. The downside of gambling enterprises is people losing money they don't have and one cannot buy a gown or bracelet with an I.O.U. So, no one gets away with not paying what they owe *La Lionesse*, one way or another. I always take pleasure in ensuring that."

"Do you really? Now what an interesting coincidence that is," Bernheim said slowly, a salacious smile curling his thin lips. "I some-times find I need to do that too, in my line of business. But of course," he looked at his own hands with their own fastidiously manicured nails, "I don't scratch people."

"*Chevalier*, how fascinating. How do you take your revenge then?" Bella purred.

"Let's say, I have my own methods," he replied enigmatically, "but I find dispensing the punishment is so rewarding."

Bella shivered inside but kept her face smiling impassively, wondering what the hell she was getting into, apparently way out of her depth or comprehension. However, she'd experienced enough for one night, her nerves were in shreds and she'd presented her lures, telling herself she deserved a standing ovation for her acting. "Each to his own then, *Chevalier*." She sat back and sighed slightly. "Well, it has been a most delightful and illuminating evening and time has flown, but as I told you, it has been a rather busy day for me, so if you…"

Bernheim interrupted her. "*Chère Lionesse*, do you have to go? Can you not stay a while longer? It's still early." Bella merely shook her head, trying to look regretful, so Bernheim pressed on, "In which case, would you give me the pleasure of your fascinating company over dinner again tomorrow? Perhaps we can try one of the restaurants in the town, then we can continue to get to know each other better?"

Bella had been aiming for an invitation to his villa, but perhaps it was a bit premature. She therefore merely smiled. "*Chevalier*, how delightful. It is somewhat unconventional of course, slightly inappropriate for an unaccompanied Lady, but then," she appeared to consider, "we are not in London now, nor even Paris. I know you are a complete Gentleman, one of your many attractions, so I should be delighted to accept."

"Capital!" he smiled at her, almost oozing gratitude as he preened at her honeyed compliments. "*Lionesse*, please, call me Frederick." Bella smiled again and rose to leave, picking up her reticule and long evening gloves. She held out her hand to him regally as he rose and bowed over it punctiliously. "Goodnight, Frederick, until tomorrow then. Shall we say six o'clock here at the Hotel? Would that be convenient?"

"Absolutely perfect, *Lionesse*." He bent to place a kiss on the back of her outstretched hand, before turning it over to place another in her palm, his tongue describing a small circle.

Bella pulled her hand back, disgusted at such a forward action, wishing she'd kept her gloves on to dine, but then remembered herself and smiled flirtatiously and batted his hand with her fan. "Oh, tut, tut, Frederick, reeeeally!" She looked at him archly, "How VERY inappropriate of you and a bit premature for a first evening for such a Gentleman, as well as a Lady such as myself. I'm tempted to change my mind about tomorrow, but you will no doubt behave properly then, I'm sure, so perhaps I won't." She gave him the hint of a knowing smile which could be taken any way, as could the word 'properly'. She turned to go, acknowledging his bow with an aristocratic inclination of her head. "Until tomorrow then. It has been a real pleasure to make your acquaintance and have such a delightful dinner. Thank you so much."

"Bonsoir. Goodnight, *Lionesse*. Tomorrow will be even more pleasant. I promise you..."

Chapter Three

Bella hurried up to her suite, her breath now coming in distressed gasps. She lurched into her room and banged the door shut behind her, leaning against it, her eyes closed.

"My God, Your Grace, are you all right? Whatever have you been doing?" Jack sprang up from the sofa where he'd been sitting waiting for her, the notes he'd been holding falling to the floor.

Momentarily distracted, Bella stared in surprise at Jack. "How on earth did you get in here, Jack?" she asked.

Jack merely rolled his eyes at her. "Now what sort of a silly question is that to ask someone like me?" He grinned, going over to her hurriedly to take her hand and shoo her to the sofa, alarmed by her pale face. "Come along, what on earth have you been up to?" He bent to retrieve her notes from the floor where he'd dropped them. "You look like you've seen a ghost. Can I get you a glass of water or perhaps something stronger?"

Bella didn't know where to start, but she desperately needed to talk to someone and Jack was her only option. Taking a deep breath, she took his hand in her shaking one. "Jack, I have to talk to you, seriously. There's much more to what we're doing here than I told you before, but I need your word you won't speak to anyone of this…and…it's suddenly become very dangerous. I need advice and help but I have no one to turn to except you." She seemed disturbed, very shaken and on the verge of tears.

Jack looked at her with a straight face. "Your Grace, I realised a while ago there was much more going on than you let on. Oh, I know you and the Duke have obviously fallen out, but what he's doing, this man he's after, there's something about him, isn't there? The Duchess, back at Firle, told me to guard you with my life and never let you out of my sight. You don't ask that of someone if you were just coming here to France to chase after an errant husband, or visit the sights, or go shopping for frilly petticoats, or a new reticule. And then, of course, there's the curious question of why I'm here at all? Me, Jack Vallance, with my, let's just refer to it as a 'somewhat interesting background', not to mention slight lack of social graces, manners or knowledge, let alone why you have no lady's maid or proper female companion with you, or even a footman; all much more appropriate than a young groom from the stables…"

The young groom from the stables stared straight into Bella's eyes. He continued to stare at the obviously distressed woman, the silence ticking in the large hotel suite as he then picked up Bella's numb hand and eventually spoke again, quietly and seriously. "I give you my word, Your Grace, that although I'm not a Gentleman, far from it as you know, my word still means something to me; therefore, whatever you tell me will stay between us." He spoke very solemnly for a youth from the streets. "Surely you realise you can trust me now? You've done so much for me since we've been away, shown me so much, taught me so much, treated me with respect, as if I wasn't just a poor lowly groom, a boy from nowhere except the gutters. I can't believe any titled Lady, especially a Duchess, would ever do that for someone like me." Jack went down on one knee in front of Bella and looked up at her, for once a serious expression on his face. "I would do anything for you, Your Grace, anything to repay you for your kindness, both you and the Duchess of Firle. I know I was just a dirty beggar, and a thief," he hung his head briefly, "but only because I had to be. I've changed now and I want to help you, so please trust me and tell me what's going on. What's happened to you tonight, for I know something has?"

Bella pulled Jack back to his feet, both moved and reassured by his simple and heartfelt words. She tugged him down on to the sofa next to her. "Oh Jack, you're such a sweet boy, not so different from all my cousins really, despite your birth. You've done so much for me already. But yes, you're right, there is much more to all this than just chasing after a French agent who caused Wellington a few problems in Spain." Over the next half an hour, as she gripped his hand, Bella told Jack all about what Nicky had been doing in Spain. About the gold, about Bernheim, about Carmelita and what evils he believed the pair had perpetrated on the young prostitutes, everything she'd found out from Ashcroft about what had really happened to Nicky and what he knew about Bernheim. She also told Jack a bit about what Nicky had said the night they'd found him in Paris and the note he'd left her. Finally, with a deep breath she told him about her family's connection with Bernheim's father, just over twenty years before at the start of the French Revolution. She left out mentioning The Shadow, merely saying Bernheim Senior, a corrupt, venal and evil man, had been responsible for carting off Nicky's parents to Rouen Fortress where they'd perished as a result of being tortured to reveal details of the location of the family fortune; and the same had happened to the family of her father and the Duchess. She also explained how the Duke, the Duchess and her mother had helped the de Mornays and Nicky escape from France and that Bernheim's father had subsequently been killed by the Duchess although she didn't go into details of the circumstances of that. However, Bella explained it was because of what had happened to Nicky's family that her husband had a personal vendetta against Bernheim, saying he believed father and son were out the same nest of vipers. In return, Bernheim knew who Nicky was and blamed his family, meaning Bella's family, including the Granvilles, for the death of his father. At the end of her story, she sank back against the cushions with a big sigh, glad she'd finally managed to get everything off her chest so that he would now understand the reality of what they were facing.

"That's an unbelievable tale, like something Mr Crichton might have told me in my lessons with him back at his cottage at Firle. But so much makes sense now, Your Grace. When you were in Rouen, your intense interest in that ruined building? I wondered about that at the time." Jack was fascinated with Bella's tale. "But what happened tonight? You looked terrible when you returned here? Your note merely said you'd come across someone, here in the hotel, connected with your husband's activities and to keep away from you, not to let on who I really was and just to call you Aunt if we accidentally happened to bump into each other."

"I was just sitting quietly on the terrace, where you left me, when this man, a complete stranger, effected an introduction. I didn't like him, something about him gave me the chills, but just as I was about to take my leave to have dinner, he introduced himself." She grasped Jack's hand again, "Oh Jack, you'll never guess, it was HIM! Bernheim."

"WHAAAT? NO!" Jack's mouth dropped open in shock. "Bleedin' 'ell, Mum," he gawped.

"Precisely," nodded Bella. "I didn't know what to do. And then, he asked me to dine with him. It was so inappropriate, but I had to," she whispered. "So I did. That's where I've been and, oh Jack, he's the most repulsive man. I can't explain as he looks and acts perfectly normally, quite the Gentleman in fact, but it's the feeling he gives me. Nicky, my husband, the Duke, told me some terrible stories about what he was like. His personal perversions, so shocking I couldn't possibly repeat them to you, I can barely fathom them myself. But now I understand because when he kissed my hand, it made my flesh crawl." She shuddered at the memory and flexed the hand in question. She couldn't wait to wash it.

.Jack had pulled a handkerchief out of his pocket which he handed to Bella as tears ran down her face. "Oh, Jack, I flirted with him, tried to find out more about what he was doing here. He's got a villa up in the hills behind the town, but I'm so frightened. Do you think he's found Nicky? Do you think that's where he is? Why he seems to have mysteriously disappeared and just left all his belongings and money lying around?"

A storm of weeping finally overtook Bella as Jack sat and patted her hand. "Well, Your Grace," he said, "consider this. I went back to His Grace's lodgings and had a nice little conversation with the concierge, got on really well despite the language problems, if I say so myself. My French is really coming on, it's amazing, talk about practice makes perfect; well not that perfect, but I'm getting there!" He grinned proudly for a moment before continuing. "Anyway, I paid her some more rent like you said, but she's seen nothing of him. All I found out is that the Duke went out one morning, charming as you please, said good morning to her and asked the way to the local market as he wanted to buy some bread and cheese, then…poof!" Jack clicked his fingers in the air, "or *rien*, as she put it. Nothing. Gone. She hasn't seen him since. BUT…" Jack paused before delivering his big piece of news, "she described another individual who had turned up asking questions, looking for a golden-haired man who had recently arrived. A huge, swarthy, dark skinned, foreign looking man with a shaven head, a single gold earring and no tongue; a man who had to write down all his questions…"

"Oh God, Jack, the servant from Bernheim's house in Paris, it has to be!" Bella blanched.

"I think so, Your Grace." Jack now looked at Bella worriedly. "I wandered around all the local shops and bars and one or two people recognised His Grace's description. He does tend to stand out with his colouring. He bought some cheroots from a *tabac*, also some wine and fruit at the local *épicerie*, but no one has seen him for the last few days. As we wondered and you just said, it's like he's disappeared into thin air and I'm sure he wouldn't go far and leave all that money behind… nor these." As he spoke, Jack went behind the sofa to retrieve Nicky's portmanteau from which he withdrew his stiletto and a brace of pistols.

Bella recognised the jewelled stiletto instantly. It had belonged to her aunt and she knew she'd loaned it to Nicky when he went to Spain; it was also the knife she'd used to cut his bound hands that last night in Paris. "I'm sorry, Your Grace. But when I heard about the man with no tongue, I had a bad feeling, so I crept back up to His Grace's room and brought most of his things back with me. His guitar is over there by the fireplace," he nodded towards it, "but surely he wouldn't go anywhere without these?" He held out the stiletto and a pistol. "He must have gone out on a quick errand to buy some food and been abducted on the way, that's what I reckon." Jack didn't want to mention or even contemplate he might have been killed, not just abducted, although he thought it was a distinct possibility given Bernheim had already tried to kill the Duke in Spain. The only thing against that possibility was no body had been found, but Jack knew it could easily have been quietly disposed of in a variety of places.

Jack returned the weapons to Nicky's portmanteau before taking both of Bella's cold, numb hands in his, looking at her frightened face. "You have to be strong, Your Grace, but I'm almost sure Bernheim has done something to your husband."

Bella was distraught and as she burst into another round of tears, Jack swore and pulled her into his arms and hugged her. "Look here, Your Grace, you can't go to pieces now, we have to DO something, find out exactly what's happened to him and if necessary, rescue him. We'll do whatever we have to..."

Bella blew her nose and shook herself. Jack was quite right, this was no time to have a fit of the vapours. Of course, this was all supposition. She refused to consider he might have been killed. Instead, she wondered if Nicky might have gone off somewhere, or been captured by someone else, maybe the conspirators plotting to bring back Bonaparte from Elba? Because, deep down, she knew he wouldn't go out without his stiletto; she was amazed he'd even visited a market without it. Her aunt had taught Nicky to fence with a rapier way back when he was a little boy, newly arrived from France. He'd then been coached and taught to fight and shoot by her Uncle Francis, no mean swordsman, even now so she'd heard. Of course, he'd been The Shadow so was well-versed in fighting in all its forms, as a Gentleman and as a criminal, so he'd passed on to Nicky all he knew – which included NEVER to go out unarmed. Some of her earliest memories were of watching Nicky duel or fight with one or other of her aunt and uncle, in the gardens at Firle Manor or in the long portrait gallery there, or in a spacious empty upstairs room in Firle House in London. She remembered jumping up and down as she watched them, chewing one of the ends of her plaits, shouting out and encouraging Nicky in the most bloodthirsty fashion, which had amused her uncle and aunt no end, especially if he was engaged in fisticuffs with her uncle, a very different type of duel to crossing swords with her eccentric aunt.

"You're quite right, Jack," Bella sat up and pulled her shoulders back, "this will never do. My aunt and the old Dowager would despise me for being so feeble, but we must think." She paused, "I'm having dinner again with the bastard tomorrow evening, heaven help me. You must follow him afterwards and locate his villa. I tried to encourage him to take me there tomorrow, but we are just going to have dinner in the town again." She shook her head sadly, "I'm no *femme fatale*, as in a trained agent or subversive, I'm afraid," she muttered, "but tomorrow I'll do whatever it takes to get him to take me to his home. Anything, I swear. If he's got Nicky there, you're spot on, you and I will have to rescue him. We're on our own, just the two of us, so it's as simple as that," she finished forcefully.

"Well said, Your Grace, that's the spirit." Jack tried to look positive, more than he was currently feeling. "I'll tell you what, why don't we take a picnic up into the hills tomorrow anyway and have a look around? There can't be that many houses up there, surely. It will help later if I familiarise myself with the roadways and lanes that lead there from the town." Bella nodded. "You ride quite well, don't you, Your Grace?" Jack then asked.

"Reasonably, I suppose," Bella responded, "though not very much these days now I spend most of my time in London. But I used to ride out regularly over the Downs at Firle and Arlington a few years ago, also all throughout my childhood. I'm afraid I was a terrible hoyden...why?"

"Well, I thought I'd hire a couple of horses, rather than a gig or a trap. We can go much further and get down tracks we could never access in a gig. We can be a bit more nosy. Can you manage with an ordinary saddle or do you want a lady's one? I know it's not conventional, but it..."

"Didn't I say I was a hoyden?" sighed Bella. "I'm past worrying about convention now. So long as I don't show myself up here at the hotel, no one will know or care. That's a good idea, Jack, we'll set off first thing. I'll order a picnic when we have breakfast, then you can pick it up when you return with the horses. Now, go off to bed as it's late – I'm tired too. Not that I think I'll sleep much after all this, but we must try."

Jack nodded and rose to go, bowing and kissing her hand tenderly. "Sleep well, Your Grace – and please try not to worry too much."

"I'll do my best," Bella sighed wistfully. Just as Jack had reached the door to go to his own room, Bella suddenly thought of something. "Oh, by the way, Jack, how DID you get in here? Did you get a duplicate key from the maid?"

"Who needs a duplicate key?" He winked at Bella. "There's not a door can keep Jack the Lad out, nor a lock I can't pick. I was just learning how to crack these big, new, heavy iron cabinets, safes, with complicated locks, when the Duchess found me." Then he looked serious, "However, I give you my word, Your Grace, I was telling the truth before. I've not thieved anything other than Mrs Farthing's pastries and biscuits since I met Her Grace. You CAN trust me. I might have come from the worst stews in London, but I promise, your family secrets are safe with Jack Vallance." His bright sherry eyes looked straight at her.

"I know they are, Jack," Bella whispered. "I believe you. Thank you." Bella blew him a kiss and he winked back at her before disappearing from the room.

Chapter Four

The next day, Jack appeared at the hotel with two sturdy ponies in tow, then collected the waiting picnic and met up with Bella a few streets away. Much to his amusement, in a narrow alleyway, she removed her skirt to reveal a pair of tight men's breeches tucked into the sensible boots she'd hurriedly gone to buy from a local shop beforehand. They set off towards the rocky hills behind the little town.

As they traversed what were little more than mule tracks in many places, they viewed where *La Grande Corniche* now began as it curled its cliff-fronted way towards Monaco, Menton and Italy in the east, following the ancient Roman route known as Via Julia Augusta. Bella told Jack it was the road Bonaparte had apparently commissioned for his troops to march along to facilitate his ambitious Italian campaign in 1796 and the pair of them marvelled at the men still working on it here and there in the distance. To them, now quite high up, it was a wonder of road engineering as they could see that the road was on a no more than a cliff face.

Deeper into the hills, away from the new road, little houses were dotted here and there alongside small allotments or fields where farmers grew vines or local produce; a few chickens scrabbled around the odd barn or ramshackle stable. Behind tall gates, some newly built, large villas could be seen, screened by shrubbery and palm trees. The pair followed tracks that lead right to the top and sat to eat their picnic, gazing at the stunning views of the Bay and the beautiful Mediterranean spread out below them, blue sea glittering in the sunlight. It was an even more breath-taking view than from the hotel terrace and finally Bella understood why her Uncle Reynard had rhapsodised so much.

They sat and talked over their simple meal of bread, cold meats and cheese with fresh, ripe peaches. Jack couldn't eat enough of them since he'd discovered them for sale everywhere on the stalls around the town. While insects hummed and buzzed around them, Bella asked Jack to tell her more about his childhood and how her aunt had found him and taken him to Firle. She felt the time was right, now that she had come to know him better and there was a real feeling of camaraderie between them.

Just as Cat had been, she was in turn appalled, distressed and amazed to hear details of the story of his terrible life in the gutters of the Dials, some of the worst slums of London and home to a hard core of beggars, pimps, whores, thieves, murderers and general villains of all descriptions.

Hesitantly, Jack related how his mother had died and left him to fend for a little half-brother and half-sister when he was about eight or nine, he didn't know for sure; somehow, he had taken in a couple of little boys, brothers, who'd lived downstairs from the small, rat-infested tenement garret room Jack and his siblings existed in when the boys' mother, another prostitute like Jack's mother, had died. Then one day, he'd found a pair of little girls, no more than tots, begging in a doorway, emaciated and literally starving, so he'd taken them in as well. All seven had lived in his garret room and struggled to survive and look after each other, though they all relied on Jack, the eldest. The little children had begged; he'd found what work he could, whether holding horses for the gentry or cleaning out stables or privies, anything that would earn him a coin; otherwise, he'd thieved. He'd been forced to, if it meant money for their rent and food. It had been a hard existence, literally living from day to day, until that fateful one when he'd tried to cut the reticule of the Duchess of Firle near Bond Street, desperate for some money to get medicine for one of the children who was sick.

Something about the desperate, painfully thin and dirty boy had got to Cat, so instead of handing him over to the Magistrates, when he'd begged and pleaded with her not to because his little family would all starve without him, she'd gone with him to his garret to see if he was indeed telling the truth. She'd been overwhelmed and distraught when she found it was exactly as he'd told her. It took her all of five minutes to decide to haul the bedraggled, freezing and half-starved children from there and transport them down to Firle, where she'd found homes for the little ones among the estate tenants or neighbouring country folk. Jack had found bona fide work for the first time in his life, as a lowly stableboy, intent on learning how to be a proper groom. Desperate to better himself, he was watched with interest by the Duchess, herself curious about this kind-hearted and determined boy. She had arranged for his schooling in the local village and extra tutoring from an old retainer of the family who had taught the young Granville boys before they'd left for Eton and who still kept an eye on them during the school holidays. Jack had blossomed beyond all expectations in his new environment, mentally and physically – so now, here he was, trying to repay Marie-Catherine Granville for saving and literally changing his life.

Bella was stunned and overwhelmed by his story. She said little other than she was finally glad to know about it, simply because she didn't know what else to say. Where he'd come from and how he'd managed to better himself, even if he was still working in the stables at Firle, was astonishing. She finally said she was glad her aunt had chosen him to accompany her and she didn't know how she would have managed without him. Hugely embarrassed at her praise, Jack endeavoured to change the subject to more mundane matters and focus on the remains of their meal.

Everywhere was quiet in the hot afternoon sun and Jack pulled off his shirt and lolled back against a rock, looking at the view and dozing in the heat, another new experience he revelled in. Bella simply sat quietly under a shady tree and considered the evening ahead, wondering if Nicky was inside one of the shuttered houses they had passed on their way. She was frightened but equally determined to inveigle herself deeper into Bernheim's acquaintance to gain an invitation to his home. Some deep, inexplicable inner feeling told her Nicky wasn't dead and Bernheim knew either what had happened to him or his whereabouts. Moreover, despite everything that had happened between them, she knew she would go to any lengths to find her husband and rescue him if he was in trouble, which she now believed he was. She'd told herself her imagination was running away with itself, but she simply couldn't shake off the chilly sense of foreboding that wouldn't go away.

Bernheim both fascinated and repelled her. He was obviously a well-travelled and extremely clever individual, fastidious in his manners, appearance and dress; not so much as a speck of dust or crease had marred the perfection of his beautifully tailored jacket and waistcoat and his cravat was a masterpiece even Benjy, her uncle's sometime valet, would have envied. He was also excessively punctilious, to the extreme. He'd mentioned over dinner his schooling in Austria and she'd put his almost militaristic mannerisms down to that. However, under all his various idiosyncrasies, she sensed a leashed power about him, a restless energy and deep passion. As an attractive woman, Bella was used to dealing with men, their effusive addresses, attempts to flirt and more, but now she was experienced in bed matters, courtesy of Nicky's practised endeavours, she could sense and see it in those black, obsidian eyes that had looked at her as if he was mentally removing her clothes and assessing what else he'd like to do with her; he'd licked those thin, cruel lips of his as he'd talked to her and Bella didn't need Nicky's warning to somehow know the man's perverted lusts simmered beneath the surface of his outwardly urbane, polite, courteous and gentlemanly exterior. She shivered as she contemplated their forthcoming dinner and what she suspected Bernheim would want from her afterwards.

Bella had kissed a lot of men, especially over the past year, in her efforts to shake off the hold Nicky seemed to have over her. Some of the most charming and flirtatious rakes amongst the Ton had amused and tried to take her fancy, endeavoured to please her, young and old.

Her aunt would no doubt be both amused and aghast at what she'd done in unseen quiet corners at balls and parties and out in gardens where no one else could see, although it had never gone further than kisses and some exploratory caresses. That was why there was a betting book about her. However, accomplished and good-looking lover that he was, Nicky was a hard act to follow, as legions of women could have told her, so most other gentlemen had left her stone cold, unimpressed, even occasionally disgusted. Not one of them could hold a candle to how she felt when Nicky kissed her – because she loved him. That was the difference, she realised. Nothing she did or tried could change that fact, no matter how many accomplished rakes and lotharios did their best to try.

The thought of kissing Bernheim made her feel slightly nauseous, but she was resolved to do it if it furthered her investigations. That manipulative bastard, Ashcroft, would be proud of her, she decided. Her final thoughts before she too dozed off in the heat, were of her last night with Nicky in Paris and the way he'd made love to her, before they'd fallen asleep. Even now she could remember how it felt to be held in his strong, protective arms, the way he'd kissed and caressed her and then moved inside her. Surely he couldn't pretend he didn't have feelings for her after the way he'd made love to her? He couldn't hate her, or could he? She sighed as desire for him curled round her belly and her heart ached as she drifted off to sleep.

"Your Grace? Wake up, Madam, Your Grace...?" Hands shook her. "Your nose is going rather pink." Bella came to dazedly as Jack peered laughingly down into her face. "You're not in the shade any longer, Your Grace, so you've caught the sun." His own tanned features grinned down at her, "We need to make a move if you're to be back at the hotel in time for your dinner appointment." The residue of her pleasant dreams rapidly dissipated. Bella allowed Jack to raise her up and they returned to where their ponies were themselves dozing in a little shady stand of trees.

They slowly made their way back down the hilly tracks, still silent in the afternoon sun, only the sound of crickets intruding into the peaceful scenery. As they trekked along in companionable silence, Bella's mind again wandering to her forthcoming dinner, Jack suddenly pulled up his mount when they reached a wooded pathway. He sat still for a minute or two, his head cocked to one side. "Did you hear that, Your Grace?" he turned to Bella whose own pony had now pulled up alongside his.

"Hmmm? What?" she mumbled, her mind far away.

"I thought I heard a cry," Jack said quietly, his head still bent to listen in the silence.

"I didn't hear anything," Bella said, but they sat quietly for a further few minutes, the hot air only full of the sound of crickets humming and lazy buzzing bees. Jack shrugged and let his pony move on. His ears were far more attuned and alert than his mistress's and he could have sworn he'd heard a cry. No, it had been more like a scream...a few minutes before. It had come from a distance, drifting across the hot silent air. He shuddered. Perhaps his mind was playing tricks on him, still full of the amazing and lurid story he'd heard from the Duchess the night before. He shrugged to himself and paid more attention to where his pony was now picking its way down a rocky pathway, but nevertheless, instinct told him he HAD heard a scream. An agonised, long scream. Obviously, horror was just as prevalent in this quiet, rural foreign backwater as it was in the Seven Dials in London.

Chapter Five

Before Bella left her room, Jack knocked and entered. He whistled when he saw her, making her smile. "Do you think he'll approve?" she queried with a grin, feeling like she was dressing to go to her execution and was putting on a brave face.

"Absolutely!" he smiled back at her. His face then turned serious. "Just remember, Your Grace, wherever you go, I'll be there watching. You won't see me, but know I WILL be there. Whatever happens," he paused, "if you leave together, I'll follow. If you come back here alone, I'll follow him and see where he goes. Wherever that is, I'll follow until he goes back to his villa. Then I'll come back here and we can decide what to do."

Bella nodded and ruffled his hair. "Thank you, Jack. It's reassuring to know I have a guardian angel at my back, even if he is slightly naughty and always hungry!" She chuckled then smiled at him as she turned to go, "Wish me luck, Jack; oh, and don't forget to lock the door behind you…" and with a brave, albeit slightly hysterical laugh, she sailed out.

He was waiting for her as she descended the stairs to the hotel foyer. Immaculately dressed as before, Frederick Bernheim looked up at the woman in the stunning, midnight blue, shot silk dress and his lips curled in appreciation. The shimmering threads of the material caught the light as she moved, the material clinging to her body, enhancing the tall, voluptuous figure as she insinuated herself downwards, no few eyes watching her. A delicate row of sapphires and diamonds glittered around her neck and wrist, small stones sparkled in her ears and a few more littered her gleaming, upswept curls. She looked the epitome of an upper class, Society Lady; such restrained, understated elegance; but Bernheim fancied he could perceive the sensual allure that rested beneath.

Bella held out her gloved hand. "*Chevalier*, how delightful to see you again."

He raised an eyebrow at her as he bowed and bent low to kiss the glove punctiliously, a feeling of superiority over the other staring men in the foyer that this stunning woman was his companion for the evening, boosting his ego. "Frederick, please, *Lionesse*. It is more than delightful to see you again, too," he oozed, "and may I say how exquisite you look? We should be going to a palace, a Society *soirée* or at the least a refined establishment, not the meagre offerings in this small town; you will outshine, nay dazzle, every other diner out tonight."

Bella tilted her head. "Thank you…Frederick," she purred, as he took her hand and escorted her out to his waiting carriage as if she were the Queen of France.

They dined in a discreet but elegant little restaurant, with views that overlooked the Bay. Once again, they discussed current affairs and politics, art and culture while attentive waiters hovered, but, as with the previous evening, once they got to their coffee, the conversation turned to personal matters. In the meantime, Bella had achieved nothing by fishing around Bernheim's views on the return of the Bourbons and whether France had really seen the back of Bonaparte, so she'd consequently given up.

"I see you've been out in the sunshine today. Would you consider it indelicate if I inferred your nose is a trifle pink?" Bernheim smiled at her flirtatiously.

"Oh yes, I forgot my parasol and my nephew dragged me off on a picnic. Wretched nuisance," Bella tutted dismissively, "him *and* no parasol. I do hope it doesn't peel."

"I thought he was going off sailing or fishing?" enquired Bernheim.

"Yes he was...is...but the boat apparently needed a minor repair today, or the nets, or some such thing, I really didn't want to know the details, so they won't now go until tomorrow or the day after. You know young boys, they need to be kept entertained; he bores easily," she waved her hand airily.

"Is that what he's doing this evening then?" Bernheim asked lecherously, "Being entertained?"

"Really, Frederick," Bella bantered, "the boy is only just fourteen!" But then she smirked seductively back at him. "However, I think he may have found himself some little amusements for the evening at my encouragement, so don't worry about him, it's all part of his French education after all. He really is growing up so quickly; his mother has no idea..."

Bernheim leered at her. "And what do *you* do for entertainment, *Lionesse*? All by yourself, with no husband to keep you...entertained?"

Bella sat back in her chair, alternately sipping her coffee and fanning herself. Her green eyes narrowed and she looked directly into Bernheim's black glowing ones, like hot coals. "Well, of course, I'm very busy with my business interests. But for entertainment," she shrugged slightly as she raised her eyebrows and widened her eyes to look at the man questioning her, "it depends if I come across anyone who wants entertaining and who can entertain me in turn, when I get bored." Bella purred and licked her lips suggestively, watching Bernheim watching her as she ran her tongue over her inviting smile.

Bernheim's eyes narrowed fractionally and then gleamed. "Really? And have you found yourself bored here in Nice, or even Paris, perhaps looking for some entertainment?" Bernheim reclined back in his seat, watching the beautiful, aristocratic woman across from him, waiting for her answer.

"Well, of course, Nice is such a backwater, albeit a picturesque one. I did, of course, need a rest from all our racketing around in Paris, but one only requires so much rest before one gets bored, like one's nephew."

Bella toyed with the jewels around her neck and continued to sip her coffee. She looked the epitome of relaxed grace. Inside her, the dinner was churning in her stomach. She knew her answers now would potentially determine the course of the rest of the evening or the following day. Finally, she burned her bridges. "As a result, I'm now looking for something to amuse me while my nephew explores the delights of the seaside. Perhaps you could recommend something nice for me to do on one of his fishing days? The ennui at the hotel is so tedious, all the ladies there just want to discuss their ailments, or gossip cattily about people I don't know. They don't have a brain between them to be worth bothering with at cards. As for the shops here, they aren't even worth a consideration unless one wants to buy a seashell, a bunch of lavender or a peach…"

Bernheim was totally engrossed in this conversation, desire for the woman now heating his blood. Her answer was the subtle invitation he'd been longing for. "Hmmm," he lisped softly. "Well, there are wonderful views of *La Baie des Anges* from my villa. And of course, it's very private, that's the beauty of the hills behind the town, no nosy busybodies minding other people's business. We could have a wonderful lunch in the gardens or on the terrace, then perhaps a game of cards or two? I consider myself quite an adequate player. Of course, there is always an afternoon '*siesta*' in the shade, if the heat is too fatiguing. The Spanish have precisely the right idea about how to spend the hot early afternoon hours, you know."

Their game of cat and mouse continued. "Do they really?" responded Bella conversationally. "You must enlighten me, but wouldn't that interrupt the business affairs you carry out at your home? Isn't that what you are doing here in Nice?"

"Not at all, My Dear *Lionesse*. I actually find myself free of meetings and commitments over the next few days, as luck would have it. I do have some unpleasant other business to finish off, but that will soon be dealt with and then I can give you my undivided attention."

Not by the flicker of an eyelash did Bella betray the flash of worry that coursed down her spine at Bernheim's remark. "Unpleasant other business, Frederick? Surely not in such a lovely, quiet place as this?" Bella's sixth sense was on high alert.

"Oh, nothing really," the thin lips curled. "I just have some vermin to deal with in my cellar. I need to supervise my staff in eradicating it once and for all."

"Vermin?" Bella shuddered delicately. "Rats?" she queried, "Or something else? Urrrgh, I despise rats. There are so many in London and Paris, they seem to get everywhere. My cat tends to bring one in to the garden from time to time and toys with it before putting it out of its misery; disgusting habit. I hope they aren't visible in your villa?"

Bernheim waved his hand airily. "Oh no, merely in the cellars. As I said, nothing for you to worry about, My Dear. It's just a particularly large one that has suddenly appeared unexpectedly, but don't worry we'll have dealt with it before you arrive and then I am at your service."

The conversation was quite surreal; how she didn't show any give-away reaction, Bella never understood. She was talking about Duchess, Nicky's cat. That the 'rat' Bernheim had in his cellar was Nicky, she was absolutely positive. It was the way he spoke about it. She just intu-itively knew. He made it sound so banal, it was quite unbelievable. The man was seriously sick in the head.

Her first reaction was panic, overwhelming panic, then terror, espe-cially the way Bernheim had referred to 'dealing with it', but while Bernheim summoned over a waiter for more coffee, Bella took a deep breath and pulled herself together. She simply had to persuade Bern-heim to take her to his villa as soon as possible. Maybe she could distract him while Jack tried to rescue Nicky before any harm came to him, if it hadn't already. Her mind didn't want to think about that, nor what she would have to do with Bernheim, but whatever it took, she would do it. There was no alternative. Her mind was filled with images of her uncle's terribly scarred back and the story her aunt had told her about how he'd come by it, courtesy of Bernheim's father and his lieutenant. Then she remembered Nicky's description of the whipped and beaten prostitutes; it was all too coincidental. Her feeling of sickness increased.

Bella fanned herself, unsure if she could manage to pick up her refilled coffee cup, her hand was shaking so much; instead, she sat back and smiled seductively at Bernheim. "So, Frederick, it appears you know how to relieve my ennui while my nephew fishes. You've no idea how appealing I find that," she said softly.

"Oh, it will be my pleasure, I can promise you, Dear Lady," his black eyes glittered. "I'm absolutely sure it will be something that will please us both," he lisped.

Apprehension crept up her spine at the completely inappropriate turn the conversation had taken, although of course she had known where it would go. She'd never dream of speaking or behaving with anyone in London like this, even anonymously masked in her gaming saloons, but then this was a desperate situation and she'd deliberately set out to encourage the man. Bernheim's eyes raked over her, down her body, pausing briefly on her breasts, then up to her lips again, staring at them. He shifted in his chair slightly as his body responded to his lascivious thoughts. She watched closely, though not obviously; she knew what he wanted her to do to him.

"Will it really? Then I look forward to it, immensely," Bella purred. "Indeed, Frederick, I can't wait. Perhaps tomorrow?" she said seductively, rising slowly from her chair. "In the meantime, kindly excuse me for a few minutes?" Bernheim stood automatically as she headed off in the direction of the Ladies' Retiring Room. Bella got there just in time and proceeded to throw up her dinner into a chamber pot. The thought of kissing Bernheim was bad enough, but to do to him what she'd taken so much pleasure in doing to Nicky, was too much for her and she sank down onto a sofa, weeping. Yet again, Ashcroft's words permeated her mind when he'd referred to his female agents: '...they will also do ANYTHING to get the information we need...' and Bella finally understood what he'd meant. She also realised what a protective bubble she'd lived in all her life: loved, cossetted and protected, surrounded by luxury, servants, every convenience, wanting for nothing...unlike poor Jack and his siblings. Her understanding of sex and the carnal world was now in a different league to what she'd studied, giggled over and read in books. Reading versus reality, especially the pleasant and unpleasant of the latter, were poles apart.

She wondered what her worldly-wise aunt would do in her situation and the answer was obvious. Whatever it took. That amazing woman had KILLED men to rescue her uncle, in cold blood, as well as in a fight. She'd also told Ashcroft airily she was no ninny at Almack's, nor a helpless woman like so many of her naïve peers, so, pulling herself together, Arabella de Bresancourt blew her nose, washed out her mouth, wiped her face, splashed some cold water on it and then pinched and patted her cheeks to regain some colour. Then she fished around in her reticule and applied more of the rose-tinted salve to make her lips shine enticingly, dabbed some more scent on her neck and re-sooted her eyelashes, uncaring of the mess she left in the little retiring room. Finally, she took a deep breath and sauntered back to their table, as if she hadn't a care in the world.

Bernheim peered closely at her as his nose twitched when it picked up her freshly applied scent. "Are you feeling well, My Dear?" he enquired. "You're looking a little flushed?"

"Oh, just a trifle warm, it is rather close and stuffy in here," Bella shrugged dismissively and started to fan herself. "Perhaps we could go for a short stroll in the fresh air before I return to the hotel? The Bay always looks so lovely in the moonlight and the breeze will be refreshingly cool."

Bernheim's eyes gleamed. "What a splendid idea." He rose, holding out his hand to her. He'd noted her glistening lips as well as the fresh scent and knew an invitation when he saw and smelled one. His body was almost beside itself in anticipation.

They sauntered along the deserted road that ran alongside the beach. A detached part of Bella's mind thought how wonderful and romantic it would be if she was there with Nicky, but those thoughts fled when, in the dark shadows of a pavilion, Bernheim pulled her into his arms and started to kiss her. She shut her mind to think of nothing but amusing images of Terrie chasing the cat around her little sitting room and knocking all the furniture and ornaments flying, as she forced herself to moan suggestively in Bernheim's arms, responding to his kiss with ardour and passion, one hand digging deep into his shoulders and back, the nails of the other, nails she'd deliberately filed to be more pointed, reaching up to claw into his neck.

Bernheim's head reared back as he felt her nails on his skin. "Aaaargh, *Lionesse*," he shuddered, "I knew you would have hidden passion underneath that demure exterior of yours," and he leaned down to bite Bella's neck like a vampire. "I can't wait to experience more of you," he grasped her hand in a grip like steel, "but mind your talons, I personally don't like to be marked."

"Oh, Frederick," she breathed, "I'm so sorry. It's been a while since I've met a man who can make me feel so much, a man who can light my fires." Bella groaned and pulled his head down to her lips once more as she rubbed herself against the front of his body like a cat in heat.

No one saw the dark figure huddled in the shadows across and further down the road. He stood with a grim expression on his face, his hands balled into fists. He'd been hovering round the back of the little restaurant, outside the high, curtained but open window of the retiring room when Bella had gone in and he'd heard someone retching and then weeping. He'd known it was her when he heard her forlornly sob her husband's name as she cried. It had been a long, long time since he'd felt such anger, not since he'd come across a pair of little children clinging to each other, callously abandoned, shivering, starving and sick in a stinking doorway in a Seven Dials alleyway. But he could do nothing except watch and wait, praying his Mistress knew what she was doing.

They returned to Bernheim's carriage. "Are we going to your villa?" purred Bella.

"I'm looking forward to entertaining you at my villa in a few days, but for tonight, perhaps at your hotel? The journey up to my villa in the hills is difficult at night, almost impossible in a coach, I'm afraid, as the roads are merely tracks in some parts, so it's way too risky with such a precious passenger," Bernheim replied apologetically.

Bella cringed inside but her acting was worthy of the best London theatre. "Oh, Frederick, that would have been lovely, but my nephew is next door. I cannot risk it. Even if you have a room there, if I'm not in mine..." she paused in apparent frustration. "The proprieties, you understand, he might hear, or might want me...a trifle difficult..." she looked at him with such regret on her face. "However, tomorrow morning?" she licked her lips and made a slight sucking sound, "I simply can't wait days. Could I not visit tomorrow? I'm so bored here, so restless again, I might even consider going back to Paris or on to Florence after all."

Bernheim thought about the man in his cellar and sighed. He wanted him out of the way before indulging himself with this beautiful creature, but he was so tempted. It had been a while since he'd had a woman who matched his desires and this one was something special, something that rarely crossed his path unless he paid a small fortune. Even then, he didn't think he'd experienced such beauty, such intelligence and such similar carnal tastes all in one package; he was on fire for *Lionesse*. Looking at those lips and mouth was driving his imagination into orbit. If the man in his cellar continued to be so difficult, it could take several days to get the information he wanted as he didn't know whether any associates he might have in Madrid, for example, would also need sorting out. He couldn't wait that long, couldn't risk her disappearing off somewhere, like Italy or even back to Paris or London, somewhere he couldn't follow at such a critical time in his other plans. He pondered. She wouldn't ever have to know about what was transpiring in his cellar. She was just a bored and ignored married woman after all, even if she was more intelligent than most of her kind, another one with an unsatisfied appetite, looking for a diversion to appease it, very discreetly. She was therefore ideal for his own requirements. A short affaire to slake their mutual lust and then they'd go their separate ways and she'd return to her home far, far away, never to be seen again.

"Well, My Dear, you are such a divine temptation and I'm just a mere man, so perhaps I could make a start on dealing with my vermin in the morning, then perhaps an afternoon's diversion with you? Luncheon and a siesta as I suggested, I think we can forget the cards. How does that appeal? Would you like that?"

"Wouldn't YOU, Frederick?" Bella purred. "I'll ensure my nephew will be out ALL day, fishing or sailing somewhere, so that would be perfect."

He leaned forward and ran his hand and fingernail down her neck, smelling her, feeling her shiver, delighted she responded to his touch so wonderfully. "Perfect indeed, My Dear," he laughed lecherously and Bella's skin crawled at the horror to come, despair and frustration filling her soul that visiting Bernheim's lair and finding Nicky was going to take even as long as that. She desperately hoped he would survive the morning.

Bernheim kissed her again before he helped her out of the dark carriage at the hotel. His hands roved over her body, lingering on her breasts, then found their way inside her bodice, pinching her nipples hard. Bella couldn't help herself, she shuddered and moaned. A hand then crept down her legs and up, underneath her skirts. He'd felt her response and revelled in it. "Ah, so responsive to my touch, Lovely *Lionesse*; truly, I cannot wait for our *siesta* tomorrow and neither can you, I can feel it...sense it!" He assumed her shudder was one of pleasure and the moan from his vicious fingers one of ecstasy. The reality was disgust and repulsion.

Bella didn't know whether to stop him or let him continue, images of Nicky being tortured now alive in her brain, and she wanted to ensure Bernheim came for her as soon as possible in the morning. However, her stomach was roiling again as there was only so much she could take of his pawing. The hand crept higher up her leg, reaching the top of her stocking and playfully tweaking her garter before roaming further. She gasped and he smirked. It continued higher until it reached the top of her thigh and a fingernail scratched her sex, making her jerk. He felt it, presuming she was now as excited and on fire for him as he was for her and his heated blood bubbled in his veins. "Aaaah, Frederickkkk," Bella moaned again, "you are SUCH a temptation, but not here, not now; tomorrow. As soon as you can, hmmm?" She pulled away with a teasing smirk. "I can dream of you all night, fantasise about what you'll do to me...what I can do to you... but I won't satisfy myself, I'll be so wet, so swollen, so hot and ready for you tomorrow...desperate..." she whispered tantalisingly.

His black eyes glittered down at her in the light of the coach lamp and watched as she licked her lips as she'd done so temptingly before. She was almost too much for him. He pulled down the front of her gown and suckled her breasts, then bit them, hard, listening to her mewled response. "I can't wait, oh, Mon Dieu, *Lionesse*, you taste and smell divine, a veritable banquet...so many courses, so much we can try..." Bella felt bile in her throat.

She straightened her dress and artfully shooed him off. As he helped her alight from the coach, she tapped him on the arm flirtatiously and looked at him from under her lashes. "Until tomorrow, Frederick. What time can you come to collect me? I'll be waiting impatiently, all morning." Then she leaned over finally to whisper in his ear, "I told you, I don't want to have to please myself, so don't keep me dangling too long and spoil YOUR pleasure…"

"I'll send my coach at noon, My Dear. That should allow me time to sort out my infestation, which I ABSOLUTELY have to do, no matter how much of a temptation you are. You can prepare yourself and be patient. Expectation is everything, as is being made to wait, as you know…restraint and torment are such delightful appetisers to the main course. But make sure you DO wait for me," he ordered in a suddenly rasping whisper, his black eyes alive and glittering. "I promise I will make it worth your while, many times worth your while…" he whispered finally as he kissed her hand punctiliously and watched as she nodded to him, then sashayed up the steps into the hotel.

Chapter Six

Bella wanted to run to her suite but she had to behave appropriately as she made her way from the carriage, up the steps into and through the hotel foyer, unsure if he was watching her. She'd tried as best she could to tempt him without pressing too hard, which would cause suspicion she was sure but she couldn't believe some of the salacious things she'd said to him, nor his parting words to her which were both frightening as well as nauseating; now, she would have to wait. However, tears were rolling down her face as she finally fell through the door of her room, her whole body reacting to the events of the evening and what had happened in the carriage. Jack was waiting for her and he ran to put an arm around her, helping her to a seat. He poured her some brandy from a nearly empty decanter, speaking as he turned back to her. "In case you're wondering why I'm not following him, he's got a room reservation here, so…"

"I want a bath, Jack." Bella didn't give a fig about anything at that moment and shivered as she sobbed, completely distraught and overwhelmed. "I don't care what time of the night it is," as she tipped the glass and swallowed the liquid in one gulp, shuddering as the strong liquor burned its way to her heaving stomach.

Jack sped out of her room and down to the reception desk. The clerk on duty muttered it was the middle of the night and baths would have to wait until morning, but Jack started to make a scene, quietly swearing and threatening all sorts of dire retribution from the Kings of France and England downwards if the management didn't comply, so they eventually gave in and said hot water would be sent up as soon as possible.

He then crept into the deserted bar and helped himself to a bottle of brandy from behind the counter, returning back upstairs before anyone was any the wiser.

He sat next to her, his arm around her, refilling her glass with the brandy, giving her time to collect herself and stop crying. Eventually Bella calmed down, pulling herself together. There was a knock on the door and maids arrived with a bath and hot water. Jack directed them into the adjacent dressing room and ordered one of the bemused girls to get the fire made up. The flash of a pile of gold coins in his hand suddenly galvanised the hotel staff more than his threats and they started to run about with a semblance of urgency. It was a salutary lesson for him on how money talked in such establishments. Before long, the bath was filled and logs were burning in the grate. Shooing the staff out and almost throwing a large sum of money at them, knowing now that anything he asked for, he would get and quickly, Jack shut and locked the door and turned to urge Bella into her dressing room before returning to pour himself a brandy and wait impatiently to find out what had happened. Drinking the strong liquor, he felt older than his years and wondered for the umpteenth time what had happened to his original expectation of a quiet sightseeing and shopping trip to France.

Bella scrubbed her skin, desperate to remove any feel of Bernheim's wandering hands and then washed her hair. As she relaxed in the warm water, she thought about what she might have to encounter on the following afternoon and her brain simply couldn't process it. She wasn't sure she could actually bring herself to go through with it – but then she thought of Nicky and remembered all the information from Ashcroft about Bernheim and also what Nicky had said about his character.

They'd both been adamant the man was a deranged menace. If she was worried about Bernheim's lovemaking, that was nothing to her panicking about what he might be doing to Nicky. Again, a vision of her uncle's back returned to her mind, together with distant memories of her de Mornay grandfather, who'd never recovered from the vicious beatings in the Rouen fortress and who had died in London a year before her mother, long before his time too, a virtual invalid for years, a broken man at heart.

She also remembered how Nicky's parents had both been killed by Bernheim senior's attempt to get his hands on the de Bresancourt fortune. Her Uncle Reynard limped as a result of an injury sustained at the same time as Uncle Francis had been tortured. Finally, she thought of her Uncle Gerard's daughter, Amandine. Uncle Gerard had also limped until his death as a result of the brutal treatment he'd received at the hands of the elder Bernheim, again in the Fortress, but Amandine had never married. Bella had never known why she was so withdrawn and timid, to the point of being a virtual recluse and extremely uncomfortable in any sort of male company, even her extended family, until her Aunt Cat had explained what had happened to her before her Uncle Francis had been captured. That really made her shudder with fright. Rape didn't even cover it. And Edgar Bernheim had been at the root of all of it. Both Nicky and Ashcroft had maintained the son was equally bad, if not worse, than the father.

The whole scenario was a complete nightmare for her, way beyond her comprehension; she felt completely out of her depth. All the memories whirled round in her head, now meaning so much more. For once, Bella really yearned for her Uncle Francis to come along and sort out all her problems. But this time she was truly on her own, with only Jack to help.

She finally reappeared in the bedroom, wrapped in a dressing robe and Jack jumped up to pull her over to a comfortable chair he'd placed in front of the now roaring fire. He handed her another glass of brandy which she tossed back in one gulp, coughing as the fiery liquid burned down her throat. He pulled the damp towel from her lifeless fingers and went to stand behind her, rubbing her long thick hair and doing his best to dry it. He gave up, not sure how to manage a lady's long hair and instead went round to kneel in front of her, taking her cold, shaking hands in his. He looked up into her forlorn, frightened face and casting politeness and manners and the fact he was a groom and she a Duchess to one side, whispered, "Tell me, Bella, tell me what's happened?"

"Bernheim has Nicky. I'm absolutely sure of it. I know we have absolutely no proof, but I just KNOW. If we don't rescue him tomorrow, I doubt he'll see the end of the week, even if he's been strong enough to withstand the torture I believe Bernheim has inflicted on him so far. I think he has him in the cellar at his villa." Jack's face went white. "I put two and two together from rather odd comments Bernheim made here and there over dinner and it's the only obviously conclusion. Anyway, I've managed an invitation up there tomorrow afternoon for...for...luncheon and...and..." she couldn't say any more, "and while I distract Bernheim, you've GOT to get in, see what's going on there. If you do find Nicky, try to rescue him." She took a deep breath, "Though what you can do against that tongueless giant and any more of his staff, I just don't know," and the despairing tears fell again.

Jack swore long and venomously. "Oh, pardon, Your Grace, but I can't help it," he finally muttered, collecting himself. He climbed back up to sit on a chair next to her and took her hands in his strong calloused ones, though they were considerably softer now than they'd ever been.

Tears fell again and Bella laughed forlornly and coughed, "I'm like a watering pot when I'm with you, Jack. Do you have this effect on all the ladies you work for?"

He laughed too, both of them slightly hysterical, but her face had gone back to wearing a haunted expression. "What are we going to do, Jack?" she whispered. "And what am _I_ going to do? The man repulses me...and Nicky, along with his superior in London, told me Bernheim murdered a lot of the women he...er... he...went with," she finally gulped. "I gather it was while he...while they...but if I don't go, he's going to kill Nicky for sure. I've never known another man apart from my husband...and we've nowhere to go to find help and even if we did approach someone in authority down here, how can I explain all this? And if someone did believe my husband had been kidnapped and sent some soldiers, I'm sure Bernheim would simply kill Nicky and escape, if Nicky was even still alive by that point…"

Jack might only have been fifteen or sixteen, but he had a very good idea of what Bella was talking about, in fact far more than she did. He'd grown up in the worst Hell in London, had seen more in his few short years than most people would in a lifetime, or even knew existed. Horror, pain, starvation, sickness, cruelty, crime, injustice, degradation, depravity and perversions. Everything was commonplace in the desperate stews of the Seven Dials. He thought of what he'd been forced to do to get money to feed his siblings and the children who'd come into his care. He looked deep into her eyes, "When the time comes, you'll do anything for those you love, believe me." He gripped her hands tight as they both stared into the flames for long minutes.

"You just have to close your mind to it," he muttered finally, closing his eyes at his own terrible memories. "Think yourself somewhere else; just relax. If you try and fight it and go stiff, it goes worse. Or they hit you. Breathe deeply and don't cry out, they like that too…it drives them to go harder…" he finally whispered.

Bella slowly turned her head and looked at him in utter shock and disbelief. "Jack?" she whispered, "How do you know about things like that?" She was stunned, appalled, as she looked at his still, pale face and the knowing, haunted eyes. "Dear heaven, what has been done to you?" she gasped softly. "Oh, my God, oh, Jack!" She turned and hugged the youth to her. "Oh, my poor darling, you were only a child!"

He continued to look at her impassively. "Where I come from, you have to do what you have to do sometimes, or you starve," he shrugged.

Bella was shocked to her core and sat in silence for a long moment, looking at the youth in front of her. "Someone once told me you have to do ANYTHING, whatever it takes, to achieve your ends in this dreadful line of work," Bella said slowly and quietly, "but at least now I know I'm far from alone in all this. You understand what I'll probably have to do, don't you? It's not a case of lying there, eyes closed and thinking of England. I have to put on an act or it won't work. This man is perverted too and I know you've been there. It makes it seem more bearable somehow. Thank you." She leaned and kissed him on the cheek. She sat quietly, holding his hands tightly, drawing comfort from him, a mere sixteen-year-old, if that. She shook her head at the bizarre and terrible situation she now found herself in.

Jack nodded at her silently. He'd hoped his words would comfort her somehow, make her realise he understood.

"Are you up to talking about tomorrow?" Jack took a deep breath, trying to focus Bella's mind away from the nightmare she herself would have to endure. "We have to plan, decide what to do, strategise...just like a game of chess," he finally said, wanting to prise his Mistress away from emotive and distressing subjects.

"Yes, you're right, but I need to think, assemble the facts," so Jack watched, fascinated, as she sat and gradually dried her long hair in front of the fire, muttering to herself.

"Right," she said finally, sitting back up and tossing her mane of black hair over her shoulders. "That was a complete waste of time. I have no idea what we're going to do." Jack gawped at her. "All we know is that Bernheim has a villa up in the hills, at the back of the town. It could be anywhere, near the top, or nearer here, we don't know. We've been up there to trek around a bit, so we're aware it's remote. So remote, it's unlikely anyone knows who lives up there, so there's no point asking. We presume, although we don't know for sure, that Nicky is being held and tortured in Bernheim's cellar as we know his presence in Nice was discovered by the tongueless giant – it does seem the most likely explanation for his disappearance. I am assuming Bernheim hasn't killed him outright as there are two things he now wants from Nicky before no doubt, he will dispense with him, as he's already tried to do once before; to whit, money and information. If I know my husband, which I do, very well, he'll simply tell him to rot in hell, or words to that effect." She grimaced at what that would mean for him. "We also have to presume Bernheim's dumb servant is still there and hasn't returned to Paris. I'm sure he must have other servants, although we can't guess at how many as we don't know how large the house is. However, he is always most fastidiously dressed, so he probably has a valet. Someone must take care of the general cleaning and his laundry, a housekeeper no doubt, maybe a housemaid to assist. There may also be a cook as he talked about a delicious luncheon, also a coachman for sure as he has his own vehicle, so there might also be a groom or stable hand. He talked about his gardens, so there may also be a gardener and a general handyman, unless the latter is what the Arab does as he doesn't appear a very domestic individual. That's my summary of the situation, so any ideas? You're the thief here. There are so many unknowns, possibilities and people to deal with. Oh Jack, what the HELL are we going to do?" as she finally swore herself.

Jack looked back at her, completely bemused. "I have no idea whatsoever," he shook his head. "I can barely remember what pieces go where in a game of chess and you expect me to have a strategy to rescue your husband from a house about which at the moment..." Jack counted on his fingers as he spoke, "...we're not one hundred per cent sure he is even there, never mind know its location, it's size, its layout, its defences, nor how many people reside or work there...and that's just a start. The whole situation is a joke and we are completely insane," he laughed slightly hysterically again as he gazed into the fire for a moment.

"But why should that deter us?" he turned back to Bella. "Mr Crichton, the old family tutor down at Firle, who's also been giving me lessons for a while now, he told me countless stories of battles where the odds were completely against those who won out in the end, so that's what we are, the underdogs who will prevail. They'll never suspect an attack in a million years as it's such a mad idea: an aristocratic Duchess and a thief?" He laughed strangely but his eyes were glittering and Bella suddenly realised he was relishing the challenge and was undaunted by it, now he'd got to grips with their situation.

"We are completely delusional, Jack, you realise that?" Bella started to laugh slightly wildly again too. "If my family could see me, with you, I don't know what they'd say. But what I DO know is that my aunt, the Duchess, would never contemplate defeat, were she in my shoes, nor would my Uncle Francis, my Papa, nor even my late mother and late Great Aunt, the Dowager. No matter how great the problem, failure is NOT a word any of them understand; they never have and never will. Benjy, my uncle's valet, always laughed and said we were a mad family and 'You Don't Grapple with the Granvilles…if you've got a grain of sense' and he's right. Papa, classics scholar that he is, calls us *invictus*; that's Latin for unconquered or invincible. They are my family, I'm grown up and one of them, so from now on failure is not a word in my vocabulary either."

Bella got up and marched back and forth across the room, deep in thought. "Right, My Lad, bed for you," she ordered. "We have to assume the bastard is staying here as we know he has a room reserved. He said a carriage couldn't make it up into the hills in the dark and I doubt going on horseback is any easier, unless one carries lanterns and is very familiar with the route, which he may well be but it's still a difficult journey and it's now very late. Therefore, if I was Bernheim, I think I'd get a few hours' sleep, then set off at first light to return to 'see to' my husband before I, as in his lunchtime and afternoon entertainment, arrive." She shuddered. "You," she pointed at Jack, "must therefore loiter on the main road out of Nice, near the hotel. Then follow him to his villa and reconnoitre. He's sending his carriage for me at noon, so it's unlikely you'll be able to get back in time for us to discuss a plan. It's a complete nightmare scenario but we must go with our intuition. It's served me well so far, I just KNEW something was amiss with Nicky and that Bernheim was involved. If I know you're trying to get in to the villa from the outside and I am on the inside, we must deal with the servants there as best we can and effect a rescue. We can't plan anything else. The whole situation is completely ridiculous, but Nicky's life depends on our rescuing him. I am absolutely convinced he IS in that villa." She stopped her pacing and looked very hard at Jack. "Have you ever killed anyone, Jack?" the question came out baldly and unexpectedly. "I know you were a thief, but have you? One hears tales of people having their throats slit for a mere few coins in the Dials or other such places…?"

Jack blanched and shook his head. "No, me neither," Bella mused as if she was talking about shopping in Bond Street, "but my aunt has, quite a few men actually, many years ago when she had to rescue the Duke from that little mess he got involved in. If she can do it, so can I!"

Bella said with asperity. "I have a horrible feeling it may be necessary to handle the staff, especially that giant heathen, but if I have to shoot Bernheim," she carried on talking while she wandered over to the bags belonging to Nicky that Jack had brought from his lodgings, rootling around inside to bring out various pistols and a couple of daggers as well as his stiletto, "I actually think I will do so with the greatest of pleasure."

Jack looked at her in awe. He stood up and clapped his hands. "Bravo, Your Grace. With that spirit we WILL prevail. We're English, and they are mere foreigners. Mr Crichton taught me all about Crécy and Agincourt, the Armada, Blenheim and Trafalgar. Wellington has finally put paid to them down in Spain, so these Frenchies had better watch out!" He helped her sort out the various weapons and they discussed who would carry what. He took the stiletto and put it in his boot, then armed all the pistols, slightly relieved to notice the Duchess seemed quite familiar with handling the weapons. "Can YOU shoot, Your Grace?" he asked curiously.

"Oh yes," Bella laughed coldly, "my father is a crack shot, absolutely deadly, every time, which is somewhat odd for someone so studious, I have to admit. However, he taught me when I was a young girl, just like he originally taught Nicky until Uncle Francis took over his weapons coaching. I can shoot the pips out of playing cards at quite a distance. I understand how to make allowances for any wind or weather variances, also the type of pistol. I'm afraid my hoyden tendencies were extensive. Not as much as my aunt though," she laughed, "have you ever seen her fight with a rapier?"

Jack grinned at her. "Oh yes, in the gardens at Firle with the Duke," he chuckled. "The servants always watch and lay bets. They're quite a pair when they get going, especially when they're trying to settle an argument and they're cross with each other, especially when the Duchess puts her breeches on," he chuckled. "That always annoys the Duke even more, never mind her choice language when she screeches at him. Then, they normally kiss each other when they're done – and I don't mean a peck on the cheeks, either. I've never known such an eccentric or crazy pair of people."

"Mmmm," smiled Bella. "You know, my aunt originally taught my husband to fence when he was a little boy. Then, of course, the Duke coached him as well and they practised at some club in Town, as well as down at Firle in the gardens when he grew up and before he went off to the war, so Nicky is quite a swordsman. I tried it too, you know. Oh, how my aunt despaired of me," she grinned at the memories, "but it was just never my thing. Pistols, now, that was something else. It used to irritate the hell out of Nicky that I could shoot even better than he could; I'm apparently just like my father."

Jack grinned at her and laid out the armed weapons. "I can take several pistols, but I'm not sure where you can hide one?" Bella looked at the large pistols and realised he was right. They were far too big to fit into her elegant reticules or secrete in a pocket of her coats. "I can take a small dagger, but that's about it," she sighed. "How useless is that? My aunt used to wear a sheath strapped to her leg under her skirts for that stiletto, but I've nothing like that here and I doubt such a thing exists in any shop in Nice, even if I had the time to run one to earth. Let's just hope I can find a weapon there."

They chatted for a little while longer and then Bella sent Jack off to bed. He had to get up extremely early to hire a pony on which to follow Bernheim and then it was in the lap of the Gods what would happen at the villa.

"Don't think about Bernheim and what you might have to do," he whispered as he turned to leave her room. "It will only give you nightmares. I'm sure when the time comes you will do whatever is necessary without a thought, because you're motivated by higher and better things," he said knowingly. "God and the Fates be with you. Please take care Your Grace and remember, I WILL be there, watching and helping. We'll get him out, you'll see. We don't need Wellington's army, we are our own army," and with those stirring final few words, he turned towards the door.

He was halfway out of it when suddenly he ran back to her, going down on his knees. Jack took both her hands in his and kissed them reverently. "Be careful, Your Grace. Whatever you do, if you're in danger, if there are too many of them, just run away and I will come and find you before we get proper help, mayhap hire some men, never mind the Authorities. Then we'll go back again. I promise we WILL rescue the Duke." He was surprisingly calm and pragmatic beyond his years. "What IS that saying I remember from my tutor? Aaah, bugger..." he swore as he hit his forehead lightly, "that Roman fellow? Oh, yes... 'he that fights and runs away, may turn and fight another day; but he that is in battle slain, will never rise to fight again.'"

Bella smiled sadly down at him, "Ah, Tacitus, I believe. You've learned your lessons well, Jack, it appears. I'll remember but so must you, My Dear Boy, remember your own warning." She bent to kiss both his knuckles tenderly, making his eyes widen.

Jack bowed his head and was silent for a few moments then, finally, he looked up, sherry brown eyes gazing directly into tawny green ones. "Keep your mind blank. Think of your daughter, your aunt, of Firle, someone you love...and you WILL survive it." With that, he turned and left the room, ready to follow both Bernheim and her, silently and secretly, wherever they went.

What an extraordinary lad he was, thought Bella, as she lay back on her pillows; how glad she was to have him with her. Maids and footmen would be useless and her aunt perhaps hadn't realised just how perfect and ideal a companion she had sent along with her niece. Or maybe she had? It was all too extraordinary.

As Bella lay there fretting over entering the wolf's lair with no weapon to speak of other than a little dagger, a random thought about the events all those years ago in Rouen popped into her mind. Her aunt had poisoned several men before facing Edgar Bernheim and his accomplice, Pierre Dupont, to rescue the Duke and the Fourneval family. It had been the silent and ideal solution for her to dispense with several men by herself. A nasty smile crept over Bella's face and she determined to rise very early the following morning to visit a local apothecary and procure her own deadly weapon, prior to setting off for Bernheim's home.

Finally, worn out by the stresses and strains of the evening, she fell into a restless and troubled slumber, her dreams tormented by nightmare visions of her uncle's back and what was happening to Nicky in some unknown cellar.

Chapter Seven

He sat on a damp, dirt floor, propped up against cold stone, blindfolded and naked except for his now stained, rank and ripped breeches, his manacled wrists behind his back, attached to a short chain on a ring on the wall behind him. He could not work out his location, whether it was day or night, or how long he'd been there. All he knew was that he was Bernheim's prisoner and he was starving.

He'd gone out one morning, was it days or weeks ago? He only wanted to get some bread and cheese in the local market and to get his boots repaired. The slot in them where he kept his stiletto had come unstitched with constant wear and he was going to get it mended while he found himself some breakfast since it was only a ten minute job at the most. But he never arrived at the market. As he rounded the corner from his quiet little lodging house, the last thing he remembered was a blow on the back of his head and he'd woken up in this hellish place. How long he'd been unconscious before he came round, he'd no idea.

As ever, he felt something furred with a long tail scamper over his bare feet, better that than the other biting creatures who also inhabited this hole. He kicked out reflexively but another soon followed and he gave up the effort. He was so hungry and thirsty. Periodically, they fed him some water, but it was never enough. His throat was parched and dry and he felt lightheaded. It didn't help that when they stuck the needles in him he screamed with the pain. If they didn't give him more to drink soon, he wouldn't have a voice to scream with and Bernheim wouldn't like that. Gallows humour, he thought.

Nicky didn't know how much longer he could last, not that he cared much now. He'd reflected a lot since he'd been there, given there wasn't anything else to do.

In the beginning they'd just beaten him viciously, all over his body while Bernheim asked continuously about the whereabouts of the Valenciennes fortune. He didn't believe him when he'd truthfully said he had no idea. Bernheim had obviously been digging around as he'd demanded to know where the money had come from to start the expensive restorations on the derelict chateau on the Valenciennes Estate. When he'd said an elderly relative of the family who'd adopted him in England had left him a bit of money, Bernheim didn't believe that either. It wasn't the 'bit of money' he didn't believe. He was firmly convinced Nicky had the Valenciennes fortune and nothing would persuade him otherwise. It was as if any other money was irrelevant, he only wanted the famed Valenciennes gold, wherever and whatever that was. Nicky was damned if he was going to tell him he suspected his legacy from the Dowager would dwarf anything his family had ever possessed. They'd led a luxurious lifestyle as well as maintaining a presence at Versailles, neither of those coming cheap. No wonder the tenants and local peasants were poverty-stricken and angry that all their labour brought them no benefit. He'd let his mind rove back to his early childhood, hazy memories now, but he'd never seen nor heard his father mention any golden fortune, not, he presumed, that he would in front of a three or four year old. Even so, his father had constantly drummed into him the pride he should feel for his status and the ducal title he would one day inherit – as well as how superior the family was compared to all the riffraff around them, including other upstart aristocrats, as he'd referred to the nobles with whom he'd associated at Versailles.

Here, they'd given up beating him from head to foot until he'd felt like a rag doll with every bone in his body broken; he doubted he'd ever make love to a woman again having been kicked frequently in the genitals; next they tried chaining him up and whipping him instead. He could still feel the stinging of the cat-o'nine-tails as its tips coiled around his torso, his body now covered in festering sores and weals, bloodied and broken skin. He didn't know what his back was like, but it was agony to lean against it and when he sat up, he had to ensure it was only his shoulders that pressed against the cold, damp wall. With his wrists manacled to the chain behind him, he couldn't lie down to sleep, not that he wanted his face in the rat-infested dirt, so he'd become used to dozing, sitting up as he now was. Not that they let him sleep much either. Even when he passed out from the pain, they threw water over him to bring him back to consciousness...so they could carry on.

Then Bernheim started asking him about Spain, specifically what had happened to the gold shipments, wanting to find out who had betrayed him. Nicky merely said it was Carmelita, that he knew nothing about what happened to the gold as Bernheim had shot her with him together and he'd been unconscious and ill for months afterwards. Matters then naturally progressed to Nicky's work for Wellington. Bernheim wanted to know why a Frenchman was working for the English and what he was now doing in France and, more to the point, there in Nice. Nicky didn't bother to mention he felt he was mostly English now and refused to answer any of his questions. Bernheim had raged like a madman, "Why is a wealthy French Duke working as a spy for the damned English?" he ranted over and over. "The monarchy is restored now in France so what's the point?" But he got no answer from his prisoner.

When he got bored of asking about the Valenciennes fortune, the Spanish gold and why Nicky was an English spy, including whether he knew anything about his current activities, Bernheim then started on about The Shadow and who had killed his father. Nicky merely said he knew little as he'd been a very small boy at the time and he thought everyone involved was dead. Relentlessly Bernheim had asked him and equally relentlessly, Nicky had simply said they were dead. He would sacrifice everything before he'd ever betray Francis and Cat.

They had risked their lives for him when he was a child and he would die before he'd give away their secret.

So they were at an impasse. That was when the Chinaman had arrived with his box of needles.

With his step-father's interest in all things scientific and the latest medical advances, Nicky had a vague recollection of him relating stories about a trip to the Far East on behalf of the Firle commercial empire to investigate and set up some new trading contracts out there and had come across the Chinese practice of acupuncture. He remembered the family laughing in disbelief at Eddie's description of how sticking needles in certain parts of the body could relieve pain and cure some ailments in others. It had all sounded completely absurd and far-fetched and he'd had his leg pulled about it, but his step-father had assured them it was the truth and since he'd experienced it for himself, he knew it really worked. Eddie had been interested because of his constantly aching crushed pelvis, hip and thigh, caused when it was smashed in his childhood by Pierre Dupont, a man who had eventually gone to work for Bernheim's father. A man he had ironically ended up shooting on that terrible final day in Rouen Fortress when they'd gone to rescue Francis.

But this Chinaman didn't use his needles for the benefit of mankind to alleviate pain; he specialised in creating it, and Nicky now lived in perpetual dread of being dragged off to experience his particular form of torture.

He knew he was a Chinaman as he'd removed Nicky's blindfold the first time he used the needles on him, to watch his reaction. No matter how he tried to resist the pain, Nicky's eyes told their own story. That was when he'd seen the large Arab in the room as well, who just stood, staring impassively. Of course, Bernheim was there too, his face watching unemotionally as they'd strung him up and the Chinaman had stuck needles in his spine, making his body twitch with the excruciating pains that ran down his legs. After that, sometimes they sat him in a chair and stuck needles in his neck, giving him the most terrifying headaches when he thought his head would explode, or they forced him flat on a table and the needles went in his body which made his heart race and thump; at one point, he'd thought he was having a heart attack. But mostly, the inscrutable man applied them slowly and incrementally, increasing the pain in different parts of his body until he usually ended up screaming and invariably passed out before coming to later, his body on fire or twitching uncontrollably. Sometimes they left the needles in him when they chained him up, back in his cell or wherever they kept him, making him suffer for hours...or was it days? He had no idea.

Constantly, they asked him questions. Mostly it was Bernheim but if he wasn't there, it was the Chinaman in his strange accent. Where was the money? Who was The Shadow? On and on they went. The last session he had needles in his feet so that both his legs went numb and he couldn't move. Then, as the feeling gradually returned, so did the most excruciating pain he'd ever felt. He'd screamed and screamed in agony and Bernheim had been demanding to know why he was in Nice. The temptation to tell him about Ashcroft had been huge but he'd eventually passed out before he said anything and when he'd woken up, whilst the needles and the pain had gone, his heart had again been thumping erratically. He genuinely thought he would die soon if they carried on.

Part of him wished he could die, just to put an end to it. No one knew where he was, so he wasn't going to escape or be rescued. There was no Reynard watching his back this time. He'd tried to make a getaway at the beginning, when they'd removed the manacles so he could eat the crust they'd tossed to him like a dog, along with some filthy water. But after he'd attacked the Arab and another swarthy servant who was helping him, they'd nearly kicked and beaten him to death and from then on never left his manacles off , occasionally releasing one hand so he could drink more of the fetid water, just enough to keep him alive; no food, just the dregs of some water trough. Now, he was beginning to accept the inevitable – he was to become another of Ashcroft's casualties, a further increase to his attrition rate.

His solitary reflections had encompassed his family and his life over the past few years. How much now did he realise how deeply the Granvilles and the de Mornays cared for him and how much he regretted his callous treatment of their loving concern. He could have written while he'd been away, there were always ways and means of sending letters, even if they took a time to reach their destination. He reflected sadly and guiltily over Sooty's words about them all worrying constantly, losing sleep because they didn't know his where-abouts and if he was alive or dead.

His one relief was that he'd been to see the Dowager before she died. Other than his step-mother, whom he'd loved deeply, the Dowager was the one person who had really understood him, perhaps more than his step-mother in some respects. He didn't know why but she seemed to sense something bad had happened to him before he'd come to England, something that made him keep himself slightly aloof, reluctant to give all of himself or accept the love they all offered unreservedly. He'd never told anyone the details of what had really transpired in the Fortress before he'd been rescued, the unbelievable horrors he'd experienced. Nonetheless, the Dowager had sensed some-thing and was always on at him to try to talk about it, to let go of his fears and trust again, to let himself love and be loved. In his own way, he'd loved the old lady as much as he had his step-mother, she'd truly been the grandmother he'd never had. Granny Granville. He'd never understood what she meant however, about love…until now.

He'd thought a lot about Bella, his Sooty. As he'd lain in agony, trying to stop thinking about the pain, her face would come to mind, always teasing him, laughing at him…loving him. Whether it was as a little girl, a tomboy with her black hair in pigtails when she'd been very small, then in plaits with freckles over her pert nose, or when she'd grown older, on the cusp of womanhood…and now, to the stun-ning, beautiful woman she'd become. He finally admitted to himself that he loved her; that he always had loved her.

First, like a little sister, but deep down, from the moment he'd given her that first kiss when she was about thirteen and he'd been eighteen, just to stop her nagging him and satisfy her curiosity about what a kiss felt like, he'd known there was a connection between them. Because of it, he'd offered to marry her, just before her seventeenth birthday. He realised now, deep in his subconscious, it was something he'd wanted, but wouldn't admit to. He'd always run away from it, denied it to himself and everyone else. That's why when she'd crept into his bed and he'd drunkenly taken her virginity, he'd been so angry. He was determined not to be loved by her, nor be committed to her; he was too frightened to let go. It wasn't simply his lack of money or estates – he knew she didn't give a hoot about that, although HE did, before the Dowager died – but it had given him a good excuse to push her away. He'd tried to see her as a sister, but that hadn't worked either. She simply refused to be fobbed off, to leave him alone. As he'd grown up, the way he'd dealt with the abuse he'd suffered in Rouen Fortress had been to push it to a corner of his mind, to shut away his deepest emotions, just like he'd closed them down in the Fortress as a means of survival, whilst at the same time watching his parents being tortured to death. He'd seen his cold, impassive father rise above it all, totally emotionless and he'd tried to do the same. His father hadn't been rescued in time, but he had. For him, emotions would only lead to hurt, so he had vowed to himself all those years ago never to feel anything. But the Dowager and more recently, Sooty, had kept pushing him to let go and allow himself to be loved.

He knew she loved him, everyone did. What had happened between them at *Le Lion d'Or* was inevitable, in the passion that had exploded between them. He still didn't know why he hadn't recognised her. Oh, he knew he hadn't seen her properly in years, she'd changed a lot from the tall and gawky teenager she'd been into the lovely woman she was now, but still, it was, as ever, as if his mind simply refused to see what his body obviously did. *Lionesse*...hah! It was all so obvious now and he was the biggest fool ever. He'd obsessed over the faceless woman for months and his anger when he'd returned and discovered the truth had been monumental. He couldn't believe how he'd treated her and yet, still she persisted in loving him, chasing after him to France. He'd tried running away from her, but nothing worked. He thought about her constantly but then he always had, subconsciously. He always compared every other woman to her and none could match her. He accepted it now and his feelings swept over him like a breached dam. He loved her, deeply, passionately, completely. She knew him so well, she was like another part of him. It was cathartic, knowing he cared for nothing really, except her, knowing she would love him in spite of anything and everything.

Now they had a daughter, his little Terrie, a miniature feminine replica of himself.

However, they were at home in London. He would die before he let Bernheim or anyone get to them or his adopted family. His only regret was the way he'd parted from Sooty. He'd deliberately left a harsh note for her, believing she'd be so angry with him again she'd storm back to England in high dudgeon – but at least she was safe there and Francis would see she came to no harm. Two lone tears ran down his face as he leaned his head back against the wall. The irony didn't escape him – just when he'd finally realised he had everything he wanted in life, had at last conquered his demons, he was about to lose it all. Through his own stupid, prideful fault.

When Ashcroft had visited him at Valenciennes to tell him about Bernheim, he'd gone running off to Paris without any consideration for anyone. He'd already spent months in Normandy, working day and night, even hard physical labour, breaking up stones and digging trenches. He'd made every effort to dispel Sooty from his mind, to deal with his frustration and escape his endless dreams of her, making love to her, wanting her so much, fighting the temptation to return to London. So the prospect of chasing after Bernheim and focussing his mind on that instead was overwhelming. But it hadn't worked and Sooty had found him. He had absolutely no idea how she'd done it nor how she'd wormed her way into Ashcroft's confidences but when she'd turned up in his room in Paris, he could hardly believe it. Of course, then they'd argued again and she'd cracked him over the head with a bottle.

He didn't have to try hard to remember how she'd made love to him after that. The feel of her soft mouth on his body, of her riding him hard until she imploded around him, then when he'd loved her after that, how the unrestrained, uninhibited, torrid and deep passion of it all had blown him away. He wanted to do it again, to show her how much he loved her, how much he cared. He wanted more children and this time, he wanted to be with her, watching her grow round as his son grew inside her, evidence of all the love and passion he carried for her. Another tear fell from under the rag around his eyes, but it was not to be.

He wondered idly if she'd conceived a child from that night in Paris; if not, the Dukedom of Valenciennes would finally die with him, just as so many other aristocratic French families had fizzled out during the Revolution; no more little Lions to follow after him. But he didn't care about that. Finally, his pride was worthless; his title, the recovered chateau and small amount of surrounding land, the Dowager's fabulous inheritance, all of it meant nothing. He just wanted Sooty and his little daughter, his own family at last, they meant everything to him. The Dowager was right, all the money and possessions in the world were nothing if you didn't have anyone with whom to love, share and enjoy it. What a wise and wonderful old woman she'd been. She'd been right about his father too, he knew that, deep down.

Cold, heartless pride had killed his father and mother, his father's refusal to abandon his wealth to save his pregnant mother and him and buy their lives with it, now seemed different. The Dowager's words had made him admit that fact to himself at last. He wanted a loving family of his own, just as he'd been adopted into the closest family he'd ever come across, something he'd never experienced at Valenciennes. There was his cold, remote mother who was more interested in her clothes and jewels and showing them off at Court. Then, his unemotional father, a man he only vaguely remembered, mainly as he only saw him when he was in residence, an irregular occurrence. When he was there, his son was summoned at five p.m. in the Grand Salon of the chateau, washed, scrubbed and dressed like a miniature courtier to be presented by his nanny or governess for a ten minute inspection, like a little aristocratic blonde insect. He was supposed to report on any useful instruction he'd received that day before being dismissed with a reminder he was a Duke-in-waiting and to remember who he was and to act appropriately at all times. His parents were often away for weeks or months, mainly at Versailles, so he rarely saw them at all and memories of them both were hazy; only the horrific ones in the Fortress had stuck in his mind.

Nicky wondered why he felt so strongly about their deaths, uncaring of him as they'd been, apart from the fact he was the heir, the continuation of the line. At the end of the day, they had been his mother and father and the ties of blood went deep. He wasn't even sure anymore if he was bothered about being a Lion of Valenciennes, let alone worrying about a necklace handed to him by a bloodied and beaten man who could have kissed and hugged him goodbye with the last of his strength, instead of fretting about the inheritance. It now seemed absurd. He could still feel it round his neck, the necklace. The irony of the chain and clasp being too strong to break had made him hysterical at one point when the Arab had half strangled him with it. Strangely, the only person it reminded him of now was of Sooty, *Lionesse*, not his roots and heritage. He supposed that was what happened when one confronted death. Everything unimportant simply faded to irrelevance.

He heard the sound of footsteps approaching and groaned despite himself, abandoning his emotional reverie and bracing himself for what was to come. Perhaps this time they'd end it, put him out of his misery. Hard, cruel hands dragged him roughly to his feet and unlocked the chain from the ring on the wall. It even hurt to stand now, not that he had a chance to try as they heaved him out.

"You goin' tell us wha' we wanna know tooday, Yol Glaice?" the strange Chinese accent asked sarcastically in broken English. "I have partikoolally nice tleat in stol fa you if you doan." Nicky heard a mirthless laugh. "I doan tink you goin' be abel to lesist me afta dat. I know you at you limit."

"*Va te faire foutre !* Go fuck yourself!" Nicky swore long and hard at them in coarse French in his now hoarse voice. "*Rien... rien...*I've got nothing to say." His last ironic thought was that at last he could answer Ashcroft's question of which language he thought and spoke in under extreme duress and laughed hysterically as he passed out.

However, just as they'd been tying him to the table after he'd been brought round again, a message had arrived. They'd strung him up instead, his manacled wrists hanging over a hook on the ceiling, his feet above the ground, his arms straining out of their sockets. They just left him to dangle there, the Chinaman muttering that he would, "have wait til tomollow..."

Chapter Eight

J ack dozed for a couple of hours, still dressed. It was dark when he rose and crept through the back of the hotel. He couldn't be bothered to go to the livery stable and rouse them from sleep to hire a horse. He merely entered silently and helped himself to the best pony there before leading it away, sacking wrapped over its hooves to mask the clink of its shoes on the cobbled streets. Old habits die hard, he told himself as he set off. Besides, he wasn't stealing the nag, only borrowing it…

His next stop was a gunsmiths. The lock on the shop door was no trouble and inside he helped himself to two neat little pistols with ammunition. However, this time, he left a handful of coins on the counter. He crept back out and locked the door behind him, laughing and telling himself he was now completely touched in the head. At the reception desk of the hotel he left the pistols, wrapped tightly in a large piece of velvet cloth, in the cubby hole where his mistress would leave her room key. There was a terse message inside with them.

1 for reticule
    1 for garter

The clerk on duty was fast asleep and never saw him come or go. He checked the register and noted gratefully that Bernheim had indeed checked in to stay overnight so it would be an easy matter to wait unobserved and follow his carriage when he left. Even if the man left his carriage to wait for the Duchess later in the morning and travelled home on horseback, it would still be easy to follow him, he'd just have to be quieter and more careful to remain invisible.

Jack had taken possession of the Duke's stiletto, now tucked neatly into the top of one of his boots, its jewelled hilt glinting just above the soft leather. He had his own familiar dagger as well, just in case. No one went around the Seven Dials without a weapon, least of all him. He'd actually never killed anyone, more by luck than judgement when he was younger, but he knew how to fight at close quarters and had stabbed or cut many another youth in fights over food or a few coins, or anything he could fence or sell. He also wasn't afraid to stab any member of Bernheim's staff silently in the back when he got to the villa. He had no preconceived notions of chivalry or fair play – it was him or them, kill or be killed, law of the underworld. Jack the Lad was taking no chances.

Bella wandered around her suite restlessly, gathering the items she would take with her. Unable to sleep properly, she'd given up and risen to go out early and now had a little bottle of deadly poison in her pocket. She'd told the apothecary it was to get rid of a large rat. Her laugh to herself was malevolent and hysterical. Two could play at Bernheim's game, she thought ruthlessly. She'd collected Jack's parcel on her return, read his note and ensured the pistols were secreted as per his instructions. She also had a small dagger hidden in her other garter that she'd purchased on her brief shopping expedition. Her heart was thumping and her nerves were on a frazzled edge. She paused and wondered if this was how her Aunt Cat and mother had felt before they went into Rouen Fortress each time to help her grandparents and other aunts escape; also when they'd gone in that last fateful time to rescue Uncle Francis. Their bravery almost overwhelmed her, especially her Aunt Cat. But she was a fighter, knew how to use a sword, to kill people, whereas Bella had only her brain. What use was that in situations like this, she asked herself? Her mother had possessed copious amounts of love and determination – but failure wasn't in her dictionary either and she had discovered she, too, had hidden depths and so would Bella. *Invictus*. With that final thought and a whispered prayer to her mother in heaven to watch over her, taking a deep breath, Arabella de Bresancourt, the Duchess of Valenciennes, picked up her belongings and went downstairs to meet her Fate and save her husband.

Chapter Nine

The hot and stuffy carriage wended its way up into the hills, lurching and bumping on the sometimes rough roadways and tracks and Bella fanned herself frequently to keep cool. Eventually, quite high up, the vehicle rolled to a halt and the coachman came round and opened her door. "Afraid we 'ave ter walk from 'ere, M'Lady. It's not far, but the carriage can't make it down the track that leads ter th' front door." He muttered to himself about why on earth his master didn't get it widened as he helped Bella out and she put on a large sunhat with veiling over her face. Another purchase that morning. She'd suddenly remembered in the middle of the night that the Arab might recognise her from her visit to Bernheim's house with her begging box for the Veterans' Charity. "Th' master usually uses a small gig or goes in ter town on 'orseback, 'less it's rainin' o'course," the man commented as he led her down a winding track towards a house that came into view, "but it's a noosance when 'e 'as 'is visitors come ter call..."

Bella had to gasp. The villa looked so beautiful, set amongst palm trees and gardens full of flowering shrubs, its painted stucco walls covered in bougainvillea and flowering vines. As they walked down the garden path to the main door, Bella stopped to look out at the stunning view, miles of coastline spread out below her with the blue Mediterranean sparkling in the sunlight. "What a beautiful spot," she said to the coachman. "Has the Chevalier lived here long?"

"A while, 'e comes an' goes," the man merely responded with a shrug. "The 'ouse belonged ter 'is father an' I 'ear 'e 'as an 'ouse in Paris as well, but 'e does seem ter like this 'ere little villa, even if tis off th' beaten track an' a bit of an effort ter git to."

Bella deliberately oooohed and aaaaahed over the view and took the opportunity to wander from the path to the front door and stroll around the gardens, trying to make out if there were any outside windows or entrances to the lower floors or cellar, but she could see none. "This is sooo charming," she enthused to the irritated coachman. "The villa is sooo much bigger than I thought. Does it have many floors and rooms? The Chevalier was so vague when he told me about it, just kept saying how much I'd like the view. Are there servants here or are they housed elsewhere?" She sounded quite domestic and a typical brainless woman.

"The servants live in quarters at th' back o' th' kitchens, farther down th' drive, near the stables, M'Lady," he said.

"Ah, quite so," she nodded vaguely, for all the world an aristocratic Lady not particularly interested in the lives of mere menials. "I must bear all this in mind if I ever find myself back in this part of the world, so much more private than the hotel and one can have one's own staff to hand, though, as you say, it is a bit cut off."

Bernheim appeared at the front door before she could extract any further tidbits of information from the unsuspecting coachman. "Ah, *Lionesse*," he bent over her hand and the coachman rapidly doffed his hat to his master and promptly hurried off. "Welcome to my humble abode. No more pink noses I see," he tweaked her veiling, offered her his arm and escorted her inside. There were no servants around. The house was deadly quiet.

"Where are your staff, Frederick? Don't you have footmen, house-maids? I can understand no butler if this is a little rural retreat, but one MUST have adequate servants, surely?" again the disdainful, aristo-cratic surprise.

"I sent them off for a few hours this afternoon. They should have left a buffet for us in the dining room and I wanted to have the house to myself with you here, just for a while. I wasn't sure where you would like to take your *siesta* after luncheon...upstairs, downstairs or even outside?" a very slight leer curled his lips.

"Whatever you suggest, Frederick, whatever you want will please me," Bella purred through her veiling, privately aghast at the thought of doing anything outside where any wandering servant might see.

"Good, good," he murmured, "quite delightful. I have such plans for us this afternoon..." his suggestive, soft words hung in the air. As she followed him through a cool dark hallway, Bella removed her hat, hugely relieved there were no servants to worry about, well one in particular. She idly wondered where Jack was hiding and the knowledge he was outside, somewhere near her, was strangely comforting.

"Come, My Dear, let us have an aperitif before luncheon. There is an awning on the terrace and the view is sublime." Bernheim led her through a dining room and out to the terrace where an ice-bucket containing a chilling bottle of champagne and two glasses, along with several plates of *hors'd'oeuvres,* sat waiting on a long wooden table surrounded by cushioned wicker chairs and footstools. In any other company or situation it would have been inviting and delightful. However, this was neither, so Bella strolled about to take in the view, turning her head this way and that as if looking at her surroundings, but of course merely searching for entries or windows to the cellar. She heard the cork pop and the gush of liquid pouring into the glasses.

Bernheim came up behind her and pulled her into his arms. "You, My Dear, are a perfect aperitif to what I know will be a mouth-watering, hot, tasty and delicious afternoon." He kissed her, carnal, wet, hungry and lascivious. Bella felt as though she was in the arms of a rampant, drooling snake.

"Ah, Frederick, cold champagne and a light luncheon – how perfect to put me in the mood, not that I wasn't in the mood when I woke up this morning after our lovely evening last night..." she smirked and simpered coquettishly before wandering over to the table to pick up one of the glasses he'd filled and pop an olive into her mouth, licking her lips suggestively as she swallowed. He held out a chair for her and she sat down.

"What a simply beautiful spot," she commented airily and waved her hand towards the view. "I can understand why you holiday here. Your associates must enjoy their visits?" she fished, thinking of the coachman's comments about widening the track.

"Mmmm, we often all sit out here for our meetings," replied Bernheim. "Much more pleasant than in the interior dining room, unless it's very hot in summer, of course, then the cool dimness is a welcome respite. There is normally always a very slight breeze up here which tends to take the edge off the searing heat."

Bella looked at the large table and many chairs. "You have big meetings here?" she looked amazed. "I presumed your business was in Paris and this was just a little escape in the sunshine and perhaps the odd local transaction?"

"Oh, you'd be surprised what goes on here in these little coastal backwaters," was all he commented. "I have a lot of business connections down here. They come in from the Italian states, or further afield in Europe, as well as over on the islands," he too waved his hand airily towards the sea. Elba was also in that direction, Bella thought. She was about to probe further when Bernheim deliberately changed the subject and started discussing the plants and his gardens.

After a couple of glasses of champagne they sauntered inside and helped themselves to food which they brought outside again. Bella's stomach was churning but she had to force herself to eat, partly as she couldn't escape the champagne since Bernheim kept topping up her glass.

"Did you sort out your vermin problem earlier?" she asked conversationally as she calmly buttered a small roll. "All this wildness and undergrowth must harbour all sorts of unwanted visitors and biting creatures," and a hysterical voice in her brain thought of Jack, lurking somewhere in the bushes nearby.

"Unfortunately not," replied Bernheim. "By the time I returned here this morning, I didn't have long enough to get to grips with it before you arrived, so I've put it off until tomorrow. However, that will be the rat's last day." He laughed mirthlessly and Bella shuddered.

"This is a lovely champagne," Bella commented as she savoured the bubbling liquor in her mouth. "Do you have a good cellar here? I always take care to have good wine and champagne available at my clubs. A lot of the clientele expect it, although some wouldn't know a good wine from vinegar," she blithely chattered on, "but I do love champagne myself, there've been some very good vintages lately. However I suppose red wine, port or brandy are more your taste, being a Gentleman?"

"How interesting for a Lady to understand good wine," chatted Bernheim as he cut into his cold chicken, "but of course I was forgetting about your business."

"Mmmm, yes," said Bella. "I'm always on the lookout to lay down some good wines in my cellar. My father, being French, is a particular connoisseur and I learned a lot from him. One can't really drink cheap wine and brandy after experiencing something from a renowned vineyard, especially if it's a good vintage," and for the next quarter of an hour they discussed wine, vineyards and vintages.

"I'd be terribly interested to see your cellar," Bella finally asked. "I'm always keen to pick up recommendations from an expert and you obviously are one," she'd been stroking his ego for quite a while, "and then perhaps you could show me round your lovely villa and then... we could decide where to ...er...*siesta*?" She smiled seductively and held out her glass for Bernheim to refill, knowing the bottle was virtually empty, hoping he would go himself to get another in the absence of any staff.

Bernheim was on the rack. She was such a tempting morsel. One minute all come-hither with her seductive smile and licking lips, then the next he could feel her withdrawing slightly. Undoubtedly a practiced tease, he surmised, expert at winding up her men. What's more, she was so obviously an aristocratic Lady. His perfect woman. He'd lain awake all night thinking about her, fantasising about what they would do that afternoon. He'd nearly gone to visit her room a couple of times to surprise her but she'd been quite adamant about keeping her activities quiet from her nephew, so he'd reluctantly stayed where he was. He'd wondered how far he could go with her, being a gambling house owner and obviously a woman of the world. Would she appreciate some of his milder idiosyncrasies? He would soon find out but he suspected she would, especially given her comments about dealing with problem customers who owed her money and the way she'd responded to and obviously understood his occasional innuendos. His lips curled salaciously as he wondered what she'd make of the 'rat' in his cellar, if she knew what else went on there, apart from his extensive wine collection. This current rat wasn't the first one to be dealt with down there, it was such a perfect location to investigate and exterminate two-legged vermin. He had a sudden vision of taking her in the cellar, perhaps bottom up over one of his wine barrels, or maybe tying her to one of the wine racks, tormenting her and making her beg him for release while he savoured one of his favourite vintages. He felt his body harden. He had to have her, urgently. He'd waited long enough.

"Come, My Dear." He stood and held out his hand. "I find I am thirsty for other things." He tipped the last of the champagne into her glass. "Bring it with you," he said and drew her to her feet. "I might quite like to spill it and lick the remnants off your luscious body," he whispered.

He tucked her hand through his elbow and sauntered into the main hallway and up the stairs. "I think maybe we'll start in my bedroom," he looked at her lecherously, "then perhaps I could show you my cellar later; such an interesting place, to do all sorts of things," he suggested and Bella's flesh crawled. She braced herself, the moment had come. She wondered what Jack was currently up to and sent a fervent prayer he was near and taking the opportunity of no servants around to search for Nicky.

Chapter Ten

Bernheim delicately directed Bella to a guest suite with a dressing room and water closet. While she was otherwise occupied, he hurried down to the cellar to make sure his 'rat' was secure. He'd been so frustrated after his solitary night, he'd sent instructions on his arrival to string up his prisoner so he could vent his frustration and ire on him personally with his whip. He'd been in the midst of it when Bella's coach had been spotted coming up the hillside, so he'd reluctantly abandoned his activity to go and clean himself up and send Mustapha and the Chinaman off for the afternoon. That they'd left de Bresancourt dangling was of no concern – he'd still be alive the following day when they would get the information he wanted, he'd been assured by the little Oriental.

Bernheim was a meticulous man and wanted to make sure he wasn't likely to be disturbed, nor that his prisoner would cause any trouble. He strode through the extensive wine cellars and storerooms, through a heavy oak door to another set of cellar rooms beyond. In the largest, an apparently unconscious man was hanging by his arms.

His manacled wrists were separated by a longish chain linking them and this was caught over two large hooks fixed a short distance apart in the ceiling timbers, keeping his arms spread like the upper part of an X. His ankles were also manacled and his bare feet were just above the floor, his toes barely touching it. They just about gave the body above some support, but not a lot. If they hadn't, the man would be half crucified, dangling as he was only by the wrists. Scrabbling sounds could be heard as Bernheim entered the chilled room. The man looked thin and filthy; his tawny, golden hair now dark with dirt and sweat, his face covered with a bearded scruff and he smelled foul. His head was drooping on to his chest and he had a wide dark rag tied round his eyes. His body was a mass of running sores, cuts and bruises and his wrists were rubbed raw from pulling on the rusted manacles round them. He didn't move as Bernheim entered; he looked more dead than alive.

There was little by way of furniture in the room: a couple of plain wooden chairs and a large, old refectory table was pushed up against one wall. Small barred windows were set high in the stone walls, giving enough light to illuminate the prisoner and let in a little air and Bernheim pulled a face at the unpleasant stench that emanated from the dirty captive.

He picked up a particularly nasty cat-o'nine-tails from the table, the ends of the fine leather strips shining with metal tips. He cracked it through the air to see if the man was conscious. Nicky raised his head slightly and swore in a hoarse voice. *"Je t'ai dit…va te faire foutre espèce de salaud Chinois!* I told you …go fuck yourself, you piece of Chinese shit," he whispered coarsely.

Bernheim smiled nastily and sauntered over to his prisoner. "Well, well, it appears it's your lucky day, Your Grace," he lisped and poked him in the abdomen with the handle of the lash. "I have a much more delightful afternoon ahead of me than dealing with vermin like you, so I'll have to leave you here, enjoying your own company, as I've had to send the servants off for a few hours. Can't have them in the house while I'm entertaining a Lady. Who knows which room I might want to fuck her in, delicious morsel that she is. She's just gagging for it and for me, of course. I've even a mind to bring her down here and do it. There's something deliciously erotic, explicit and apposite about a cellar, don't you agree?"

He bent nearer Nicky's head and whispered, "Make the most of your last day on earth, Your Grace, for tomorrow, I promise, you WILL tell me what I want to know or you will experience pain such as you won't believe; no one can resist that. Think about it, hmmm?" He pulled on the little lion charm on the chain round his neck. "Hah! *Le Lion de Valenciennes*? All I see is a half dead, flea infested, mangy cat."

As Nicky hung there, listening to Bernheim's taunts, unable to see which made his other senses more attuned, his nostrils flared as he caught a familiar scent on the man's jacket. It was so familiar, he'd know it anywhere. It was the same as Sooty always wore; *La Lionesse* too.

It had to be a coincidence. It was rare for a perfume to be that exclusive, unless the wearer was wealthy enough to have a perfumer create one, just for them alone, but his mind reeled with the memories of smelling it all over her soft body and creamy skin. That he could smell it now on Bernheim made him nauseous.

"I hope she fucks you to death," he whispered hoarsely, "or gives you a permanent dose of the clap, whoever she is, the trollop. You'll not get anything from me, EVER. I'll take my secrets to the grave, You Evil. Perverted. Sick. Bastard."

The lash cracked and Nicky couldn't help crying out as it tore through his already tender and lacerated skin. "Hah, that's what you think," rasped Bernheim softly. "My oriental friend with the needles disagrees. As for my woman, she's a Lady," Bernheim sneered, "an aristocratic Lady. She appreciates a man when she finds one and I can't wait to take her, every way I want. Aaah," he sighed, "that long black hair, those green eyes and voluptuous breasts. I'll make her beg for it," he whispered tauntingly, "and you can just dangle here. You might even hear her scream with pleasure, perhaps dream about what I'm doing while I fuck a lioness," and with a malevolent laugh and a vicious jab in his sore testicles with the handle of the whip, Bernheim turned and left the room, secure in the knowledge his prisoner wasn't going anywhere.

He never saw how the man's body stiffened, nor how his jaw dropped at Bernheim's final word.

Left once more in his silent, agonised darkness, Nicky contemplated what had just happened. When he'd heard the door opening, he'd braced himself for the return of his oriental tormentor. Instead, carried on the draft of fresher air, an evocative, remembered perfume had tantalised his nostrils, mixed with Bernheim's cologne. Unable to see, his other senses were more alert than normal. When the scent had come closer he'd thought it a dream or hallucination and visions of Sooty had filled his mind. Then Bernheim had touched him, played with his necklace and he'd been confused by the strong, evocative scent coming off his jacket. When Bernheim had described the woman waiting for him, Nicky's mind had gone into overdrive with visions of Sooty. But then, Bernheim had mentioned the word 'lioness' and he was struck dumb. The coincidence was too great; his mind simply couldn't deal with the reality.

That Sooty was there, wherever there was, he had to believe, hope, but a heart-wrenching disgust crept over him as images of her fornicating with that evil, depraved bastard overwhelmed his mind. It was beyond his comprehension that she could be sharing the bed of the man willingly or because of him. He thought of Carmelita and shuddered, even as he hung there in his chains. He then remembered Rosita and the other dead girls and a numbing wave of terror filled him. He simply didn't understand any of it. Had Bella traced him and come across Bernheim herself? Had she any idea what she was doing? He doubted it. She was obviously by herself. She was completely deranged, worse than Cat.

He wondered if she actually knew he was there? If she did, had she come to try and rescue him? Having reached the point of welcoming death as an escape from the pain and torment that currently filled his days and nights, it was a tantalising prospect. But she wasn't a solitary rescue party, she wasn't her Aunt Cat. Worse, her precious life was at stake.

The thought of her, the love of his life, giving herself up to Bernheim's depravity because of him was too much to contemplate and as he hung there, tears cascaded down his face and he howled hoarsely into the silence, "Nooooooo, my Soooooooty," before he sank into welcome oblivion.

The ragged peasant youth who was wandering aimlessly along the track blended seamlessly with his surroundings. He looked like a goatherd or shepherd; a tattered, wide-brimmed straw hat was pulled down over his brow; his dirty, frayed smock hung long and loose over baggy trousers and in his hand he held a typical herder's stick. But there were no sheep or goats in his vicinity and if one were to look closely, one would notice boots poking out under the trousers instead of the expected sandals. But one would have to look very carefully and the boots were well worn. The shepherd sauntered along, chewing on a piece of straw hanging out of his mouth, looking gormless and miles away.

Jack had explored all the land surrounding the villa and was now looking for a way into the grounds other than the track that led directly down from the pillared entrance gateway. It was hot and quiet in the noonday haze and the sound of crickets filled the scented air. He pushed his way through the undergrowth and climbed over a broken fence, finding himself near a group of outbuildings and stables. A handful of chickens pecked around in the stable yard but everywhere was silent. He crept around the back of the main outbuilding and peered in through the shuttered windows as best he could. It looked like living quarters for staff but all appeared quiet and deserted. As he turned to move on, he heard the sound of quiet foot-steps and, peering in again, he watched as a thin, small man with oriental features, sallow skin and a long black pigtail hanging down his back, came into view. He was dressed in the traditional garb Jack had seen on the inscrutable men working in the opium dens in London, especially round Limehouse and the docks: loose black jacket done up to the neck with a mandarin collar, baggy black trousers, a matching small round hat on his head and simple sandals on his feet. His narrow, slitted eyes were black and he had a vivid thin scar running down one side of his face from temple to jaw. A long droopy black moustache hung either side of his thin lips and a narrow beard grew down from his chin. The man gave Jack the creeps as he watched him enter the room, take his hat off, loosen his clothes and then lie down on the bed; he settled himself comfortably and soon appeared to be asleep.

Jack crept away, shivering slightly despite the heat and, keeping to the cover of the prolific shrubbery, made his way over towards the main house. Careful to keep out of sight of the villa and the outbuildings as best he could, he stole around the perimeter, taking note of the location of various windows and doors and looking expressly for lower floor windows, skylights or vents. The villa was built on a slight slope so appeared to have several floors. Most of the upper windows overlooked the gardens and distant views of the sea and were shuttered against the strong sunlight to keep the rooms cool. On the ground and lower floor, most of the windows were either shuttered or barred.

As Jack crouched behind a thick hedge of rosemary, he could just make out the distant murmur of a voice coming from one of the lower ground floor rooms. He listened intently but couldn't make out what it was saying. A few minutes later he heard the sound of mocking, cruel laughter and a sharp cry. Then it went quiet again and only the bees buzzing around little pale blue flowers on the fragrant herbal shrub could be heard. He'd pinpointed the source of the voice: a small, barred, basement window with no glass. As he assessed the other windows on either side of the barred window for possible entry, an unearthly cry emanated from the room with the barred window. It wasn't the same as the previous one, this was a cry of such agonised despair that the hairs on Jack's neck stood on end. It went silent again and peace returned to the gardens. Jack didn't know the Duke that well, but the cry had definitely sounded like his voice and he sighed with relief that he was still alive and in the house. What condition the man was in remained to be discovered, however.

Jack crept speedily over towards the shadowed wall where the windows were located and keeping himself hard against the side of the building, dropped to all fours to peer into each window. All he could see were cell-like storage rooms, some containing bottle racks or barrels of wine, others were cold and deserted. He noted one had iron rings bolted into the stone walls with a short length of chain attached but the cell was empty. Then he reached the window from where the voice and the cry had seemed to come. Bracing himself, he peered in, then sucked in his breath at the sight of the man suspended by manacles from large hooks in the ceiling. From the way his head drooped on his chest and his body sagged, he looked to be unconscious or barely alive. Jack's eyes narrowed in his grimacing face as he took in the bloody, oozing sores, cuts and bruises that covered the man's face and entire battered torso. It was the Duke.

Jack wondered how on earth they were going to get him out.

Chapter Eleven

She thought as she pleasured him that she had reached the nadir of anything she could ever experience. As Bernheim stretched out on the luxurious bed in his shaded bedroom, naked, jerking and sighing with ecstasy under her teasing lips and hands, Bella tried with no success to blank her mind from what she was doing. His body was lean and hard, freshly clean and he smelled of a musky cologne; she felt she should be grateful for that small mercy – at least he wasn't fat, dirty or stinking of any type of sordid body odour, nor was he excessively hairy – but there was something about him that repelled her beyond explanation. As he finally climaxed in her mouth with a rapturous moan, she thought she was going to be sick, yet again. Instead, she shut her eyes for a moment and thought of Nicky to try and give herself strength, then opened them again to smile seductively at the man now lying back on the covers.

"My Dear, that was quite divine, simply heavenly," Bernheim crooned, his black eyes glimmering with passion. "Now, if you would like to slowly strip the clothes off that delectable body of yours, I'm sure you know how, I will no doubt get aroused enough again to entertain us both. I'm told I am quite the man and can last for hours; I have it down to a fine art and can even climax sometimes without losing myself…especially now you've taken the edge off my urgent desire for you."

Slowly, Bella peeled off her clothes. She wasn't remotely interested in his amorous prowess although she grimaced at the thought of putting up with him for hours. Apart from the disgust, she didn't have hours; she would have to do her best to hurry him along, if she could manage it. She'd bought her under-garments in Paris, hoping to entrance and please Nicky. That she should be using them for Bernheim's entertainment, she'd never contemplated. She decided to burn them after this.

As she started to perform in front of him, momentarily she remembered how Nicky had stripped for her that first night at *Le Lion d'Or*, but she shut her mind to that memory and concentrated on watching Bernheim, noting what appeared to please him and simply followed her instincts.

She twirled, writhed and caressed herself salaciously, peeling off each item slowly and seductively until she was left in merely her silk stockings and a nonsense of a half corset. Bernheim was as hard as a rock by the time she'd finished, caressing himself as he watched her performance. He crooked a finger and beckoned her over, moistening his fingers to then rub along her sex. Before she could say anything he moved like lightning and slid off the bed, bending her over to slap her buttocks, hard and cruelly. As she shrieked with the shock and pain, he thrust himself inside her and continued to slap and beat her. She was dry inside and the discomfort was intense but the more she cried out, the harder he thrust and the more he hit her. "Aaarrgh, oh yes, *Lionesse*, the pain, it's so wonderful. You like that so much, do you not?" Bella was speechless with shock as she writhed to escape but he grabbed her by the hair and pulled back hard, making her screech again. She stayed where she was, realising finally that the more she screamed, the more pleasure he got. Just as Jack had said.

He used her body in a number of degrading positions and became violent, vicious and seemingly insatiable. She tried to pretend she was enjoying it, crying out encouragement to him, but when, after no little effort, he forced himself into her bottom, she nearly fainted with the pain and sheer shock.

Bella's attitude to prostitutes underwent a complete alteration. She couldn't comprehend doing this night after night with a never-ending stream of strange and no doubt horrible men. Although she doubted many, if any, would do what Bernheim had just done to her, not that she actually knew how many men did enjoy sodomy, just taking him in her mouth had been difficult enough. She felt ill and her brain numb. Every inch of her body ached and she was sore inside and out. She was sure she must be black and blue all over.

Something in Bella changed that afternoon. She'd never get over what she did with Bernheim; to say he abused her was an understatement, but she did as Jack said. With a monumental effort, she finally closed off her mind and shut away her emotions. She laughed and cried out with simulated ecstasy as he fucked her, she couldn't ever call it making love. Then, having climaxed again inside her, he didn't stop, but simply continued and got even more carnal and depraved and his perverted appetites started to take over as he seemed to get more and more excited. He slapped and spanked her to arouse himself to further heights and then he drove into her ruthlessly, invading every orifice of her body in turn. He was vicious, he was rough and he was surprisingly strong. It was like trying to stop the incoming tide.

She pleasured him with her mouth frequently to try and keep him out of her body, she was so dry other than the remains of his previous release so at least that helped ease the pain for a while, she thought hysterically, but he was relentless and still insatiable. He took her into different rooms of the villa, dragging her by the hair, to force her into all sorts of depraved positions, contorting her and pinioning her in them with anything to hand, like the sash cords from the drapes, smacking her again, until finally, when she didn't think she could take any more, he bent her over the desk in his study, gripping both her wrists high up behind her back in a ruthless, iron grip as he thrust once more into her soft, tender bottom. As he thrust, hard and deep, making her screech in pain, which he took to be pleasure, his own moans of ecstasy grew louder and more distracted. Then he let go her wrists and his hands went around her neck. As his climax approached, his hands grew tighter and tighter around her throat and Bella pulled at them ineffectually, terrified he would strangle her as he had the prostitutes in Madrid. She was choking and coughing, her breath coming in gasps as his release finally overtook him and his hands relaxed as his body collapsed over her back.

"You drive me to such ecstatic heights, *Lionesse*," he panted in her ear, "so keen to suck and service me, so pleasurable to find someone who enjoys pain and submission and understands my needs."

Bella had merely sighed back at him, acting in a terrible nightmare "Aah Frederick, I enjoy giving and receiving pain, usually depending on my mood, but THIS is all about YOU, because you're such a man. So desirable, so insatiable, you lasted so long. I couldn't keep up with you…you overwhelmed me."

He'd pulled out of her then, finally exhausted by his efforts before returning upstairs with her to his bedroom as if what had just occurred had been a trifling social interlude over a cup of tea. He pulled her into bed with him and fell fast asleep. Bella lay next to him like a soiled, broken doll and felt hot tears course down her face. She felt like a prostitute, worse than a prostitute. She felt as if she'd been torn in two, dirty and used, thinking she could never contemplate going near any man, ever again. Just like the tragic, innocent Amandine Fourneval.

Listening to Bernheim's snores, she crept out of bed, feeling like a cripple she was so sore, but she forced herself to dress hastily in the dressing room where she'd left her weapons secreted under her large hat and shawl, gloves and reticule. She ensured her pistols were now easily to hand as she stood and looked down at the man on the bed, her fingers around one of the pistols and thought about her dagger. She loathed Bernheim with every fibre of her being but, as she stood there, she knew she could never bring herself to murder him in cold blood and despised herself as feeble, the pistol trembling in her hand as she battled with herself. She told herself her Aunt Cat or Great Aunt Elizabeth wouldn't have had any qualms were they in her shoes, but it made no difference; she simply couldn't do it. She wondered if she could tie him up but was worried he'd wake up before she had him secured, so hoping against hope he would sleep for a long while and that Jack had found a way in to the cellars, she turned and hurried out of the room and made her way downstairs. Her whole body ached unbearably but Nicky's life depended on her so she forgot her own problems, totally focussed on finding the man who was her entire *raison d'être*.

She half hobbled and half ran out into the gardens and round the back of the house, now inspecting the barred windows that obviously were set into the cellar room walls and wondered where Jack was. She would rather investigate the cellars with him than by herself, as she didn't know if there were guards down there, despite Bernheim saying his retainers were elsewhere. She eventually peered into one barred window and reared back in horror at the sight. The vision of Nicky, unconscious and covered in dried blood, suppurating sores and weals all over his torso, bedraggled, filthy and suspended from the ceiling in chains, would haunt her forever and her hand went to her mouth as she felt her stomach heave. She nearly jumped out of her skin when a firm but gentle hand grasped her shoulder and another came over her mouth to stop her crying out. "Ssshhh! It's only me," whispered Jack. "Come away quickly in case you're seen. There's servants around here."

He pulled her into some shrubs and looked at her closely. "Are you all right? Where's Bernheim?" he said quietly, taking in her ashen, haunted face and trembling hands. He didn't miss the marks and slight bruises he could see on her skin above the neckline of her dress and one on her cheek. Deep anger roiled through him.

"I'm fine," she said stonily. "That perverted bastard is asleep. I know I should have killed him but I couldn't bring myself to do it in cold blood." She suddenly looked distraught. "I'm sorry, Jack, I'm so feeble, I know I am. I'm weak and useless," she said brokenly, "but I simply couldn't do it."

"Of course you couldn't," Jack replied softly. "If you had, you'd be no better than they are. Don't worry, we'll go and get your husband. I've been reconnoitring. I think Bernheim's men are going back down to the cellar to start on him again later, so we'll have to be careful, though how we get him out in his state I'm not sure."

Bella looked back in the window and shivered as tears ran down her face. She turned to Jack, "The bastards, they're worse than animals. I've got to get him out, I don't care what happened to me, it was nothing to what they've done to Nicky."

Jack stared carefully at his mistress. There was something slightly different about her somehow... shock yes, but a hardness that wasn't there before. He knew what had happened, had seen it several times in the Dials. People lost their innocence there, their goodness, in an effort to survive. He hoped this change in his mistress was only temporary and his eyes were saddened.

Chapter Twelve

Bella followed Jack to where he'd climbed over the broken fencing. It was now late afternoon and the servants' quarters were deserted. They quietly entered the grounds through a rear gate and made their way outside the villa from room to room. Five showed signs of occupation, one of which was obviously a woman, a housekeeper by the signs of the spare clothes in her closet. They now knew potentially how many they were dealing with.

They saw the housekeeper first. She was hanging some washing out on the clothesline in a kitchen garden, hidden from view of the back door by a hedge. Jack turned to Bella and put a finger to his lips and then crept up behind the middle-aged woman. A hefty blow from his pistol butt felled her without a sound and, with help from Bella, he pulled her back into the bushes near the fence. They left her limp body, tightly bound and gagged with her stockings and torn strips from her petticoats.

There were four left. They waited for a while and, as they'd hoped, a grumbling man walked out of the kitchen door, calling for the missing woman. He was dressed in an apron and was obviously a cook. As he came round the hedge he met the same fate and was left near the housekeeper.

Then there were three left. Jack and Bella had a whispered conversation and decided to make their way into the house through the now open door.

Pistols cocked and ready, they approached quickly and quietly and were just going through to the kitchen when a muted but terrible scream rent the air. It came from the direction of the cellar window. Jack gripped Bella's arm as her eyes widened with horror and she gasped. "Be strong, we'll get him," he muttered resolutely and went into the house as a second agonised scream followed the first.

They crept through the silent kitchen, pots now boiling over as they cooked. Bella raised her eyes at Jack as he moved the pots off the range. "Just in case anyone comes in this way," he shrugged back at her.

They moved out of the kitchen and into the hallway. Jack followed Bella into Bernheim's study, a sitting room, morning room and then a dining room, watching her curiously until he realised what she was up to. Wherever she found any decanters or carafes of liquid, she poured a few drops of her poison into each. She hoped Bernheim was thirsty when he woke up, or his business acquaintances were when they came to visit for a meeting. This somehow didn't bother her, but why she couldn't kill Bernheim in cold blood, she still couldn't fathom.

She led the way towards the door to the cellar that Bernheim had casually pointed out during their depraved afternoon and found it locked. Undeterred, Jack produced a couple of small tools from his pocket and, with raised eyebrows from Bella, he opened the door in seconds. "Wherever did you get those from?" she whispered, amazed.

"I thought they might come in handy," he smirked at her, "so I brought them with from Firle. No idea why since I thought this was going to be a 'sightseeing and shopping' trip. But they're useful for Duchess's suite doors and all sorts of things." Bella shook her head and smiled, momentarily distracted from the horror surrounding them.

They crept carefully down the dark stairs. Someone had left a wall sconce burning in the wine cellar at the bottom. Making their way carefully past the barrels and hundreds of wine bottles, they reached a second door. As Jack was about to investigate that lock, they heard someone approach on the other side so quickly ducked down behind some large wine racks and held their breath. The door opened and the large dumb Arab lumbered through and made his way towards the staircase, leaving the door open behind him.

"You didn't lock the upstairs door behind us, did you?" Bella whispered.

"No, it was too dark, and anyway, I wouldn't have in case we needed to make a quick exit; trust me, that's more important," whispered Jack back at her. He was in full-on thief mode now.

"Let's hope our tongueless friend doesn't think anything of it then. What shall we do? Go through or wait to see if he comes back?"

Distant agonised cries emanating through the open door made up Jack's mind. "I think we have our answer. Come along, Your Grace, I can't sit here a moment longer; I was about to go in myself when I spotted you coming outside." He stood up to creep through the open doorway, Bella hot on his heels, cocked pistols now in her hands.

The barred gate to one of the cellar storage rooms was hanging open and beyond that was a door leading to the chamber where she'd seen Nicky hanging in chains. It was half open and Bella and Jack carefully peered through the gap between the door and the frame.

The long wooden refectory table had been pulled into the middle of the room and Nicky was now lying face up on it, spread-eagled, his wrists and ankles tied down with thick rope. The Chinaman was standing over him and long needles were stuck into his body, all over his chest and torso. As they watched in shock, the little oriental man inserted another, causing the man on the table to cry out in obvious pain. "Whey is Valensen gol?" his sing-song voice asked, twirling the last needle as he spoke.

Bella strained her ears to hear the response. "*Sais pas...*" A hoarse voice barely whispered back.

"Ah, but you do, Yol Glaice; why you not tell me and save all pain?" He twirled another needle, causing a further agonised cry.

"*Sais pas,*" Nicky murmured, his voice now not even a hoarse whisper.

"Tly again." Another twirled needle, then he placed another couple further up Nicky's chest, near his neck, causing further tormented moans and cries of pain from the restrained and painfully writhing man.

"Fuck yo… aaaaiiiiieeeeeeeee," the hoarse scream was all Bella and Jack just about heard.

Bella moved before an alarmed Jack could stop her. She raised her pistols and stormed into the room. "If you stick one more needle into him, I swear to God you'll regret the day you were ever born," she cried, suddenly noticing a second large Arab lolling back in a chair against the wall who lurched to his feet at her entrance. "You too!" she waved her other pistol at him.

"Take the needles out and release his hands and legs," Bella spat at the Chinaman.

"Monsoo Belnheim, he no likee if I do dat," replied the little man.

"Well I no likee if you don't," replied Bella venomously. "Now, do as I say!" But the Chinaman didn't move, merely stared at her inscrutably.

"Who you?" he asked but Bella ignored him.

The Arab took a step nearer to her and she waved her pistol at him. "Don't think I won't shoot you," she threatened but he looked at her as if she was an irritating fly, standing there in her elegant day dress. He started to lumber towards her, his hands reaching out and dark eyes glinting nastily. "I'm warning you," she threatened once more but the Arab ignored her, so Bella raised the pistol, took aim and fired. He dropped like a stone, the report of the firearm bouncing off the walls around them. The Chinaman suddenly took advantage of her momentary distraction and leapt at her. With a chopping movement he knocked the second pistol from her hand as one of his legs came up and he kicked her hard on the chest. Stunned by the movement, Bella fell to her knees but rose to her feet to watch in disbelief as he spun round and kicked her again. She fell back for a second time and hit the table, causing a moan from the man on it as it rocked and she slid to her knees again, stunned, her head rocking forward as she tried to gather herself. The Chinaman smiled evilly at her and raised his hand in the air to bring it down in a chopping motion against her exposed neck but suddenly, a second shot rang out and, his expression stunned, he collapsed to the floor, a ball from Jack's smoking pistol lodged deep in his back.

Jack ran into the room and helped Bella to her feet. "Are you all right?" he exclaimed anxiously and Bella nodded, gripping the side of the table to support herself. They both turned to the man on it. Bella ripped off the rag over his eyes and he blinked in confusion.

"Sooty?" he croaked. It was all he could manage, disbelief written over his face.

"Oh, Nicky," Bella wailed in anguish, "what the devil have they done to you?"

Jack was about to bend to untie the ropes and release his hands as Bella eyed the needles askance. Tentatively she pulled one out and Nicky let loose an agonised cry. "I've got to take these out, we can't move you with them stuck in you like this, you're like a horrifying pin cushion," as she pulled another, causing him to cry out again.

"Oh God, Jack, what can I do? I can't bear to cause him more pain."

Jack stood up to inspect for himself and started to speak, "You've got to, Your Gr..." but he got no further. The large dumb Arab had silently crept into the chamber and suddenly appeared behind them, making a grab for Bella. She screamed as he caught her by the arm in a grip of steel and pulled her to him, his other arm snaking around her neck.

"Let 'er go," shouted Jack as he pulled his own second pistol from his belt, cocking it as he pointed it at the man. But the Arab merely looked at him blankly.

"Er... *libérez la femme*," Jack essayed again, suspecting the man didn't understand English, but the Arab merely opened his tongueless mouth and directed a strange sound at Jack, his version of a laugh, then tightened his grip round Bella's throat, causing her to make choking sounds as her feet kicked uselessly against him.

"Oh, fuck you," Jack snarled, aimed the pistol and fired. Bella screamed again as she felt the ball whizz past her head to bury itself in the forehead of her captor, who slowly sank to the floor behind her, pulling her with him as he fell.

"Christ, Jack," she stuttered as he helped her up, "that's two I owe you." Bella looked into the face of the young man in front of her as she rubbed her neck. "How can I ever thank you?"

He bent his head, embarrassed. "It's nothing, you'd have done the same for me." He turned, releasing Nicky's bonds once again.

"Sooty?" Nicky begged in a hoarse whisper she could barely hear. "Water. Pliss...so thi'sty." Bella looked angrily at his cracked, parched lips and then around the bare room but there was no water to be seen.

Jack had just released the ropes holding down Nicky's wrists and was about to free his legs when Bella said urgently, "Can you go and find him something to drink, Jack? It might give him some strength. But remember, I've poisoned all the decanters." Jack nodded and hurried out of the chamber as she turned, intent on undoing the rest of the ropes. But first, she leaned over Nicky and gently kissed him lovingly, on his bruised and filthy face. He raised his head slightly to look at her through bloodshot, pain-glazed, golden eyes. He blinked again, unaccustomed to the light. "'lo Trouble..." he murmured hoarsely, trying to lift an arm and failing. "Are y'ever goin' t' stop f'llowing me 'round?" But his head fell back to the table once more, a momentary smile on his face before his eyes closed again and he lost consciousness.

"Oh, Nicky," was all Bella could manage, her voice choked as her hand tenderly caressed his battered, dirty face and ruffled his hair. "Never," she whispered lovingly, "never ever. I'm a hopeless case."

Wincing as she did so, she removed the remaining needles and released Nicky's ankles while he was unconscious then bent towards his face once more to try and bring him round. "Nicky? Nicky? Wake up, pleeeeease!" She slapped the sides of his face gently. "Nicky? Oh, please, My Love, you've got to wake up. We have to get you out of here, quickly, before anyone else comes." She bent once more, trying to bring him round, eventually hearing him groan quietly.

Well, well, well," a sibilant voice hissed behind her. "I catch one rat and now I find I have two in my trap. How pleasing."

Bella turned and gasped to look into Bernheim's malevolent back eyes, a pistol in his outstretched hand.

"Can you imagine how surprised I was to wake up to the sounds of pistols being fired and find myself alone in my bed? And now here you are, making a mess." He looked disparagingly at the dead bodies of his men and tutted, "How very inconvenient of you, My Dear. Ling Fu was such a useful and talented individual."

"That evil bastard," bit out Bella, "is no loss to anyone, and neither will you be when the Authorities catch up with you and your friends."

Bernheim laughed strangely. "I don't think so, My Dear. In fact, I and my associates will be long gone before anyone is any the wiser and the Emperor will be back in Paris, not that I much care who rules, just so long as I get paid for my trouble." He shrugged nonchalantly as Bella looked back at him with utter loathing. "However, the immediate question is, what shall I do with you?" He looked at her thoughtfully. "So, this man, who is he to you, I wonder, not just another agent it appears?"

Bella didn't hear the whispered, "Nooo, say nothin'," Nicky's voice was too quiet and hoarse as he struggled to come to his senses again and lift himself.

She pulled her shoulders back, her voice withering. "He is my husband. As you have seen, I would do ANYTHING, put up with ANYTHING, even your disgusting depravity, in order to retrieve him from your clutches." She looked at Bernheim disdainfully as he stood there in a black velvet dressing robe, an elaborate set of initials embroidered in gold on a large breast pocket.

"Amazing! *La Duchesse de Valenciennes* no less, come to rescue her husband. My, how touching. Do you work for Wellington too?" he enquired conversationally.

"I just want my husband back. I have no interest in your machinations or anyone else's, but if I happen to put an end to your nefarious activities, so much the better," Bella responded with considerable hauteur. "Unlike you, I am a patriotic Englishwoman and love my country. We are far from perfect, but our politics are considerably better than those on offer from revolutionaries or a megalomaniac. One hopes the restored monarchy will be an improvement on the former one and has learned its lesson and that your compatriots realise that, but, as I said, that is secondary to concern for my husband.

"Really? How very noble of you, My Dear. But, I wonder, we didn't seem to be getting very far extracting information from your husband." He paused, looked her up and down and then over at Nicky. "Maybe if we start on you? I've learned quite a bit from my Chinese friend, you see, even though I prefer to whip or beat my women. The noble Duke might be a bit more forthcoming with a few needles stuck in your abdomen or neck. What do you say, Your Grace?" Bernheim looked at Nicky's horrified face. He'd managed to rise very slightly but his whole body felt numb and his muscles wouldn't respond properly due to the effect of the needles, on top of his other injuries.

"Let 'er go an' I'll te' yo' what'ver yo' wan'. You c'n 'ave everythin', 'vry guinea I 'ave, what'ver yo' wan' but jes' leave 'er 'lone," he whispered, coughing in his effort to speak, loud enough to be heard, nonetheless.

"Quite fascinating," muttered Bernheim, raising his eyebrows. "We couldn't persuade him to say anything before except curse, like a cretinous, uncouth peasant, but threaten to lift a finger to your beautiful face and body...*et voilá!*" He snapped his fingers as he started to walk towards Bella. "Now then, *Madame Duchesse*, where should I start to persuade my canary to sing?" He gazed at Bella consideringly, "I must say you look quite fetching, My Dear; well-fucked, not at all the aristocratic Lady you usually appear to be. Though I must say, after what you did this afternoon, the way you performed for me, 'Lady' isn't perhaps the right word?"

Bella heard Nicky's choked gasp as she moved backwards as Bernheim approached, but she was then hard against the table. "Let him go and I'll give you whatever you want," she said with as much ice in her voice as she could muster. "I'm a wealthy woman in my own right and I really do run two gaming establishments. I know all you want is money, so how much will it take? I can also call upon my family if I don't have enough; just name your price."

"Oh, so that part of your story was true then? I wonder how much else is? It'll be interesting to find out." He was almost upon her when he heard a footstep behind him.

"She might be too good to kill you in cold blood," said a venomous voice in English behind him, "but I have no such qualms, given where I come from. I've already shot one of your bastards in the back, so two will be no problem. Come away from her and put your pistol down." Jack was standing in the doorway, a carafe of water in one hand, a raised pistol in the other. But Bella knew he'd fired both his pistols and her eyes widened with fright at his bravado.

Nicky lay frozen with dread and frustration at his inability to move properly, not that he would have been able to do anything. He felt as helpless as a new-born kitten, in the midst of the surreal and dangerous tableau currently playing out.

Bernheim noted Bella's expression with interest. He turned his head slightly to see who was behind him, never taking his aim from her. "Ah, your 'nephew' I take it?" he mused sarcastically. However, he had mistaken her frightened expression. "You do well to look worried, My Dear. If he shoots me, my pistol has a hair trigger and you will go down too, I promise. So, an interesting situation we find ourselves in, what?"

"Do it, Jack!" cried Bella, wondering perhaps if he had reloaded after all, or found another pistol.

"Noooo," the terrified hoarse whisper emanated from Nicky.

Slowly, Jack went down on one knee and theatrically placed the water and his pistol on the floor, making Bernheim smirk with his apparent success and step back slightly to encompass the room. Now all three of his prisoners were in view. His pistol was still pointed at Bella but he had lost his concentration momentarily when Jack put down his weapon. Nicky watched in fascination as it returned to Bella as Jack's hand inched towards his boot and in a swiftness of movement that took Nicky's breath away, he watched as his stiletto suddenly appeared and flew through the air to bury itself in Bernheim's upper back, just as the man turned to take aim once more at Bella. At the split second he threw the knife, Jack yelled, "MOVE, BELLA!" The pistol exploded but she didn't move fast enough and Bella staggered for a second then slowly sank towards the floor.

Jack rushed forward looking distraught and caught Bella up in his arms. The ball had gone through her right shoulder and although she was unconscious, she was still alive. He sighed with relief. He turned to the Duke, "Can you move, Your Grace?"

"No' much," Nicky whispered back, "bu' ne'er min' me." He looked panic struck, "Where's she hit?"

"In the shoulder, the right one, she needs a doctor, but she'll make it, I know it. She's stronger than she looks."

Nicky collapsed back, his eyes closing in relief and pain. "Than' God," he whispered, "Wa'er, pliss, then look after 'er."

Jack carefully laid Bella's head on the floor and ran to get the carafe of water and take it over to the tortured man. He propped him up in his arms and helped him drink, shocked at how thirsty he was. When Nicky had drunk his fill, Jack gently laid him back down again and stood back to survey the room and take stock.

He was the only one on his feet. The Duke was conscious but obviously severely beaten and injured so was incapacitated, and the Duchess alive but unconscious. He couldn't give a damn about the rest of them. But he knew he had to get out and away as quickly as possible. He went over to speak to the Duke, "I can see you've been through Hell, but do you think you can walk?" he asked. "We have to get out of here, but I can't carry you both."

"I'm 'relevant," Nicky's voice was slightly stronger now his throat wasn't so parched and his brain was starting to work again. "Jus' get 'er out of 'ere an' to a doc; she's your pri'rity." He looked up at Jack, "Who ARE you, by th' way? You look vag'ly fam'liar, but I can't place you."

Jack grinned at him, feeling lightheaded. "I'm Jack Vallance, Your Grace, a groom at Firle. The Duchess of Firle ordered me to accompany your wife over here to France and look after her. I thought she was going sightseeing and shopping, but this is the strangest shopping trip I've ever been on." He chuckled briefly and slightly hysterically before turning serious again. "If you'll excuse me saying, Your Grace, we've traipsed across the whole of this bloody country looking for you, messing with all these damn Frenchies and I'll be buggered that now we've found you if I'm not going to make sure you get back to London, safe and sound!"

Nicky smiled back at the youth, feeling his mind coming more and more together, even if he still felt like he'd been run over by a coach and four. "I'm a damn Frenchie I'll 'ave you know, but tell me, you don't speak like a groom?" he was puzzled by the lad's accent which was almost as cut-glass as his at times.

"Well, you're excused because you're really English, aren't you? I got my education from Mr Crichton, the old tutor at Firle, the Duchess saw to it."

"Ah," chuckled Nicky, understanding immediately. "Another of her waifs and strays. I was one too, y'know, she found ME in Rouen Fortress and helped me escape, so we have something in common. And I know Richard Crichton. He had his moments with me, too, in my youth. But enough of this, we have to get away from here. Can you help me up?" Nicky grimaced as he struggled to rise and Jack bent to help him. With a monumental effort of mind over matter, Nicky finally managed to sit up on the table, feeling his head swim again for a moment, but when he went to stand, his legs gave out from under him and he fell back again with a deep groan.

Jack left him temporarily and knelt down. Blood was oozing from Bella's shoulder so he tore strips from her petticoats and wadded them into a pad which he pressed under the material of her dress bodice. He stood up, making a decision. "Right," he said. "I've dealt with the servants outside so I'm going to carry the Duchess upstairs and lay her in the sitting room. I saw a small cart and a horse in the stables, so I'll go and get that and bring it round. Then I'll come back for you and we'll all go back down to Nice in that. I'm not sure where the coachman is, nor the carriage Her Grace came in, but I'll deal with him if he appears, don't you worry. He'll be a piece of piss after this lot of bloody foreigners!"

Nicky looked at the lad in amazement. "I can see why Cat, er, the Duchess, chose you to escort my wife. How old are you?"

"Sixteen, Sir, well that's what Her Grace thinks, as I'm not too sure. I could be seventeen, or fourteen or fifteen."

"Fifteen? Sixteen? Good God, and where on earth did she find you?"

"I was trying to thieve her reticule in Bond Street. I grew up and lived in the Seven Dials."

Nicky's eyes widened in astonishment. "The Dials? Damn me! But that explains a good deal." He shook his head in bemusement as he watched Jack heave Bella's unconscious form up and over his shoulder and disappeared out through the door to make his way upstairs.

Nicky stared for a long while at Bernheim's prostrate body with the Duchess's stiletto protruding out of his back, then at the lifeless forms of his tormentors, strewn around the cellar room floor. Sooty and Jack had come at the eleventh hour. He knew he'd been at the end of his tether and couldn't have survived another day of their torture. But his mind reeled as he remembered Bernheim's words and he shuddered to think of his beautiful Sooty in Bernheim's bed. A stream of tormenting images filled his head until he put his face in his hands and wept at what she must have done to get to this place and rescue him.

Jack eventually hurried back into the cellar and found the Duke still weeping, a tormented look on his face. "Your Grace!" he cried in alarm, "whatever is it?"

Nicky looked at Jack. "Do you know what happened with my wife and Bernheim?" he asked quietly, his expression agonised.

Jack looked him directly in the eye. "Yes, Sir, but she did what she had to, it was the only way to find out where you were and then distract him. She, well, she's taken it hard. You'll have to be very understanding and go careful with her." He gave Nicky a very mean-ingful look. "I tried to help her deal with it, best I could. I knew what she was facing, what it's like, the sort of man he was…" he shrugged.

"Bloody hell!" Nicky swore softly as he instantly understood the implication in the words.

"Exactly," said Jack pithily, "but I can explain more later. Come along, Your Grace, we've got to get you upstairs and into the cart."

Jack was strong for his age but he struggled with the taller, much bigger and heavier man. Nicky gasped in pain and frustration once more when Jack pulled one of his arms round his neck and half dragged, half carried him towards the cellar door. As they were about to go through, Nicky bade Jack stop. He forced himself to lean against the wall, sweat at his exertions running down his face, his body on fire and fresh blood oozing from several of his cuts and weals. "Go and get that stiletto, Jack," he panted. "It belongs to the Duchess of Firle. She loaned it to me as a sort of lucky talisman, saying it would keep me safe. It means a lot to her. The Duke gave it to her a long time ago when he helped her and her family escape from Normandy and she used to carry it with her for protection for years, until she gave it to me when I went to war. She used it to kill a very unpleasant man in Rouen Fortress a long time ago, to save the Duke's life and end an unspeakable reign of evil by his associate, so it has sentimental, not monetary value. I don't want to leave it to rust in that bastard as he rots."

Jack hurried over to Bernheim's body, pulled out the knife and wiped it on his baggy peasant's trousers as he rushed back to the Duke to continue to virtually drag him out the cellar. Neither heard the almost silent groan that emanated from the body in the long black dressing robe as the dagger was removed from his back. The man's brain silently seethed at the patches of conversation he'd overheard while he'd drifted in and out of consciousness on the cold cellar floor, including those final words from his nemesis about the history of the dagger and its owner. At last! He had a definite lead as to who these people were who had put paid to his father's activities in Rouen. Firle, in England. That was the clue to everything…and he passed out again.

Getting him through the cellars and up the stairs was a nightmare, but Nicky literally crawled and forced himself forward on his hands and knees as best he could. Jack dragged and heaved him by the shoulders and legs until his own muscles screamed with the effort of moving the big man who was virtually a dead weight. Eventually, gasping and breathless, to Jack's enormous relief he finally toppled Nicky unceremoniously into the back of the cart where he passed out, sheer bloody-minded determination on both their parts having carried the day. Jack hurried back into the house and retrieved Bella and set her down in the back of the cart too. Finally, he ran inside yet again, did a quick search and collected her reticule and other belongings from the bedrooms upstairs so no identifying trace of her would be left behind. He thoughtfully tore off some blankets from Bernheim's bed and, with the Duke and Duchess covered, the little cart set off and wended its bumpy way down the hilly tracks, back to Nice.

Chapter Thirteen

Jack's next decision was where to take them. As the horse slowly plodded along, he turned in his seat and looked at the figures in the back. The blankets had partly slipped off them and the unconscious Duke looked like he'd been in a pitched battle and lost. The Duchess looked pale and drawn with blood all over her dress, her skirts and petticoats ripped and torn from Jack's desperate efforts to make some bandages. He needed to find a doctor for them both. Feeling exhausted and overwhelmed at the events of that terrible afternoon, Jack pulled the cart over to the side of the road. Finally, shaking with delayed reaction, the boy put his head in his hands and simply cried his eyes out.

His bout of weeping over, Jack gave himself a good talking to. If he fell apart now, it would all be for naught and he had to think. Money. He needed money. He'd learned he could achieve anything with enough of it and there was plenty in their rooms at the hotel. So, parking the cart in the shade of a stand of trees in a little park, he crawled into the back and shook the Duke, hard. Nicky groaned and opened one eye. "We're back in Nice and I've got to go and get some money. You HAVE to stay awake while I'm gone," he shook Nicky's shoulders again, "d'you hear me, Sir?" Nicky nodded. "I'll be as quick as I can and the reins are tied up. I don't think the horse will go anywhere but you need to keep a look out." With that, he jumped down again. "I'll return as soon as I can," he added and hurried off in the direction of the hotel.

He crept through a back entrance that was used for deliveries, realising his bloodstained peasant attire would alarm both the guests and management, to make his way up to their rooms where he picked the locks to enter them. He hurriedly changed clothes in his room, packed up his things and went through to the Duchess's suite. He retrieved all the money he'd discovered in the Duke's portmanteau, thankful it was still there and not thieved by the staff, then rummaged through the Duchess's cases until he forced open one of her locked bags to find a large hoard of gold. He packed a change of clothes into a small bag for both the Duke and the Duchess and hurried furtively out of the hotel and back to the cart.

On his way, he called into a livery stable and in broken French enquired about some discreet, clean lodgings. With his aching head full of left and right turns and instructions in French, after trying one or two which he didn't fancy, he finally pulled up in front of a quiet house on the outskirts of the town. He went in and took two rooms for a week and with a hefty tip to the concierge, then half dragged and heaved a blanket-covered Nicky into one of the rooms where he collapsed with an agonised groan on to the large bed. As it was evening by this time, Jack explained away the moans and groans and Nicky's inability to walk by himself by telling the concierge the man had drunk too much and had fallen badly. He then went out and picked up the Duchess, draped a blanket over her and carried her into the room to deposit her on the bed next to the Duke. He told the concierge Bella had imbibed too much as well, hoping the money he'd given the elderly woman would ensure she kept her mouth shut about the strangeness of her new temporary tenants.

He went out to visit the concierge once again. A lot more gold exchanged hands and soon a bath and steaming hot water arrived in the Duke's room together with a tray of food from a tavern round the corner. Finally, a servant was sent off to summon a discreet local doctor.

Jack helped the unsteady Duke strip off what was left of his stinking rags, gasping as he took in the full state of his battered and bloodied body. With a great deal of swearing and effort, he finally helped him get into the bath and sink into the steaming waters. He grimaced as he carefully inspected the terrible sores, torn flesh, weals, cuts and bruises that marked Nicky's face and torso, bathing and tending them as best he could. Staring at the horrific lacerations and tortured flesh, Jack wondered in amazement how on earth the Duke had stood what had been done to him, let alone remain alive.

Nicky literally groaned in torment as he sank into the warm water after the effort it had cost him to struggle into the deep tin bath and he told Jack he reckoned several of his ribs were broken or fractured. He shuddered and shook with pain from those and the various torn muscles in his shoulders, arms and back as a result of being suspended. He gradually relaxed down into the hot water and let Jack gently sponge off the dirt from his hair and face, sending a silent prayer of thanks to the Old Moor who had tended him so well the previous year. His wound had held firm and appeared not to have been too badly affected, although as he ached and hurt everywhere inside as well as out, Nicky simply didn't know for sure. He was pale and shaking like a leaf when Jack literally heaved him out the filthy water and he collapsed, dripping, into a towel covered chair with Jack mollycoddling him like a little child. There were so many wounds on his body, Jack didn't know where to start, so simply pulled a clean, soft shirt over him and helped him into some clean breeches, looser on him than usual due to his period of virtual starvation in his cellar prison and then resolved to go straight to the apothecary for salves and bandages for his wounds. Nicky's face was virtually unrecognisable, a battered mass of cuts and bruises, his lips swollen and his eyes puffy, reddened and half closed, but Jack prayed everything would hopefully heal in good time and the Duke's stunning looks wouldn't be too spoiled. He didn't offer to find a mirror, suspecting it might distress the man quite a bit if he actually saw what he looked like beneath the accumulated beard.

The doctor arrived with a young assistant and after much huffing and tutting, removed the ball from Bella's shoulder and dressed her wound. They covered her in her nightgown and left her to continue sleeping, the doctor saying she should return to consciousness soon but to call him again if not and to keep a watch out for any infection.

He looked at Nicky's battered face and enquired what had happened to the pair of them as he'd noted the bruises and marks on Bella's body. At his most cutting, Nicky merely said he, his wife and young brother-in-law were travelling along the coast for a short holiday but his wife and he had been set upon by footpads on their return from visiting friends who had a new home up in the hills and they'd been beaten soundly, especially himself, to hand over their money and valuables. Obviously, he'd tried to put up a good fight, hence his sore face; fortunately, his brother-in-law had come looking for them and brought them back to Nice where they would spend a few days recovering before returning back to their home in Paris. Jack had kept his back turned the whole time and his mouth shut. The doctor, decided Nicky was a Person of Some Standing and clearly not in any way nefarious, so he merely tutted in sympathy, asked his assistant to leave some salves for his battered and bruised face and told them they should report the matter to the Authorities. The man then bowed and departed, clutching a generous bag of gold coins handed over by a silent Jack with a nod.

Finally, the three of them were alone. Bella slept on; Jack and Nicky struggled to eat some of the food from the tavern while Jack told Nicky the whole story of where he and Bella had been since arriving in France and what they'd been doing. He privately told Nicky how he'd found him in the slums of Paris the first time, and then followed him that last morning to the prostitute's tenement, then the livery from where he'd left for Nice and finally, how he'd traced him in Nice to his lodgings.

Nicky was completely taken aback and shook his head at how this enterprising young lad, not Bella, had managed to track him so closely and it explained how Bella had found him. He looked over at the youth and realised his head was lolling – he was completely exhausted and overwhelmed with what he'd achieved in rescuing them all. So, after asking him to help him over to the bed again, he sent him off to his own room, rolled over next to Bella and fell fast asleep, thanking his lucky stars for the day the soft-hearted Duchess of Firle had taken in the young groom and had the forethought to send him with Bella on her travels.

Jack slept like the dead around the clock and finally came to the following afternoon. Embarrassed, he hurried into the Duke's room to find him sitting by the bed, watching over the Duchess. She was shifting restlessly and after laying a hand on her forehead, Jack said he thought she was developing a fever and went to summon the doctor. He also visited the apothecary for some more healing salves, bandages and strapping for the Duke's body plus some clean shirts, noting the bloodstains on the one he was wearing. After an argument about strapping up Nicky's ribs and checking for more internal damage, which a worried Jack wanted to do, they'd finally agreed he could live without the nosey doctor seeing more than necessary and Jack would have to tend his sores and open wounds as best he could.

For the next two weeks, Bella tossed and turned and her body was periodically racked with fever. The doctor found a nurse to tend her and Nicky refused to leave her side. She moaned and cried in her sleep for Nicky and Terrie, then other nightmares tormented her dreams, making her cry out in anguish. Nicky was distraught but eventually the fever lessened and the doctor pronounced she had turned the corner. During this time her monthly courses had come and gone and privately, Nicky had breathed a enormous sigh of relief there would be no child as a result of whatever she'd done with Bernheim. That her anguished nightmares were a result of this he had no doubt, but they would have to deal with that once she recovered both her consciousness and her strength.

In the meantime, Jack had removed all their belongings from the hotel and checked out, so to all intents and purposes, he, the Duke and Duchess had disappeared. But he still worried some of Bernheim's accomplices, or even the Authorities might come after them and he was anxious to leave as quickly and quietly as possible.

Nicky and Jack eventually agreed the best way was to take passage on a ship to England. They had no idea if the liveries were being watched, nor if someone was looking for them, but a nervous Jack didn't want to take any chances by hiring a coach which could be too easily followed and stopped. Disappearing off on a boat or packet would make them less likely to be spotted. While a worried Nicky kept vigil over Bella, Jack went to see what he could do about finding a vessel that would quietly take them away from Nice.

Chapter Fourteen

"Hello, Sooty." Bella finally opened her eyes to find Nicky's concerned golden ones looking down into them, his hand holding hers on top of the coverlet. He lifted it to his lips and kissed it lovingly. "You can never tell ME off again for oversleeping," he smiled gently.

"Where are we?" she asked anxiously, not recognising her surroundings and panicking slightly.

"Still in Nice, but safe," he said quietly, "don't worry."

"Where's Jack?" she looked around in concern.

"That young lad is out finding us some lunch. I've no idea where he puts all his food," he chuckled, "I thought I ate a lot when I was his age, but I'm sure it wasn't as much as he does."

Bella looked up into Nicky's beloved face, noting the now yellowing bruises around his eyes and remnants of cuts and scratches. She raised her hand and stroked his cheek, now just covered with a bit of stubble, simply because he couldn't be bothered to shave every day. "Are you all right?" she whispered. "I thought they were going to kill you," her eyes looked haunted.

"I'm still a bit sore, a few broken ribs and my old wound is playing up again, even though I thought it was all right...but, I'll live," he smiled. "You know us pussy cats, nine lives," his hand moved to catch hers and bring it to his lips again. He looked at her more seriously, "You've been quite ill, you know. Jack and I have been worried sick. How does your shoulder feel now?" he asked softly.

She brought up a hand to press on the bandage around her shoulder, under her nightgown. "Sore," she whispered, "How long have we been here?" she asked curiously.

"Two weeks. Your wound got infected and you've had a fever."

"Two weeks?!" she gasped and he nodded. "My God!" she stuttered.

"We couldn't leave while you were so ill," Nicky explained, "but we're keeping our heads down and don't go out in daylight unless we absolutely have to. We're not sure if anyone is looking for us."

Bella lay silently for a few minutes, trying to recall what had happened two weeks previously. Nicky watched her face as the memories gradually returned and her eyes suddenly closed in remembered fright. "He shot me," she whispered. "That's the last thing I remember. What happened? Did Jack kill him?"

"I presume so. The last time I saw him he was lying on the floor with Cat's stiletto sticking out of his back. I wasn't in a position to check, it was all Jack could do to drag me out before anyone else arrived to take a pot shot at us."

Bella shivered. "He was a monster," she whispered and tears started to run down her face. "I had an opportunity to kill him," she sobbed, "but I couldn't bring myself to do it; he was asleep and I could have shot him, or stuck my dagger in him, but I couldn't do it, Nicky, I just couldn't do it. I'm so feeble, so useless," and she put her hands up to her face.

"Bella, my precious, whatever are you saying?" Nicky gasped. "You could never have done that, that would make you as bad and callous as them. Besides, you're the bravest, most determined woman I know apart from Cat, so don't you dare ever call yourself useless." He sighed feelingly, "I'm sure he's dead, but quite frankly I don't care. All that matters to me is that you're safe and you get better so we can go home, back to London."

Bella looked up at him, more tears in her eyes. "You don't want to go back to Valenciennes?" she whispered. "Take Terrie there, away from me?"

He looked down at her, his golden eyes glittering with emotion. "No, My Sweetheart, I'm only going back to Valenciennes if you come with me and bring Terrie as well. My home is with you in Hertford Street, or Litlington. We can go to Valenciennes any time to visit, as I do want to finish restoring the chateau. It's a matter of principle, to make a statement, if you like, that there are some things you can't and shouldn't destroy, like history, heritage and family; not because I want to go and live there by myself and be the Grand Duke again like my father. When we do visit, you can go shopping in Paris while the work continues, but only if I can go shopping with you and spoil you, because I'm not leaving you ever again." He leaned down to kiss her gently. "How can I?" he whispered, "I love you far, far too much."

Bella gasped in disbelief. "Nicky? Whatever do you mean? What happened to 'you're my sister' and all those excuses you made?"

"I was a fool and anyway, you were never my sister. A dreadful nuisance, trouble with a capital T and a complete baggage; yes, most definitely, but never my sister," and he bent to kiss her lips again.

"Where did this epiphany come from?" she whispered.

He picked up her hand and started to rub it gently. "A lot of things go through your mind when you know you're going to die," he said quietly. "I had nothing else to do but think, stuck in that hole," he shuddered. "I didn't expect to be rescued, didn't think anyone knew where I was. Hell, even I didn't know where I was; actually, I still don't." He shook his head, "I passed out when Jack dragged me out and shovelled me in his cart and didn't come to again 'til we were back in Nice."

"Oh, Nicky," was all Bella could mutter, she was so choked. "Are you sure? You fought me off for so long. I couldn't bear it if you're just saying this because I've been ill?"

"Arabella de Bresancourt, *La Duchesse de Valenciennes, La Lionesse de Valenciennes*," and he grinned at that second title, "I love you now, I realise I've loved you for years. You drive me mad now, you've driven me mad since the day you learned to toddle; you've always been a part of my life and I simply can't live without you. I don't care about anything anymore: my title, the estates, the money… I just want you, Terrie, my own family; that's all that's important to me. Bless her, the Dowager was so right," he finally whispered and kissed her hand reverently.

"Oh, Nicky," Bella burst out again, tears running down her face. "I never thought I'd ever hear you say that. I love you so much," and she started sobbing.

Nicky laughed. "Why are you crying about that?"

"Because I'm so happy," she sobbed. "I need a handkerchief."

He fished one out of his pocket and shook his head. "I don't think I'll ever understand you in a million years," he grinned, "but so long as you keep following me around, I won't complain."

She finally laughed through her tears and blew her nose. "Do you think I could have a cup of tea?" She looked around, "Are we in a hotel?"

"No, Sweetheart, some quiet lodgings, it's more private. I'm afraid the establishment doesn't run to tea. It's water, wine or brandy at the moment, so I think I'll get you some water." He got up and went over to a carafe on the table.

"I'd rather have some wine."

"Ah, that's the Bella I know, well, perhaps just a little," and he returned to the bed with a small glassful. He helped her sit up, watching her groan as the effort hurt her shoulder. He swore silently to himself, then handed over the glass and settled back down to let her sip it slowly.

They sat quietly for a long while. There were many things Nicky wanted to talk to her about, mainly connected with what had happened with Bernheim, but he knew that would have to wait for the right moment. Bella looked at her husband, thought of Bernheim and wanted to burst out crying again; the prospect of letting any man touch her, even Nicky, made her cringe.

Jack burst into the room, saw Bella sitting up and hurried over to the bed. "You're awake!" he cried joyfully. "Thank heavens!" He picked up her hand to kiss it. "How are you feeling? Have you got up yet? Aren't you hungry? The tavern is sending over some roast chickens for us shortly," he smiled at Nicky. "When do you think you'll be fit enough to leave?" he said, looking at both of them.

Bella laughed at him. "Give me a moment, You Wretch. I've not long woken up. I didn't know I'd been out of it for so long."

Jack looked embarrassed. "Oh, I'm so sorry, Your Grace, please forgive me. Shall I go and let you rest? Can I get you something else to eat or drink? Is there anything you need? Something to read perhaps?"

Bella looked at Nicky. "See what I've had to put up with all these weeks?" she grinned.

"Personally, I think he deserves a medal, traipsing around after you all the time," chuckled Nicky. "I'm amazed you haven't driven him to the nearest asylum for the insane; you normally drive me to distraction."

Jack looked at the pair of them, confused. "Oh, come here, Jack, sit down, we're only playing," Bella laughed and indicated the chair on the other side of the bed. "Now then, about lunch," she grinned. "A bit of chicken sounds delightful but only if you can spare some for me, maybe a wing? How many birds have you ordered for us? Five? Ten? I can't have you fading away, now can I?" and Jack and Nicky burst out laughing.

Several days later in the gathering dusk, just before it sailed, the three quietly and furtively boarded a small boat that was headed for Marseilles. Bella was carried on board by Nicky from the anonymous coach that delivered them to the dock. Once there, they transferred to another boat headed for Cadiz in Spain and from there, they boarded another bound for England. Before she left Nice, Bella penned a very short note to her Aunt Cat with which she sent Jack to the local posting office.

Dear Auntie,

Well, you will no doubt be Pleased to Hear I finally caught up with My Darling Husband, at long last, and we have been enjoying the Delights of Nice, here on the Côte d'Azur. There are plenty of Charming English People visiting here too, although, as with all pleasant towns, it does house some Unpleasant Visitors too. I am sure you can Imagine. Unfortunately, we had to associate with One or Two, but I am glad to report we think we've now seen the back of them, Permanently, one hopes. The Perils of Travelling to Unknown Places, as I am sure you will agree.

We have decided to take the Long Way Home so expect to see us in a Few Weeks' Time. I simply cannot wait to see Terrie again - give her a Big Kiss and Cuddle from her Mama and Papa and tell her she will see us very soon.

B

PS: I trust Uncle liked the Items I sent you from Paris! I am sure he will also be Delighted to hear we are on our way home, Safe and Sound, with all my Husband's Business Matters completed satisfactorily and that he will tell all Other Family and his Friends.

It was as vague as she could make it but it would reassure her family they were all safe and on their way home. No doubt Uncle Francis would pass the message on to Ashcroft.

As they sailed out of the little harbour in Nice, Bella looked out of the small porthole in her cabin and decided she never, ever wanted to see the Côte d'Azur again.

Chapter Fifteen

A pale, drawn man sat on his terrace up in the hills, reflecting as he watched the sun set over the harbour and the comings and goings of the little boats. He'd escaped death by a hair's breadth, the knife in his back glancing off a vertebrae, diverted from its path and puncturing the side of his lung instead of going through his heart. He owed his life to his coachman, the housekeeper and the cook who'd found him in time on the cellar floor and fetched a doctor post haste. His housekeeper had done some nursing in her time and she and the cook had managed to keep him breathing until the doctor arrived and worked a miracle, according to the pair of them.

He'd only just recovered and managed to rise from his bed, horrified to discover that some of his associates, who had come to visit him for a pre-arranged meeting a few days after his prisoner's escape, not knowing he was wounded, had helped themselves to some liquor in his dining room and had all been fatally poisoned. As a result, he had been disassociated from the plot to bring Bonaparte back from Elba and he was seething. Yet again, his promised gold had disappeared out of reach. His only consolation was the knowledge he had gleaned that afternoon while lying on his cellar floor at death's door.

Firle. A small hamlet in the eastern part of Sussex, near the coast and the little fishing harbour of Newhaven. It was not far from Brighton where the British Prince Regent had his summer palace, his Pavilion, an eccentric building with domes and Chinese influence in its design. On the outskirts of Firle, buried deep in the quiet countryside and apparently difficult to find if you didn't know it was there, stood the inconspicuous country home of one of the wealthiest and most reclusive aristocrats in England, the Duke of Firle; so early enquiries had already told him.

As soon as he was better, Bernheim decided he was going to visit England, London and Brighton in particular. From there, he would see what was at Firle and learn more about the reclusive family of that name who lived there. For instance, why did such a wealthy and aristocratic man like the Duke, who also lived in a luxurious mansion in one of the most exclusive squares in central London as befitted his title and station in life, like to spend so much time in an unassuming, nondescript, relatively small and rambling house in the countryside, when he owned so many other magnificent homes on estates around England, far more appropriate to his title and lineage. The man was a mystery and Bernheim's instinct told him that people who kept a low profile for no obvious reason, often had something they wanted to keep hidden. He intended to find out what the Duke of Firle was hiding. He also wanted his revenge...and his gold.

Of the three agents who had caused him so much trouble and loss of money, again, not to mention nearly killing him, there had been no sign. Even close to death, he had sent people to watch the roads out of Nice and keep an eye on the various stables and posting houses where carriages could be hired. The Duchess and her 'nephew' had checked out of their hotel and disappeared into thin air. Bernheim knew he'd injured her so she couldn't have gone far very quickly and the Duke certainly wouldn't have been fit to travel anywhere after his taste of Bernheim 'hospitality'. But they had all vanished, despite combing all the hotels, inns and main lodgings in and around the town for a week. He'd abandoned the search after that, concluding the group had made a run for it as soon as they'd left his villa, just as he had run that day when de Bresancourt had broken in to his home outside Madrid and he'd been shot by his associate.

But he would have them all, in London, Firle, or wherever they were. They would never expect to see him in England and would be off their guard. Frederick Bernheim smiled grimly. Revenge would indeed be sweet and he'd have the Duchess of Valenciennes again before he killed her. Even now, the scent of her soft skin haunted him as he remembered their torrid afternoon. A salacious, malicious smile curled his lips as he sat and sipped his wine and watched a small packet sail out of the harbour on the evening tide.

Chapter Sixteen

LONDON: WINTER 1814/1815

The sunshine and sea air brought the colour back to Bella's cheeks and her freckles reappeared. Jack now sported a deep tan and Nicky's body gradually healed, although the scars left behind told their own tale. His handsome face slowly returned to its usual humorous mien, with no obvious signs of the beating he had received. Miraculously, his nose hadn't been broken and the now fading marks would gradually disappear.

But Nicky was troubled. Outwardly, during the day, Bella was her usual sunny self with everyone but when they were alone at night, just the two of them in their cabin, she was withdrawn and quiet and stiffened when he pulled her into his arms in bed. When he tried to kiss her, lovingly, deeply and passionately as he increasingly yearned to do, she shrank from him and turned her head and he knew something was very wrong. But whenever he tried to talk to her about it, she just looked at him with a hurt and frightened expression, said she couldn't talk about it and ran away, or pulled away, stiff and frozen in their bed. Something had happened to make the loving and passionate woman he knew disappear. He was sure it was to do with the events in Nice, but he couldn't deal with it if she wouldn't talk to him.

It was late autumn when their ship finally docked in London and the weary travellers arrived back in Hertford Street to be greeted by a relieved and delighted Carstairs, who'd been increasingly worried about his employers' long and mysterious absence. Jack helped bring in their luggage and disappeared straight down to the kitchens, preparing to make his way back to Firle House, thence down to Firle Manor, to resume his duties as a groom. However, he was summoned to Nicky's study.

He entered the room and bowed, standing quietly with his hands behind him while Bella and Nicky regarded him seriously. She was sitting in a chair in front of the fire, Nicky standing behind her, a hand hovering over, but not touching her shoulder.

"I'm afraid we can't possibly allow you to go back to Firle after everything that has happened," announced Nicky gravely. Jack looked up at him, a worried frown on his face. "There's nothing there for you anymore, nor at Firle House here in London. You're not suitable now..." Nicky waved his hand in the air dismissively.

"But... but, Your Grace, I need to work. I didn't realise going away would mean I would lose my place in the household. I still have my little family to oversee, even if they are living with some good people nearby. Have I displeased you? I thought... I thought..." he was at a loss for words and suddenly looked distraught.

Bella couldn't keep a straight face any longer and couldn't bear to hurt him. "Oh Jack," she smiled, "you can't go back because after everything you've done for me, for us, how could we send you there to a life of servitude? You're far too good for that and the debt we owe you is immeasurable." She held her hands out to him, "I know you're almost grown up now, but we, the Duke, Nicky and I, we'd like to adopt you, formally, as a ward or whatever is appropriate; take you in to live with us, not as a servant but as one of us, be your legal guardians and provide you with the rest of your education properly and help you find your way in the world. Yes, of course we could simply throw money at you, reward you for what you did and send you on your way...but we want to do more, help you more than that... money alone isn't everything..."

Jack looked stunned at her words and his mouth dropped open. Nicky smiled. "I owe you my life, Jack Vallance, Bella's too and I can never repay you for that," he said quietly. "This is the very least we can do and what we hope will be the best for you. I also assure you, your family, all of them, related to you or not, will all be taken care of and you, personally, will never want for anything again."

Jack was still speechless and stood with his mouth gaping like a floundering fish. "For a start, I'd like to send you to Eton to finish the rest of your education," said Nicky. "I've thought about it a lot over the past few weeks and discussed it with Bella. It'll be devilish hard for you of course, at first. Although we'd obviously never say a word about your background and you must learn never to recourse to the language of the gutters," he grinned, "sometimes gossip gets out, but we'll simply say you're the ward of the Duke of Valenciennes, thereby part of the Duke of Firle's extended family; that should convince everyone to think twice about mocking you." Nicky looked at him very seriously. "But, having been to the place myself and experienced it, I daresay your life will still be a misery at times as the boys there can be cruel to outsiders. I discovered that, being French. However, on the positive side, you WILL make friends, you'll gain an education, confidence and polish that will take you anywhere, that is what Eton does for you. You're strong, you see. With your background and after what's happened over the past few months in France, I'm sure you can take anything they throw at you."

He smiled again at the astonished young man in front of him. "After that, if you're up for it, Oxford, a bit of travelling to see the world if you fancy and then..." he waved his hand in the air again, "a commission in the Army if you like, like I had, or I'm sure Francis, the Duke of Firle, will take you into his organisation. You see, you'll be bored out of your mind with nothing to sensible to occupy yourself, you're very bright, so if your mind has a business leaning, he's your man. But in reality, whatever you want to do, wherever you discover your talents lie, I'll support and help you so far as I'm able." He finished his speech and regarded Jack with a pleased look.

Jack stood silently for a while, taking in everything Nicky had said to him. "I...I don't know what to say, Your Grace," he finally mumbled, still shocked.

"I know it won't be easy for you, Jack," said Bella. "Even here at home or when we all go to Firle. Unfortunately, the servants will know where you came from and might be a tad awkward, no matter what orders we give. However, with our support, plus I know my aunt and uncle will assist us, you'll deal with it, the staff will eventually accept it and you'll become a Gentleman." She leaned forward and regarded him assessingly. "There's something about you, Jack. I don't know quite what it is, but properly dressed and away from the stables, apart from your definite charm," she grinned, "there's a quality about you. I mean, just look at your hands..." Jack looked down at his elegant, long fingers and currently immaculate nails that hadn't seen the inside of a stable or any manual labour for months. "You've no idea of your real background, have you?" she queried musingly, tilting her head to one side for a moment as she looked at him. "But you WILL be a Gentleman, very easily, I'd swear it's in your blood somewhere. What's more, I guarantee you'll have the young ladies of the Ton falling at your feet in a few years' time."

A wicked smile finally curled across his face. "Do you really think so, Your Grace?" Jack's eyes sparkled. He didn't know anything much about what Eton was all about, but he understood pretty young ladies.

Bella burst out laughing. "You Wretch, I absolutely know so. My feminine instincts tell me you come from the same mould as my Uncle Francis and this reprobate here," she cocked her head in Nicky's direction, "so heaven help all us ladies if the pair of them decide to take you in hand."

Nicky chuckled and winked at Jack. "So, what do you say, Young Man? Fancy throwing in your lot with the pair of us? Bella and me, that is? Her Uncle Francis and me, now that is a whole other matter..."

Jack was still overwhelmed and went over to Bella. He went down on one knee in front of her and, taking her hand in his, he bowed his head and kissed her knuckles reverently. "I never looked for such a reward, Your Grace, truly. It was an honour and pleasure to serve you and to pay back the Duchess of Firle for her goodness in taking me and my family in and off the streets. I...I could have been hanged or transported if she hadn't been so kind. You don't owe me anything, truly."

Bella bent down, patted his face and lifted his chin to look at him. "We DO owe you, Jack. You saved our lives and there is such goodness inside you, despite your unfortunate background. You are a truly remarkable young man and I want to see you grow into a truly remarkable Gentleman." She stood up and pulled him to his feet, "Now then, the decision is made. I've got a daughter to collect from my aunt so you can sort out all the arrangements for schooling and everything else with Nicky. I've already arranged for your room UPSTAIRS," she grinned, "and when you want some food, just ring the bell. You won't need to raid the kitchens anymore, nor thieve from the cook, the kitchen will come to you," and with a rippling laugh she left the two men to it.

Chapter Seventeen

L ife returned to normal in Mayfair. Nicky privately told
Francis exactly what had happened to him in France, a
different version to that which he'd received second hand
from Cat, then from Jack in a quiet moment, then directly from Bella.
Francis now had the whole story about their adventures, including
Bernheim and the man's obsession with The Shadow and those associated with him. Privately, he was deeply concerned.

Ashcroft was also brought up to date, privately satisfied his ruse to
get de Bresancourt's wife involved had paid such dividends. They all
assumed Bernheim was dead, but Ashcroft being Ashcroft, was only
ninety-nine per cent sure. He didn't like loose ends and had therefore
sent people to investigate quietly in Nice and also at the address in
Paris. The information trickling back to him only increased both his
scepticism and concern. There had been no funeral, no confirmation of
a death anywhere which niggled at him, even in a Europe that was still
in chaos. The whole story about the mysterious Shadow was still unre-
solved too, but since Bernheim, if he was still alive, had disappeared,
Ashcroft had other matters to worry about. For the time being, he put
the whole affair to one side.

Jack went to Eton, escorted by none other than two Dukes, Nicky and Francis, which did not go unnoticed at that venerable and renowned establishment, as had been their intention. He was now set to forge his new identity – Jack Vallance, young Gentleman of leisure. Nicky threw himself into picking up the reins of running the vast business holdings and investment portfolio he'd inherited from the Dowager while Bella returned to mothering her precious daughter and running her two gaming establishments.

Increasingly, whenever she could, Bella now escaped to *Le Lion d'Or* and away from spending nights with Nicky. She loved him to distraction but couldn't bring herself to let him make love to her or do more than kiss her on the cheek. Images of what she'd done with Bernheim taunted her day and night and she froze every time Nicky touched her. She was a tormented soul. She didn't want to behave like this, but she couldn't seem to help herself and the more she tried to grapple with and overcome her problems, the more depressed and withdrawn she became. She toyed with unburdening herself to her aunt but realised she would have no answer to help her this time. She cried herself to sleep, night after night, in her empty, lonely bed at *Le Lion d'Or*, her memories of what she'd shared with Nicky there tormenting her even more.

Nicky knew she had problems, he was sure related to Bernheim, but she wouldn't talk to him. To the world they were a happy young couple, but he knew differently and he now kept away from her room and her bed, knowing it distressed her. He was beyond frustrated, but he loved her. Relieving his frustration with another woman now, as he'd done before in his anger, held no appeal whatsoever. He threw himself into work and exercise instead to relieve the physical ache. He returned to his club and the various establishments frequented by his aristocratic peers to keep themselves fit – boxing, wrestling, fencing, riding and driving his racing curricle – the more physically and mentally demanding, the better. They all exhausted him, but nothing eased the deep pain in his soul.

Before he'd taken him to Eton, Nicky had finally had a long, quiet talk with Jack, picking up on an earlier conversation on the boat back to England. Over several bottles of wine and brandy he'd eventually discovered what that young man had suffered to support the gaggle of children he'd taken into his care and he was both horrified and humbled. The depravity Jack had experienced to earn a few pennies was sordid and Nicky, remembering his horrific treatment in the Fortress at Rouen at the hands of Bernheim's lieutenant, empathised with the youth and, peering into the bottom of a brandy bottle, finally, for the first time in his life, shared just some of the torment he'd endured so long ago, which had made such an impact on him as he'd grown up. To say Jack was shocked was an understatement, but he could well understand the man's anguish. A strong bond between the two men was forged that night and Jack had told Nicky as much as he knew and surmised about what Bella had done with Bernheim and how deeply it had affected her.

Christmas came and, as ever, all those related to the Firle family gathered at Firle Manor for the festivities. Jack had returned from his first partial term at Eton and quietly asked Nicky to teach him how to fence properly. He was a very good shot already and could fight anyone with a knife, but the gentlemanly art of engagement with a rapier hadn't been necessary in his world. At Eton it was, so he and Nicky spent every available hour practising. Nicky enlisted the aid of Cat and Francis, so between the three of them, including their new adept and determined pupil keen to train from morning to night, Jack made good progress. Unsurprisingly, Jack got his own sword for Christmas and a beautiful stiletto from Cat with his initials engraved on the blade.

Eddie was now romantically involved with Lady Elise Montgomery, the Widow of Hertford Street. Bella and Nicky were hoping he would soon pluck up courage to marry her and, sure enough, on Christmas Eve, Eddie stood up at dinner and announced that he and Elise were betrothed. The whole family was delighted and a happy group departed for the local church for Midnight Mass.

When everyone returned to the house after the service, as was family tradition and following everyone else, Nicky pulled Bella under the large dangling bough of mistletoe in the hall and kissed her soundly. The kiss changed from a mere peck as he held her in his arms and the familiar pull of passion gripped him. As his tongue delved into her mouth more hungrily, he'd felt her stiffen in his arms, until it was as though he was holding a statue. Her initial response, which had gladdened his heart, had disappeared without trace. While Bella had crept up to bed in tears, he'd joined the younger Firle offspring and drunk himself into a stupor with Alex, the young Earl of Jevington, eldest son of the Duke and with a reputation as something of a lothario himself amongst the Ton. After a long and inanely philosophical conversation about the mysteries of women, he'd woken up with a sore head to find himself still in the drawing room the following day.

On Christmas Day, Nicky presented Bella with an identical golden lion charm to wear around her neck. Several sets of amused eyes watched as he fixed it on her and Cat nudged Francis in pleasure as Nicky bent to place a kiss on the back of Bella's neck. They were the only other people who knew what had gone on in *Le Lion d'Or* and the story of the missing necklace. Bella was overwhelmed as she fingered her gift constantly. The knowing look that had passed between them was electric, especially when he'd whispered in her ear as he'd fastened the chain, "Now you won't have to steal mine again... *Lionesse!*" When the family dispersed to bed later, full of food, all happy and slightly inebriated, Nicky was hoping against hope Bella might finally let him love her, as he was so desperate to do.

Bella, meanwhile, was wound tight as a spring and at war with herself. Her will was to roll into Nicky's arms and lose herself in him, but deep down there was another part of herself stopping her. She lay in bed, in the shadows, eyes screwed tight shut, feeling Nicky join her. As his hand gently roved up her body under her nightgown, she felt herself stiffening again and no matter how much he tenderly kissed and encouraged her, she couldn't bear his touch, images of Bernheim roiling around in her head. At the end of his tether, Nicky reared up and tried to enter her, but it was impossible. She was dry and unaroused and with a muttered stream of oaths, he rolled off and to the other side of the bed, angry, frustrated and hurt. Bella lay still as stone and tears rolled down her face until with a strangled cry she ran from the bedroom and despite chasing after her, she disappeared down one of the endless passages of the old house and he didn't see her again until the following morning.

They made their excuses and left Firle to return to spend the rest of the holiday at Litlington, driving in silence back and forth during the day to go to their own separate bedrooms in the privacy of their country home at night; as soon as they could, they returned to London. Bella buried herself in the affairs of her gaming saloons and contemplated opening a third. Nicky threw himself into his business affairs and became more and more short tempered. Bella withdrew even further into herself.

Chapter Eighteen

And so the winter weeks passed. It was a cold, damp afternoon in early March. Bella was playing with Terrie in her little sitting room and Nicky was ensconced in his study with his secretary.

A polite knock on his study door and Carstairs entered. "Two Gentlemen to see you, Your Grace."

"I told you," Nicky bit out, "I don't want to be disturbed. I'm not at home to anyone," returning to the papers he was studying.

"But, Your Grace, it's the..."

"Didn't you hear me the first time, Carstairs?" Nicky's temper was deteriorating daily as frustration boiled within him. "I'm NOT at home."

Carstairs was getting used to this state of affairs and merely ignored him. "His Grace, the Duke of Wellington is in the drawing room with Her Grace and a Lord Ashcroft," he intoned icily, almost smirking when he saw Nicky's jaw drop open.

"Whaaaat? WELLINGTON?! Here? Are you sure? Why the devil didn't you say so?" Nicky gasped. "What in Hell is he doing here in Hertford Street? I thought he was in Vienna?" he muttered to himself, rising instantly, struggling into his jacket and hurriedly straightening his cravat. Brushing past the affronted butler, he rushed out of his study, brusquely dismissing his secretary as he went. That man merely rolled his eyes at Carstairs who nodded back at him and sniffed.

Bella was sitting, deep in conversation with both men when Nicky strode into the room. "Your Grace," he bowed low, "Ashcroft," a mere nod of the head in the second man's direction before turning back to the Duke. "What on earth are you doing in London, Your Grace...and here?" his voice rose in astonished puzzlement. "I thought you were still at the Congress, in Vienna?"

"Ah, de Bresancourt, good to see you again," Wellington tipped his head. "I was just telling your delightful wife that I'm not really here at all, officially, just a short, quick visit to see a few people in London. I'm on my way back over to the Continent shortly, events have overtaken my plans somewhat, but I wanted a few words with you while I was still in Town."

Nicky looked from Wellington to Ashcroft and back again. Such a powerful and august pair could only be there for one reason, he surmised: Bonaparte. A frisson went down his spine. "Perhaps you could spare me a few minutes in private?" enquired Wellington. "I'm sure Lord Ashcroft and the Duchess won't mind?"

"Of course, Your Grace. Please, follow me." Nicky ushered Wellington out from the drawing room and down the hallway to his study.

The two men sat in a couple of armchairs in front of the fire, Nicky still slightly overwhelmed at the great man's presence. Wellington came straight to the point. "I'm not sure how up to date you are with the news, but Bonaparte escaped from Elba last week, landed in the south of France near Cannes and is heading inland as we speak, towards Paris one assumes. His old soldiers are flocking to him in their droves. I left the Congress to come back and catch up with the Prime Minister for a few days, apprise him and the Foreign Secretary on the latest negotiations amongst the main Powers in Europe and get their views on the situation. All this suddenly happened while I was travelling, so I have to turn around and go back, quick sticks, as you can appreciate." He looked straight at Nicky, "You don't seem surprised? How much have you heard? I know news of his escape will become common knowledge in the next day or two but I didn't think it had percolated out much beyond Whitehall yet. How up to date are you?"

Nicky sighed. "I did hear Bonaparte had escaped, alarming information of that sort travels fast. Naturally I try to keep abreast of events across the Channel and the Duke of Firle, Francis Granville, has his own lines of communication on the Continent, especially from France, which are very speedy, so he told me a couple of days ago as soon as he himself heard. As for the actual escape, Ashcroft suspected last year something along those lines might happen and sent me off to chase after that French agent, Bernheim, again. He suspected he might be involved with plots to facilitate that very eventuality and I actually ran him to earth in Nice, just along the coast from Cannes. Did you know about that?"

"Yes, he told me," said Wellington succinctly. "I gather you thought Bernheim disposed of?"

Nicky looked at Wellington's impassive, hawkish features. "The last time I saw him, he was on the floor of his cellar with a knife in his back. He's not dead after all, is he?" he concluded quietly.

"No, I gather not, but he's Ashcroft's problem in the main." said Wellington. "I'm afraid I'm going to have a War to get to grips with again and we both have need of you."

"But I've retired. I told Ashcroft. I can't do his dirty work anymore. I have a wife and family to consider now; he always maintained he didn't use married men, even more so, ones with a family."

"I appreciate that, of course," responded Wellington. "Many of my officers are married with families, as are half the army, including me, but these are now desperate times, very desperate, you mark my words. At least it will focus the Congress, hopefully stop their bickering and pull the Powers together for one last concerted effort to get rid of Bonaparte once and for all, because that is what it's going to take to defeat him."

Nicky bowed his head. "Of course, Your Grace, but despite my rank, I was never in the field, have never had command of even a squadron or a company, you of all people know that. Therefore, why am I so important for you to visit now, at my home, given what's obviously going on in France and further afield? Europe will be in uproar once the news spreads."

"A lot of my most experienced men from the Peninsula are still in the Americas and Canada, even though we've signed the peace treaty and the War over there is officially at an end," Wellington said in frustration. "Although we can find soldiers – there are the other Allied forces of course – I will have need of every competent man I can lay my hands on to match Bonaparte and his French veterans. You are an exceptionally determined, capable and resourceful individual with a set of skills unmatched by most."

Nicky nodded his head in embarrassed acknowledgement of Wellington's compliment but remained silent as the man continued. "I understand from Ashcroft there were personal reasons you became involved with him and his organisation before, including the money," the Duke said disdainfully, "but that is no longer the case now, I gather? So, tell me, de Bresancourt, this is me, asking for England. Are you English? Or French? Are you willing to risk your life for our British King and Country one final time, to rid the Continent of this pestilential bastard and those that work for him who will destabilise France and put the whole of Europe in turmoil yet again?"

He leaned back and watched Nicky's face.

Nicky considered the question, yet again, the one several people had asked him over the years. He'd always considered himself English, although deep within him there remained a pride in his Gallic title and a yearning for the country of his birth; not as it was now, war-torn and in chaos, but in peace, to enjoy its culture, way of life, its food and drink. He felt he was neither one nationality nor the other. As for risking his life to fight Bonaparte and Bernheim, privately, the first could go hang as far as he was concerned; he loved his adopted country, but he'd done enough for England over the past few years at no considerable risk and personal cost to himself. Bernheim, however, was another matter. A deep, suspicious dread filled his soul at the knowledge the man was still alive and intuition told him he would be a danger both to him and his whole family until he was truly dead and in his grave.

He looked across at Wellington. "I was brought up here. England has always been my home and always will be. But I am French by birth, so there will always be a small part of me that yearns for the better things that France has to offer. Quite frankly, I have no love for either Bonaparte nor the Bourbons, both have plenty of faults. I just hope that one day, the country will settle down and let Frenchmen live their lives in peace and prosperity with a proper Government of men who are honest, capable and efficient, who also don't ignore the plight of the people, especially those in the struggling lower classes."

"Very diplomatic and hopelessly optimistic," said Wellington acerbically, "and Bernheim?"

"He should be rotting in hell for what he's done to me, my wife and countless others. I'll put him there if it's the last thing I do," Nicky said with passion.

"Interesting," murmured Wellington. "So, then, de Bresancourt," he spoke slowly, "will you join me as an officer, a part Aide-de-Camp, on my Staff? I'm heading to Brussels in the first instance, then onwards, but will probably headquarter myself around there eventually. Near enough but not too near…like we did down in the Peninsula when we sat in Portugal and observed events from there and launched our attacks over the border when the time was right. You might have to fight a battle, more likely go undercover again for reconnaissance, as you were originally doing for us in the Peninsula, or you may well have to tackle Bernheim again if we find he's making mischief, but I really can't say. I just want to know if you're with me? I'll be leaving England in a couple of days at the very latest, time being of the essence now, so I need a prompt answer."

Nicky thought about his life. He didn't have one at present without Bella in it to love him. She'd changed and his days and nights were barren and empty, barring his beloved imp of a daughter who was the light of his existence. He didn't want to spend his days engrossed in papers and business or his nights tossing and turning in frustration. He needed to escape from everything in London, yet again, to find an opportunity to deal with Bernheim once and for all.

He looked at Wellington. "I don't fit in any pigeonhole, English or French, a soldier or a spy, but if you want me, Uncle Arthur," and he winked at Wellington, "I'll fight for you. I'm your man, I give you my word."

Wellington looked glacial. "As ever, de Bresancourt, your disrespect for any sort of authority is absolutely appalling. I'd no more put you in charge of a troop, never mind a squadron or a company, than a chimney sweep," his words dripped with acid sarcasm, but then a slight smirk creased his lips. "However, if I had a few more men like you, I'd be far more confident of sending Bonaparte back into exile than I have to admit I am at this moment. And I do mean exile, somewhere far away and far more difficult to escape from. So, de Bresancourt, welcome to my personal staff." His acid expression turned into a slight curl of the lips. "I'll send word when and where to report for duty in the next day or so," and getting to his feet as he spoke, he nodded his head at Nicky and strode towards the door. "For now, I'll retrieve Ashcroft from your dear wife's clutches and be on my way. Urgent meetings in Downing Street…"

He turned, actually to smile at Nicky, "You know, if I didn't know better, I'd swear Ashcroft had a soft spot for her. She must be quite some woman to beard that cold fish in his lair and then go haring after you across France, and risk her life to rescue you like she did."

"Yes, Your Grace, she is quite some woman. That's why I'll put Bernheim in his grave if it's the last thing I do…for almost destroying her," he rasped with deadly promise.

As Nicky saw the Duke into his coach, Ashcroft quietly bent his head and whispered, "I'll see you before you go. I have news of Bernheim," and with a few more hurried whispers, he took his seat next to Wellington.

Chapter Nineteen

While Nicky was ensconced with Wellington, Ashcroft was having his own private conversation with Bella, the real reason for his own appearance in Hertford Street. They made desultory small talk over a cup of tea and then, Ashcroft sat back and looked at the beautiful woman sitting across from him.

"So," he steepled his fingers under his chin, "you managed to run him to earth, twice. No mean feat, if I say so myself."

Bella sat and watched the man across from her impassively. "Yes, though it wasn't really my doing. It was Jack who actually found him."

"Aah, yes, the groom you've…ah…adopted," Ashcroft mused. "Your husband told me about him. Interesting young fellow by the sound of it. Tell me about him…?" He sat back and sipped his tea.

So Bella related what she knew of Jack, his background, and how the Duchess of Firle had recommended he accompany Bella on her trip to France, then what she knew of how he'd managed to trace Nicky, both in Paris and in Nice.

"Amazing," said Ashcroft, "quite an intrepid young man it seems, for a mere groom and former child villain?"

"Yes, indeed," replied Bella. "There's simply something about him. He's not quite the feral youth you would expect from his background and he has a heart of gold; taking in all those children. I hate to think what he must have done to procure food for them all and keep a roof over their heads," she grimaced and shuddered eloquently.

"Mmmm," considered Ashcroft thoughtfully, "The Dials is certainly not for the fainthearted," and he shivered theatrically. "How old did you say he was?"

"He actually doesn't know how old he is," shrugged Bella. "I personally have him at sixteen or so as he's a strapping lad, but of course he could be fourteen or fifteen, or seventeen if you go the other way, we simply don't know for sure." She smiled as she reminisced, "He's quite the chameleon, you know. One minute a creature of The Dials and the next a budding young Gentleman. It's extraordinary, plus he has the charm and intelligence to go with it." Then she laughed jokingly, "He's far more secret agent material than I would ever be," and she continued to chuckle at the silly thought as she sipped her own tea. "Nicky and I have adopted him formally, you know; it's the least we could do, given he saved our lives."

"Yes, so I gather," said Ashcroft laconically, putting down his cup and saucer and examining his fingernails. Not by a twitch of his eyelashes did he reveal how interested he was in this young man. The ability to be chameleon-like, with his obvious skills, was of huge interest to Ashcroft, even if the lad was only sixteen or thereabouts.

"Nicky has sent him to Eton to gain some polish, though I'm not sure if that environment will be a trifle harsh for him. He had little or no education until the Duchess of Firle picked him up, well not the sort of education most young men aspire to, unless you count lock breaking or pocket picking," she giggled.

"Eton?" shuddered Ashcroft. "Oh dear. They'll make mincemeat of him if they find out his background. Never mind The Dials, if they knew he was a groom that would be bad enough."

"I know," said Bella quietly, "but Nicky said it would be the making of him if he could deal with it and he's right. In any event, after what we endured together, it should be a piece of cake for him."

"Quite so, My Dear, quite so," nodded Ashcroft, making a mental note to keep a quiet eye on this young man for the next few years, perhaps engineer an introduction at some point if he was going to be living in Hertford Street. He'd found out what he wanted on that matter and changed the subject.

"But now, what about you, My Dear? You were the one who finally found Bernheim and persuaded him to take you to his lair. Don't dismiss your part in all this."

"That horrible, foul, evil man," Bella shuddered as she spoke the words, slowly, feelingly and with venom, her green eyes closing for a moment as a haunted look flashed across her face. Ashcroft, watching her closely, didn't miss it.

"That bad, hmmm?" he said softly. "Well, I did try to warn you..." he continued, shaking his head sympathetically.

"I know," Bella sighed, "but I didn't understand how...how difficult...how difficult some things could be. It was terrible, it plagues me, what I had to do," Bella whispered. It was the first time she'd mentioned it to anyone, but for some reason she knew Ashcroft would understand.

"Mmmm," he murmured, "it's always bad the first time. The well-brought-up Ladies who work for me, I've heard it before; the horror and disgust..." he let the words hang in the air.

Ashcroft watched Bella's face as his words struck home, so he continued, "Everyone is different, of course, but I gather one way they deal with it is to mentally consign it all into a box, like one does with old clothes or items unwanted any more, such as packing things into a trunk; visualise shutting down the lid firmly and then place it in a far, dark corner of the attic, never to be seen, used or opened again, unless absolutely necessary. Out of sight. Out of mind. Over and done with, permanently," he said descriptively and continued watching Bella's face. "It's like something that happened and has no meaning to their normal lives. Something to be forgotten. Irrelevant. I think your husband probably does that. He needs to deal with what he's had to do as well; it means nothing, purely a means to an end. I think you probably understand that now, hmmm?" He watched as Bella's eyes widened and stared hard at her. "If you let events haunt you and some are now haunting you, aren't they?" he said softly, "It means the enemy has won, got the better of you. But we can't have that...no...absolutely not." He sat back, drank more tea and let his words sink in.

"You understand..." whispered Bella, "don't you?"

Ashcroft leaned forward and patted her hand. "Of course I do, it's just some people can handle it better than others; those with no heart or emotions or feelings, cold fish, just like they call me," he said slyly. "But the more sensitive ones, it does affect them and they learn to deal with it in their own way. Of course, one gets used to it, if one does it often enough, like a necessary, albeit unpleasant or dirty chore, like a foul chamber pot, for instance. But whatever happens, you MUST understand it, My Dear, or it will destroy you, and your life." Ashcroft sat back and looked her in the eye. "It's easy to talk, isn't it? 'I want to help my husband, I'll do whatever it takes...' etc, etc," he parroted what she'd said to him in his office that morning months before, "but the stark reality is somewhat different," he said tellingly and there was a long pause. "You wouldn't listen to me, so you had to find out for yourself, the hard way, unfortunately. But don't let him win, Bella," he finally whispered.

They sat and looked at each other for a long time while the logs in the fire popped and the clock on the mantel ticked. "You let me win, didn't you?" Bella finally said quietly.

Ashcroft looked at her with an unreadable expression. "You nearly won anyway, it was touch and go." He smiled. "We must have a return match one day, with nothing to play for, eh? I've never met a woman who has ever come close to me, not even the Dowager," he said, "until you."

"And I've never come across a man like you," said Bella quietly. "I still can't make you out," she put her head to one side. "I'm never sure whether you're playing me like a fish on the end of a line, or actually telling the truth."

"Well, that you must decide for yourself," said Ashcroft enigmatically, "and I won't even ask if you'll help me again as I don't think you've yet recovered from what happened in France. However, you must, you know that? And you will, won't you, My Dear? England and your husband, need a woman like you."

Bella looked at the grey man in front of her and shrugged. It was neither a yes nor a no. "But I'm afraid WE need your husband again. That's why we're here," said Ashcroft and Bella nodded, her face finally showing the fright she'd felt when the two men had walked into her drawing room that late afternoon. She'd known straight away they had come for Nicky.

"Who is it this time?" she asked shakily. "Bonaparte, I take it?"

Ashcroft nodded, unsure how much she knew. "He's escaped from Elba; he's on the French mainland and his old soldiers are flocking to him. Our latest information, received by pigeon just this morning in fact, is that the 5th and 7th Infantry Regiments were sent to intercept him near Grenoble on the 5th of March, but Napoleon stepped out in front of them, ripped open his coat and said "If any of you will shoot his Emperor, here I am." The men joined his cause *en masse,* so this is what we're now up against. We also understand Louis is panicking and making ready to flee; no backbone, probably gone already," Ashcroft tutted disdainfully, obviously thinking little of the new French monarch, "so I'm afraid it's War again and Wellington HAS to grapple with him personally this time, deal with the menace once and for all."

Bella gasped and put a hand to her mouth. "Oh noooo!" She sat back and considered his words. "Uncle Francis told Nicky he'd escaped from Elba a couple of days ago, but that was all I heard. You foresaw this, didn't you?" she looked at him as memory returned. "That's what Bernheim was involved in down in Nice, of course," she said thoughtfully and Ashcroft nodded.

"Ironically, he landed in the south of France, just outside Cannes, not that far from Nice, so it all fits, even if Bernheim's involvement was stopped. However, there is also an additional problem," said Ashcroft finally. He wanted to tell her himself, she deserved to know. "Bernheim isn't dead."

Bella's face went ashen, her body rigid. "Oh dear God," she whispered, clutching the arm of her chair and her cup and saucer tipped in her other hand. "But Jack...I thought he killed him?"

Ashcroft took her cup and saucer from numb fingers before she dropped them. "Unfortunately, it appears not. The man must have nine lives." He looked extremely frustrated. "We investigated his villa down there of course, but there was no death reported, no funeral and we finally discovered the owner had been 'ill'," Ashcroft highlighted the word, "then disappeared. Went back to Paris possibly, or wherever, we're not sure," he shook his head. "He hasn't returned to his house there, that we do know, because it's under constant watch now even though it's all closed up. We're sure he'd suspect we would have it under surveillance given how we've tracked him down twice, so I think he'll dispose of it if he hasn't done so already. Therefore, the key questions are, where is he now and what is he up to?" Ashcroft shrugged his shoulders again looking angry. "He's undoubtedly making mischief, you mark my words. France is in turmoil with Bonaparte's return, so a situation like that offers all sorts of opportunities for a creature like Bernheim. I'm sure Napoleon will have need of a man of his 'capabilities' to cause trouble amongst his enemies, internally in France and amongst the Allies. And of course," Ashcroft paused meaningfully, "he'll want his revenge on Nicky. This is the second time your husband, now with you, his wife, have scuppered his plans. I'm talking of personal gain here, not altruistic endeavours for his Emperor. Of course, this brings us back to the whole business with his father and The Shadow."

Bella gasped quietly again "You know, My Dear, I've never come across a family quite like yours," Ashcroft opined conversationally, putting down his own cup and saucer. "Quite extraordinary, quite extraordinary," he murmured, "and the most extraordinary of the whole lot of you is your dear Uncle Francis." He actually grinned then, a rare expression on his face, lighting it up and making him look pleasant and approachable, as opposed to cold, distant and forbidding. "I know he was The Shadow and, My Dear Girl, please believe me when I say wild horses wouldn't persuade me to divulge his secret to anyone. In fact, I find the whole situation quite amusing. Your uncle and I play endless mind games around the whole matter. He knows I know, but of course he'll never admit to anything. As for your aunt, well! Words fail me, what an extraordinary and dangerous woman she was, still is. No wonder your uncle remains entranced with her," he sighed. "Quite extraordinary", he repeated. " If only Society had half a clue," and he laughed, sitting back and watching her reaction intently.

Bella was dumbstruck. "Oh, it's perfectly all right, My Dear," Ashcroft leaned forward and patted her hand again. "I don't expect you to say anything, just remember," he tapped the side of his nose with a finger, "I KNOW. This whole Bernheim problem is now inextricably linked with your family. Irrespective of whatever he does for Bonaparte, he just wants to feather his own nest, as he always has, and your family is now his primary target."

He got up from his chair then. "I think I can hear Wellington," he commented but turned to Bella, saying "just remember, My Dear, we need your husband to help us. These are desperate times, as Wellington says, but I'm always here if you need help or advice and we really must have another game, soon. What say you?" With that, he picked up her hand, kissed it punctiliously and then strode towards the doorway to the hall.

Bella was shellshocked by the whole conversation. That Ashcroft had finally plumbed her uncle's secret she wasn't surprised by and she simply knew, deep down, he wouldn't tell a soul. He just wanted to know for his own ends that they were patriotic and not malicious. It was his statement that Wellington wanted Nicky which terrified her. In fact she'd been frightened from the moment the Duke of Wellington and Ashcroft had arrived at the house. News that Bonaparte was on the move again was bad enough, but the knowledge that Bernheim was still alive was truly the stuff of her nightmares, as shocking, vivid images started to cross her mind of Nicky either dead or terribly injured on some foreign battlefield or else strung up again as she'd seen him in Bernheim's cellar.

She rose and tottered over to a tray of decanters on a sideboard, pouring herself a full glass of brandy. She tossed it back in one gulp, shuddering as the fiery liquid burned its way down, then poured another. The images got worse and, tears streaming down her face, she fled the drawing room and ran up to her bedroom, flinging herself down on her bed, weeping copiously, her mind full of horror, fear and remorse. Everything Ashcroft had said to her was going round and round in her head. She finally fell asleep, only to have nightmares full of the terrible images she'd already pictured: Nicky's dead, mangled body shot to pieces at the hands of Bonaparte's army with Bernheim in the distance crowing with evil laughter.

Chapter Twenty

She never appeared at dinner and having dined alone, Nicky spent an entertainingly playful hour in the nursery with Terrie and her toys before retreating to his bedroom, staring in frustration at the closed door between his room and Bella's. He prowled back and forth, dressed merely in breeches, boots and a half open shirt, gradually working his way through a bottle of brandy until at last, with a muttered oath, he stalked through to his wife's bedroom, still carrying the bottle and his glass.

She was sitting in a chair in front of the fire in an undone dressing robe, with a long and enveloping nightgown beneath, her hair cascading loose and unbrushed down her back. She was lost in thought, the fingers of one hand playing with the little golden lion around her neck, the fingers of the other twirling her wedding ring round and round on her finger. She looked terrible: pale, drawn and haunted; she'd obviously been crying. Nicky sighed. He had no idea what the matter was this time as she'd looked fine that afternoon.

There was no easy way to say it and he'd lost patience with her anyway, so half-drunk as he was he simply came out with it. "I know I promised I wouldn't," he announced baldly, "but, well, things have changed between us now." He started to prowl up and down her room as he spoke. "Wellington needs me and I'm afraid I'm going away again. You know Bonaparte has escaped and he's being welcomed with many open arms in France, therefore we're going to War once more, Wellington has got to get rid of him or there'll never be any peace in Europe." He looked at her but his words evinced no response. He toyed with the rest of his news, still wondering if he should tell her, but finally he shrugged, " Bernheim isn't dead. He's on the loose. I have to find him and settle this vendetta between my family and him once and for all."

There, he'd told her. He tossed back his brandy and poured himself another measure. A whisper reached him. "I know. Ashcroft told me what's going on in France; and about Bernheim."

He went and sat on the other chair by the fire and looked at her. "Aaah. That explains the tears, I presume," he said sarcastically. "Well then, you'll understand why I have to go. He knows too much about us. We're all vulnerable and in danger and I can't allow that. I won't let him destroy my family and it's MY mess now, not Francis's, so I must deal with it." He took another deep breath, "I gave my word to Wellington I'd go with him as part of his personal staff. There'll be a big battle, it's inevitable, Wellington has to confront and deal with Boney, once and for all. I know the Prussians are capable but in my and everyone's opinion, he's the only man in Europe who can pull everyone together and do it."

Another whisper. "I know," then utter silence.

Nicky downed another gulp of brandy and rose from the chair in frustration. "Is that all you have to say? 'I know'," he parroted her whisper theatrically and facetiously. "I'm leaving here in a day or two, you might never see me again and all you can say to me is 'I know'?" He threw his glass into the fireplace in a fit of frustration where it shattered and caused blue flames to spark as the alcohol caught light, then he swigged another mouthful straight from the bottle. There was still no reply.

"Is that all I mean to you now?" he asked belligerently. "You can't even be bothered to express worry, or concern that I'm going, never mind the love you used to profess to constantly? Whatever happened to that?" he queried nastily as he took another swig and paced the room. "I don't know what's happened to you, Arabella, you've not been the same since we left France. I know it has to do with events there, but if you won't explain or talk to me, I can't understand or help you," he bit out in angry frustration.

Bella sat as still as a statue, the expression on her face impassive as he ranted irrationally, "What IS it? Did you enjoy what Bernheim did to you? Did you discover you actually liked it? What you did to me at *Le Lion d'Or* and in Paris was more than most inexperienced, newly married young women would even contemplate, let alone be aware of, but of course that would never apply to YOU, now would it? So, maybe you have extreme tastes, but how should I know? You never talk to me now. You never told me what happened anyway, what Bernheim did to you. Perhaps I should try and do the same? Believe me, I've got a very good idea about what it was. Would you like that? I'm damned sure I could do what he did, I've done just about everything to a woman in my time, whether I wanted to or not, whether I enjoyed it or not. Or maybe you met someone else while you trailed across France, in Paris I presume, or even in Nice? And I'm just the nuisance husband now that you're stuck with because you knew no different." He swore venomously, getting himself worked into a serious temper at her continued stillness and non-response. "Is that why you lie there like an ice cold, marble statue while I try and make love to you? Is that why you shrink from me and run away when I touch you? You never even kiss me and freeze if I so much as peck your cheek."

Still Bella sat immobile as he raged at her, all his hurt and frustration boiling over. "So you should be relieved now I'm going away again. God knows why I'm here anyway, frustrated as Hell with a wife who doesn't want me, and Heaven help me, I don't want any other woman and nor will I force you to do something you obviously find distasteful. That's what love does for you." He swigged yet more brandy, "How's that for a great ironic joke? Nicholas de Bresancourt, serial womaniser, lothario, lover and rake, hoist on his own petard by a wife who doesn't want him and can't even stand his touch." The bitterness poured out of him now he'd started, "Well, I'm off to war again, not to mention going after Bernheim. No doubt, if one doesn't do for me, the other will, so you'll be the rich, merry, titled widow. Perhaps then you'll smile your seductive smile and spread your legs for some other poor fool who succumbs to your charms," and with that he took a final swig from his bottle, threw it angrily in the fireplace to shatter on top of his broken glass, then stormed back into his bedroom, slamming the door behind him.

Bella was still as a statue while he ranted and for a while after. She was still grappling with what Ashcroft had told her, trying to consign what Bernheim had done to her to a box in her brain's attic. She knew she was destroying her marriage, everything she had with Nicky, but so far she'd battled in vain. Now she was trying, one final time, to consign her horrific memories somewhere else. Ironically, that afternoon's news and the gruesome images of Nicky lying dead on some foreign battlefield, or in some dank cellar, was helping push all her own tormented images and self-pity into Ashcroft's box. Now, her only concern was losing Nicky or being responsible for his death; it was her own fault. If they'd been happy and she hadn't driven him away, perhaps he would have refused Wellington and Ashcroft. After all, what could Bernheim do when they were all safe in England? London and especially their various country homes around Firle were a whole world away from Nice.

His declaration of love had shocked her too. She had not been at all aware he felt so strongly about her. She'd really believed his words to her in Nice had been just to make her feel better, to help her recover, but she'd obviously been wrong. Slowly, as if in a trance, Bella got to her feet and wrapped the robe around her, tying the belt as if girding herself for a battle. She walked across her room, opened the connecting door to his and went through.

He was standing in front of the fire, an arm on the mantelpiece and a booted foot on a coal scuttle, staring down into the flames, another bottle of brandy in his hand. As he turned to stare at her, taking another swig of liquor from the bottle, her eyes took in his handsome face and body. She'd been enthralled by him since she'd been a teenager and before she really understood what lust was. Her feelings had only grown stronger as she'd become a woman. The tall, strong, muscled torso; the thick, tawny blond hair; the charming smile, the glowing golden eyes with their sooty lashes. He was truly every woman's dream and he was her husband, apparently now hers alone, yet all she'd done was reject him. But she loved him to distraction, passionately and suddenly, she knew she wanted to feel his arms around her, wanted his kisses, his caresses, to have him make love to her; before he went away...to risk his precious life, again.

He turned to look at her, anger and frustration still alive on his face. "What do you want?" he bit out.

"You," Bella whispered.

"Hah! As you once told me, you caught me years ago, but it's all a bit late now," he said bitterly.

"No, it's never too late if you love someone. I can't cope with you going away again. You could be killed."

"Oh, that bothers you now, does it? I thought you'd be pleased," the drunken sarcasm was venomous.

"If you die, my life would be over. I love you too much. I've always loved you, for as long as I can remember," she whispered, her voice breaking.

"Then you have a strange way of showing it. I assumed Bernheim's brand of love was more to your taste, now you've experienced it."

"Love? Depravity is a better description. Love isn't a word in his vocabulary. You have no idea what I had to do with him," she cried. "It was more than sordid; I don't think I'll ever get over it, it's haunted me every hour of the day and night, the nightmares..."

"How should I know? You've never mentioned it." His response was cold.

"I couldn't," she whispered in despair, "I thought I'd read about most things by now, even de Sade, but I never knew some of the things he did existed or understood how it actually felt...and the pain," she winced, "I felt torn in half and so sick and DIRTY afterwards," tears started to fall down her face. "I still feel dirty. Degraded. Disgusting. You don't want a wife who's done that; I'm spoiled for you now, defiled, not the innocent girl you married. I can't deal with that. I wanted to be so perfect for you, just like you've always been my perfect man," she sounded broken.

Nicky looked at her, at the tears in her eyes, the haunted expression and he couldn't help himself. "Dear heaven, Sooty, what the hell did he do?" his expression was horrified as he froze.

"He... he...and then, when he..." she gave up, merely choking out, "he tried to strangle me as he climaxed." Then it started to come out, "It felt like he was in ecstasy doing that, but I couldn't see, couldn't breathe...he was behind me...in my...up my...oh Nicky, the pain, so deep, he was so big, it was too much," she sobbed. "It tore me, made me bleed, then choke, I couldn't get my breath...but he ignored all that, wouldn't stop, he was so strong, so rough, so insatiable, he bragged about it," she whispered again, unable still to get out the words to describe what she'd experienced, her hands wringing in the folds of her robe, her torment obvious, speaking about such personal and depraved things that had been outside her comprehension. "And...and...I couldn't, or wouldn't stop him...had to pretend, encourage him...because...because I needed to distract him, we needed to rescue you..."

"Oh nooo...oh my God, Sooty, My Sweetheart," it was Nicky's worst nightmare, just what he'd suspected. He dropped the bottle from lifeless fingers and strode over to her, pulling her into his arms.

"Oh Nicky, I need you. Please, please, if you can, if you don't care too much, just love me. I can't stand it all any longer. I feel so wounded and lost...and you, you're going away to war, again. Can you forgive me? Do you mind what he did?"

He hugged her tight. "Mind? You're crazed, what sort of a man do you think I am? I love you. Why should I care other than he hurt you terribly and you did it because of me? I want to make it, you, better, whole again, back to who you were if I possibly can. But Sweetheart, when I touch you, you just freeze."

"Please, please, try again. I've tried to put it all in a box, shove it away to the attic at the back of my mind. Ashcroft told me. H...he understood."

Nicky looked stunned. "Ashcroft? A box?" he was confused.

"He's not quite the cold fish everyone thinks. You obviously told him what happened at the villa and he knew, he understood; he tried to warn me before I left England, but I didn't take any notice."

"Bloody hell," was all Nicky could mutter.

"Nicky? Please..." Bella simply looked at him pleadingly and held out her hands.

He didn't answer, merely swung her up into his arms and strode over to his bed. He fell down beside her and tenderly, warily, kissed her face and she rose up and clutched him to her desperately, tears on her cheeks. Their lips met and long withheld, mutual desperate passion caught fire. Nicky kissed her deeply and hungrily, relentlessly and mindlessly...all the months of abstinence finally catching up with them both.

All Bella could think about was Nicky leaving her, risking his life in a far-off War yet again, possibly dying; any thoughts of herself and Bernheim just disappeared. Nicky was all over her body and her senses. She wanted him like she needed air to breathe and her belly flipped and spasmed, heat and moisture pooling between her thighs.

She felt his hands undo her robe, rove up under her nightgown. "Please, please, Nicky. Inside me... now...I need you, I'm ready, I have to have you, make me better..."

Was that her begging him so needily? She simply couldn't believe herself, she never talked like that. At least Bella didn't. *Lionesse* did... and had with Bernheim, but that had been a performance, a caricature of a high-class courtesan, a theatrical act. And she was Bella, not *Lionesse*. But she didn't know who she was any more, not that she cared. She frantically pulled her nightgown upwards, her legs splayed open invitingly as a hand ran over her naked torso.

"Jesus...Sooty..." Nicky almost gaped, stunned at her inviting, uninhibited display. He tore open the front of his breeches and thrust into her, making her gasp, her eyes widening at the immense feeling as he filled her, becoming part of her...pulsing and throbbing deep inside. He rose over her on his elbows, gripping both her hands in his own on either side of her head, looking down into her eyes, part worried she would freeze on him again; but she was lost, starting to writhe under him, striving, hot, wet, on fire, her green eyes alight with love and lust as she stared up into his golden ones.

It was over in moments. He thrust only a few times, driving hard and she convulsed around him, crying out his name, her muscles contracting as the waves overwhelmed her. As she climaxed, he lost himself and a forceful stream erupted out of him, making him cry out as blackness momentarily threatened to overwhelm him.

As they lay there, panting breaths all that were audible in the silent room, he felt the first sob rise up from her chest. Then another and another, until she was heaving with them. Deep, emotional, heart-breaking sobs that tore at Nicky's heart as an unstoppable flood of tears coursed down Bella's face. He rolled to his side pulling her with him, holding her hard against his chest, unwilling to break the close contact between them, unwilling to pull out of her. "It's all right, My Sweetheart, My Precious," he crooned and stroked her like a distressed kitten, "let it out, nothing matters, I love you. I love you..."

She sobbed as if her heart was breaking. "I felt so dirty, debased, used, unclean. I still scrub myself but I can't get rid of the nightmare of him inside me. I didn't think you would want me any more... couldn't face another man touching me... it was so horrible, he was so repulsive, like a voracious snake. I felt sick, he actually made me physically sick," and she continued to weep. "He hurt me, Nicky, so rough, so VICIOUS, so violent... like a man possessed. He smacked and hit me, bit me, pinched me, forced me every which way, tied me... to the furni-ture, the bannisters, in different positions. All afternoon, he was insa-tiable. He went places... I've read about it but never imagined people really got pleasure from it and I had him in my mouth, frequently, it was so foul, but I didn't dare stop him, couldn't stop him and then, then..." her final wretched admission. "When he was asleep, I should have killed him. I had the chance, I stood over him with a loaded pistol in my hand and I couldn't do it. But now he's not dead anymore and you're going after him, going hunting AGAIN. The guilt, Nicky, I simply can't BEAR it!" she was completely distraught, traumatised and emotional, sobbing pathetically as if a dam had broken inside her, as she clutched and pulled at his shirt.

Nicky had never known anything like it. He felt helpless anger such as he'd never known roiling inside him at what Bernheim had done to her. What she'd suffered, simply because of him. He felt worse than a worm.

"I'll kill him, Sweetheart, I swear to God, I'll kill him," Nicky grated. "Nothing is your fault, you mustn't blame yourself for anything." He hugged her even more tightly. "You have to forget it, forget it all. Nothing matters. All that matters is I love you. I love you, I've always loved you and I always will. I just want to make it better," he finally said helplessly, totally at a loss as to how to comfort her.

Bella felt suffused with his tenderness and love; he was so kind, so gentle and caring and he understood, just like when she'd been a little girl and tumbled off her pony or fallen out of a tree, or simply tripped over nothing and scraped her knees and hands. He'd always been there to make it better, kiss it better, cuddle her better...and now he was going away.

"Nicky," she breathed, "what am I going to do without you, when you're gone?" a last tear dropped to her cheek.

He leaned down and kissed her. "Wait for me, My Sweetheart," he whispered. "I'll be back," as he kissed her again, then again. "Nothing," another kiss on her neck, "nothing," and another, lower, at the tender spot on her collar bone, making her sigh, "will keep me from coming back to you," he breathed, like a vow.

He raised his head and looked deeply into her green eyes. "When I was in Rouen, in the Fortress, someone was watching over me. They sent Cat and your mother to save me, that gypsy friar and Francis... then in Spain, Reynard came and in Nice, you came and there was Jack. I think I must have a Fairy Godmother," Bella giggled and sobbed, choking back another tear, "or a Guardian Angel, on my side. I'm trusting in them yet again to bring me home, safe." He kissed her once more, tenderly, his deep soothing voice a balm to her shattered and frightened soul and she responded to his kiss fervently. It deepened and he hardened inside her, making her sigh and then gasp as he moved over her once more. He bent his lips to trace a pattern down her neck again and to her breasts where he teased and nibbled her nipples, until she squirmed and moaned ecstatically beneath him.

"You're so responsive to me," he muttered. "I still can't believe the little nuisance in plaits I used to play tricks on has turned into such a beautiful, passionate woman."

"I've always responded to you," Bella sighed, revelling in his caresses. "Even when you were horrid to me, I always put up with it as I was so infatuated with you... and I was NOT a nuisance!" She rolled over on top of him, suddenly and amazingly starting to feel cleansed of her trauma and she actually grinned down at his laughing face, kissing him on the nose. "I was a just a better shot than you, as well as a much better card player. We won't even mention chess," she laughed too and kissed him, "you simply couldn't cope with it."

He rolled her back, "I still can't, You Baggage, though my aim has definitely improved," he leaned down, grinning wickedly and bit both of her nipples very carefully, but noted she revelled in the tormenting pleasure, much to his delight.

"Ooooooch," she moaned, "you're being horrid again. I'll get my revenge, just you wait: pistols at dawn, in the garden. Just like we used to when we disagreed. I bet I can still shoot more pips out of the playing cards than you..."

"Sweetheart," he drawled, "if you think I'm going down into a bloody cold and draughty garden, to shoot pips out of playing cards at dawn and no doubt wake up half of Hertford Street and Shepherd's Market, frightening them to death, you're completely delusional, as usual. Not when I can think of much better ways of being horrid to you and enjoying your revenge on me up here in my nice warm bedroom."

"Is that so, Your Grace?"

"Sweetheart, you've noooo idea," he drawled again wickedly, then, with a searing golden look he bent his head and all thoughts of playing cards disappeared from her mind.

He loved her all night, making her cry out and climax again and again, spending himself inside her until he was drained and they were both mindless with exhaustion.

At a quiet time in the early hours when she was lying limp in his arms, Nicky finally coaxed out of her in detail, exactly what Bernheim had done. "Why did you never tell me all this before, Sweetheart?" he asked in disgust and despair. "Am I such an unfeeling brute you thought I wouldn't understand? Surely you must know that I, more than any other man," he paused, hesitating over his words, "given what I've had to do, would understand?"

She shook her head. "I... I know, but I couldn't. I couldn't find the words to tell you. I've never spoken about things like that, even with

Aunt Cat when I asked her for advice about how to, er, how to... do things to you," she stuttered to a halt momentarily, blushing.

He knew what she was trying to say but the temptation to tease was too much. "How to do what 'things', Sooty? Tie my cravat? Comb my hair?" he looked at her innocently.

"Ooooh, you know," she went even more pink and thumped him in his belly, then leaned over to whisper in his ear.

"Oh that," he grinned. "Does whispering it in my ear make it easier to say than out loud to my face? It's the same words and there's no one else here but me!" He burst out laughing at her silliness.

"Stop laughing at me, You Oaf," but she was serious again. "I was terribly embarrassed, but she was a woman and made a joke of it all, so I got over it then, but with you, it was somehow different, difficult... oh, I can't explain!" She buried her face in his chest and then more muffled words wandered upwards, "Anyway, I thought, hoped it would gradually go away, that I'd forget... but it just got worse."

As she'd haltingly recounted what had taken place that torrid afternoon, Nicky realised what a terrible impact Bernheim's depravity had made on her and how naïve she was in some respects, no matter how high her intelligence. "... I'd read about it in books, most of the things he did, except the strangling thing," she said raggedly. "I know some people are supposed to do it, including men with each other, you know, but it was all terrible, he was like a wild, rutting animal and so vicious," she shuddered. "It was so perverse, sooo painful. It's not pleasure like I share with you, so why do people do it? I take it they actually do, don't they?" she sighed.

"Some of it can be very pleasurable, if done in the right way," he'd said to her softly. "For instance, I seem to remember you didn't mind too much when I spanked you, over your desk," and she heard the teasing in his voice.

"That was different," she whispered back, feeling herself blush again and finding it easier to unburden herself in the warmth of his arms in the darkness, now the candles had burned themselves out. "That was you, I loved you, you were just playing. I knew deep down, even though we were both so angry, you'd never hurt me."

"Precisely, My Darling. Everything can be so delicious, such a delight, so arousing, or a silly, pleasurable or teasing game, if you love or simply care for each other, or lust after one another and leave your inhibitions outside the bedroom door, just like the games we played in *Le Lion d'Or*. I promise I'll show you. I'll make you forget every damn thing he did," he swore under his breath, "and replace it all with memories that will keep you warm at night when I'm away, yearning for me to come back and do them to you again," his deep and sensuous voice oozed over her, making her shiver.

Bella shook her head. "I'm not sure, Nicky, really, I don't think I can. Please My Darling... not that, no...."

"Hush, just trust me, let me love you, don't think and fret about it now," and he kissed her deeply, his hands roving her body to start to arouse her yet again, determined at some point to bury her terrible memories and experiences and replace them with something far, far more pleasurable which would teach her properly about making love in all its varied and erotic forms.

They eventually fell asleep and Bella woke to find Nicky propped up against the pillows, fingering his necklace with one hand, watching her, a thoughtful expression on his face, twirling a random lock of her hair round and round a finger of his other as the first birds began to twitter outside, heralding the approaching dawn. She yawned, stretched and then snuggled up close into his arms again. "Pistols at dawn?" she chuckled sleepily and he shook his head.

"No thank you, You Lunatic, I don't need to get pneumonia or make the neighbours think Boney is invading London," he laughed. "But I do need to get an heir, a little *Lion de Valenciennes*." He tugged the chain around her neck. Bella yawned again and rolled back on the pillows, looking up at him curiously. "Is that what you're thinking about? But you've got a little Lioness, how many more cubs do you want?" and she giggled sleepily.

"I need Lions," he chuckled. "The estate and title is strictly entailed to male heirs down a direct line; Lionesses can't inherit, though I have to say I'm not sure about male heirs of little Lionesses, as in Grand-Lions or Great GrandLions, in the direct line." He laughed at his silliness, "It's complicated and I've tried to find documentation about it. I have lawyers looking into it now in fact, but so much has been lost or destroyed, so in the absence of it, only a Lion will do, or two or three; I'm not fussy, the more the merrier... a whole pride?" Now Nicky was back in the civilised world and his life had all been put to rights, the deep-seated, indoctrinated, niggling pride about his ducal heritage had resurfaced, in spite of his strange thoughts in the cellar when he assumed he was about to die.

Bella burst out laughing. "Great GrandLions? What are they? And as for a pride, what do you think I am? I can't produce a litter."

"You're my *Lionesse*," he grinned, tugging the lock of hair he was playing with. "Remember, *Chérie*?"

"So I am," she grinned back at him, a wicked look stealing across her face, suddenly wide awake. "So, you want more cubs, do you, *Mon Cher*?" and she poked him in the chest playfully.

"Well, it seems like a good idea, since I'm going away." The unspoken risks of the battles to come and Bernheim's threat hung unmentioned in the air between them for a few moments.

Bella didn't want to think about any of it so she turned to him. "Hmmmm, so you're too chicken to face me in the garden over a playing card, too feeble to deal with a bit of cold weather, or pacify irate neighbours, yet you think you're manly enough to ensure I provide you with a little Lion, or a litter of them?"

He grinned at her, "Something like that."

"For someone so feeble, how are you going to manage that?"

"Oh, I expect I'll think of a suitable plan," his look was beyond suggestive.

"Reeeally?" her own look was deadpan. "Well, it appears to me I'll have to think of something desperate, quickly, before you come up with any plan, seeing as how you're such a useless weakling," as she poked his smoothly muscled biceps and ripped torso dismissively, tutting, "useless, absolutely useless."

He chuckled, watching as she licked her lips, tapping them with the tip of her forefinger. "Hmm, Your Grace, I think I may have a solution to your predicament," she said after a few moments. "Just a minute." She leaned down over the side of the bed, groping around on the floor, allowing Nicky an enticing view of her pert bottom which he couldn't resist leaning down to kiss and start to caress.

She sat back up. "Tut, tut, that's no way to make Lion cubs," swatting his hand away playfully.

"Oh, I don't know," he grinned, "it seems like the start of a good plan to me."

"Not as good as my plan," she smiled sweetly at him. "Anyway, mine definitely works."

"It does? How do you know that?" he looked puzzled for a moment.

"She's sleeping in the nursery upstairs," Bella said knowingly, her look mischievous as she lifted up the sash to her dressing robe which she'd just retrieved from the floor.

Nicky took one look at it and at Bella's saucy smile. "Oh no, not again, not that," he shook his head. "ABSOLUTELY, DEFINITELY, NOT!" He wriggled back against the pillows again as she advanced on him, finally straddling his lap as he was backed up against the headboard. "I swore I'd never let you do that to me again."

Not by the blink of an eyelash did he reveal the horror at the prospect she was jokily teasing him with, the nightmare of what he'd been subjected to in Bernheim's cellar, his own private torment with which he had to come to terms himself. Terrifying memories of being in constant darkness and not knowing where he was when he's awoken after being kidnapped on his way to the market, were still vivid in his mind. The unknown prospect of what they were going to do to him, of being dragged back and forth from his rat-infested cell by the silent Arab thugs, either to Bernheim or the vicious Chinaman, to be strung up and kept waiting for he knew not what, unaware of his surroundings or who was there, whether it was day or night or how long he'd been there...and then tortured unmercifully until he couldn't think straight and simply passed out. The agonising pain; he'd never, ever, forget it. The scars on his body were a constant reminder and he knew they would never fade completely. The nightmares and images still woke him in the night in a cold sweat. He couldn't sleep with the curtains drawn now, he hated absolute darkness, he always had, but now it was so much worse. He loathed rats and mice, spiders, anything that crawled in dark corners. The thought of being blindfolded again terrified him as he tried to rationalise with himself that this was Sooty he was with, loving and playful again, not the sadistic and evil Chinaman or the vicious and perverted Bernheim.

"It's my revenge," she smirked at him.

"But I haven't done anything horrid to you at least, not yet," he smirked back, swallowing hard.

"You're going away, isn't that horrid enough?"

"I can't help that, Sweetheart, I've given Wellington my word," he sighed.

"I know," she said softly, "but it's still horrid." She smiled determinedly at him, "Anyway, look what happened last time I did this to you and you went away. Who knows, now you've had some practice at it," and she winked at him, "I might well produce a Lion cub this time."

Nicky sighed theatrically, trying to look hard done by and smiled sorrowfully, "Once again, I don't have a choice do I?" She didn't understand the truth in his comical plea, parroting what he'd said previously in *Le Lion d'Or*, but this time his fists were curled in tension, hidden under the covers, as he braced himself, his nails digging hard into his palms as he willed himself not to stop her, his fierce pride once more governing his emotions.

Bella chuckled at him, "Not if you want me to procreate small Lions and I'm completely immune to your theatrics," she leaned forward, raising the sash. Her mind roved back nearly three years, "Any last requests from the condemned man before I carry out his sentence?"

He laughed in torment, his body stiffening as she tied the sash tightly round his eyes and everything went black. "You'd better make sure it's a male cub, torturing me like this! Why have I earned this sentence, despite being innocent as the day I was born?" Nicky breathed deeply, feeling sweat break out on his brow, admiring his acting skills and repeating to himself he could handle this...he could handle this... Sooty was playing and she loved him. Slowly, he calmed down and some of the fear and anxiety dissipated as he relaxed and smiled at the woman he loved and now trusted. It appeared love was the solution to both their problems. He shook his head and laughed at his irrational fears as he pushed them away.

"Innocent? You? What rubbish! And don't you laugh," she prattled, "let me see now, what have I got on the charge sheet? Desertion. Isn't that a capital offence in the army? Then there's Cowardice, for not going out into the garden for pistols at dawn against a mere woman; then a second charge of Cowardice for worrying about catching a cold, then a third for being frightened of Lord and Lady Bartholomew next door, who are so old and decrepit, they'd give Methuselah a run for his money." She laughed then as a final item struck her and he heard her wicked, lecherous mirth. "And finally, Dereliction of Duty," she choked at her joke.

"Dereliction of Duty?" he burst out laughing. "What on earth is that for?"

"Well now, let me see," she paused and wriggled in his lap before kissing him hungrily. "I've only climaxed, hmmm, I can't even remember how many times tonight, so they must have been quite forgetful incidents, definitely not enough nor memorable enough. How's that for utter Dereliction of Duty?"

"Appalling," he was still laughing, "and what form of capital sentence does all that get me?"

"Oh, definitely hung, drawn and quartered," she said airily, "but that's sooo gruesome and sooo messy, I'll just have to love you to death instead!" She kissed him again, sighing in lustful pleasure, "Or on the other hand," she paused and watched as he tensed apprehensively, "this is much more appropriate for such a villain," as she started to tickle him mercilessly.

Nicky howled and doubled up in mirth as her fingers ruthlessly caught him under his ribs, just where she knew he was most sensitive. "Ooooh noooo, Sooty... aaaaaaaarghh, You Witch, I'll kill you, I swear!" He rolled around on the bed, trying to escape her teasing and it wasn't long before he caught her tormenting hands and held them in a vice-like grip above her head. He rolled over on top of her and kissed her ruthlessly, "I'll get my own back," he warned, "I'll spank you and fuck you so hard you won't sit down for a week," he chuckled and suddenly paused as, what he'd threatened in his unseemly coarse language, carried away in a spur of the moment joke, suddenly hit him and he wished he could have bitten his tongue off as images of what Bernheim had done to her rushed to his mind. But she merely giggled and he breathed a huge sigh of relief that she really did seem to have put the terrible episode behind her, not that there wasn't a huge difference between his idea of spanking and the vicious beating Bernheim had obviously meted out.

When she breathed naughtily back at him, "Is that a promise? What else will you do?" he finally relaxed completely and caught her hair round his other hand to pull her close enough to whisper a torrent of wicked, licentious suggestions in her ear, making her gasp out loud in complete shock and blush bright red if he could have seen, before letting his lips roam down her body, setting it on fire.

"Hey, You Wicked Villain, you're supposed to be my prisoner, not the other way round," she managed as she struggled to roll him on to his back so she could finally get access to his body as she yearned to do. "Perhaps I should tie you to the bed again?"

"Oh no. Absolutely no. NO and NO." Nicky tried to be firm, but Bella could hear the thread of amusement in his voice. "Not this time. THAT," he whispered in her ear, "is a whole different game, and only if I want to play, which I absolutely am not going to do today, Madam," and she giggled, pushing uselessly against his tautly muscled arms and chest. It was like trying to move a wall, so she gave up. "Besides," he continued wickedly, "it's your turn now. You've never been my prisoner and it's high time you were," he started to caress her body again as he spoke, switching suddenly to French. "*Chérie*, you've no idea of how much I can make you suffer," his voice had never been so soft and sensuously teasing and Bella's stomach lurched, the words somehow sounding more *risqué* and seductive in that language. "Far, far worse than anything you did to me at *Le Lion d'Or, Ma Belle*. I'm such an expert torturer, it can go on for hours, days even," he crooned. "Tantalisingly, erotically, until you're so strung out, so desperate, you won't know yourself and you'll beg, cry, plead with me for mercy and then, being the terrible villain I am, I'll refuse you, until finally, when you're at the end of your tether, I promise I'll make you scream so loud, with such intense pleasure you've never, ever, dreamed existed or imagined possible." He rather fancied he could hear her mouth drop open and he smiled salaciously to himself. "Maybe when I come back? I'll look forward to it..."

"Hours? DAYS?" she wondered what that was all about, what he'd done in his past with other women. "Oh. My. Lord," was all Bella could whisper, going hot and cold at the same time as her mouth gaped and she shivered as a myriad of sensations ran down her spine and deep into her belly.

Nicky rolled over onto his back in uninhibited abandonment, stretching out like a big, blind, indolent golden cat, amused and pleased at her reaction to his wicked words, wishing he could have seen her face, before saying quite conversationally, "But in the meantime, if you want to carry on killing me... help yourself."

She teased and tantalised him endlessly to her heart's desire, just as she'd done at *Le Lion d'Or*. He simply lay back and let her do as she wished, even letting her have her way as she decorated his neck with a series of bites, revelling in the pleasurable torment of it all, before she gave in to temptation and impaled herself on top of him with a deep sigh.

"At least I know now who's doing this to me, even if I can't see you," he groaned finally as she bent to kiss him, feeling his fingers seek out and toy with her breasts, tweaking her nipples gently. Then his mouth curled in a salacious smile. "I will get my revenge for this as well you know, as I promised I would the last time at *Le Lion d'Or*. I haven't forgotten, I just haven't got around to it; but I will, that's another thing I owe you, *Lionesse*."

"Ooooh, I'm petrified," Bella giggled and heard him groan as she raised herself up, pausing tantalisingly before lowering herself slowly, inch by inch, and repeating the action several times more.

"Are you dead yet?" she queried.

"Nearly," he muttered. "Why I let you do this to me, I'll never know," he groaned again.

"Mmmmm, you love it really," she whispered. "Just like I love you," and she moaned as the spasms started deep within her as she sank down on him one last time, hearing him cry out to himself unexpectedly as he experienced a deeply emotional release, exploding inside her as she collapsed on top of him. She felt his strong arms snake about her tightly, pulling her close to him as if he needed a rock to hang on to in his darkness. She sighed, snuggling into his safe, secure and loving embrace. After a few moments Nicky reached up and pulled off his blindfold. He looked at it impassively for a while, what it represented, the memories it conjured up, but with Bella in his arms he'd overcome them; finally he smiled to himself as if he'd climbed a mountain and consigned it back onto the floor.

They dozed intermittently. "Why should I ever want anything else beyond that," Bella murmured. "It was so perfect. I wonder what my next cub will be, a baby Lion or a Lioness?" and she sighed as a big smile curved her lips.

"But you know there's so much more, You Witch," he said in amusement. "You and your salacious and curious reading," he chuckled. "You just have to ask and you can experiment on me as much as you like."

"Oh... but..." she started hesitantly.

"Sweetheart, look, you know I'll never ask you to do anything you didn't want to, but you must learn to talk to me, tell me what you like and what you don't, I'm not a mind reader."

She buried her face in his neck again. "Ooooh no, I like everything you do, but Nicky, I COULDN'T, it's just too much. I'm not like you, you're such a scoundrel, so uninhibited, you don't give a fig for anything you say or do."

"After all the things you've done to me in bed, you couldn't find the words to talk to me?" Nicky shook his head in bemused disbelief. "Dammit, Sooty, that's completely ridiculous! I thought I understood women, especially you. Oh, Sweetheart, you've never found me difficult to talk to before, expressing your endless opinions and ordering me about," he laughed. "You always used to come to me with your problems when you were younger. In fact, my ear has frequently been sore from the tongue lashings you've given me."

"I know, but this is different; we're grown up and you're a man."

"Oh Lord, am I?" Nicky couldn't help but chuckle. "But what about all those disgraceful things you whispered in my ear at *Le Lion d'Or* that last night before I left for Spain? That wasn't exactly a shopping list," he asked curiously in amusement.

Bella sighed, caught on his hook like a fish. "Well, you see," she idly drew circles with a finger through the light mat of golden hair on his chest, trying to decide what to say. "That wasn't really me, Aunt Cat told me what to say," she whispered in embarrassment, "and it was all in French and although my vocabulary is second to none usually, it certainly didn't extend to some of that, er, graphic and, er, coarse terminology; in fact I didn't understand half of what I said to you at the time."

Nicky burst out laughing at her revelation. "Cat told you? I might have known. Damn Francis, he's the very Devil; that's no doubt where she got it all from; the bugger," he carried on laughing, "and that's no doubt where you picked up some other of your delightful little tricks, eh? I found it hard to believe you'd got those from a book, that's why I was so jealous, I was convinced someone else had taught you." He continued to chuckle, "Oh Sweetheart, you're quite impossible, you and Cat, I love you both dearly, but whatever am I going to do with YOU?" He raised her chin and kissed her tenderly. "You're never to keep such terrible worries like you've had over the past few months from me again, do you hear? I'm here to share your problems, Sweetheart, whatever they are, in or out of bed, I'll cure you of your embarrassment if it's the last thing I do," he smiled wickedly, "'didn't understand what I said'" he parroted and shook his head as he guffawed. "Do you want a translation? I've never forgotten, y'know, I was quite transfixed myself at the time at what you suggested."

"Ooooh noooo, that bad?" she cringed and reddened with embarrassment as he nodded.

"Worse than what you whispered to me earlier?"

He nodded again. "Much, much worse! Let me remind you," and he bent down to whisper in her ear, repeating all the erotic, perverted suggestions to her again, translating into English as he went when she didn't understand the pornographic or slang French expressions.

He watched with enormous amusement as she went an even deeper beetroot, the flush moving from her chest up to suffuse her face, up into her hairline. He was fascinated.

"I suggested we did all THAT?" she finally whispered. "Ooooh noooo," she put her face in her hands and then remembered who had told her what to say. "I'll murder her," she said as Nicky chuckled. "I'll absolutely KILL her, how COULD she? She must have known I wouldn't understand it!"

"You should also complain to Francis. He was a renowned rake in his younger days, him and Ricky Ambrose and their friends; he was the most shocking womaniser in his time, especially when he was being his alter ego. Reynard told me some appalling stories when I was convalescing with him, so it's definitely all his fault," he drawled idly, examining his fingernails as Bella ranted on about her Aunt Cat. "Disgraceful behaviour for a Duke, a pillar of the British Establishment, to suggest such things to his wife; absolutely shocking! I dare say they've done them all, frequently." His face was a mask of inconsequence.

"Nicky! No, I can't believe it. I can't imagine it! That's outrageous. They're my aunt and uncle, they're old, well, not old, but you know what I mean, not that that's got anything to do with it, I suppose, but... oh noooo!"

"Oho, believe it, My Darling, and DO imagine it," he teased. "I know Francis exceedingly well and he claims he's taught me all he knew," he chuckled. "Well, perhaps not all I know. I have discovered quite a lot for myself," his chuckling increased, "so I suggest you think about all that and let your imagination run riot the next time the family sit down for dinner." His mirth got the better of him again. "Preferably over the soup. I'll watch you choke and blush and know exactly what you're thinking," and he doubled up at the expression on Bella's face.

"Nicholas de Bresancourt, you are quite the most disgraceful man I have ever met, simply impossible," scowled Bella, waggling a finger at him and trying to look scandalised but she couldn't maintain her straight face as she gave in and started laughing too. They fell back amongst the pillows, exhausted, Nicky cuddling her in his arms; within minutes the pair of them were fast asleep.

Chapter Twenty-One

B ella slept like the dead, exhausted by the rollercoaster of emotions and continuous lovemaking during the previous long night, but Nicky had an appointment.

He dragged himself reluctantly from the bed soon after dawn, looking longingly both at his pillows and then at the temptation of the naked woman he'd just peeled off his torso. He sighed but he needed to see Ashcroft and early morning was the time they'd agreed. He wanted to spend all of his last days and nights in London with Bella, uninterrupted. He'd already determined what he was going to do as he'd lain awake, listening to the birds twittering, watching Bella sleep, thinking about his meeting with Ashcroft and what lay ahead across the Channel with Wellington.

He left his room and went silently through to hers, ringing the bell before telling his wife's sleepy maid to order him a bath and to leave her mistress undisturbed before he summoned his valet.

Ashcroft had acquired a dog. An exceedingly ugly mutt of indeterminate age and colouring, certainly with no breeding. It wasn't particularly big, possessed only one eye, a torn and bent ear and a rough, wiry coat, neither long-haired nor short. It had appeared from nowhere and started to follow him one morning as he strolled across Green Park from his Mayfair home towards St James's Park and Whitehall.

The spymaster enjoyed his morning walks, eschewing a carriage unless it was pouring with rain. Walking gave him time to think and reflect on the many State security problems that came across his desk on a daily basis, the fresh, crisp morning air a pleasant and stimulating change from being cooped up in a coach and then his office for the rest of the day, often well into the night. It was also the only exercise he tended to take and he found it relieved the interminable backache he now suffered as a result of sitting for such long periods of time. He enjoyed going home the same way, for the same reasons, mainly in spring and summer; he was no fool and walking across a deserted park, or through dark and empty streets at night, on one's own, was not for anyone with any sense – not if you wanted to avoid being robbed or your throat cut.

After a few days of being followed each morning, Ashcroft had produced a large bone from his previous night's dinner from his capacious overcoat pocket and tossed it to the starving dog. It had caught it neatly in its jaws, despite its size and trotted off with a satisfied gleam in its one eye. The following morning, it got a piece of ham, then a lump of cheese and soon the dog was padding after Ashcroft all the way to his office entrance in Horse Guards. The first time it had attempted to follow him inside, the burly doorman had aimed a nasty kick in its direction to consign the flea-ridden cur back to the gutters, but a cutting admonition from Ashcroft had saved the hound. All day, it had sat patiently outside the entrance door, eyed malevolently by the doorman, while it waited for its saviour to reappear and had followed him home across the Park.

The next morning it had trotted behind Ashcroft inside and up the stairs, then waited calmly outside the door to the Department of Information for the rest of the day.

The day after, the dog followed him inside, much to the consternation of Chalmers and Ashcroft's own strange entertainment, then lay in wait again outside his office door, causing Chalmers nearly to trip over it more than once. He was not amused.

The day after that, the dog merely padded through into the inner sanctum itself, as if it was HIS office and calmly lay down on the rug in front of the fireplace, dozing there all day in utter contentment. And that was that. The dog followed Ashcroft all the way home that day where, with a deep sigh, he finally allowed it in through the front door. He handed it over to his shocked housekeeper, telling her to bathe it and see to the many sores and marks evident under its fur and to treat the fleas which made it scratch itself so frequently.

The dog sat at his feet in his study, clean, de-flea-ed, slightly fluffy and smelling of Ashcroft's cologne which his housekeeper had informed him with a commendably straight face that fleas and lice didn't like. It was now well-fed on the remains of Ashcroft's dinner and had its own bowl of water, formerly a rather nice silver finger bowl from the dining room table. The man looked at the besotted animal and began to talk to it, discussing potential solutions to State secrets and problems as he grappled with them himself...and so it continued.

Ashcroft had named it Nelson, for obvious reasons and one-eyed Nelson now sported a jaunty, patriotically coloured collar while he and Chalmers developed a mutual antipathy to each other. In fact, the dog would growl at almost every individual who invaded his Master's office, with two exceptions. One was Colonel Melrose, the man who had introduced Nicky to Ashcroft and was still the latter's main conduit to all things military in the War Office and the other, was the Duke of Firle.

Francis Granville had sauntered into Ashcroft's office one morning, not long after the dog had taken up residence, to see if the spymaster had received any word of either Nicky or Bella in France. They had enjoyed their usual fencing around the issue of The Shadow and, over a glass of fine Madeira, while they discussed current political events in France, Francis had quite happily fondled the dog's head, uncaring of its ugly demeanour which invariably put off most visitors, had scratched its ears and even bent down to rub its stomach as it had rolled onto its back in open invitation. Ashcroft had been surprised at the dog's acceptance of the Duke, given its seeming dislike of most other individuals on two legs, with the exception of himself, his housekeeper and Colonel Melrose, who always brought him a bone or tidbit. Much to Ashcroft's bemusement, a new collar with a large tag arrived at the Department of Information a week after Francis's visit. The collar was red, white and blue and came in a large box addressed simply to:

Special Commander Nelson,
Security Officer,
Department of Information.

The over-large, gold, bone-shaped tag which hung very visibly across Nelson's furry chest, sported his name on one side over a small, expensively bejewelled in diamonds, rubies and sapphires, White Ensign flag of the Royal Navy. On the other side a short inscription read: *"England expects every dog to do his duty, but preferably not in the Department of Information"*. The famous orders to Nelson's fleet before the Battle of Trafalgar back in 1805 were now well known to every Englishman, but this parody of them was both ridiculous and hilarious. Ashcroft very rarely laughed out loud, but when he saw the parcel, which came with no note, and opened it up, he knew immediately where it had come from and he simply guffawed uncontrollably, then chuckled with mirth intermittently for the rest of the day every time he looked at the tag, much to the stunned amazement of his staff.

And so it was that Nicky met Ashcroft on an extremely early morning walk with Nelson in Green Park. They sat on a bench for a short, private discussion while Nelson wandered off to investigate interesting smells among the familiar trees and bushes. Ashcroft had met Francis several times in the same place, the latter arriving with Bubbles. The over-large, beautiful, indulged, cream-coloured, very furry, apparently brainless Pyrenean Mountain dog and the small, ugly, clever, one-eyed and multi-coloured mutt with no breeding whatsoever, had bounded off to bark and chase each other in mutual antipathy around the park, while their owners discussed serious matters of National Security.

"... So, you see, I sent a couple of people to Nice to find out what they could about Bernheim's death and..." explained Ashcroft, watching in fascination as the immaculately dressed young man next to him encouraged Nelson onto his lap with a flick of his fingers, seemingly uncaring of the animal's dirty paws and ugly mien, then proceeded to scritch it round one mangled ear while crooning into the other in French, which made the dog's tongue hang out in bliss. "Good lord, how did you manage to get him to let you do that?" Ashcroft was distracted from his chain of thought. "He usually can't abide strangers, or anyone for that matter and you haven't even given him a biscuit or tidbit...and how come he can understand French?"

"No idea," smirked Nicky, "but I assume HE, at least, approves of me and he's obviously multilingual: Woof-Woof-speak, English, French, who knows what else?" He tried not to laugh as he spoke to the dog in Spanish and then in German. "Perhaps he's an international spy in disguise, sitting and listening to you discussing State Secrets in your office on a daily basis, to pass on to his doggy connections here in the park on the way home?"

"Don't be nonsensical," was the tutted reply, "but it seems nothing, even Nelson it appears, is immune to your charm," Ashcroft observed acidly. "No sense at all," he muttered under his breath. "Understands French, German and Spanish?" he muttered again. "Doggy connections? Where do you get these brainless ideas?" causing Nicky to chuckle as he answered.

"Oh, my wife is quite immune, I can assure you," he said airily, "not to mention the rest of my family."

"Your wife, eh? No doubt that's why you agreed to marry her," commented Ashcroft knowingly. "No doormat there and what a combination: beauty, charm, determination, all along with a considerable brain," he leaned back on the bench smiling a strange smile.

"Just like me," said Nicky humorously. "I thought that was why you selected me to join your little Service?"

"I suppose you do have some of her attributes," said Ashcroft facetiously. "You're tolerably decent to look at, have some charm, but I agree you do have determination, I give you that."

Nicky chuckled. "Ashcroft, are you insinuating I have no brains?"

"Absolutely," replied the other man impassively. "Allowing yourself to be captured like that, going out unarmed to get your boots stitched, for goodness' sake. What sort of an agent are you?"

Nicky looked directly at Ashcroft and then burst out laughing. "Ashcroft, I do believe you're trying to be funny. Whatever is the matter with you? First you adopt a decrepit dog, now you're trying to be a comedian. Are you feeling quite the thing this morning? Perhaps I should go and get you some hartshorn or a burnt feather to sniff to bring you back to normal?"

Ashcroft huffed. "I am quite serious, believe me – and you are as idiotic as Francis Granville, making out everything is a complete joke. I know perfectly well he was The Shadow, but all he does is prevaricate and play the fool every time I bring up the subject or try to have a serious discussion. The man is quite ridiculous and you are exactly the same," he tutted. "I am absolutely appalled you went out without weapons and got yourself taken. Good God, if it wasn't for that wife of yours and your, er, Ward, you'd be at the bottom of the Mediterranean, feeding the fish in an unmarked watery grave. Can't the pair of you understand that man is a menace to the Allies, as well as your family? The more I understand about his background and what is motivating him, the easier it will be for us to put him out of reach once and for all."

Nicky smiled at Ashcroft inanely. "Oh, I couldn't agree more, Lord Ashcroft. My going out unarmed was a shocking oversight, even I concur with you about that. But, of course, that's what happens when a man wants his breakfast so badly. I simply couldn't think straight on an empty stomach and naturally the worry over my poor boots was causing me nightmares; YOUR boots if you remember: Chalmers threatened me no end to take the greatest care of them."

"Oh, for heaven's sake," ground out Ashcroft in despair. "You're quite impossible, I don't know who is worse, you or Granville."

"Do you know, someone else told me I was quite impossible just a couple of hours ago, so there must be something in it, don't you think?" Nicky sat back with a beatific grin and continued to cosset the enraptured dog on his lap.

"I presume that was your wife. I'm glad we at least have the same opinion of you," said Ashcroft sarcastically. "Now then, where was I before I got so distracted? Oh yes, Bernheim," he sighed. "So, as I was saying, we could find no trace of his death and after a good deal of digging by a couple of very thorough contacts down there, we managed to unearth a local woman who had been summoned to help nurse the bastard after your Ward stuck him in the back. Apparently, between him and your wife, they had done away with most of his retainers, foreign individuals apparently, not much liked by the villa's domestic servants, I understand. Two of the latter, to whit the cook and the housekeeper, were merely knocked unconscious and incapacitated. The coachman had been given a few hours off so had sloped off for a quiet drink with a friend who was caretaker at a neighbouring property. The doctor who was fetched by the coachman to treat Bernheim, organised for a nurse to help the housekeeper look after him as he needed twenty-four hour nursing apparently. We gather it was touch and go for a while, but the cook and housekeeper managed to keep him alive until the doctor arrived and regrettably, he pulled through. The knife went in at a slightly off angle, glanced off a vertebrae, so apparently was deflected from his heart and only punctured a lung." Ashcroft shook his head, "Shockingly unfortunate."

"Shockingly," agreed Nicky bitterly.

"Anyway, he recovered, then left the villa and promptly disappeared to, we know not where. He certainly hasn't appeared at his home in Paris yet and I doubt he will, so we must wait and see where he resurfaces. Now Bonaparte has returned, we expect him to take the opportunity to start causing mischief as no doubt there will be money to spend for anyone willing and able to cause trouble on behalf of that megalomaniac. As we know, Bernheim will do anything to line his own pockets."

Nicky nodded in agreement. "HOWEVER," said Ashcroft leaning closer to make his next point, which is why he was meeting Nicky in the park and not in his office so their conversation would be completely confidential, "although that is what concerns Wellington and me, unfortunately you, your wife and Ward are still the only people who know what he looks like, which is why we want you back in France, or in Brussels where I think Wellington will make his HQ. You and Granville might be interested in my other little tidbit of information. I'm going to tell him about it later today when I go there for tea; this is all about The Shadow, whether he likes it or not."

Nicky looked impassively at Ashcroft, alarm rising inside him. "What about The Shadow?" he enquired tonelessly.

"I'm glad to see you're finally admitting you know all about the fellow and his... ah...'connection' with your family."

"I'm doing no such thing, Ashcroft."

"Of course you're not," replied the older man sarcastically, "so why should I tell you then?"

"If anything concerns Bernheim, then I need to know," Nicky replied evasively. "I owe him. He goddamn near killed both me and Bella in Nice."

"Quite so," said Ashcroft, "therefore anything about The Shadow has nothing to do with that I suppose?"

"Oh, stop playing games, Ashcroft," bit out Nicky.

"Very well," said Ashcroft, smirking. "Well, the old woman, the nurse, helped care for Bernheim for several weeks while he was bedridden as he caught an infection at some point and became very ill, delirious in fact." He watched Nicky's face intently as he spoke. "According to the woman, who of course only spoke French, Bernheim was raving about shadows a lot, or rather one in particular, *L'Ombre,* she said, as opposed to *les ombres,* or shadows in general. She assumed he was seeing things in his delirium so didn't take much notice. Interesting that, don't you think?" he commented with narrowed eyes. "Another word she couldn't understand which also didn't mean anything to my people, but they, fortunately, still wrote it down as part of their report into his ramblings – very thorough, very thorough..." he muttered, pleased with himself, "... was *Ferle,* Bernheim said continuously; *ferle*, or, of course Firle, as you, Francis Granville and I would say."

Nelson yelped as Nicky suddenly gripped him tight and promptly jumped off his lap. "Exactly, Nelson," Ashcroft murmured as he watched the dog depart. He looked at Nicky, "I somehow thought that might interest you," he said quietly.

"You had better tell Francis," responded Nicky impassively, "and discuss it with him. He's the Duke of Firle. I couldn't possibly comment."

"No, I rather thought you wouldn't," tutted Ashcroft, "but no doubt you're exceedingly interested. Pity I won't be a fly on the wall next time you find yourself in the estimable Duke's study, which I presume will be tomorrow after I apprise him of all this intelligence later today. Then, maybe SOMEONE will finally see fit to trust me enough to tell me the full story!" he ended angrily. Losing his temper was a very rare occurrence in the controlled Ashcroft's life.

"Well, you'll just have to tell His Grace that," said Nicky calmly.

"I most certainly will," ground out Ashcroft. "I'm not having that dangerous and crazed Frenchman coming over here, causing trouble, because he has some obsession with you and your family." His silvery grey eyes looked keenly at Nicky, "If it were just a personal matter, I wouldn't care a jot, but his underhand activities have always involved politics and I'm not having this country's security put at risk because of some decades' long feud... THAT NOBODY WILL TELL ME ABOUT!"

"Dear me, Ashcroft, there's no need to get so animated," replied Nicky quietly, "you'll upset Nelson," he smiled serenely.

"Now you listen to me, You Facetious Young Pup," Ashcroft said icily, "I WILL get to the bottom of this, if it's the last thing I do. With luck, the man has come to his senses and simply gone to live in the sunshine somewhere and enjoy the fruits of his and his father's ill-gotten gains, which I suspect are quite considerable already, despite the family obsession for yet more, in which case there will be nothing for any of us to worry about. But if there is the REMOTEST possibility of that not being the case, I want to be prepared."

"Ah, quite so," said Nicky, in an almost identical tone of voice as that often used by Ashcroft . The man glared at him.

Nelson had reappeared and jumped onto the bench between the pair of them. Nicky twirled his collar, admiring its patriotic design and picked up the jewelled tag to peer down and read its content. He grinned, suspecting only one man in London who knew Ashcroft's dog would be idiot enough to produce something so valuable, silly and apt, for the ugly mutt. That man certainly wasn't the dry and ascetic Lord Ashcroft.

"Fascinating collar, Nelson," he scratched the dog's head again. "Do you whisper, 'kiss me, Ashcroft,' before you go to sleep at night?" With that, he rose to his feet and bowed exquisitely, smiling hugely at the almost apoplectic expression on Ashcroft's face. Francis wasn't the only one to capitalise on the famous sayings connected with the late naval hero at the Battle of Trafalgar.

"Thank you so much for your information, Lord Ashcroft, I'm sure it will be appreciated in the appropriate quarters, wherever they may be," Nicky was all aristocratic politeness. "In the meantime, I presume you would wish me to continue to communicate with you as before? In which case, is there any chance of another pair of boots? I seem to have mislaid mine on the way to the mender's, how terribly remiss of me. I should be whipped or tortured for my carelessness so I learn my lesson…"

"You know something, de Bresancourt," said Ashcroft slowly and frostily, looking up at the man in front of him who was idly examining his perfect fingernails, wondering if he should grow them again and take his guitar away with him, "I called Bernheim dangerous and crazed just now, but I think it was the wrong description. The man is definitely unhinged. Anyone trying to take on two complete lunatics, which is what you and Francis Granville are, is obviously seriously deranged and deserves everything he gets, for as God is my witness, I swear he will never get the better of the pair of you." He shook his head despairingly, "You two should be in Bedlam, never mind serving Wellington or gracing the House of Lords. I think it my considered duty as a dedicated servant of the Crown to inform the Prince of Wales and the Prime Minister to that effect." He looked at the bemused dog, "Don't you agree, Nelson? You may kiss me now..." and he literally doubled up with laughter, for the second time in all his years of devoted service to his King and Country.

Having quickly discussed some final bits of information about Wellington's plans for the rest of his time in London and just before he was due to depart, Nicky strode off in the direction of Piccadilly, Bond Street and thence towards the less salubrious area of Berwick Street and Soho, to pick up some items of shopping on his way back to Hertford Street. As he hurried along, he wondered if he should warn Francis about Ashcroft's intended grilling later and his increased knowledge of The Shadow, but decided Francis was obviously well aware of the fact Ashcroft knew his secret. It was up to him to decide if he would share any further details with the spymaster. That Ashcroft would keep the information to himself, Nicky now had no doubt, but it wasn't his decision, so he would wait until he visited Firle House to make his farewells before leaving for the Continent with Wellington; he would discuss it all with Francis then. In the meantime, he could do nothing about Bernheim other than be on his guard and wait for news of his reappearance. With those decisions made and still chuckling over Ashcroft's response to his jokes, he smiled wickedly to himself and turned his mind to his shopping and errands list and the pleasurable events he'd planned for the rest of his short time left in London with his beloved wife.

Chapter Twenty-Two

B
ella twitched her feet away from the tickling sensation. "Gerroffff..." she muttered grumpily and buried her head under a pillow. She felt chilly and realised there was a strong current of cool air blowing across her naked torso. She groped around for the covers to pull over herself but they seemed to have disappeared.

Moaning, she peered out from under the pillow with one eye open, fumbling around for some covering as she shivered. "Where'reth'covers?" she grumbled, "'s'cold... goWAY!" she mumbled again as her feet were tickled once more.

She finally emerged from under her pillows, sat up and glared at the wide-open window which was allowing the cold March air to chill her body, giving her goosepimples. She finally found the pulled back covers and drew them over herself as she shivered again. She turned and looked at Nicky, sitting relaxing in a chair near the bed, calmly stroking a purring Duchess on his knee and drinking a cup of coffee.

"Good morning," he said conversationally, "what a lazy person you've become lately, Your Grace. Can I interest you in some coffee to help wake you up? Isn't the fresh air bracing, though it appears we're in for some rain later by the look of all those black clouds?"

Bella peered at the clock on the mantelpiece and groaned. "What on earth are you doing up and dressed? I thought you'd be out for the count 'til at least noon, knowing you; it was way past dawn before we went to sleep and for Heaven's sake, shut the window!" With another groan, she fell back into the pillows and pulled the sheet up over her face.

It was wrenched out of her hands and Nicky's grinning face loomed over her, "Tut, tut, there's no time to stay in bed, we've got so much to do today. Come along, Lazybones."

She slowly sat up again as he perched on the bed and resumed drinking his cup of coffee. The cat was now sprawled out lazily on his side of the bed, purring and dozing off to sleep; he continued to stroke her when he put his cup down.

"Well at least someone is happy and allowed to go back to sleep around here," she grumbled.

Nicky chuckled, "Poor puss, she was very offended at losing her sleeping place to another Duchess last night. I'm afraid there's only room for one Duchess in my bed so you'll have to discuss with her as to which one it's going to be."

"Has she been sleeping with you then?" Bella sighed and smiled at him. "Is that why she's got her own little hinged panel in your door?"

"At least one female in this house took pity on me and decided to keep me company. I even received gifts at two o'clock in the morning. Mind you, dead mice or rats just aren't the same if they don't come nicely wrapped with a ribbon." Bella giggled and shuddered. "Don't worry, Sweetheart, there can't be many mice left in the whole of Mayfair, given the number of presents I've had over the past few months. I just wish she wouldn't decide to picnic on them and leave me the half-eaten remains to clear up. The housemaids cringe if I don't do it for them, or invariably call a footman to do undertaking duties." Nicky chuckled but Bella had no idea of the horrors he felt every time the cat had brought her prey into his room. Nightmares of his cellar and having his toes nibbled and the feel of scrabbling feet and furry bodies would take him a long time to get over. It had also brought back memories of his dark cell in Rouen Fortress where he'd been locked up by himself as a small boy. Harrowing memories, compounding more terrifying ones.

"She'll miss you when you're gone," Bella said sadly as Nicky handed her a cup of coffee from the tray sitting on a table in front of the fire. "She's extremely attached to you."

Nicky smiled and sighed, "I know, but I dare say Terrie will keep her distracted. I'm amazed she never gets scratched, no matter how many times she grabs her."

Bella laughed. "She's no doubt inherited your magic touch. Duchess doesn't think twice about having a go at me if she's feeling all contrary. Anyway," she changed the subject, "what on earth are YOU doing up and dressed so early? I didn't think wild horses would drag you out of bed before you needed to eat again, given the time we went to sleep. You're not exactly famous for being an early riser, except when you were in the army no doubt."

"Oh, I don't know about that," he winked at her as she blushed slightly at the unintended innuendo in her comment, "but, well, I had things to do, you see," as he tapped the side of his nose and smiled mysteriously, "places to go, people to see."

"Yes, yes, I'm sure. You've been the biggest Lazybones between Mayfair and Sussex all your life, Nicholas de Bresancourt, I don't believe you for a minute."

"Once upon a time, maybe, but I HAVE been out, really," he grinned. "In point of fact, I've been rushed off my feet with being so busy, organising this and that."

"What a tall story," she said, shaking her head with a smile and resumed sipping her coffee as he poured himself another cup before sitting in his chair again, perching his booted feet on the end of the bed. Nicky gazed over at Bella and sighed. She looked simply delicious, all rumpled and voluptuous as she leaned back innocently amongst the pillows, long hair loose and tumbling over her shoulders in abandon, lips swollen and red. The rake in him would describe it as a 'well fucked' look, and it was all he could do not to shed his clothes and climb back into bed with her as he felt himself harden. But he had more interesting plans for her, for the day too, so he resisted the temptation with great reluctance.

"Well, Duchess, whatever you may think, I've made plans for the day and they can't wait while you loll around here impersonating my cat," he smiled. "Just because you had a busy night, it's no excuse."

"Busy night?" she grinned "And who's fault was that? Not mine," she commented.

"It was most definitely your fault, Madam. Whose room are you in? Who came in here and dragged me off to bed and wore me to a frazzle?" He curled his lips in a wicked smile. "As I'd like to remind you, I told you I was completely innocent hours ago, but of course you took no notice and had your wicked way with me, regardless." He watched the blush creep over her cheeks.

"Nicholas de Bresancourt, you are an extremely dangerous man to be allowed in anyone's ballroom or drawing room, let alone a bedroom and in any case, you haven't been innocent since you were about sixteen, or possibly less, knowing you," she protested.

"Fourteen, actually," he grinned. "Or was it thirteen? I can't remember."

She put her cup down and threw a pillow at him which he and his cup just avoided. "You're absolutely disgraceful, beyond redemption," she laughed.

"I know, you told me that last night too. So, what are you going to do about it?" he smirked.

"Absolutely nothing," she whispered and looked at him under her lashes as she reddened again.

"Well, that's a relief, I was seriously worried you'd consign me to a monastery and then go off on retreat and become a nun," he smiled and listened to her laugh. "Now then, Your Grace, as I was saying, unfortunately I've been summoned and this is my last day before I go abroad with Wellington, so you've got to get up and organise yourself as we can't lose a minute. I've got everything planned."

"You have?" she asked curiously. "What's that?"

"Well, first of all, we're going on a little trip; only a short one mind, then it's a surprise."

"Ooh! Where are we going?"

"I told you, it's a surprise. So hurry up and bathe and get dressed and then we can have some breakfast and leave. I've ordered your bath already, so off you go. I'll tell Carstairs to serve breakfast in, what? Half an hour at most? Will that do? Don't be any longer, time and tide wait for no man, nor woman, you know the saying…"

She nodded and jumped out of bed, scrabbling on the floor for her discarded robe and hurried through to her room where she found her maid waiting by a hot and steaming bath in her dressing room. Bella was soaking in the scented water when Nicky poked his head around the door and at the sight of him, her maid scurried out, blushing. "Why the Devil does everyone blush whenever I appear around here?" he asked.

"I told you, you're a dangerous man," she laughed at him. "What do you want now, You Villain? I'm being as quick as I can. What should I wear when I don't know where we're going?"

"Ah, now then, what to wear? Didn't you do some shopping when you were in Paris?" he looked at her knowingly. "Francis happened to mention Cat had acquired some interesting additions to her very personal night-time wardrobe as a result of your endeavours. I assume you must have FORCED yourself to acquire something for you as well, knowing how much you HATE shopping?" he grinned.

"You and Uncle Francis seriously need taking in hand," opined Bella acidly. "I'll have a word with Auntie Cat, you're obviously worse than a pair of gossiping washerwomen."

"Well? Did you?" he winked, muttering to himself, "I must tell Francis his latest soubriquet, he'll be overcome with pleasure," he chuckled to himself before looking back at her.

"I might have done," she responded airily, thinking about the mound of 'interesting' undergarments, corsets and nightwear she'd purchased hopefully, that had lain untouched in her armoire since her return from France. She was already running through them in her mind, deciding which to choose that would please him the most.

"Aha! I'll look forward to inspecting it later," he grinned lecherously. "A simple day dress will be fine. Don't worry about a bonnet and gloves and which pelisse or reticule; we're not going anywhere that special, I promise, just spending time together. It'll be only thee and me," he smiled mysteriously.

"What about Terrie?"

"All organised. I've sent her round to Berkeley Square to play with Lizzie; Double Trouble at Firle House," he grinned. "I want to spend the rest of my time tomorrow with her. So many women in my life to please," he sighed and chuckled, "but today is for you, Sweetheart. Is that all right?"

"Whatever you like. Now, go away and let me bathe in peace. Have a word with your other Duchess and tell her I don't want any night-time presents left outside my door, thank you, while you're away."

"Yes, Your Grace; whatever you say, Your Bossiness. I'll have a forceful conversation with her immediately, in Spanish, so I know she'll understand and follow your instructions to the letter." He bowed and disappeared, laughing and calling out to the cat in Spanish as he returned to his own rooms.

He didn't give her time to eat more than a roll for breakfast and seemed in such a hurry to usher her from the house and into the carriage waiting at the kerb, only then to disappear back into the house for a while.

In the hallway he addressed Carstairs. "Her Grace and I will be away all day, Carstairs, also overnight. We'll be back in the morning and will collect Lady Thérèse from Firle House on the way as I've already sent her round there, as you know. He looked at the impassive, long-suffering butler and smiled at him. "I know I've been a bit short-tempered lately and I apologise most humbly and sincerely." Carstairs' eyes widened slightly as he wasn't used to his aristocratic employers and their visitors apologising, certainly not like that. "You may have already heard I am off again," he knew what the servants' grapevine was like and sighed. "Tomorrow, probably, to join Wellington in Brussels, more than likely. Bonaparte has escaped Elba, unfortunately, as we've heard and he's now in Paris, so it's War again," he grimaced. "Therefore, while I'm gone, I want all the staff to take particular care of Her Grace and Lady Thérèse."

"Of course, Your Grace, you surely know you can rely on us all, absolutely."

"Good," said Nicky. "Any problems, go straight to Firle House and inform the Duke, in person, but you know that anyway and please don't forget what I said about the letter in my desk."

"Yes, Your Grace, of course," the butler bowed. "I fully understand." The man's face was impassive, but he cringed inside and hoped it never came to pass that he'd need to deal with that letter.

"Good man. Thank you. Also, since Her Grace and I, as well as Lady Thérèse, are all out for the rest of the day and overnight, I thought you and ALL the staff here might like a day off as a treat." He pulled a large bag of gold coins from his coat pocket and handed it over to the astonished butler. "Tell them to go and enjoy themselves at Vauxhall, if the weather holds, or the theatre, or dancing or drinking. They can go to Brighton if they like, if they've got the time, though it's a bit far for just a few hours looking at the beach and the sea and it's a trifle inclement at this time of year, but I don't care; whatever or wherever they want, they can go or do. I'll leave you to sort it out, just take the coaches, or hire whatever is required, but the cost is back to me. If you need any more money, just ask my secretary, though he should be joining you too, no boring estate work for either of us today, thank Heavens, or anyone else in my household. The only living thing left in the house should be the cat, so just leave some food out for her, unless you want her to forage for herself and bring in more vermin to picnic on!"

Nicky looked at the speechless man and chuckled. "Good Lord, Carstairs, have I finally shocked you into silence?" he patted him on the arm. "Never mind, I'm beyond saving, I do assure you. Tell everyone to enjoy themselves – you all deserve a treat," and with that, he turned and hurried out of the front door again, leaving the astonished butler clutching the heavy bag of money in the hallway, still gaping like a beached fish.

They arrived at *Le Lion d'Or* and Bella looked at Nicky in puzzlement. "What are we doing here? I thought we were going out for the day?"

He grinned at her, "We are, Sweetheart, we've just arrived." He tugged her from the coach and up the steps, unlocking the front door himself and ignoring the large notice pinned to it.

CLOSED FOR 24 HOURS DUE TO UNEXPECTED BUILDING REPAIRS

La Lionesse d'Or remains open as usual

He directed the footman who had followed him from the coach to leave a large picnic hamper and other packages from the back of the vehicle in the hallway, then sent him on his way, telling him to hurry back to Hertford Street with his coachman and report to the Butler. He then shut the door behind him.

Bella stared at Nicky in perplexed concern. "What on earth is going on? I didn't know there was a problem here. Where is everyone, anyway?"

"Ah, yes, WELL, *Lionesse…*" Nicky began, "EVERYONE has been given the day and night off, there isn't a problem at all. I just wanted to come somewhere quiet where we won't be disturbed. At short notice, this was all I could think of." He shrugged but looked like a small boy pleased with the mischief he had wrought.

"Whaat?!" she exclaimed. "The day and night off? You've closed *Le Lion d'Or?* Whatever are you doing?" she expostulated.

"Well, I do own this little concern after all…er, don't I?" he laughed.

"Not that you've ever shown the remotest interest in it," she said sarcastically, "but my apartment is very private, no one will bother us if I give instructions."

"Nothing is private when half the Ton is downstairs," he said pithily, "and if they know you're here, there's always the chance someone from the staff will still bother us. No, this is the best way to get undisturbed peace and quiet. No one will be back until tomorrow morning."

"But whatever for?" Bella was still puzzled.

Nicky didn't answer and merely ushered her up the stairs to her apartment where fires had been lit and it was warm and cosy. The building seemed eerie and still without the usual bustle of staff and clientele thronging its rooms, although it was only staff in the mornings until noon when the gaming house opened for business. It was turning cold and blustery outside and finally starting to rain, so he part drew the curtains before sauntering over to a sideboard and an ice bucket where a bottle of champagne was chilling. He opened it and poured them both a glass, surreptitiously adding a dash of brandy to Bella's before handing it to her. She was sitting in a chair in front of the fire watching him in bemusement. "Are you going to tell me what all this is about and isn't it a bit early for this?" she held up her glass.

He peeled off his jacket and sat opposite her, toasted her in silence and tossed back the golden liquid. "Not at all, it's never too early for champagne." He smiled his big teasing smile before taking a deep breath. "Well...you see, Sweetheart, it's like this," he began again, twirling his empty glass in his fingers as he spoke, choosing his words carefully. "You and I have had a rather strange relationship over the past few years since you...er...grew up. Our wedding was hurried and furtive, just because of your inheritance, and we never had a proper wedding night, never mind a honeymoon; then I was away, either travelling or in the army, so I hardly saw anything of you and when we did finally...ah...get together," he grinned, "that was a bit of a disaster. It wasn't until I tipped up here, what was it, nearly three years ago?" He shook his head in disbelief at how quickly the time had passed since that fateful week, "Then, I finally got to make love to you properly – but I thought you were someone else at the time and that whole situation was bizarre, to say the least." His look was wicked for a moment and Bella finished off her champagne with a gulp.

Nicky got up and refilled Bella's glass, adding brandy again, his intention merely to relax her and remove some of her nerves which he knew would soon surface when she discovered his intentions. He sat down and continued, watching her sip the drink absently. "...And since then, I've been away again and, well, you know what's happened in the meantime, or, more to the point what hasn't. In fact, I don't think I've made love to you properly when I've known who you are, or haven't been angry as Hell, apart from that one short moment in Paris but even then, I wasn't my usual self... until last night." He sat back looking more thoughtful and continued, "As for you..." he cocked his head on one side, "well now..." he paused and gave her a penetrating stare as he gazed at her, looking her over assessingly, "for a start, you're far from an ordinary woman like your Society peers, or indeed the vast majority of women. Incredibly intelligent, well-read and far from naïve, as I've discovered. To the outside world, you're a well-brought-up young Lady, very much in control of yourself, most of the time. In fact, the only time you let yourself go with me, lose your inhibitions and express yourself, is either when you've totally lost your temper, had too much to drink, or are hiding behind a mask, being someone else; or I can't see you; which I find very interesting... or after I've fucked you." He used the word deliberately and smiled. "It really is all quite surreal. In fact, if I regaled the whole story about *La Lionesse*, our history together and our adventures, to anyone, they'd think it utter, unbelievable tosh, not even worthy of one of those ha'penny romance novels you Ladies like to read.

"Well really," sniffed Bella, "there were all sorts of extenuating and unusual circumstances involved. It was never that simple."

"Whatever you call it or however you want to explain yourself, extenuating, unusual or even bizarre, those are the facts. But now, just when we FINALLY seem to have sorted ourselves out and begun to confront our own personal little problems, I have to go away again. It's all very unfortunate, not to say frustrating and I have one day and just one night left with you, before I leave." He sighed. "Therefore, my lovely Duchess, I intend to make the most of our time and try to mend some of what is still an issue between us. I want to make sure that when I do go, you won't get any more crazy ideas in your brain which I'm not here to address, as well as giving you some memories which should keep any more of your nightmares at bay, permanently, which will help you forget you're a Lady, when it's appropriate."

"Oh my," Bella muttered, eyes widening. "But why here? We could have stayed at Hertford Street, surely?"

"Ah, yes, *Chérie*," he smiled, his tone changed, his voice turning deep and seductive. "We could have, but you see, My Sweet, *Lionesse* lives here and I've been looking for her for years. Sooty lives in Hertford Street and although I love you both the same, it's *Lionesse* with whom I want to spend my time today and...tonight."

A slow blush crept into Bella's cheeks at his hot, lecherous look. "There you are," he chuckled, "Sooty always blushes, *Lionesse* never did. SHE didn't have many inhibitions when she was with me."

"You couldn't see what she was doing most of the time," giggled Bella, "so how would you know if she blushed or not?"

"I knew, I just knew," he smirked. "So, is she here? Do you think she'd like to spend the rest of the day and tonight in bed with me?" He smiled a wicked smile in Bella's direction.

"Well, this is where she lives, but you know how fussy she is about her companions. She doesn't sleep with just anyone, y'know," Bella prevaricated.

"Who said anything about sleeping?" His lips curled, "She seemed to enjoy my company and other things, last time I was here. I'm sure she's got a soft spot for brave soldiers," he said softly.

"Only the most irresistible, rakish ones," Bella said slowly. "Do you know anyone like that? They have to be tall, handsome, strong, charming and able to sweep any woman off their feet."

Nicky rose and approached her chair, leaned down over her and kissed her on the nose. With one swoop, he picked her up in his arms and carried her through to the bedroom. "Consider yourself swept, My Dear. Now, do I fulfil your other criteria?" he grinned.

"I suppose you'll pass," Bella huffed and he chuckled down at her prim expression before she spoiled it by giggling. He paused at the entrance to her bedroom, "Ah, the scene of the crime," he said softly to her as he gazed around, "it looks just the same."

"You remember then?" Bella smiled at him.

"How could I forget? Your terrible deeds on my poor innocent body are scorched on my brain forever."

"Serves you right. I've still not really forgiven you for carrying on with another woman."

"But it was you!"

"You didn't know that though, did you, You Villain?" she poked him in the chest. "See, guilty again; innocent, my foot!"

"Does that mean you're going to punish me again?" he asked as he tossed her on the bed, his eyes glinting down at her, his lips curling lecherously.

Bella giggled. "You know, dealing with you is like handling an Indian snake: fascinating, slippery and very deadly." She shook her head, "I never know what you're going to do or say next."

He threw himself down on the bed on top of her, "Well if you don't know what I'm going to do next, You Saucy Baggage, you're even sillier than I know you are already," and without giving her a chance to say anything else, he pulled her into his arms and started to kiss her.

He rolled off her and she came up for air, dazed and panting. She turned to watch him as he scooted up the bed and propped himself up on the pillows. She crawled up after him and smiled, her lips once again pink and swollen from his ruthless attentions. "You see, I was right," she whispered. "I may be silly, but you are utterly deadly," as she leaned down again to kiss him. His hands roved up and down her back, caressing her bottom through her dress and then he pushed her on to her back and let them wander up and down her torso, lingering to tease her breasts, making her nipples harden painfully and her belly to spasm.

"I think it's about time you showed me what you've got on under your dress, *Lionesse*," he whispered and pushed her back, putting his arms up to cross them behind his head, looking expectantly at her.

"Why don't you undress me, then?" she responded naughtily, kneeling up next to him.

"No, *Lionesse*, I want you to strip your clothes off for me," his sensual voice crawled over her and she shivered, "but do it slowly and think about what I'm going to do to you after."

"What are you going to do after?" she whispered, eyes widening.

He looked at her impassively. "I'm going to make you scream and screech and wail with pleasure," he finally whispered, "just like I promised last night."

Bella swallowed hard. "Noooo," she whispered.

"Oh yes, *Lionesse*, it's time."

"What are you going to do?" She was transfixed, like a startled rabbit.

"Everything..." the one word conveyed such sensual and wicked promise, Bella shivered again. "Take off your clothes, *Chérie*..."

Bella retreated backwards and slid off the bed, as in thrall to Nicky as ever. She stood a few steps from the end, watching him watching her and, taking a deep breath, she slowly started to undo the bodice of her dress. As he'd asked, she began to peel it off tantalisingly slowly, watching his eyes narrow, then gradually she forgot her apprehension and enjoyed herself as she realised how transfixed he was. The dress was undone and half off and she stopped, turned around and put her hands up to her hair. One by one she started pulling out the pins until she knew there were just a couple left holding it all up, random locks now falling down her back. Slowly, she let her dress fall to the floor and then undid her shift. She'd not bothered with a corset, knowing the froth she was wearing would be spoiled by the tight lacing. The ordinary, plain shift slowly slid down her body, revealing the black lace underneath and behind her she heard Nicky's indrawn gasp. From the back, only three quarters of her bottom was covered, leaving nothing between the end of the lace and her black stockings, held up by red lace garters decorated with a confection of black ribbons and bows at her knees. The camisole, what there was of it, was held up by more black ribbons which were also threaded through the lace. Slowly, she raised her hands and took the last remaining pins from her hair, the whole heavy mass dropping down her back while she tossed her head, running her hands through it as she sighed in pleasure and let her head drop back.

She stood poised for several moments, still with her back to him and then ran her own hands slowly up and down the front of her body, teasing his imagination as to what she was doing. Gradually, she turned her head over her shoulder to look at him. He hadn't moved a muscle but was staring at her hungrily.

Slowly, she moved around and his narrowed eyes widened. A ribboned drawstring in the camisole was pulled tight under the bodice, creating the fashionable empire line, pushing her breasts up so they overflowed out of the lace top, the pink of her areolas visible, her nipples only half covered. The lace was so fine, they could be seen right through it anyway.

She watched and smiled to herself as he shifted on the bed and ran his hand over the front of his tight, tailored pantaloons, his eyes still glued to her. Slowly, she ran her hands over her body again, pushing up her breasts and caressing herself, writhing slightly and swivelling her hips suggestively. More long-ago lessons from her unconventional and sometimes outrageous aunt. Another woman who could also never be described as ordinary.

She licked her lips slowly, biting and nibbling them as she continued to caress herself until she heard the soft moan emanate from the man watching her intently. She smiled wickedly and turned her back on him again, slowly sauntering from the bedroom, turning at the door to whisper, "If you want me, you'll have to come and get me," then walked through to her sitting room to pour herself another glass of champagne which she tossed back in one gulp, breathing deeply. She was mid-way into refilling her glass when he came up behind her and pulled her into his arms ruthlessly. He kissed her hungrily, devouring her, his hands cupping her bottom and holding her tight against the hardness in his pantaloons.

When he raised his head to draw breath, she smirked up at him, "Not so silly now, hmmm?"

"Oh, I don't know," he grinned lecherously, "that's not much good to keep you warm under your thin dress in this cold weather. Silliest damn underclothes I've ever seen, hardly worth putting on and I..." he paused, doing a double take as he looked at her decolletage. "Jesus, Sooty, have you rouged your breasts?" He almost gaped in astonishment.

Bella smirked up at him again and pulled away to carry on refilling her glass. "Oh, you noticed," she said airily. "The assistant in the shop suggested it might...er...enhance the presentation of the outfit." She grinned saucily as she turned back to face him, sipping her drink. "I think her normal clientele weren't exactly ladies Grandmama would care to meet...and she assumed I was starting to travel down that path myself. Very high class, of course!"

"You Witch. That's disgraceful behaviour for a young, respectable married matron, a Duchess, no less. Your grandmother would be more than shocked," he tutted as he eyed her breasts appreciatively.

"Well, between you and Auntie, you're obviously doing your best to turn me into a disgraceful Duchess, so what do you expect? Do you think I'll start a new trend at Almack's?" she asked innocently.

"You're not going out anywhere wearing that, My Girl, rouge or no rouge. I wouldn't be able to think straight all evening."

"I know," she laughed salaciously, "that's exactly why I bought it, and a lot of other things like it. You're going to have a lot of distracted evenings on your return, Your Grace."

"Heaven help me," he sighed and went to pour himself another drink.

"Don't you think YOU'RE rather overdressed now?" Bella looked at him from under her lashes, over the top of her glass.

"Extremely. If you ask me nicely, I might take my waistcoat off, and if you ask very nicely, I might even take my shirt off. Now why don't you take your excuse for a chemise and your champagne, go back to bed and I'll see what I can do…"

Chapter Twenty-Three

Bella sauntered back into the bedroom. Nicky picked up one of the packages he'd brought with him and followed her.

She was lolling on the bed when she eyed the parcel suspiciously. "Have you been shopping?"

"I had to knock up a couple of shop owners to open for me, I was so early running about my errands. Didn't I tell you I'd had a busy morning while you were snoring away?"

"I don't snore; so, what did you buy?" she asked curiously. "Anything for me?" she laughed in expectation.

"This is all especially for you," he announced as he upended the parcel and a pile of multicoloured lengths of wide ribbon fell on the bed.

He picked up a red one and sauntered over to the side of the bed, pulled her champagne glass out of her now nerveless fingers and put it down on the nightstand before lifting her wrist.

Bella stared up at him and he looked back down at her enigmatically. "You're not going t...?"

"Oh, I most definitely am," he interrupted, "didn't I promise I would?"

He could feel the tension in her stiff arm and paused momentarily as he wrapped the length round her wrist. "If you really, really don't want me to do this, just say and I won't," he said seriously. "I'm not here to upset you, Sweetheart, you know that don't you? And you mustn't EVER be afraid to say if you don't like something, or do it because you think I want it but you don't." It was a telling moment as they stared at one another.

Bella looked at him for a long minute, tempted to say no, but knowing deep down she could already feel a knot of sensual excitement inside herself at the erotic promise of what was to come, so, despite her apprehension, she took a deep breath, relaxed and let her arm go limp, opening her clenched fist. Feeling her acquiescence, Nicky bent down to kiss her briefly. "So, *Lionesse*, what's sauce for the gander is now sauce for the goose," and he proceeded to tie her wrists to the bedposts on either side of the headboard.

Nicky sat back and looked at the tethered woman on the bed in front of him in the miniscule scrap of black lace. He was sure deep inside her there was a well of restrained sensuality and passion he wanted to mine and encourage her to release permanently, just for him, as he'd experienced some of it when she was playing at being *La Lionesse*, and his eyes roved up her long, shapely legs to the perfect figure above, the voluptuous breasts oozing out of the low cut, teasing chemise affair. Her long black hair drifted around her shoulders and down her back, her lips were red and swollen from his ruthless kisses and her green eyes were now glittering back at him. She was so beautiful and tempting, he could hardly keep his hands off her. Of all the women who had passed through his life, aristocratic and common, he now wanted her like no other, with a deep ache that he knew he'd carry with him all the time he was away, in fact forever, he didn't doubt. That he lusted after her obsessively, as well as loving her deeply, was such a new experience for him, he could hardly cope with the maelstrom of feelings and emotions coursing through him. He mentally shook himself and returned to the task in hand, allowing himself the pleasure of letting his hands slowly crawl and caress up her restless legs to the tops of her thighs and the enticing, damp warmth they found there. His fingers delved and teased...she was already aroused and wet; he smiled at her knowingly.

Bella writhed under him, pulling on the ribbons that held her wrists tight. "What are you going to do now?" she asked softly, green eyes staring into his golden ones.

Nicky took a deep breath and sat back again "Hmmm, I might take my waistcoat off?" he suggested.

"And then?"

"Patience is a virtue, *Lionesse*, we have all day," he winked at her.

He gazed at her as he slowly rose from the bed and tugged at his cravat. Then, just as he had the very first evening he'd turned up at *Le Lion d'Or*, he stripped himself of his waistcoat, cravat and shirt. Slowly and seductively, he peeled them off and caressed his body and across the front of his fitted pantaloons; as before, Bella was riveted, despite herself. His tan had mostly gone, so had a lot of the superficial scars from his ordeal in the cellar in Nice, but many others were still visible and would never fade, just like the big one below his ribs, his memento of Madrid, also the one she'd seen when he'd first appeared at *Le Lion d'Or*. Nonetheless, his torso was still firm and tautly muscled, his biceps big and strong, his chest and abdomen rippled with shaped muscles, testament to the exercise he'd disappeared off to do on most days. Bella knew he fenced with her uncle or one or two of her uncle's old friends, at Captain Carnie's very discreet establishment. She presumed that like his peers, other Corinthians, he boxed and wrestled and indulged in other physical activity at his club or elsewhere. It was a body to tempt most women to drool over and she was no more immune than any.

She grinned at him slowly as he paused and stood in front of her. Almost as tall as her Uncle Francis but not quite, Nicky was still over six foot of incredibly handsome manliness, arms crossed, leaning against the bed post nonchalantly. "You know," Bella said reflectively, "if you sang as you did that, you'd probably bring the entire female population of London to a standstill. You're completely outrageous. You'd probably make some Ladies faint with lust," she giggled.

"I thought you'd appreciate it. You did the last time."

"How do you know that?" she enquired archly. "You couldn't see my face."

"I watched your reaction. I didn't need to see your face, your body told me."

"Is that so? But you're still half dressed, you've even got your boots on. I got a much better show before," she complained.

"Unlike you, I'm in no hurry, *Chérie*." He sat down next to her and kissed her, slowly and thoroughly, his hands now caressing her provocatively rouged breasts, teasing the nipples until she sighed and shifted restlessly, pulling on the ribbons. "Devilish inconvenient not being able to move, isn't it?" he commented conversationally. "You can't stop me touching you wherever I want, but of course if you want me to touch you somewhere particular, you're going to have to ask."

"On no, Nicky," she gasped softly.

"Oh yes, you will; I promise, by the time I've finished with you," he replied and leaned over to kiss her again. His lips roved over her face and then moved down to wander around her neck. "My turn," he whispered, then sucked and bit until a large bruise flowered, ignoring her gasped protests.

"You Moron," she raged. "How can I go out to Almack's, or any social events, with that mark on my neck?"

He ignored her ire. "That's your problem for when I'm gone. Perhaps you could start a new fashion in woolly scarves or wear a fichu differently. Anyway, I've had enough of them from you."

"But you're a man, you wear a high starched collar and cravat," she ranted. "Ooooh, what have you done to me?" She tugged on the ribbons yet again.

"Tsk, tsk, temper, temper! I was having so much fun..." He returned to kissing her neck then moved back to her lips, pacifying her ire with a deeply carnal kiss that left her panting. He moved lower, down her neck again until he reached the juncture with her shoulder where he nibbled and bit, sending frissons down her spine before moving lower, down her chest to her breasts. He laved and sucked her nipples, sending spasms down to her belly as his hands moved lower. Bella started to wriggle and moan under his ministrations as heat and more spasms roiled through her. He kissed her until she was mindless, his tormenting fingers teasing and caressing, never quite giving her the pleasure she sought.

Her eyes glittered up at him. "Please..."

"Please what, *Chérie*?" he crooned.

"You know," sighed Bella, "you know what I want."

"No, I don't. Tell me..." his soft deep voice crawled over her. "You weren't so bothered about asking me last night and you're not some reserved, conservative or naive young matron like a lot of your ilk, you know what we're doing here. This is real life, this is nothing to do with procreation or fulfilling one's marital duties; this is pure lust and erotic sex, or however you want to describe it. The greatest free entertainment and enjoyment since the dawn of time and what really goes on in the wider world out there for those who wish to indulge mutually, explore and enjoy its many and varied forms; so, *Lionesse* tell me..."

"I was...last night was...the thought of you going away, it was all too much." Bella couldn't get her words out straight. She took a deep breath. "I want you, Nicky, all of you. I want you to make love to me; properly...you know what I mean..." she finally burst out.

"Ah," he leaned down to kiss her. "Do you now." The knowing, caressing hands returned to tease her further. He kissed her yet again, long and passionately until she was begging him to touch her intimately, almost incoherent with need.

"So, *Lionesse*, I've found you again at last, so now you're getting your payback. But this is just the start." He slowly rose from the bed and sauntered out, back into the sitting room, leaving her panting and wanting behind him, determined to let her crave and wind herself up so she'd be hot and ready for what came next.

Nicky drew in a deep breath as he left her, controlling the raging lust that thrummed through him. He poured himself another glass of champagne and wandered over to the window, contemplating what he was doing. She was so like her mother if she but knew it, full of unrestrained passion when she let go. He remembered his step-mother, Carlotta, dancing round their sitting room while he'd learned to play the guitar, lost in the feisty sensuousness of her flamenco dancing, tossing her head and twirling around, clapping her hands and flashing her eyes enticingly at her husband and his mind roved back to a conversation he'd had with his step-father.

In a late night, drunken reminiscence just before Nicky had first gone to War, Edouard de Mornay had opened up and talked to him about Carlotta, the love of his life. How passionate, wild and uninhibited she'd been, how his scars and disability had meant nothing to her, she'd loved and encouraged him to love her, be himself, let go and indulge himself and pleasure her however he wanted, right from the very first night he'd met her, to forget the women who'd cringed away from him. So, he'd taken her at her word and their life had been a relationship most men only dreamed about. Nicky had remembered seeing them kiss passionately, often, then disappear up to their bedroom. As a curious young boy on the cusp of adolescence and curious about the facts of life, he'd crept out of bed sometimes and stood outside their bedroom door at night, listening to the soft moans and cries of pleasure that had emanated out, wondering what they'd been doing, but the house had been filled with love and laugher and his step-mother had loved and cossetted him too; always laughingly encouraging him to be 'nice and charming to the ladies and please them at all times', ruffling his hair as she'd smirked at her little golden cherub, telling him he would be a heartbreaker one day and that, if he was a real man, if he gave pleasure and love generously or selflessly, the more pleasure it would give him; he'd never forgotten that. And now she'd grown up, Bella had turned into her mother in so many ways as well as resembling her with her long black hair and creamy skin. She no doubt had her father's intelligence, but she had her mother's capacity for love, and her innate passion, and Nicky wanted it all for himself. Unrestrained, uninhibited and sometimes wild, as her mother had obviously been.

Nicholas, however, although he hadn't inherited his father's vain and selfish indifference, or his ego, and had grown up in the midst of a loving and caring family which coloured and directed his view of life and general behaviour to others, had inherited his father's pride and determination, indoctrinated into him from when he'd started to toddle. He'd also inherited his leonine good looks, roving eye and lust for women and, as he'd grown up, he'd indulged his appetites to the full, amusingly encouraged by his adopted uncle, the Duke of Firle, the erstwhile Shadow. That man had seen so much of himself in the young boy he'd helped to rescue. But although Nicky was like his father in some ways, unlike him, this Duke of Valenciennes had fallen in love and had found a woman who not only stood up to him she matched his passionate and carnal appetite when he let it loose, tempering any inclination to let his title and heritage get the better of him or continue his womanising now he had a wife with whom he could love and indulge himself.

Having poured himself another glass of champagne and fed up with watching the rain outside, Nicky tossed it down before rummaging amongst the parcels and returning back to the bedroom.

Bella knew what he was going to do as soon as she saw what he had in his hand. "Well, what did you expect?" his lips curled wickedly at her doubtful expression. "I promised, remember?" As he leaned down, holding the long length of thick black silk ready to tie round her eyes, he asked, "Any last requests from the condemned woman?"

Bella looked up at him, suddenly serious. "Don't go away," she pleaded passionately. "I beg you, explain to Wellington, or tell him you're ill, anything; surely you've done enough for them?"

He shook his head. "I can't do that, Sweetheart. Whatever else I may be, I'm a man of honour and gave my word. I'm a Gentleman as well as a Duke, not a ne'er-do-well without principles, aristocrat or vagrant. 'An honest man's word is as good as his bond', as that old proverb says. Therefore, much as I regret it now, I am committed," he said quietly, smiling sadly at her. "But I don't want to talk about that now, not here, so, anything else?" the sad smile changed to a lecherous grin. Bella ignored the grin and responded seriously, trying once more. "I know you've given your word to Wellington, but you have to promise me, you won't go after Bernheim. I don't care what he's done to us, we survived, so leave him be. Let him be Ashcroft's problem now for someone else to manage. The man is evil, keep away from him, please, please, My Love; he's not worth risking your life for again, I couldn't bear it."

Her worried concern touched Nicky deeply but his answer was evasive. "I know, but you've got to stop thinking about him, or worrying about me. I swear I'm going to put that man, Ashcroft, Wellington, the whole damn lot of them, out of your mind," and Nicky wound the long length of material round and round her eyes, tying it tightly, just as she'd done to him.

As *Lionesse*, she'd simply been fearful of him getting any clue to who she really was, but being blindfolded was completely disorienting, she'd never realised, unnerving too, as Bella listened to his soft voice. "Today is about sex, in all its varied and erotic forms, about passion and love...and what I make you feel and what we'll share between us. That's what I want you to think about to the exclusion of EVERYTHING ELSE. You can't see anything now, can you? Absolutely nothing except the dark," he whispered knowingly. "No light, no time, no place, so just let yourself FEEL, your other senses will be enhanced. This isn't like a parlour game, this is a whole other game, erotic and sensual," he whispered seductively. "Feel how your senses respond, just give in to them and forget the whole bloody rest of everyone else except ME." Nicky paused then kissed her tantalisingly briefly. "I will be the centre of your universe, the source of your torment and pleasure. You didn't really understand what you did to me before, last night neither. In your innocence, you thought you were simply stopping me from recognising you, but now experience and learn and enjoy what the game really is about, *Lionesse*, and you'll understand what it can do to you."

Bella shivered slightly at the unintended consequences of what she'd done and the erotic promise he'd described, but was silent for a while, thinking over his words about the other people who currently had such an impact on their lives, especially Nicky's; but she wasn't going to spoil their last day subsumed in worry and regrets. So finally, her lips curled upwards and she joked, "Nicky?" she whispered, "I'm hungry."

He burst out laughing. "You Baggage! What for? Me, or the breakfast you didn't have?"

Her smile broadened wickedly. "What do you think?"

"I think, you think and talk far too much; now then, *Lionesse*, where was I...?"

Finally, after what seemed to Bella like hours of unbearable, sensuous teasing and torment, Nicky rolled over on top of her. "Oh yes, yes, please, Nicky, please, no more teasing," she sobbed, her body twisting and turning to encourage him closer, her wrists pulling uselessly on the knotted ribbons.

"Yes, I want you, I can hardly bear it, but it's time for something else before I give you what you want..." Nicky took a deep breath as he prepared to lay the first of Bella's demons. As she squirmed restlessly he reached over and released her wrists, moving quickly to toss her onto her stomach and hold her there while he bound them behind her.

Bella immediately stiffened like a board as she felt his hands move knowingly over her bottom, holding her breath for a repeat of the pain and horror of what Bernheim had done to her. But Nicky was a vastly experienced man and knew what he was doing. There was no way he was going to hurt her and he simply wanted to unpick the harm Bernheim had wrought. He bent down and whispered in her ear, "Relax, *Chérie*, this is ME, I'm not going to hurt you, I love you far too much," as he kissed down her back. "I just want to pleasure you beyond anything you've ever known; open your mind, just relax and this WILL be pleasure...your climax will come, with an added sparkle on the top...and I can't wait to hear you shriek in complete ecstasy..."

He was as good as his word and afterwards, Nicky lay, cradling Bella in his arms. "Are you all right, *Chérie*?" he finally whispered, her screams of frenzied rapture having almost deafened him, making him grin with relief.

"I...I...I had no idea," she whispered, still feeling stunned and bemused. "But why didn't you do what he did? Bernheim. Why did it feel different?" she finally whispered.

"Because I'm not an animal, *Chérie*," Nicky said softly. "I just wanted you to have a taste of the different sort of feeling, a different type of immense excitement it can bring, especially if it's done gently, carefully, with someone you love and trust," and with that, he kissed her again and put a tick next to the list in his head, ready to move on to the next item.

Chapter Twenty-Four

T hey adjourned back to the sitting room to picnic from the hamper of delicacies Nicky had brought with him and to drink Champagne, the frisson of awareness and connection now pulsing between them as if it was alive.

"It's been a long time since I was here," said Nicky reflectively, sipping his Champagne. "I remember EVERYTHING," he looked knowingly at her, "as if it was yesterday." He shook his head, "And you say I own all this? You're such a Witch. Mind you," he waggled his glass at her, "I just knew you were up to something when I was home before I went back to Spain and that Bernheim business with the gold, but however did you conceive the idea and get it all off the ground? There's a sizeable investment here, especially as you have two clubs, not just one," he laughed. "Trust you never to do anything by halves! You're such a baby to run a business, let alone a gaming business – and you, a Lady of the Ton as well, running a commercial enterprise. Disgraceful!"

"I am not a baby!" she squawked then smirked, "Babies don't do what we've just done." Bella sat back and explained how she'd come up with the idea and approached her uncle for a loan. Nicky was enormously amused when he heard how Francis had been involved. "Trust him to have his finger in another profitable pie; from smuggling to gambling now. Whatever next?"

"Oh, he's got nothing to do with this, he never did have, apart from lending me the money to buy the leases and get it off the ground. He wouldn't let me pawn Mama's rubies or offer them as collateral against a loan." Nicky's eyebrows raised both in horror and love at the thought of her risking something so sentimentally precious for his benefit. "Anyway, I paid off all his loan ages ago, at the end of six months if you must know." She smiled in cat-like satisfaction at him. "Uncle Francis was very impressed. This is a VERY profitable business and it's all yours, not that you need it now," she grinned.

"Well, I certainly don't want it, haven't I got enough bloody paperwork? So you can have it all back again to play with, just as long as I'm the only customer you entertain up here in your lair, *Lionesse.*"

"Is that so?" she bantered, "Says who?"

"Says your husband, your Lion. The King of my little pride," he smiled a wide, sexy smile and crooked a finger at her. "Now come here, I haven't nearly finished with you yet, *Lionesse.*" Bella didn't move, just poked her tongue out at him saucily as she'd done as a child when he'd tried to boss her about, so he leaned over. "Rawrrrrrrr," he said softly, "do as you're told, Baggage, or I will truss you up again and repeat the exercise." Watching her appalled face in amusement he said airily, "I might just do that again anyway, seeing as how you seemed to like it so much. I wonder how much more you could take next time around?"

Bella shivered at the tingle that ran down her spine at his words and rose up slowly to sit on his lap. She put her arms round his neck and looked into his golden eyes, suddenly hungry for him again. "You are completely wicked," she muttered. "Whatever are you up to now? You've got that funny look on your face, I know it so well. But I really don't think I could deal with another morning like I've just had." She laughed as she kissed him teasingly on the mouth, "I'm not sure I'll ever recover from that."

"Oh, I don't know," Nicky crooned over her, his fingers playing with the lace around her breasts, "some people say the more you have, the more you want," and his sensual laugh sent more shivers down Bella's spine.

"That's shocking," gasped Bella. "You're shocking to suggest such a thing."

"Not at all, *Chérie*, it's a fact of life, although women are able to climax far more frequently than men. That's down to anatomy and how we're made, but there's an art to fornicating and some men can harden and climax without losing themselves, just like some women can have multiple climaxes and some are done for after just one or two...but I won't go into all that now. What I will say is that there's a deep well of sensuality and passion inside of you, now you're learning to let go, so appreciate and enjoy it. It must be your fiery Spanish blood," he mused. "Your Mama was full of it, you could see it when she danced and in her eyes and your Papa loved her for it. Even Francis wasn't immune." He sighed at long ago memories, "Apart from Cat, who Francis is completely besotted with as we all know, *Madre* could also wind him round her little finger when she needed to." He bent to kiss Bella hungrily, "Just like you now have me in your coils, but remember," he raised a hand in the air in a claw-like gesture, waggling his fingers and then drawing his nails across her bare thigh, "when you capture a Lion, you have to be prepared to face the consequences." His eyes glittered as he laughed at Bella's comically apprehensive expression. He kissed her again passionately, his hands now caressing her breasts and roving down her body to worm under the bottom edge of the black lace. As Bella started to squirm in his lap, he suddenly pushed her off and rose. "Come along, *Lionesse*," he announced with a wink, "we're going downstairs." Taking her hand, he led her out of the room, ready to tackle the next item on his list.

They made their way down the stairs, the club rooms eerily silent without customers or staff. The house of *Le Lion d'Or* was deceptive – it looked innocuous and inconspicuous from the front, but once inside, the many rooms were tastefully decorated and spacious and the building extended quite a way back. There were several gaming rooms, a large dining room, an entertainment room, a quiet sitting room, a bar and drinking room, cloakroom and retiring rooms, other offices, kitchens and staff rooms; everything to keep the many guests and gamblers occupied, amused and happy and the staff efficient. The drapes and blinds were drawn in most areas and the rooms were dim and shadowy. Nicky made love to her in a variety of them – it was a surreal afternoon. He was determined to drive out Bella's nightmares of what Bernheim had done to her and replace them with their own light-hearted and erotic memories. They made love on dining tables, gaming tables, armchairs and dining chairs, on rugs and carpets and even on the stairs.

Bella was initially scandalised, embarrassed and inhibited at some of the positions she found herself in. By the end of the afternoon, in the loving hands of Nicky's humorous and playful tuition she was over-whelmed, laughing uncontrollably at some of what they got up to, uninhibited and completely exhausted. Nicky finally pulled her into the main gaming salon and over to a corner table. He scooped her into his arms and laid her down on the soft green baize top. As an idle hand played down her sprawled, limp body, he smiled down at her. "Do you know where this is?" he asked, a thoughtful expression on his face.

"Of course, it's the Main Salon?" Bella responded, puzzled at the obvious question.

"Oh, no, *Chérie*," he smiled. "This is the very table I was sitting at when *La Lionesse* first came and introduced herself to me."

Bella propped herself up on an elbow and looked around. "So it is," her lips curled in a seductive smile. "You remember then?"

"As if I could ever forget," he grinned. "I was strangely drawn to you from the moment you sat down. That was quite some night, You Wicked Baggage."

"It certainly was," she whispered. "I was overwhelmed. I had no idea making love with you was going to be such a..." she hesitated, smirking, "a pleasant experience."

"Just pleasant, *Chérie*? You unman me." His curling smile teased, "I seem to remember you were somewhat overcome with it all the first time." His eyes momentarily lost focus as his memory took him back to her bedroom upstairs the first night he had gone there and made love to her. "Of course it all makes sense now."

"I appear still to be somewhat overcome by what I'm experiencing at your hands today," she shook her head in bemused wonder. "Is there no end to all this?" she waved her hand in the air. "You're turning me into a... a... er... wanton; a terrible trollop," the waving hand turned into a finger that dug him accusingly in the abdomen.

Nicky burst out laughing. "Arabella de Bresancourt, you're my precious, personal, wanton trollop now, and if I didn't think you were enjoying it, I would never have shown you or done half the things we did today. You did enjoy them, didn't you?" his knowing look was comic, "and don't you dare blush at me now after all that."

Bella felt the heat rise up her face and watched as Nicky threw his head back and guffawed at her. "Oh *Chérie*, you are just wonderful," he chuckled before adding, "and it's only late afternoon. We have the rest of the evening and all night...and believe me, there's so much more. Loving and playing games have such endless possibilities," he teased as her blush deepened.

"You're a truly shocking rake," she said, laughingly scandalised. "But you're MY shocking rake," another dig in his chest as her face momentarily went serious, "and I love you, so you just remember that when you're away and resist the lures of all those women I know will chase after you. I just presume you won't be chasing after THEM." She gave him a very meaningful look. "Because I'll chase after you and hunt you down and you know what a good shot I am, never mind Boney and his army."

Nicky's face also went serious. "The same applies to you, *Chérie*." His golden eyes looked deep into her green ones as his deep velvet voice spoke softly. "I WILL come back to you and Terrie, you're everything to me and more – and you're MINE. I have to trust you won't share what we have with anyone else, no matter how long I'm away. It works both ways, Bella."

The long silent look they exchanged spoke volumes. Their history and current situation miles apart from that of most couples. Slowly, Nicky bent over the table and kissed her. It was a kiss of promise, of love and commitment, a vow to come home safely back to her if the fates allowed.

The kiss deepened and without taking his eyes off her, soundlessly he rose onto the table and lay down across her. He took her suddenly, on the table, with a fervour and passion that was somehow different to what had gone before, Bella could sense it. The charm and humour of the afternoon's loving and frolicking was temporarily gone. In its place was a strong emotion that reached out to the very depths of her soul, a wordless expression of his love and need of her. Her hands grasped tightly in each of his, each time he drove deeply into her he paused to look down into her eyes, his golden ones glowing with love and a passionate, overwhelming desire that made them glitter. The green baize of the card table was soft under her back as they climaxed together in an emotional conflagration of love, passion and commitment that moved Bella to tears.

"Oh Nicky," she whispered, moved almost beyond words. "I love you, Nicky, I always have. There'll never be anyone else." Two tears ran down her cheeks, "That was..." she stuttered, "that was... what was that?"

He looked at her. "Special," he whispered, as moved by what they'd just shared as she'd been. "Like you and me." He was still grasping her hands and he gripped them tightly again. "I love you, Bella. You're silly Sooty and luscious *Lionesse*, everything mixed up in my Duchess. I'm damned if I'm going to lose you now," he stared down at her, eyes glimmering in the dimness of the room. There was momentary silence between them before he continued. "I said last night, we've had a strange relationship. Childhood friends, siblings but not siblings, a wedding that was hurried and secret, then I went away...and you," he paused, seeking the words, "grew up," his fingers left one of her hands and roved down the side of her face, "Then I came back and was so confused. I didn't know you, you weren't the little girl in pigtails who'd followed me constantly, so I avoided you, or tried to, then you seduced me that night." He bent and kissed her lightly, "Then you were *Lionesse*, so tempting, so alluring, then Sooty, chasing after me like a ten-year-old, except you weren't ten and look what you went through, for me." He shook his head, "It's all been so surreal. Here we are now and you're my wife but you run gaming houses...and I...I'm a..."

"Spy?" Bella whispered softly, but he shook his head.

"No, *Chérie*, I'm not a spy, just one of Ashcroft's agents. There is a difference."

"Is there? I'm not sure. You do whatever it takes don't you?"

Their eyes met, understanding humming between them as he nodded. "Yes, but you understand now, it means nothing to me, it's only you."

"Yes," she whispered. "I don't like it, but I do understand now," she said quietly. "Which reminds me," an amused and curious smile on her lips, changing the subject away from the emotional and traumatic morass that loomed and not wanting to dwell there, "where did all that singing come from?"

He grinned at her. "Aha! Madam Know-it-all, you thought you knew everything about me, didn't you? I sang in the choir at Eton and it sort of went from there."

"You did NOT learn to sing like that at Eton and you most certainly were NOT a scrubbed, cherubic choirboy," she pronounced, struggling to raise herself on an elbow. "Absolutely not. You certainly did NOT learn to play a Spanish guitar like that at Eton either!"

"I did actually. I'll have you know I had my moments being scrubbed, if not cherubic," he grinned. "Perhaps I didn't learn all of it there, or the guitar, but remember, I went to Italy and everyone sings there, well they seemed to and well, oh I don't know, it just went from there. So, you see, I have all these hidden talents," he grinned. "You're only just beginning to discover them," his smile was lascivious.

"Never mind your hidden talents, my bottom is aching. Do you know how heavy you are, You Oaf?" She laughed at him as she pushed at his chest playfully, "You're not the scrawny wretch I grew up with anymore."

"Oho, are we complaining again? Well you shouldn't be such a tempting morsel should you?" he chuckled as he pulled himself off her and then off the table. Before she knew it, he'd scooped her up in his arms and strode from the room. "I think it's about time we retreated back upstairs, it wouldn't do for any nosy, confused gamblers to see us cavorting around naked in the gaming rooms," he chuckled.

"I'm not naked," Bella remonstrated.

Nicky looked down at the dishevelled, virtually naked woman in his arms, her lips reddened and swollen from being kissed endlessly, her eyes with that just pleasured look in them, her creamy breasts teeming over the top of the bit of black lace froth that was still miraculously hanging on the top half of her torso by one bedraggled ribbon. "No, of course you're not, you look almost ready for a polite evening at Almack's," he commented conversationally as he climbed the stairs.

"What are we going to do now?" she asked as he strolled back into her apartment and plopped her down in a chair in front of the now dwindling fire. He bent to put more coals on it and lifted his head. "You've worn me out, You Wanton," he sighed. "I need a rest," he smirked, "well just a small one. How about we play cards? Or do you want to sleep a while?"

Bella was exhausted but didn't want to waste her last night with him asleep. "Cards?" she laughed. "YOU want to play cards, with ME?"

"Oh, you never know, my luck or my prowess at cards might have changed," he grinned. "Why? What else are we to do? Are you hungry? Or mayhap you have another interesting outfit to change into to tempt me with?" his smile was lecherous.

Bella shook her head, getting up to retrieve a pack of cards from a nearby cabinet. She strolled over to the table and the remains of their picnic and nibbled on a piece of cheese. "I'm not particularly hungry, at the moment," her sly smile at him was equally lecherous, "and I might change later, if you ask me nicely. I am rather overdressed after all." She adjusted the bit of black lace, trying but giving up covering her breasts, watching him watching her as she lightly caressed herself teasingly, "and who knows, I might have something else to wear that may...er...catch your interest?" She was now in full *Lionesse* mode again and wondered how she'd changed into this wanton, demanding woman in the space of a day. She wandered around to pour another drink for herself, then sat down at the small card table in front of the fire and started to unwrap a pack, riffling through the cards.

Nicky sauntered back through from her closet and bedroom. He'd washed and droplets of water still clung to his chest and there was a towel wrapped around his waist. "So, Your Grace, you want to play cards do you? And what are we going to play for? Guineas? Or something more interesting? I seem to remember saying, a long time ago, that money was sooo boring…"

Nicky wandered over to her desk and found a sheet of paper and a quill and some ink. He brought them over to the table and tore the paper in half. "Write down a forfeit you want from me on there and I'll do the same for you," he grinned. "We'll play for that. Whoever loses must pay their forfeit."

Bella looked at him with a raised eyebrow and then pulled her piece of paper towards her and hurriedly scribbled down a few words before folding the paper over. He looked at her and grinned to himself before writing something very brief on his. "What are you smiling at?" Bella asked curiously.

"Aha, my secret. I'll tell you afterwards," he sighed and smiled humorously. The two folded pieces of paper sat in the middle of the table under a small paperweight and Bella dealt the cards.

They played for a while and Nicky got up, helped himself to another drink, lit a cheroot and sat back in his chair, smoking nonchalantly. He started to win and Bella couldn't make it out. He was either truly getting absurdly lucky or his card-playing capability had reached new levels of excellence. She got up and lit one of her own long, thin cheroots and sat down with another glass of Champagne, looking indolent but actually watching him intently. He continued to win until Bella finally twigged. He was cheating. She continued to watch and the penny dropped. She knew exactly what he was doing as that young scoundrel, Jack, had taught her the self-same tricks over some bored afternoons and evenings in Paris and on the long coach journey to Nice.

Slowly but surely, she started to win again and smiled to herself at Nicky's slightly perplexed expression as she did so. She caught him watching her but kept her face impassive. Finally, he threw his cards on the table in frustration as she won their last round. "You cheated!" he expostulated. "You can't do that, you own gaming houses. You'll be ostracised, ruined, if your clientele found out."

Bella shouted with laughter. "Me? I cheated?" she cackled. "You can talk, You Knave! So what, pray, were YOU doing?"

Nicky realised he'd been had and sighed. "There's no beating you is there," but then he grinned slyly. "What's it worth to keep my mouth shut and not tell anyone?"

Bella laughed even more. "I never need to cheat, as well you know, especially when I play you. I was taught by the same source as you," she tutted. "That jackanapes, I'll box his ears for teaching you," she shook her head as she laughed and sat back quaffing her Champagne. "I warned him NEVER, EVER, to cheat when he plays now, even at school, or he'll get a reputation and be ostracised by Society before he knows it. I only asked him to teach me how to do it so I could recognise anyone here who tried the same tricks; but I still won, I BEAT you despite your best cheating efforts." She grinned at Nicky's chagrined expression and reached forward to hand him his forfeit.

He put his hand over hers. "Can't we call it quits?" he smiled his curling, appealing smile at her, knowing without looking what she'd written on her piece of paper. He'd had a bet with himself and was absolutely sure he'd win that gamble, at least, he'd stake his life on it. He groaned to himself at what was to come.

Bella's lips curled humorously. "Absolutely not," she said forcefully. "And don't look at me like that, I'm completely immune." She pointed a finger at him, "When did he teach you? You're very good, though it pains me to admit it," she asked curiously.

Nicky sighed again and laughed. "While you were injured and unconscious in Nice, Jack thought it would take my mind off worrying about you. We didn't dare go out in case we were seen, not that I wanted to show my poor battered face anywhere; I nearly had a fit when I first looked into a mirror to shave." His face went serious for a brief moment before his smile returned, "Also on the voyage home, over some drinks one rather long night." He didn't go into all the details of his and Jack's discussion. "Then out of curiosity, I practised on the family over the Christmas holidays. No one's noticed except you. My dear Papa simply told me my card-playing skills had improved immeasurably," he chuckled at the memory of his step-father's confusion at being beaten occasionally – he'd been very careful not to win every round with him so as not to arouse suspicion.

"That's shocking!" Bella remonstrated, "Cheating your own family. You definitely deserve to pay your forfeit now," she giggled and went to pick up the other folded scrap to see what Nicky had scribbled. "Oh no you don't," he snatched it back from her. "I'll tell you what, I'll submit to you, provided you pay your forfeit too. After all, you cheated as well," he grinned.

"That's not fair," Bella laughed. "I only did it to stop you winning crookedly."

"But you still cheated," he bantered, "you should be like Caesar's wife, above reproach."

"Caesar's wife?" Bella hooted with mirth. "Since when have you been familiar with Caesar, or anything Latin? You hated Classics at school, I seem to remember. Either Papa or poor Mr Crichton were forever trying to coach you to improve."

"That doesn't mean I didn't pay attention," he smirked. "I'm not a complete moron even though you think me brainless, you AND Ashcroft," he added laughingly, thinking back to his conversation that morning.

"I don't think you're brainless at all," Bella knew he was no such thing when he applied himself, but looked at him and smiled wickedly. "I just happen to think your considerable talents lie in other directions."

Nicky's smile was pure lechery. "Do you now? Well, well, at least they're more useful and pleasurable than declining Latin verbs," and with a laugh he went over to Bella's desk and rummaged in a drawer until he found some sealing wax. He warmed it over a candle and sealed down the folded paper he held in his hand before returning back to the table. "Now then, you can't peek until it's your turn and you WILL have your turn." His eyes gleamed at her in amusement. "If I survive what you have in store for me, of course."

"Why are you looking at me like that? You don't know what I wrote," Bella giggled.

"Oh yes I do. That's why I was smiling before." He smiled at her again, "I bet myself and I'm sure I won."

"How can you possibly know?" she spluttered, confused.

"Because I know YOU," he chuckled. "You're so predictable and anyway, I dare say I would have done the same."

"All right then, tell me what's written on the piece of paper," Bella challenged.

Nicky looked at her and sighed feelingly. "You're going to do to me what I did to you this morning." He shook his head, looking resigned. "Aren't you?"

"How did you know?"

"I just knew," he sighed. "Well? Aren't I right?"

"Of course," she grinned. "Do you mind?" she asked curiously. "I won't if you don't want me to?" she asked, noting his rueful expression. "What you said to me works both ways."

He burst out laughing. "Mind? Of course I bloody mind. I've been there before with you, remember? Only this time I suspect it will be ten times worse and I'm not sure I'll survive the experience. You nearly killed me when you had me in your clutches then and you weren't very experienced. Dear God, what on earth will you do to me now?" He looked comically apprehensive.

"It serves you right for what you put me through this morning," she purred. "As you so succinctly put it, it will give you something to remember when you're off gadding around France at Wellington's behest, chasing Boney's henchmen, or hench-ladies," she waggled a finger at him.

"Hench-ladies?" he was still laughing, "What on earth are they?"

"Mysterious *femmes fatales*, female secret agents and spies, villainesses, you know what I mean," she said pointedly.

"Oh, you mean like you. Ashcroft's latest secret weapon," he chuckled. "I'm completely terrified."

"So you should be." She leaned towards him, "You have no idea what I'm going to do to you," she laughed evilly.

"Oh Lord, I knew it, you really will kill me," he chuckled resignedly and got up to pour himself a large brandy, then sauntered over to the dining table to nibble at some leftover food.

"The condemned man ate his last hearty meal," she quipped, giggling, "and had a large drink."

"The condemned man needs to keep his strength up," he sighed, "and fortify himself against the terrible torture he's about to face. I think I'd better have another brandy," he chuckled.

"No time for that," Bella rose from her chair and pulled the glass from his hand with a salacious smile. "Come along *Monsieur* Secret Agent, it's time you found out what happens to cheats in this particular gaming establishment."

With what sounded like a humorous groan, Nicky followed her into the bedroom.

Chapter Twenty-Five

S he tied his wrists carefully and efficiently to the bedposts, knowing how strong he was and how hard he would pull on the ribbons which ironically, he'd brought to use on her. Then she tied his ankles in the same way. His lips curled in a sensual, amused smile as he watched her, propped up on a mound of pillows against the headboard. "Christ, Sooty, this is only a game y'know. I'm not intending on going anywhere," he joked, surreptitiously tugging hard on the ribbons, realising he was tethered tightly and couldn't move an inch.

Bella smiled down at her captive. "I know you," she poked him lightly on the chest, "I don't trust you an inch, but you're damned right, you're not going anywhere for quite a while," and she bent to kiss him hungrily before wandering back into the sitting room, returning with the thick black silk he'd used on her earlier. He groaned theatrically. "Do you have to?" he asked, knowing full well it was a pointless plea.

"Silly question," she retorted ruthlessly. "Anything else?" she purred. "Last requests and all that?"

He sighed. "Be gentle with me," he pleaded, "have mercy, I've had a hard day." Bella burst out laughing. "I'm only a poor, innocent man, striving to hold his own against a ruthless gambler; besides, you're so cruel, no one else would carry out the death penalty for a little bit of cheating," his amused voice continued to plead.

"I'll have you know this is a very upstanding, respectable establishment and its very upstanding and respectable proprietress won't tolerate any misdemeanours, so your plea is refused," she purred and wound the long silk blindfold tightly around his head several times, ensuring he couldn't see so much as a chink of light before knotting it tightly, just as he'd done to her.

"Oh Christ, Sooty, I can't see anything, do you have to tie it so tight?"

"Good and yes." Now she knew and understood what it was all about she wasn't going to pay any attention to his nonsense. "An upstanding and respectable proprietress can't have it coming off, especially after they've discovered how much prisoners REALLY like it," she whispered seductively in his ear and received a speaking groan in response as he shook his head in denial. She just laughed and ignored him.

"How can you claim to be an upstanding and respectable proprietress?" he jokingly asked. "Not since this morning, given what she's been up to all day, not to mention cheating this afternoon," he tutted. "Shockingly depraved behaviour; it will be punished, she WILL get her just deserts."

"Oh no, she won't, she was led astray by a depraved villain," Bella purred in his ear, "so she's about to get her revenge, in spades. Oh, how appropriate," she giggled at her witticism and she leaned over and started to tickle him.

Nicky's whole body jerked as her ruthless fingers drove him insane. He shrieked in mirth but couldn't escape, merely tightening the knotted ribbons that held him captive. "So, you thought you could cheat me, did you, You Wretch?" she whispered in his ear as he writhed under her tormenting fingers, swearing at her venomously. "Well, this is payback for that. As for the rest," she threatened, "you'll just have to wait and find out what I've got in mind. It's going to be a long night, Your Grace," she laughed.

"Oh noooo, Sooty, please," he begged, laughing in despair. "Not all night, you really will kill me, what by the Heavens are you going to do?"

"That, my captive agent, is for me to know and for you to find out; eventually," she purred over him. "Actually, there is something you can tell me though?" she leaned over and ran a couple of fingers lightly over his lips, letting them tiptoe down his neck and across his chest, tweaking a nipple as they went, making him gasp lightly. "Have YOU ever screamed, or screeched or shrieked really loudly when you climaxed? Really, really shrieked, let go, like you made me do this morning?"

Nicky drew in a sharp breath. "Oh Jesus," he swore. "No, oh no, Sooty, you can't torment me that badly."

"That's not what I asked," she said softly. "Well, Nicky? Have you? In all your rakish, womanising meanderings around London and God knows where else on the Continent, with all the countless ladies, high or low born, you've seduced, fucked and done God knows what else with?"

"Why do you want to know?"

"Humour me. Just a yes or no will do and tell me the truth, for once, not what you think I want to hear, we've gone beyond that now. I don't want to know any details, just one word."

He lay quietly for a moment as Bella waited for his reply. Finally, he spoke. "I've had my moments," he said reflectively, "but no, never like you let go and lost yourself this morning, but then," he paused, "it's different for a man."

"I don't see why," Bella said softly, "but thank you for telling me, all part of my continuing education." She bent down to kiss him again, as her fingers continued their journey downward, pulling off the towel that was still wrapped around his waist and then, avoiding the throbbing hardness that was now exposed, they continued to weave patterns down his legs to his feet.

She stood silently and looked down at him. She had her challenge now and with a thoughtful look at his restless, captive torso, obviously waiting expectantly for her to do something sensual or erotic to him, she walked silently through to her sitting room where she lit one of her cheroots and sat down in front of the fire to think, ignoring with a sad smile the venomous language now emanating out of the bedroom behind her at her absence.

As she sat and contemplated, smoking and sipping from a glass of champagne, she reflected on how inexperienced she really was. She'd read countless books and tawdry leaflets on all matters of love and sex after her torrid week as *La Lionesse*, searching high and low across London in all sorts of disreputable establishments to acquire such salacious reading matter, invariably kept under the counter and unofficial, only to those in the know or willing to pay. She'd been determined to educate herself to hold the attention of the demanding, very experienced, sensual lothario and womaniser that she'd realised Nicky had been and possibly still was. Despite his protestations and promised commitment, she was nobody's fool and didn't believe for a moment that a man like him would go away for months, or a year or more, without finding some woman or women to relieve his physical frustration.

She sighed to herself. She'd also spoken many times to her Aunt Cat on the subject of sex in general and holding the attention of a man like Nicky, as her aunt had managed to do with her Uncle Francis, also a renowned rake and womaniser in his youth – talking seriously and often amid much embarrassed laughter. In Paris, she'd trailed around seedy bookshops and other insalubrious establishments and had discovered all manner of erotic and pornographic literature, pictures, leaflets and pamphlets, even some hand-written instruction sheets for sale at one very strange address she'd been directed to which had made her eyes goggle as she'd read and studied them; she'd decided she didn't want to know any further details about what went on in that little building although she had a good idea. Jack would have been horrified if he'd known what she had been up to that day when she'd merely told him she was going dress shopping! But as with all her reading during her life, her knowledge and awareness of 'fornication matters' had been considerably extended.

Theory was all very well, but putting it all into practice on a real man, an experienced man, was a whole other matter, not least if she could bring herself to do even a quarter of the things she'd read about. Plus there was another problem. Being the man he was, having told her he'd never shrieked, screamed or let go to the extent she had that morning, with all the women he'd bedded, how come none of them had ever managed to do that to him? If they hadn't, how on earth could she? She well knew what a self-possessed and emotionally contained man Nicky was in some ways and breaking through that strong will and hold he had on himself was quite a daunting prospect.

There had to be another way, a key to give him something no other woman before her had done. Something to make him remember her while he was away.

She thought about what he'd done to her that morning, the things he'd talked to her about, how SHE'D felt as he'd tormented her and she pondered on what he'd said to her during the few times they had made love and actually communicated. Then she thought about Nicky, the person. What went on behind those glittering golden eyes and outward show of amusement and charm, his self-possession, the driven, proud character who rarely let anyone in. It was his mind she needed to connect to, she realised, something all the other women no doubt ignored, only seeing the surface man, the consummate charmer with the perfect body and experience, the willingness to please which-ever woman he was with. She sat and smoked another cheroot and then, with a deep breath and a determined expression on her face at what she was going to attempt, she sauntered back into the bedroom.

His mouth was mutinous and he swore venomously at her. "Where the fuck have you been?" Bella smiled. "I'd never have let you tie me up like this if all you were going to do is wander off somewhere. What the Hell are you playing at?" he tugged uselessly on the ribbons and Bella watched his muscles flex and relax as he pulled. It was very entertaining. "Let me go, damn you. I don't want to play your games anymore," he raged.

"Tut tut, aren't we suddenly impatient and grumpy? You'll never get those knots loose, believe me, no matter how much you pull," Bella commented blithely. " I've told you before," she ran her fingers over the muscled arms and chest, "I'm never going to let you go and besides, I was thinking..."

"THINKING?!" he raged. "THINKING! You've got months and months ahead by yourself to bloody think. Why do you need to do it now? Let me loose, You Wretched Woman," as he continued to pull on the ribbons.

"You really don't like being bound do you?" she mused. "You hate being powerless, especially with a woman."

He was beyond angry at her. "Of course I hate it, all of it, not being in control, especially not being able to see," he burst out.

"Reeeally?" she raised her eyebrows. "Why ever didn't you say? Before, you know, when I was *Lionesse*? We don't have to do this now if you didn't want to, I just told you."

"Because you won," he raged bitterly. "You won and I lost and you wanted to do this, didn't you? Besides, it's only fair. I did it to you, though I suspect, unlike me, you really liked it; didn't you?"

It was an amazing answer. She understood part of it, the part where she'd won, the endless amusing competitiveness that had existed between the pair of them since childhood, his innate fairness to pay a debt. But the rest, his perception of what she'd felt that morning, something she herself hadn't come to terms with, was a surprise. Dominance and submission, she'd read about it but never really understood until now. Again, theory and actual experience were two different things. She looked down at him. He was hard and throbbing, obviously supremely aroused despite his words to the contrary. "It doesn't look to me like you're hating it," she whispered, running her fingers down the centre of his chest to his belly where they hovered and stopped, eliciting a tight groan. "I think you're protesting a mite too much, Your Grace, but being such a *macho hombre*," the Spanish was a better description of what she was trying to say, "you'd never admit it." Her index finger poked him in the belly, "The question is, of course," she mused, "what shall I do with you now?"

His replied request was coarsely pornographic and Bella's ears burned, but she knew this was going to be the pathway to the evening ahead so she braced herself. "Well of course I, we, could do that, but I have far more interesting things in mind first."

"You do? My, my, Your Grace, you surprise me." His temper had eased but the sarcastic reply was icy. He'd have given a lot to see the expression on her face at his deliberately obscene request.

"Yes, I do," she said matter-of-factly, "but first, I think I need a bath."

His expression under the blindfold was bewildered. "A bath? How in Hell are you going to have a bath? There are no staff here to heat the water and anyway, that will take hours now. What about me?" his rage began to rise again.

"Ah, now," she leaned down to kiss him tantalisingly, pulling away before it could deepen, "you haven't actually seen my new bathing room here, have you?" she said conversationally. "It's an invention of Papa's, based on the Roman baths system. It's all about gravity and hot water rising. It comes up in pipes from downstairs. I only have to go and build up the range *et voila*! Hot water from a tap. It was an experiment here and I was thinking of installing a system like it in Hertford Street, but the pipes are..."

"I'm not interested in your father's inventions or your bloody plumbing arrangements," he interrupted wrathfully. "We're supposed to be doing something else," he swore again, "but we're obviously not for some bizarre reason in your head, so for God's sake unbind me, I've really had enough now, Bella."

"Ah, but I was just getting down to it, my little game with you," she purred and he momentarily stilled his restless tugging. She noted his wrists were red already and grinned. What an unsympathetic baggage she was turning into, she thought, wondering what they'd be like by the time she'd done with him. He seemed so irrationally angry.

"Now then, while I'm in my bath, Nicholas, I want you to think and imagine," she purred, "what I'm doing to myself in my tub, for I'll be thinking about last night, this morning and what you did to me. Caressing myself in the warm soapy water, playing with the soap..." she prattled on for a few minutes, scandalising herself with a description of her erotic bathing intentions, intently watching him and his body for his reaction and smiling like a cat at the result as he moved restlessly. "Then, when I get out and I come back in here, all fresh, clean and sweet smelling, you'll be here waiting for me: hot, hard, deliciously tethered and hugely, desperately frustrated and beyond grumpy...and all mine to play with," she purred. "But of course, I'll be slightly frustrated too, as whatever I do to myself, it's not the same as when you do it to me, so you'll have to make me climax." She sighed theatrically, "Ahhhh, I'll be sooo hot, wet and moaning, how shall I make you make me do that, hmmmm?" she paused for effect and then whispered the answer to her own question in his ear. "After that, well then, I shall have to start again and I think we'll do," and for the next five minutes she described in minute, completely licentious detail the most depraved, pornographic acts she thought they could carry out on her bed with him tethered. She could hardly believe what she was saying but the effect on Nicky was dramatic. His jaw almost dropped open.

"Oh, Nicky," she breathed as she finished her speech, "do you like the thought of doing that? The image of it, you and me, has made me wet, so wet," she gasped, "I need to feel you inside me but no, I can't let you have that," and as she stood there, examining a catch in one of her fingernails, she panted and theatrically moaned before throwing herself down on the bed beside him, writhing around and sighing while stifling the most enormous urge to giggle. Not for the first time, she decided she'd missed her calling and should be in Drury Lane.

The bound man on the bed next to her stiffened as if shot. "I don't believe you," he whispered, stunned. "I don't know where you got all that from. Christ, some of the best courtesans in London would struggle to do it, including acts I promised we wouldn't do again," he muttered knowingly. "Besides, the woman in bed with me last night couldn't bring herself to say 'sex' before blushing and now, you're suggesting all that?" he actually laughed.

Bella rolled over and lay partly on top of him. "A lot has happened between last night, this morning, this afternoon and this evening," she whispered. "You've changed me now and you know what happened to Pandora when she opened the box. Believe it, Nicky, think about it, all of it, picture it in your mind," she whispered seductively. "I found a lot of interesting pamphlets, flyers and let's call it, reading matter, in some seedy little shops and bars in some of the less salubrious parts of Paris, while I was looking for you. Extremely educational," she whispered, leaning over to bite his nipple, "extraordinarily pornographic and salacious," she crawled over his body and bit the other, making him swear and writhe. "I just need a body to practise on." She wriggled further up his torso and kissed him, hungrily, like a voracious snake, her hands running caressingly all over his body, except where he wanted her to touch him the most.

He suddenly kissed her back and it was different. No consideration now for her innocence, inhibitions or inexperience, this was full of debauched carnality and erotic, depraved promise. Bella's belly spasmed and as she thought about some of the things she'd suggested, she felt herself go hot and wet, just as she'd pretended a few moments before. She knelt up and spread her knees over one of his thighs, rubbing herself sinuously against the muscled hardness. "Can you feel it, Nicky?" she whispered. "How wet I am, how swollen already? Think about it, think about it all. I WILL do it to you. I'm going to make you beg me to touch your delicious body, but I won't. Just like you promised me; you'll plead, curse me, threaten me, but you WILL beg and you'll hate me for making you do that and then," she kissed him again, "when I do touch you, suck you and lick you and everything else, you'll crave your release but I won't give it to you, until like I was, you'll be mindless, lost, desperate...and you WILL scream your heart out and never, ever, forget me. I'm not Sooty. I'm not *Lionesse*. I'm Bella. Your wife and your Duchess."

She rolled away from him, panting and got off the bed. A whispered voice reached her. "I don't believe you. You'll never do it; no one else has, ever."

She turned back and knelt over him. "Oh, yes, I will. I'm as single minded as you when I decide to do something."

"You won't."

"I'll bet you I will." It was a bizarre conversation.

"How much?"

Bella grinned. "Five guineas."

He laughed throatily. "Five guineas? Is that all my 'delicious body' is worth?"

"Why? What do you suggest? It's just a body," she bantered, tickling him playfully, watching, drooling almost, over the play of muscles in his ripped abdomen, well over six feet of every woman's fantasy who had blood in her veins.

"Something you don't necessarily want to give me, ouch," he muttered and squirmed at her tickling.

"Very well, if you win, you can do whatever you like with me for one night. Anything, absolutely anything at all, no matter how strange, or seriously perverted, or painful, obscene or depraved."

"I don't do perverted or depraved and certainly not painful at all," he said softly. "Well maybe a bit perverted and depraved for a laugh, if I've drunk a bit too much and the feeling and pleasure is mutual, like this or a bit worse, but certainly not the other, believe me, whatever you think and we've joked about; pain and serious perversion gives me no pleasure at all." He was very serious. "I'm not Bernheim or his ilk, no matter how much of a rake I was. Do you believe me, Bella?"

She nodded, then realised he couldn't see. "I believe you, but, whatever you like, I'll be your willing slave. And if I win?"

"Yes?"

"When you come back and you WILL come back, you'll give yourself to me again, like this, MY willing captive and slave, no complaints, for another night, because I may want to try something else."

His body shook with laughter. "Oh, Pandora, what a box of tricks I've opened. But you won't win, you know and I'm NOBODY'S captive plaything, not even yours, except for tonight, so make the most of it while you have me."

"Don't be so sure of yourself, You Big Oaf. There's nothing more uncertain than a certainty," and with a quick kiss, she slid off the bed once again. "Now I'm off to sort out my fascinating plumbing and my bath, but you..." her fingers danced down over his body tantalisingly, watching him squirm and jerk, "can simply lie here and contemplate your upcoming torture. Anticipation and expectation is everything..."

"How long are you going to be?" he groaned.

"As long as it takes, but not that long," she laughed. "It'll be worth the wait, I promise. Just remember what I'm going to be doing in my bath," and he listened in frustration as she walked out of the room. He felt her suddenly bending over him as few seconds later, "Oh, I nearly forgot," she whispered. "Think about after my bath, what I'm going to want from you." Her tongue crawled around the shell of his ear and down his neck and he shook his head, trying to escape her tormenting mouth which was sending shivers down his spine. She whispered in French next, "*Soixante-neuf* should be a relatively INNOCUOUS pastime to start with, wouldn't you say?" and then she was gone, leaving him slightly bemused and considerably shaken as his mind conjured up graphic images that left him sweating, hard as a rock, his balls aching in growing frustration.

Chapter Twenty-Six

Nicky couldn't guess how long he'd lain there awaiting her return. She'd obviously moved her little chiming clock from the mantel over the fireplace deliberately. It could have been ten minutes, thirty minutes, even an hour, though to him it felt like ten hours. Endless visions went round and round in his head, driving him mad with lust and frustration and taking his mind off his aching arms and legs. The silly baggage had no idea of how it hurt to be confined so tightly in one position, even on a soft bed – that practical aspect was never covered in whatever salacious literature she'd discovered. Half of him couldn't believe she'd carry out what she'd promised but the other half, who'd grown up with her, suspected she had every intention of doing them.

Bella rarely made idle promises or threats, he knew full well. Visions of her haunting little Parisian bookshops, dirty stalls and vendors in the dangerous back streets and alleys haunted by prostitutes and their potential customers, reading the pornographic flyers or leaflets there made his mind boggle and his body break out in a sweat at the thought of being left hanging endlessly on the precipice of a climax. That was on top of the fact she'd been there in the first place, some of the most dangerous parts of Paris she should never have gone near. He didn't know if Jack had been with her and therefore knew what she was buying; he suspected not which made it all an even bigger nightmare! Impossible woman!

He pulled and pulled at the ribbons, wondering if he was strong enough to shake loose the bedposts but nothing moved; the wretched lengths of satin he'd bought that morning from an innocuous haberdashery store just dug further into his sore wrists. Again and again he cursed for allowing himself to end up in this predicament – it wasn't at all what he'd intended. He'd imagined spending the day frolicking and romping around Bella's private apartment and the gaming house, laughing and playing somewhat lecherous games to dispel her terrible memories and experiences, with just a bit of what he considered relatively harmless perversion. His final little forfeit for her would be the finale, before they eventually caught up on some sleep and returned to reality the following morning when he could spend time with his captivating little daughter.

Nicky had told Bella the absolute truth when he'd said he had never been and would never be anyone's captive plaything. He'd played erotic games like this with various women but they were usually the captive and if he ever did submit, it was only occasionally and a frivolous short game of foreplay, because he didn't trust them enough. It was nothing like what Bella had threatened, though it was only a game to her too, but she seemed to want his ultimate surrender, something he couldn't handle. The only other time he'd ever capitulated was with *Lionesse* and he remembered that night of sensual torment well enough. But now, this was on a different level. He swore to himself he'd never capitulate to her, certainly he'd never beg or plead but as for the rest, he'd never, ever, in his life lost control nor let himself go to that extent, always holding something back and not just during sex.

For a short while Nicky's memory roved back to Rouen and what had happened in the Fortress. It had coloured his personality and his life. He'd never shared the sheer horror of it with anyone, only partially with Jack that one night when they'd been drinking and he'd discovered what the youth had done to keep his little tribe of children fed and a roof over their heads. The lad had voluntarily sold himself and put up with all manner of perversions, but amazingly had come through it relatively unscathed, though who knew what went on in his mind now. Just like his own. That was one of the reasons he had willingly adopted the lad. He empathised and admired him hugely for what he'd gone through, not for himself, but for others and he wanted to be there for him, to care for him if what he'd done came back to haunt him.

As a little, aristocratic, four-year-old boy in pre-Revolution France, a Duke in waiting, tended by nursemaids, Governesses and tutors, Nicholas de Bresancourt had dutifully loved and respected his parents, remote though they were, in total contrast to the loving Granville and de Mornay family he'd subsequently grown up in. How his father could have watched Dupont and his men abuse, rape and beat his mother and then abuse and sodomise him, he now couldn't imagine. The idea of the aristocratic Duke of Valenciennes standing there silently, impassively, watching and refusing to hand over a *sou* of his fortune to save his pregnant wife from being raped and beaten to death and then his four-year-old son experiencing a similar depravity, then even further perversions at the hands of Dupont after his father was taken away, was scorched in his brain forever. The only way he could deal with it all was to close his mind, now as then, even as a small boy, to keep separate from what was done to him and bury it so deep in his subconscious he could forget it all forever. He could remember vividly asking Francis to rescue his father, aristocratic pride and family loyalty having been indoctrinated into him from birth, but it was too late for the icy Duc de Valenciennes, the man who had always instructed his son to rise above and ignore everything and everyone around him, unless it was to his advantage.

So he'd lost people he thought he loved and he'd come to England, putting the horrors of Rouen behind him, always holding back slightly, fearing to love or let himself go in case the recipients of his affection betrayed him, violated him in some way, or were killed too.

The only person who suspected what was going on in his head was the Dowager, but she had never forced him to talk to her about it, merely tried to get him to confront it all in his own way and come to terms with it, not to let it destroy his life. She had been so wise and he missed her dearly. Francis's wife, Cat, had risked her life to save him from Dupont's perversions, but she too had never mentioned that day she'd found him and what she'd seen in Dupont's rooms, deciding it best left forgotten. She never knew the little boy she thought she'd saved had already been defiled terribly. His stepmother had lavished endless love and affection on him and he'd loved her as much as he was able...and then she too had died, desperate to give her husband the son he craved because she loved him so much, despite the doctor's warnings not to get pregnant.

So many people had loved him and he'd lost two of the most precious ones to him...his stepmother and the Dowager. Then there was Bella and Terrie, his daughter. That he loved Bella now was not in doubt and he'd come to terms with that demon in the cellar in Nice. He had now given her all the love and commitment he thought he was capable of. He couldn't imagine allowing anyone to do to his little girl what had been done to him, to simply stand there and watch. He'd give his fortune, indeed his life, if anyone so much as laid a hand on her. He knew Francis Granville was the same, his words to Nicky before he'd gone to Spain about spending his fortune to rescue him if necessary, were no idle promise. Nicky was fully aware the man was not the laconic, amusing, aloof Duke everyone assumed him to be, but a man of deep love and serious commitment to those he held dear. He understood what was important in life and would therefore risk his own life and everything he had to save any one of them, without a thought or regret. His beloved step-father, his Papa, was exactly of the same mind.

So here he was once again, bound and captive in a different way, analysing himself as he had in the cellar in Nice. Wondering why he found it so difficult just to let go and enjoy the silly, erotic bedroom game his wife was playing. He'd helped her to confront her nightmares and in doing so, she'd discovered a deep well of sensual, carnal passion buried within herself that matched his own, so he wondered why he couldn't simply confront his own most recent demons and put the past behind him once and for all? It was so simple; just a game...

Ironically, Bella had inadvertently made him confront other traumas. It had been so simple, finally admitting his love for her and his adoptive family, the previous night when she'd waggled the blindfold at him. He'd been terrified, the memories of the Nice cellar and the dark, the same as in the Rouen Fortress, a torment he'd suffered for months, years. Why he'd not said something to her he had no clue, again unwilling to let go his very deep private self and his fears, his pride – but he'd confronted it internally and the nightmare had simply dissipated. He realised, rationally, he should do the same now for he had nothing to be frightened of. He loved Bella to distraction and she loved him back, had always loved him and had never been afraid to show it. She wasn't going to hurt him, well, torment him, yes, but only for his ultimate pleasure, not physically hurt him. So why he couldn't simply let himself go? His ironic, puzzled laugh was his last coherent, sensible act for a long time....

Chapter Twenty-Seven

"And what are you laughing at may I ask?" He could smell her scent from across the room, the bewitching fragrance he associated with *Lionesse* had haunted him and his dreams across Spain and it was now inextricably Bella, his tormentor and torturer for however long she chose that evening.

"Nothing," he smiled. "Just cursing myself for letting you do this to me and deciding what terrible things I'm going to do to you when I win our bet."

"Is that so?" she murmured. "I wonder why I don't believe you?" She paused, staring hungrily down at him, relaxed, obviously miles away in his thoughts until she'd entered the room. "Still, never mind, I have other things on my mind. You should be very afraid, not laughing like a schoolboy."

"I'm terrified," his lips curled in a salacious grin.

"You should be. So, my delicious captive, have you been thinking about me while I was in the bath?"

"Oh, here and there," he grinned.

She looked down at his relaxed body. "Hmmm, obviously not enough," she tutted. "Perhaps I should remind you of what you should have been contemplating," and she crawled up on to the bed and leaned down to kiss him voraciously. By the time she'd finished, he was rock hard again. "That's better," she purred. "I can't do anything if you're not hard and ready."

Nicky couldn't help himself, he burst out laughing. "What's so funny?" she enquired.

"You," he chortled. "You're no more a *femme fatale* than the Dowager, God rest her dear soul."

She poked him in the belly. "Nicholas de Bresancourt, when we're finished here and before you go away, I'm going to sit you down, tell you a story and show you a picture that will make your hair stand on end. Your venerable Dowager was quite some woman, you have absolutely NO idea." For a moment, she stared at the gold signet ring on her little finger.

"Really?" he was instantly curious. "What about her?"

"Not now, not here and anyway, it's not really my secret, it's Uncle Francis's, but I know you can keep secrets so I know he won't mind. Anyway, that's for later," she laughed, "now then, where was I? Oh yes, your delicious body, worth five guineas if I remember."

"Far more than that," he chuckled. "I'm worth a fortune now, Heaven help me and I'm lying here, waiting for you to do your worst."

"I'd better get on with it then, hadn't I?"

Bella had spent the past hour confronting what was left of her inhibitions, drinking two full glasses of brandy and bracing herself for what she was determined to do. She had drunk quite a lot during the course of the day but for some reason still remained relatively sober. "Would you like a glass of brandy before I start, condemned prisoner that you are?"

"Do I need one?"

"Definitely," she leaned over and took a long swig from the full glass she'd silently placed on the nightstand and let it slowly drizzle from her mouth into his, following it with a hungry kiss.

"Mmmm, delicious," he purred. "More?" Instinct told him he was going to need more of the fortifying liquor. She took another mouthful and repeated the action, then again, until the glass was empty.

"What are you wearing?" he asked curiously. "Won't you at least take the blindfold off so I can enjoy looking at you?"

"Not at all," she growled softly. "I know you hate it, or do you love it really? I'm not totally sure, I never get the truth out of you, so I'm leaving it there anyway, it's your punishment," she laughed softly then asked conversationally, "but which is worse at the moment? Being bound or not being able to see?"

"Both," he answered truthfully.

"Wrong answer," she tutted.

"I'm not going to tell you," he smiled. "Bernheim never got a word out of me so what makes you think I'll tell you anything?"

"I'm far more frightening than any little Chinaman with a pigtail," Bella bantered, relieved and glad that he could joke about his terrible experiences in Nice.

"Do your worst and you'll see," he chuckled back. "Did you enjoy your bath by the way?" the salacious grin was back.

"Oh yes," Bella said. "You'll see, actually no, you won't, you'll just have to picture it." Nicky wondered curiously what she meant.

Bella leaned across his body, letting him feel the creation she was wearing. It was the most suggestive piece of lingerie she'd bought in Paris, an afterthought she'd been almost too embarrassed to look at, never mind purchase. She had consigned to the back of her armoire in her *Lion d'Or* apartment, not even wanting her maid in Hertford Street to see it. One look in her glass after her bath and she'd known why. She writhed against him, her exposed, pushed up breasts rubbing his chest, the piece of crimson satin, what there was of it, soft against his skin.

"Are you wearing anything at all? It feels like a small fichu, if that?" he laughed. "What colour is it?"

"Crimson," she murmured, "like the rouge on my nipples and else-where, deep crimson."

She watched his engorged length weep slightly. "Elsewhere?" he choked.

"Imagine, Nicky. Where else would you like to see me crimson? Well, deep pink, swollen and wet?" Bella didn't know herself and the language she was using and she almost giggled, she was so appalled at herself.

"Jesus," Nicky groaned and swore. "What the Hell have you done now? Please, take it off, let me see," he pleaded.

"Oh no, just picture it, in your mind," she whispered, her fingers starting to tease him, back and forth across his chest, tweaking his flat nipples until he groaned. Her lips followed her fingers, nibbling and biting then gradually, they worked up his chest to his neck, hovering as she neared his mouth.

"Tut, tut," she muttered, "I'm going in the wrong direction," and as she'd promised, she turned her body around to work her way downwards, her pert bottom now inches from his face; far enough so he couldn't reach it, but near enough to know it was there.

"Christ, Bella, you weren't joking," he muttered as he realised what she was about to invite him to do.

She wriggled backwards. "Do your worst, Nicky. I've been thinking about this for the past hour." Bella taunted softly and paused, waiting for the reaction she knew would come shortly. As she felt the familiar mouth on her, teasing, tantalising, making her gasp, she smiled wickedly to herself.

"Bella?" she felt his tongue lick her and she spread her legs wantonly, the pleasure intense. "Bella?" the penny was starting to drop and she wriggled back a bit further. "BELLA? BELLAAA!" his stupefaction was almost comical as silence reigned for seconds. "What the...?" his language was obscene, the long hard length in front of her twitched and seeped more from the top. If she hadn't been so aroused she would have doubled up in mirth at his reaction.

"What the HELL have you done to yourself?" he was choking in disbelief, lust almost blowing his head off.

She crawled forward, away from his mouth and slid off him. "You like it then?" she purred.

Nicky was incoherent as a surge of heat roared through him and he swore as he pulled on the ribbons. "Take the blindfold off," he choked. "I don't believe it. I want to see, come back here," he ordered and then swore as she moved further away from him and sat up.

"It was all the rage in Paris when I was there, well obviously only in certain rather select quarters, but I was told more and more ladies were doing it, although I'm not sure 'ladies' is quite the right description, but that might have just been the assistant in the establishment trying to encourage me. I really couldn't comment about high society, proper Ladies though, not that there are many of those left in Paris at the moment, not like here in London, they're all so-called liberals or *nouvelle riches*, capitalising on the chaos caused by the Revolution and then Bonaparte, but now the Bourbons are back, who knows? Anyway, that's somewhat irrelevant, so I had time on my hands while looking for you," she continued to prattle. "Women have been doing it for centuries of course and in certain cultures overseas, it was par for the course for all women," she continued blithely. "I read all about it, naturally, to inform myself further and I'm sure you've encountered plenty of ladies of a certain ilk who do it. I mean, when you look at classical paintings, the women all appear to be hairless, don't they, well, there you are. Anyway, I digress, it was an assistant in a lingerie shop suggested you might like it; it was a very particular shop I came across, in a very narrow and dirty back street," she said calmly. "I think she thought I was a high-class courtesan and you were a client I wanted to please. She sold me the sugar, said my maid would do it," she shrugged, "but I didn't have a maid with me and I only had the time to visit a certain house where the lady offered that service, so I could see what it was all about before we left for Nice. It's mainly done with sugar or wax by Arab, Turkish, Indian or other Far Eastern women who have found their way to Paris. I really didn't fancy some of the other strange creams or lotions for sale with odd ingredients, so I've just done it myself tonight. My maid in Hertford Street would no doubt have a fit if I asked her, so I really must try and find somewhere here in London where they do it as it's a bit awkward by oneself and definitely a bit painful. Tweezers must take forever!" she added conversationally, as if discussing buying a hat. "However, I'm glad you seem to approve," she finally added lecherously and looked down at her denuded lower body, under her arms and down her legs. The latter were all hairless and smooth but all affected parts still a bit red and blotchy, a bit tender here and there, but that would all soon dissipate and he couldn't see it the marks anyway. She smiled like a satisfied cat with its prize mouse as she looked down at his stunned face. "Such a shame you can't see me," she added wickedly.

"You... you..." Nicky was still incoherent. "Please, let me see," he begged, thrashing against his bonds, angry at her laughter.

"Oh no, just imagine, it goes rather well with the rouge," she added suggestively, "even if I say so myself. I'm becoming quite the harlot."

"You Witch... Baggage... how could you?" he was frustrated beyond belief and swore obscenely.

She continued in a chatty tone, still determinedly winding him up. "Personally, I can't see the attraction myself, other than the practicalities," she chuckled, "but there's no accounting for taste. Now then, where were we?" as, ignoring his muttered pleas and curses, for the next hour she did exactly as she'd promised.

She teased and tantalised him until he was even more incoherent; writhing over his body and mouth in all ways, avoiding touching him no matter how much she was tempted. It was completely pornographic, salacious and more than a bit depraved. Her family would have been appalled. SHE was seriously appalled. At one point, she wondered what high class harlots charged for what she was doing!

"So, how much do you want me to touch you?" Bella panted down into his mouth as she kissed him yet again.

"I'll never give in," Nicky muttered brokenly, his body on fire with longing for a proper touch of her hand to relieve the aching lust he felt; she'd taken him to the edge and then retreated so many times he thought his balls were going to burst, they were so painful, especially when she'd experimented with some little tricks she'd picked up somewhere from her reading matter.

"Oh, I rather think you will." She resumed the position she'd adopted when she'd begun her new torture. "I need to climax," she breathed, "make me...feel it...just ask me and I'll touch you."

"Noooo," he shook his head, his mind at war with his body.

"Suit yourself," she muttered and rolled across him, her back across his sweating abdomen. "Do you know what I'm going to do, I'll just have to pleasure myself," she whispered and for the first time in her life, Bella started to do just that. "Do you think I should go down into the kitchens and find myself a nice large, long, fat, carrot? What about a small parsnip? If I can't have you, they might touch the spot and give me what I want...too bad I didn't buy one of the interesting items I came across in the same lingerie shop I bought this shift...the assistant did ask me but I told her I didn't need one..." and she mewled as she rubbed herself, wondering what Nicky was picturing in his mind, nearly laughing out loud. "Ooooh, it's too much now, I'm nearly there...oh God!...oh God!..."

Nicky lay there, body on fire, listening to her mutterings, moans and cries as Bella caressed herself, his imagination running riot with torrid images of an enormous carrot pumping in and out of her naked and hairless body as he sensed what she was doing, feeling her body grind on top of him on the bed. She heard his whisper as the spasms started, "Please...."

Bella paused, on the brink and took several deep, ragged breaths. "I don't think...I can stop," she whispered brokenly, her own body now truly on fire.

"Let me... pleeease... just touch me. You're driving me insane," his soft, broken voice entreated her.

"Just a moment." She took several more deep breaths, forcing her body to calm down. She slithered back over him, the crimson satin, no more than an artful design of lengths of cloth wound around her torso and caressed his sweating muscles. Nicky swore in French, his body craving the feel of her even as his mind tried to deny it. His mouth razed over her bare, wet centre and his tongue drove inside. Bella cried out as her hand finally grasped his hot length, lightly, not firmly enough for him, but she had to let go as the spasms rocked through her.

When it was over, she slumped limply over him and he swore long and softly in French again, his heart pounding, frustration oozing from every pore with the sweat that covered his entire body.

Now that he'd given in and she could touch him, the torment was worse. And so the evening continued. Eventually, Bella drove Nicky to beg her to take him in her mouth, but that was another torment that had no end. She climaxed again, rubbing his length against her hairless lower body, but still she tortured and denied him. She progressed and impaled herself on him, but only momentarily, then left him hanging. She did it again and again until he lost count. He swore, threatened and thrashed around as much as his restraints would allow, his wrists red and raw. The sweat ran off his body in rivulets, his hair was wet. He was mindless, lost in a world of agonising pleasure and torment he never imagined. She gradually did all the salacious things she'd promised, completely lost now in her own pleasure and his erotic torture. Inhibitions were a thing of the past as she used his body mercilessly.

At one point, Bella was so worried he was going to climax and erupt spontaneously, she threw the freezing remains of the ice bucket over him, causing him to emit a tortured shriek. Well, that was one shriek she told herself. He yelled at her in a stream of gutter French invective she couldn't begin to understand but got the general drift. She listened to him, thinking the whole street would hear his yells and ranting, but she smiled evilly, got off the bed and came back to stuff a large, scrunched-up linen napkin into his mouth. She thought smoke was going to come out of his ears, he was almost apoplectic with anger and humiliation as she listened to him trying to speak. She laughed down at him, watching him splutter as his head thrash back and forth on the pillows. He obviously hated the whole thing beyond reason, her too at that moment.

She was exhausted and wondered how much more he could take as they lay there on the damp bed, heaving and panting. She disappeared out of the bedroom periodically to calm herself down as much as let him recover from his latest near climax, only to return with more instruments of torture: hot oil to massage up and down his length followed by frozen sorbet from the ice-cold, deep cellar beneath her kitchens which she licked and sucked off him; it was endless and he was half dead from the torturous pleasure and frustration.

Finally, she crawled up his body, pulled out the napkin and whispered down to him, "Beg me and I'll give you what you want."

Nicky was incoherent, almost crying, his mind had given up fighting, nothing in his entire rakish and debauched existence had been like this. He'd never let it, submission and definitely masochism wasn't on his agenda. He truly thought he was going to die of the intense agony his body felt, all centred in one place and he gave in with a broken sob, "Please, no more, I give in." The whisper was almost silent.

Bella saw the tear slip out from under the black sash and knew she'd won. She had one final arrow to fire.

She slid off him and reached for the remains of the oil she'd slathered over him earlier. She poured copious amounts into her palm and smoothed it over his hardness; he was almost too overcome to gasp at the feeling, so sensitive now to the merest touch and then, she rose over him. Slowly, she sank down; not where he'd anticipated, but where she knew he was not expecting. The feeling was strange but familiar and she persevered, just as he almost rose off the bed with a strangled gasp as he recognised what she was doing. She gave him no time to say or do anything as she rose and sank again, excruciatingly slowly and carefully, bit by slow bit. Her soft hands crept around behind her and cupped his balls, feeling them contract as his release surged up through him and then it happened. A loud, tearing, screaming wail rent the air as his body jerked and he climaxed. Another series of jerks and a strangled scream followed and she watched with a strange pleasure and intense love as more tears rolled down his face to mingle with the sweat now pouring off him, as his whole body was racked with pleasure as she continued to move slowly over him.

"No!" he begged finally. "Oh God, aaaaaaaarghh, stop, stop. Please, I can't stand it. No more," and with another cry, his head fell back and he collapsed on the pillows. Bella stopped moving, rose up and off him and sank on to the bed next to him, half lying across his chest, feeling his erratic, thumping heartbeat and shaking breaths. She realised he'd temporarily passed out and her smile was triumphant.

Nicky's body was on fire and he knew she'd beaten him; he didn't have the will to fight her nor himself any longer and for the first time in his life, just gave in and let go. As he felt her sink down on him, realising what she was doing, what it meant to her, what she was offering to him in her inimitable way, he couldn't breathe. Apart from the emotion, the physical feeling was so intense, he couldn't think straight and his long held back, climactic release surged up through him like a torrential, overflowing river, churning and tumbling from the highest waterfall. He couldn't stop the rapturously tormented scream that started deep in his chest and burst out of him as ecstasy, such as he'd never known, exploded through every inch of his body and mind. He wailed again as the indescribable pleasure went on and on until he couldn't take the intensity or pressure on his over sensitised flesh anymore and he heard a voice... his voice... begging her to stop moving. He saw stars and blackness filled his head and he knew no more.

"Nicky? Nicky? Are you all right?" He felt her slapping his cheek gently as reality returned. He opened his eyes and realised he could see again. His arms and legs were free too and he winced painfully as circulation returned to his tortured limbs. He felt lost and disorientated, still almost speechless.

"I'm going to kill you, I swear to God," he slowly whispered up at her. "Don't you ever, EVER, do that to me again."

Her grin was beatific. "But I won, you lost and you promised. A Gentleman never reneges on a bet."

Movement was beyond him, his muscles still in spasm and he was exhausted, mentally and physically. "I don't care," he whispered. "I thought I was dead for a moment anyway, you'll kill me for sure next time, unless I kill you first," he closed his eyes and opened them again, trying to gather his scattered wits.

"Are you trying to tell me you didn't enjoy that?" she purred exultantly.

"I hated every damn minute."

"Is that why you screamed in pleasure, more than once? Talk about shriek, wail and yell," she chuckled then tutted, "I must try and do better next time."

"There will be NO next time," he stated forcefully, managing to pull her down next to him and he rolled over on top of her, "do you hear me, You Witch? NEVER, NEVER, EVER, NEVER AGAIN."

She giggled "Oh yes, there will, you're too honourable to back out of our bet and I won."

"I won't let you do it."

"Oh yes you will."

"Oh, for Heaven's sake, you're impossible."

"Well, that makes two of us then, doesn't it," she laughed.

"You're completely wicked, depraved, deranged and weird. Why would you want to do that to me again?"

"Because it gave you such pleasure, eventually," she answered simply. "That's why and that's all I want to do. Give you pleasure."

He sighed. "It was extraordinary," he muttered to himself. "I've never experienced anything like that," he still felt shaken from the intensity of pleasure. "I'm still going to kill you," he grinned, "and your father, it's all his fault."

Bella looked puzzled. "Papa? Why? What on earth has he got to do with this?"

"He taught you to read!" The pair of them burst out laughing and Bella pulled the covers up over them, blew out the spluttering candles on the nightstand and snuggled down into his arms.

"I won. I WILL do it to you again," she yawned in the darkness, "when you come back from France. We'll go to Valenciennes. It's quiet there, you can scream all you like and frighten the tenants. They'll think I'm taking you to *La Guillotine*."

"How many times do I have to tell you? NEVER AGAIN!" he yawned as well. They were still arguing as they fell asleep.

Dawn was barely breaking when Nicky woke up. He lay for a long while reflecting over the previous evening and his relationship with Bella as he listened to the occasional twittering of the birds. He still had one final unopened package lying in the sitting room, connected to her forfeit. He hadn't been sure if Bella would cope with it when he'd made the purchase on the spur of the moment in the discreet little shop in Soho he'd visited the previous morning, but now he knew she would. That her carnal appetites appeared to match his now she could let go of her inhibitions both thrilled and delighted him and his love and desire for her knew no ends, knowing she felt just the same. After what she'd done to him and what she'd apparently discovered in her little shopping expeditions, he doubted his last little erotic tease would faze her. His smile was lecherous as he contemplated what her reaction would be, but the erotic and slightly depraved goings on of the previous evening reassured him her passionate nature would revel in it, if she'd open her mind further and, most importantly, trusted him.

Quietly, he got up and stretched languorously. His limbs ached pleasurably as he flexed them and he strolled through her dressing room into the closet, emerging a short while after, droplets of water glistening on his body from the water he'd sponged over himself to wash. Then he wandered through into the sitting room. They had a couple of hours before reality caught up with them and he meant to use them for their final bit of wicked, slightly perverted pleasure.

Chapter Twenty-Eight

Bella stirred when Nicky got up and she watched him stretch and flex his body with the usual pleasure. Idly, she wondered if she'd ever get bored of drooling over his torso and she giggled to herself as a random thought crossed her mind, wondering if her disreputable aunt still lusted over her Uncle Francis in the same way. She decided they were much too old for such lecherous antics, trying and failing to picture the pair of them doing what she'd recently done to Nicky. She watched as her husband wandered about, disappearing into her dressing room and then coming back out to stroll into the sitting room where she heard him rummaging around.

She got up, washed and refreshed herself, then shrugged into a dressing robe before hurrying through to see what he was up to. "You're up early. What are you doing?" she asked curiously. It was still dim in the room, the weather outside was dismal and wet and she grimaced at the dark clouds. He turned to her, holding the package in his hands behind his back. His smile was bland. "Oh, nothing much. You still have to pay your forfeit you know. I'm not going to let you off that."

She'd forgotten about their card game and her eyes narrowed as she eyed his expression. He didn't fool her for a moment. "What have you got there?" she asked suspiciously and wandered over to the abandoned card table where the sealed scrap of paper still sat. She ripped open the seal and read the scribbled words.

"How much do you trust me?"

Bella was mystified. "What on earth does this mean?"

"Do you trust me, Bella?" he asked, completely serious.

"I don't understand, what do you mean by that?"

"It's very simple, Sweetheart, do you trust me? Implicitly?"

"Do you mean when you go away?"

He nodded. "But not just that, though I give you my word you're the only woman in my life now. I'm not interested in anyone else, EVER. I do know what you think," he looked at her knowingly and Bella gasped, slightly wondering if he was a mind reader, "but this is about us, you and me. I want to know you trust me in everything, because I trust you now, implicitly, despite what I said all those years ago about *Lionesse*, my necklace and everything."

"This is all very serious and profound for five o'clock in the morning or whatever time it is."

"Mmmm, I know, but I wasn't intending to have this discussion at four or five o'clock in the morning," he smiled, lightening the mood, "so just answer the question."

Bella looked at him and the love in his golden eyes as he looked at her, so she sighed. "Yes Nicky, I trust you. I have to, I love you too much not to."

"Good. I love you too, My Sweetheart; remember that when I'm away, hmmm?"

She nodded. "But what's that got to do with the forfeit? I don't understand?"

"You will," his smile curled wider.

"Nickyyyy, what are you up to now?" Bella asked suspiciously again.

"Go into the bedroom and put on another of your, er, 'interesting' bits of lingerie, if there are any more here. I might as well enjoy as many of them as I can before I leave. Oh, and bring back two of the ribbons and the black sash."

Bella's eyes widened. "Now why should I do that?" she asked saucily.

"Do as you're told, Bella," he ordered with a grin.

"You're not back in the army yet, y'know," she riposted, "this is Mayfair."

"Bellaaaa…" he threatened.

"All right, all right," and she turned to do as he asked.

She came back a few minutes later, still wearing her wrap and handed over the ribbons and sash. "What are you going to do to me? Will I like this game?"

"Eventually," his grin widened. "Now, close your eyes."

"Why? Tell me what you're going to do first."

"Damn woman, you're such a bossy boots at times, opinionated too. I should have taught you a lesson long ago," he chuckled.

"Hah! You can talk, ordering me around. Some chance," she smiled saucily again.

"I'm your husband and there's only one Master in this household and that's me, not you, Madam, no matter you think you've got me wrapped around your little finger," he grinned.

"Who me?" she giggled. "Well, you were a few hours ago if I remember rightly and I," she poked herself in the chest, "run this little establishment, if not the household."

"Oh, dear God, you're impossible," he sighed, laughing.

"Aren't I just?" She poked her tongue out at him and waggled her fingers on her head, just as she'd often done when she'd been a cheeky little girl.

"Close your eyes." She finally acquiesced to his order and he moved closer to tie the sash tightly round and round them, just as he'd done to her before and she'd done to him. "Now, remove your dressing robe."

Bella slowly undid the robe, letting it drop to the floor. She was wearing another froth of red lace underneath, a miniature corset of sorts, rouged nipples once again oozing over the top and Nicky felt himself harden instantly at the sight of her. Bella was now glad she'd secreted some of her more salacious French purchases there instead of at Hertford Street, out of sight of her maid and she wondered randomly what that kind but slightly naive individual would have made of it if she had purchased one of the ivory phalluses she'd seen but been too embarrassed to buy. She remembered how she'd tittered at the thought of getting one for her aunt as a surprise gift, wondering what that eccentric lady or her uncle would have made of it...and had decided that was something she'd rather not know but somehow suspecting they would undoubtedly enjoy playing with it if they didn't have one of their own already!

While she was momentarily lost in her amusing musings, Nicky picked up one of the ribbons and wound it around one of her arms, just above her elbow, then pulled back her other arm to tether it the same way, tightly, pulling them and her shoulders both tautly backwards. The effect made Bella's breasts jut out and pour voluptuously over the red lace, exposing all of her rouged nipples. "Very picturesque," he commented, kissing them in turn. "Your nipples match this excuse for a handkerchief and your corset, if you can call that a corset," he chuckled.

She could picture how she looked and grinned, then tossed her head saucily. "We aim to please."

He tied her wrists loosely behind her with the other ribbon, but it was the effect on her breasts he was after. He spun her around so she was confused about where she was in the room and left her to stand and wait, watching her frustrated impatience with delight.

Nicky picked up the package he'd placed on the chair behind where he'd been standing and drew out a long silver chain. Little charms hung from some of the links and there were two small silver clamps at either end.... and so it began again. Another erotic episode that shocked, excited and rendered Bella completely and passionately mindless.

After he'd sent Bella into paroxysms of tormented pleasure and she'd experienced another thing she'd read about, the intoxicating mix of mild discomfort and extreme arousal, Nicky left the sash in place. He'd collapsed on the bed next to her, completely and utterly drained, exhausted after an unbelievable night. As Bella gradually came back to earth, he lifted her up on to the pillows to lie next to him in his arms, the covers loosely draped over them.

He gently tweaked a nipple. "Ow! Ooooh noooo, gerroff me," she muttered, making him chuckle.

"They won't be sore for long, it's just the circulation returning to normal. So what did you think of that then?" he asked quietly. "Another experience to add to your list. I told you to trust me, didn't I?"

"You Devil, that was terrible; shocking, obscene, depraved. I give up, I simply give up," she muttered darkly, completely overcome at what he'd just done to her and the myriad of feelings she'd experienced. "It's a good job you're going away, I can't cope with any more of this," but he saw her smile, breathed a sigh of relief and grinned.

"Oh, was that someone else ordering me to fuck you harder?" his grin widened. "Tut, tut, Bella, My Love, I can barely believe that was you, sooo unladylike, you sounded like a trollop from the local tavern, your poor father would be appalled!" He bent down to kiss her as he tried and failed to picture his stepfather's face. Then Nicky sighed "Actually, Sweetheart, I can't cope with any more of this either. I think I could sleep for a week and then some. You've completely drained me, but we've got a little girl to collect in an hour or two so don't be thinking you can snore away all day," he laughed.

"I don't snore," she muttered as her hands came up to grapple with the tight knots in the sash, but he pulled them away.

"You most certainly do," he chuckled. "But just a moment," Nicky said softly, holding down Bella's hands; he didn't want her distracted, he wanted her to listen to him. He wanted to speak to her seriously before they slept and suddenly felt too overcome with it all himself, at everything that had happened that torrid evening and night, which had turned out to be far more than he'd ever planned. He felt embarrassed and unsure of himself for her to see the strange emotional tears he could feel bubbling inside him, still slightly fearful of the answers to questions he needed to ask.

"Now tell me again, do you really, really trust me? You see, you didn't believe me when I told you the clamps were pleasurable, did you? You must believe me, Sweetheart, believe IN me, always. As if I'd put anything else on you that would cause you pain," he whispered. "I told you to trust me, but did you? You should have faith in what I say, realise when I'm teasing. Believe me, Sooty, NEVER would I hurt or humiliate you to the point you were seriously upset!" he rasped in a forceful whisper. "That is NOT me, never in the past nor in the future. I need you to have faith in me, to trust me, in EVERYTHING." There was a soft plea in his voice, "I know you always go to Francis with your problems, but do you think you could come to me in future? When I come home? I know what I've done in the past, but I don't want to be looked on as the family rake and irresponsible fool any longer. I have a family now, a future, you and my little pride." He sounded momentarily forlorn, hopeful yet unsure.

Bella was touched and terribly moved. "I wouldn't trust you to hang out the washing," she whispered, "or even feed the cat. You're completely impossible, absolutely useless and brainless." She heard his sudden indrawn breath and gave up her teasing with a soft laugh. "But Nicky, I love you to death and I couldn't give a toss about your title or your money, you know I never did. It's always been just you, Nicky, the person you are, rake, charmer, fool, now a card sharp," she joked lightly. "I'd trust you with my life and Terrie's, surely you know that You Idiot. So, if you're home with me and being a proper husband," she dug him in the ribs playfully, "why would I need to go to Uncle Francis?" She took a deep breath before admitting, "You see, I do need a man to lean on sometimes. I want it to be you, My Love and don't you ever dare throw that back in my face, or tell Auntie," she laughed, despite her deeply serious answer and he loved her for it.

Nicky laughed softly at her teasing and felt choked with emotion at her admission. Once more he stopped her hands from reaching up to take off the blindfold and held on to them firmly. "I love you, Bella," he then said quietly and he bent to kiss her. "Don't think of anything else, just lay back and feel this and listen to me for a moment more." He caressed her face and held her tight and then he kissed her with all his heart, deeply, tenderly, and passionately. "Don't ever leave me or betray me. I'm giving you my heart on a plate. I've finally managed to open up to someone...you...and I've let go tonight. I never thought I ever would, or could, but if I lose you I'll die. I couldn't bear it. What we've done, what we shared yesterday and last night has made us close, very close, nothing at all between us now… emotionally as well as physically. Do you feel it too?"

Bella could hear the anxiety and distress in his voice, "Nicky, oh Nicky, I've always loved you, I'll never stop loving you, I promise. I'll give you your little Lion cubs, however many you want and anything you want…and don't you even think about not coming back, for I'll come and look for you again. I'll follow you to the ends of the earth. I'm never letting you go…you truly are the other part of me now."

He kissed her again until she was breathless. "I'd like to make love to you again," he whispered, "but I can't, you've worn me out," he laughed hoarsely, choking. "It's because I feel so close to you when I'm inside you, as you've just said, like you're another part of me. It's not always about sex, games and carnal pleasure, the physical closeness is a mental connection too. Oh, Bella, I do love you so," and with that he started to weep, the emotional tears a catharsis to drive away memories and demons that had haunted him, since that terrible time in the old Fortress in Rouen.

Bella finally managed to wrench off the tight sash and pulled him into her arms, realising something profound had affected him and sensing that finally, he had really let his emotions go. He was at peace with himself and somehow she was his rock in the middle of all his emotional turmoil. "Will you tell me about it one day, Nicky? When you're ready? I won't push you, but I'd like to understand. I know it's your past, what happened long ago with Mama and Papa, Aunt Cat and Uncle Francis, Uncle Reynard too, but if you let it out, it will be gone for good and you can forget it, up in your attic," she spoke softly.

"I will, My Sweetheart, I promise, one day when I come home to you," he murmured and he fell asleep, feeling safe, secure and completely loved in her arms.

Chapter Twenty-Nine

The staff had reappeared early in the morning and Nicky had risen, bleary-eyed, to send a footman to summon their coach to take them back to Hertford Street. They decided to stop on the way and collect Terrie as Nicky had no idea what time he would be summoned by Wellington. He expected a message to arrive for him at any time.

He'd dressed hurriedly and carelessly in just his shirt, pantaloons and boots and virtually dragged Bella out of bed. The pair sat in sleepy silence as the coach pulled up outside the portico of Firle House.

Nicky jumped out and left a dazed Bella sitting inside, still trying to come to terms with what had happened to her organised, slightly conservative, sterile and mundane life in the past thirty-six hours. As their coach had pulled away from *Le Lion d'Or* Nicky had said that had been their belated honeymoon, something they would both never forget. It had certainly been that, and more…almost more than her mind could handle. Never mind her outrageous aunt and uncle, did other people do things like that on their honeymoons? Did other people do that at all? She didn't know but doubted it as she thought of her lovely but sedate and conservative married friends and their various husbands, trying to picture them doing what she and Nicky had been up to. She couldn't, but as her knowing aunt had once said to her, one never knew what went on behind closed doors and people were often not at all like the public face they put on...which made her think of the late Dowager. What secrets had she taken to her grave with her Alex...a man who she'd admitted had been quite the lothario and had swept her off her feet? Even the idea of her having a torrid affair had boggled her mind at first, unable to imagine the frosty old woman most people knew being carried away in the thralls of passion, rolling around naked in bed, and...doing what? Not lying back and thinking of England with him withdrawing, that was for sure, knowing Elizabeth Granville as she had. That woman had never done anything by halves and Bella suspected it had been the same with her love life, short-lived as it had been with her Scottish lover. Whatever the pair had done, she'd ended up pregnant as a result of it. Bella's head went round and round as she contemplated everything until, worn out with it all, she fell asleep.

Meanwhile, Nicky ran up the steps and, on entering the hallway, asked a bemused and ever punctilious Browning, who looked slightly disdainfully at the untidily dressed young Duke whom he had known since he was in short coats, if Lady Thérèse could be brought down as soon as possible.

As chance would have it, Francis had just strolled out of the breakfast room on the way to his study, carrying a cup of coffee, while Nicky was waiting. The Duke looked at the dishevelled younger man with a raised eyebrow and tilted his head in the direction of his study. He sat behind his desk, looking in apparent fascination at Nicky's appearance as the latter sank down with a sigh on a comfortable armchair, looking for all the world like he was ready to fall asleep.

"Well, good morning," Francis drawled. "Welcome to the home of the deranged, delusional and criminally insane."

Nicky looked at him, entertained as ever by his droll wit. "To whom do you refer? You, the family, or the servants?" he asked.

Francis waved his hand vaguely, "Oh, the entire establishment here, as well as my illustrious family," he continued airily. "You included of course – in fact, especially you."

"Me?" Nicky grinned. "What have I done? I don't live here anymore…"

"Ah, but you're part of the family," sighed Francis. "You are the delusional one and you're the cause of yesterday's catastrophe."

Nicky chuckled, looking innocent and pointing at his chest in confusion, "Me?"

"Yes, YOU," Francis continued, his face deadpan, looking him up and down and trying to restrain the grin on his face. "Lovely weather we seem to be having, wouldn't you say?" as he looked out of the window at the torrential rain, still as bad as it had been all the previous day. "Just perfect weather to go on a picnic, of course, but perhaps it was warm and sunny round the corner in your part of Mayfair yesterday? Unlike here, two minutes away in Berkeley Square?" he sipped his coffee. "Of course, just perfect weather to send one's entire staff out for the day to Vauxhall Gardens, or Brighton, or wherever, it being March and of course ideal weather to make exceedingly sudden building repairs to a house that was completely and extensively repaired and refurbished not that long ago, but now appears to be in imminent danger of falling down to the extent everyone had to be evacuated and the building closed for twenty four hours?" Francis tutted. "Delusional. To go on a picnic in March. So where, pray, did you sit? Under an umbrella in the middle of Hyde Park? I'm told it rained so hard yesterday, the place was virtually under water. It must have been simply IDEAL for a glass of wine and some bread and cheese, *al fresco*."

"It was an indoor picnic," Nicky choked out, trying to keep a straight face but wondering why Francis invariably seemed to find out what was going on, no matter how they all tried to keep things secret from him.

Francis continued, "As ever, you've obviously not anticipated the wildlife at your picnic destination, again delusional, the rats must have been simply terrible," as he eyed the bites on Nicky's neck, exposed by his open shirt. His raised eyebrows moved to the red wrists, exposed by the rolled-up sleeves of Nicky's shirt, now rapidly rolled down.

"Oh dear," he pronounced, quite deadpan still, "did they capture you, hold you hostage and try to eat you for their lunch?"

Nicky chuckled at the salacious innuendo. "Your mind doesn't get any cleaner as you get older, Francis," but his expression was dazed and happy and Francis was inordinately pleased, not that he showed it.

He and Cat had suspected something wasn't right between Nicky and Bella, but whatever it was seemed to have been sorted out if the look on the younger man's face was anything to go by. Francis recognised the look well – he'd seen it in his own mirror enough times when he was younger – dazed, tired and blissfully fulfilled. But he continued as he drank his coffee, "So, that brings me to the deranged…"

Nicky lolled back on the soft cushions and grinned as he listened to the droll Duke. "You decided to abandon your offspring here, as usual, for your nefarious and obviously salacious purposes, as if the one Anarchist currently residing at this establishment isn't bad enough. Do you know what they did? Encouraged by YOUR daughter's inherited predilection to engage with anything furry on four legs?"

Nicky shook his head, chuckling again. The anarchist was Elizabeth Granville, the three-year-old daughter of the Duke. She was naughty beyond all reason and completely uncontrollable. Even at a mere three, she was the despair of her mother, a nightmare to the household servants and the bane of the life of her besotted father. In fact, he was the only person who could do anything with her, when she chose to let him. With her black hair and striking blue eyes, just like her father's, she was going to be stunning when she grew up, if someone in Firle House or Firle Manor didn't murder her first. "No? What did they do? They're only three for God's sake, actually mine isn't even three yet."

"Old before their time, they're two and three going on twelve and thirteen. Deranged with it. They should be locked away for the safety of the nation," Francis declared darkly. "They decided to have a tea party with their dolls and YOUR daughter decided to invite Bubbles."

"Oh dear," Nicky chuckled, "that seems like a recipe for disaster. What did he do, eat all the cakes?"

"I wish he had, but of course nothing so mundane. Disaster doesn't BEGIN to describe the events that took place. You see, YOUR daughter decided Bubbles couldn't come to tea without a bonnet on. See what I mean about old before their time? How does a two-year-old know that? MY daughter therefore crept out of the nursery while Nanny's back was turned, stole her mother's latest new hat, specially designed by some extortionate and exclusive milliner in Bond Street and designated exclusively to go to some big charity tea affair next week, attended by several august female members of the Royal Family, no less. It cost ME a small fortune and WAS sitting in splendour in her dressing room and WAS a confection of enormous feathers. So she kidnapped the dog from where it had been shut up securely in the kitchen and took both hat and dog back up to the nursery – how, without any member of the staff stopping her, only the Devil knows. To cut a long, painful story short, they somehow locked the nursery maid, who was SUPPOSED to be supervising them, in a water closet; Bubbles took a dislike to the hat, so attacked and ate it instead of his cake; Cat threw a voluble, blasphemous, serious French fit and I," he sighed, "was sitting quietly, minding my own business, having tea in my study with Ashcroft and Nelson, who was calming sleeping in front of the fire. THAT was why Bubbles had been shut in the kitchens. They're not too fond of each other," he sighed again. "Anyway, all hell broke loose as Bubbles escaped with feathers coming out of his mouth, Cat chasing after him swearing like a French fishwife, the girls shrieking at her to leave him alone, chasing after her, the Nanny chasing them, Cat's maid, Clara, having hysterics, the nursery maid banging on the closet door to be let out and the rest of the staff in complete pandemonium; and then Nelson woke up with the noise as everyone erupted down the stairs into the main hallway, screeching and shouting. Bubbles burst into my study, barking his head off and spewing mangled feathers everywhere, instantly spotted Nelson and started chasing him, knocking everything flying and the whole house turned into complete Bedlam. Ashcroft finally managed to rescue Nelson, but Bubbles got so excited and irritated at losing his quarry he vomited the bits of bonnet and feathers he'd ingested all over Ashcroft's shoes in the middle of the new, vastly expensive Aubusson rug I'd just put down in my study, which came all the way from Paris, then lifted his leg on him for good measure as he was a trifle stressed, Bubbles that is..."

Nicky was in complete hysterics as Francis stated, still completely deadpan, "So you see, it's all YOUR fault, and everyone here is DERANGED as no one can seem to manage to look after two three year olds for two minutes while I, with the head of the Government's most efficient Security Department, discuss the state of the nation and Bonaparte's arrival in Paris, with his army flocking back to serve him, which will have the whole of Europe in turmoil again; plus, I now have to buy him new shoes, stockings and pantaloons, not to mention another new rug for my study and another bloody feathered bonnet for Cat. Not to mention new furniture for in here, ornaments and all the rest. I won't begin to tell you what happened to all the files of papers and important documents that flew everywhere or were destroyed, my senior secretary is currently prostrate and lying down somewhere dark, trying to recover..." he sighed theatrically.

Nicky was rolling around, holding his sides and weeping with mirth at the picture of what had happened the previous day while Francis sat and calmly drank his coffee, now grinning all over his face. When Nicky finally managed to speak, he asked, "Well that explains the delusional and deranged. Who is criminally insane? Is that me too?"

"Not at all," replied Francis, now with a serious expression. "That's me. I need locking away for continuing to live here in this lunatic asylum and putting up with the madness and for not emigrating to China years ago when Lizzie was born." He calmly finished his coffee. What he had omitted to mention was that while his entire household had descended into extreme chaos, he'd simply sat amidst them and cried with laughter, just as Nicky had, much to the frustration of his wife, screaming obscene French invective over the demise of her new hat, barking dogs, feathers flying everywhere, papers all over the floor getting mixed up, torn and trodden on, shrieking children, broken ornaments and furniture, hysterical maids, panicking servants and a speechless and shellshocked Ashcroft, who was clutching his little one-eyed dog to him as if his life depended on it. That latter scene had convulsed Francis the most.

As Nicky wiped the tears of laughter from his face, the subject of Francis's wrath erupted into his study, hurtled across the room and threw herself onto his lap. "Hah! I 'scaped," she announced, panting. "I wanna go back wiv Terrie an' see Duchess. Pweeease Papa, we had such fun yest'day wiv Bubbles. We wanna have 'nother tea party wiv Duchess an' she can have one of Auntie Bella's bonnets."

Francis rolled his eyes at Nicky who had fallen into hysterics again when a harassed and red-faced nursery maid burst into the study as well. "Aha! There you are, you WRETCHED little girl," she puffed. "Oh Lordy," she bobbed a curtsey as she went even redder, "beg pardon, Yer Grace, I didn't realise you was in 'ere and 'ad a visitor." She bobbed another curtsey at Nicky who was still crying with laughter. "I'm afraid Lady 'lizabeth GOT OUT the nurs'ry again wivout permission and, er, Lady Thérèse is waitin' fer you in the 'allway, Yer Grace," she advised Nicky, looking hopeful he'd disappear soon with her other charge.

The little girl on Francis's lap turned to look at the maid who was in turn looking at her venomously and poked her tongue out. "I'm goin' too," she announced haughtily before turning back to Francis, all sweetness and light and planted a big kiss on his cheek, "aren't I, Papa?"

When she didn't get a response, she slid off his lap and sidled over to a still laughing Nicky and scrambled up on to his lap. "'lo Un-cul Nicky," she beamed up at him. "You know you're my FAVE'RIT un-cul in the WHOLE world, don't you?" she crooned and leaned up for a smacking kiss on his cheek. This was followed by a chubby hand that started to twirl some of his uncombed hair round her fingers as she whispered loudly in his ear, "You don't mind if I come to tea with my dollies, do you?" and she kissed him again. It was Francis's turn to laugh at Nicky's bemused expression. Francis sighed an enormous sigh, "See what I mean?" he said, "the house is an asylum, and as for that one..."

Nicky grinned down at the entrancing tot in his lap and then up at Francis, "Where on earth did she learn to do that?" He looked accusingly over at the other man. "That's disgraceful. She's not even four," he chuckled, "Francis, it smacks of you all over."

Francis held up his hands, "Don't look at me, I'm completely innocent. Actually, I thought she got it from you," he laughed.

Another Little Person toddled in. "Where's my Papa?" an indignant voice chirped.

"Oh no, here's the other villainess," Francis sighed. "He's over here, Poppet," he crooned and smiled as a little golden cherub wandered over and clambered on to his lap, a lopsided ribbon dangling undone in her tawny blonde hair. She turned and smiled at her father, "'lo Papa," and blew him a kiss, trying to wink at her partner in crime sitting on her father's lap, but it merely looked like a screwed-up face and Nicky chuckled. She then turned to her uncle, "Un-cul Fran-sisssss," she smooched, "c'n Lizzie be wiv me? Peeease, we ownie wanna havva lickle tea party, wiv my poozzy an' my dollies. Peeeease," she leaned up and kissed his cheek, running a chubby hand through his thick dark hair. "'ny-way," she continued with an aristocratic air and amusing baby prattle, "s'my 'ouse, so if I wan' Lizzie wiv me, that's per-ficky all right. Peeease?"

Francis and Nicky looked at each other in comical horror. "Oh, dear God," sighed Francis. "I can't compete with two of them and it appears it's not YOUR house anymore either!" he grinned.

Nicky knew when he was beaten and sighed. "I'll take them both and provided they don't destroy Hertford Street in the next few hours, I'll send Lizzie back later, unless you want to come and get her? I want to talk to you about Ashcroft and Bernheim anyway. He told you, I take it?"

"Yes," Francis's face was momentarily serious. "We MUST talk before you go so I'll come round. Ashcroft said Wellington was waiting on some papers and intends to sail as soon as he can tomorrow. Not sure if he's going from Tilbury or driving down to Dover, but I think there'll be a message waiting for you when you get home. Then come back for dinner later with Bella. Fortunately, Eddie will be here tonight too, he's on his way back to London from a meeting up North, so we can all dine together *en famille* before you go off and have a last 'picnic'," he winked, "and for God's sake, wear some long cuffs and a high collar," he drawled. "Cat's got eyes like a hawk and she'll know what you've been up to; I'm not having her get any ideas along those lines when she's had too much wine, thank you. I'm too old for all that nonsense now."

Nicky's ribald chuckle was filthy and for once, he was too tired to remember his language in front of the little girls. "Too old, You Dirty Bugger? Hah! That'll be the day," he smirked. "I've a good mind to show her deliberately, it'd serve you right. I KNOW you taught these two. I still remember you dragging me into the kitchen at Firle that first Christmas I was in England and showing me how to charm Mrs Farthing. Bloody hell, I was barely five," he laughed again at Francis's comically panicked expression. "I know you claim to have taught me everything I know," he chuckled, "but there's a whole lot more I've picked up since, so I might well give Cat a few ideas." He shooed Lizzie off his lap, "Go and put your coat on and get your dollies, Sweetie Pie, then take them out to the coach. Auntie Bella is asleep in there so wake her up," he smiled wickedly. "Come along, Terrie, let's go home and find Duchess and Mama's best bonnet," and with another chuckle he started to saunter out of the study. "See you anon, Un-cul Fran-sisssss," he smirked.

The last thing Francis heard was his daughter's query as she trotted from the room behind Nicky. "What's a dirty bugger, Un-cul Nicky?" Francis put his despairing head in his hands and started laughing all over again.

Chapter Thirty

They were sitting in Nicky's study later that afternoon. Bella was fast asleep, the cat had gone to ground long ago and the little girls were 'helping' make jam tarts for tea down in the kitchen while creating more chaos there.

"So, my final words on the subject are quite simple, Nicky," Francis intoned gravely, "DON'T be a hero and keep your head DOWN. Heroes tend to end up very dead in my experience." His advice was brutal and he looked Nicky dead in the eye as he spoke. The latter had rarely heard Francis speak so seriously, or frighteningly. Then Francis continued, just as directly, "I've always felt that, at least working for Ashcroft, your life was in your own hands as a lot of the time you could assess the risks of what you were at, but in a battle," he shrugged eloquently. "Well, Ashcroft and I both agree there's a monumental one coming soon, when Wellington finally squares up against Boney. It's often in the lap of the Gods or Fate and no man is safe on a battlefield, you can simply be in the wrong place at the wrong time. You fall and the man next to you still stands; it was the same on board ship, back in my Shadow days, when I dabbled in a bit of piracy and His Majesty's Navy had their guns on us, or other pirate vessels wanted what we had. Fate is a strange mistress and we all want you back in one piece." Francis sat back in his chair with a worried sigh.

Nicky had always wanted to know about Francis's pirating adventures and this would have been the perfect opportunity to delve, but it was simply not the occasion as they had no time for reminiscences. "I know, Francis," he said quietly. "I'll be as careful as I can, I promise. I'm not the headstrong, silly bastard I was a year or so ago, things have changed. I've got Bella and Terrie to worry about now, believe me."

"I'm glad to hear it and I can see you've changed. If you don't mind me saying so, I think you've finally matured, grown up if you like. In fact, you're just like me when I was your age. You wake up one day and suddenly realise there's more to life than whatever demon or thrill you're chasing or running from, In the end, there's other, more interesting, more serious or more important things in life."

"Mmmm, exactly." Nicky was thoughtful for a while, staring into the fire and changed the subject. "What are you going to do about Ashcroft, Francis? Are you going to tell him the truth about you and The Shadow?"

For the first time ever between them, Francis looked at Nicky and asked him for his advice. "I still don't know. What do YOU think I should do?"

Nicky was touched beyond words. Francis had been his hero, his mentor, the man he'd admired and idolised his entire life and who he'd tried to model himself on. In turn, Francis had tried to guide and teach him everything he knew about being both a Duke and a simple, ordinary man, as well as a lover, a fighter and an English Gentleman. He'd never tried to be a loving father to him, that was what Eddie had done, splendidly in his opinion. Somewhere along the line, as Nicky had grown to adulthood, Francis had morphed from uncle to being like a benevolent, rascally, big loving brother, even with twenty-five years between them. So Nicky looked the older man straight in the eye.

"I personally think you should tell him. Everything. He knows a lot already anyway and God knows, he's nobody's fool. Oh, I know he can be a ruthless and manipulative bastard, but then doing what he does, he has to be." He sat back and watched Francis consider his words. "I trust him implicitly, Francis and for me that applies to very few men, other than you and Papa, Reynard and Benjy. He knows so much about so many powerful people, I'm sure he won't say a word. He's even taken to meeting me out of his office if he wants to bring the subject up, which is no doubt why he was with you at home yesterday and I met him in the park. Chalmers is his right-hand man, been with him for years, knows everything about everything else, but Ashcroft is even more secretive and wary than us, it appears. He's fascinated, y'know and he admires and respects you a lot. Besides, what can he do? Lock you in the Tower?" he finally chuckled. "I'd stake my life there's plenty more members of the Establishment and the Ton out there who've done far worse. You were only a smuggler after all, even if I think there was a lot more to what you did than you've ever told me about...like your pirating days with Benjy...?"

Francis ignored the fishing comment. "It's a capital offence, I could swing. Not only did I have a price on my head, I killed a lot of people over the years ," Francis said quietly. "Not that they didn't deserve it in my opinion. However, I never killed anyone just for the thrill of it, unless it was accidental or couldn't be helped when we fought at sea and ships went down, unlike many others I ran with; I knew a lot of ruthless pirates as well as smugglers," he sighed. "Most were utter scum: vicious, merciless, greedy bastards, but there were one or two like me, not many though; most would sell their own mothers. Anyway, I broke more laws than I could count from murder downwards, plus I defrauded His Majesty's Government of a fortune in taxes while I made myself a tidy sum from it all, in stolen goods and booty."

"On top of the Firle one," Nicky grinned, fascinated as Francis started to reminisce. "What DID you do with the money? I always wondered?" he asked absently.

"I gave a lot away, I didn't need it," Francis shrugged. "I gave a lot to Reynard who didn't know what to do with it either, being an itinerant gypsy, although I think he's finally going to settle down somewhere more permanent soon, a vineyard last I heard and make wine; drink it all more like," he chuckled. "I helped set Benjy up in business and gave him a load, so why he's still pottering around here, I don't know; but he says he misses me," he chuckled again. "Uncle Gerard had his own little pot, but I topped it up so he could live in comfort for the rest of his days and poor Amandine and Aunt Florence will be well looked after. I set up charities, helped as many French *émigrés* as I could," he laughed, "that was accidental when I brought Cat and Eddie and their family over from Rouen and things just went from there. I tried to give you some but you wouldn't have any of it," and he shook his head. "I helped as many of my old crew and captains as I could find, a lot of army veterans and the wounded back from the wars, poor bastards; Cat spends a great deal on helping waifs and strays where she can, you know what she's like, just look at Jack…and there's still a load left, which I really must do something about…" he spoke almost to himself. "I keep forgetting about it. It's sitting in a cave I had dug, deep underground in some remote fields at Firle, far away from prying eyes. Benjy and I brought a lot of it back from France when I'd recovered from my last little adventure with Bernheim's father, then gradually, Benjy and I brought the rest over bit by bit on a few, quiet and quick trips back to Normandy, which no one knew about, especially Cat. The Revolution and the Terror were really getting going, so don't you EVER say anything! I used to store it in a cave under a ruined marble temple in the grounds of Uncle Gerard's old house in Normandy," he sighed at the memories, "which is where it all began. Did I ever tell you the whole story?"

For a while, finally, over a glass of brandy and a cheroot, without being pushed, he reminisced to Nicky about some of his old adventures with Reynard, Benjy and his late uncle. Nicky was completely riveted and fascinated, trying to picture and reconcile the urbane and handsome aristocrat sitting opposite him, a pillar of the British Establishment and High Society, friend of Prime Ministers and Royalty, with the strong, ruthless pirate he'd been for a short time. A man who'd started out helping his Uncle Gerard smuggle the odd bit of brandy and tobacco across the Channel, which was how he'd originally met Reynard, had built up a vast smuggling empire in a very short space of time. The same man who had squirreled Nicky with Bella's family out of France at the start of the Revolution, falling in love with and marrying Bella's aunt in the process. He'd only gone pirating because he was bored with smuggling and wanted more of a challenge and distraction from his Ducal responsibilities; it was too surreal for words, Nicky thought. However, Francis didn't go into any details about his piracy shenanigans and skirted around some of his nastier smuggling enterprises, so Nicky drew his own conclusions. He just assumed that part was an aberration the man regretted and had simply locked away in his attic. They all had their personal crosses to bear: him, Bella, Francis...so he didn't push, he understood only too well.

"I still think you should tell Ashcroft. It'll help him understand what's motivating Bernheim," Nicky finally said thoughtfully. "He half believes the bastard is going to come over here at some point to go after us and I'll tell you something, I happen to think he's right. For God's sake, don't tell Cat or Bella that, but maybe you should warn Papa?"

"Do you REALLY believe that?" asked Francis with a look of concern.

"Yes, I do. It's my worst nightmare," Nicky said softly. "His work for Bonaparte is nothing in my opinion, a sideline, a means to an end, to line his personal pockets; Ashcroft knows that now too. Bernheim is a menace with an ego the size of France and is mentally disturbed with it, seriously and properly so; and he's obsessed by us. He's got some weird idea in his brain that your fortune, The Shadow's ill-gotten gains and mine – the famed Valenciennes gold and family fortune we never found – should be his by right. I mean, why, for God's sake? He's mad, Francis, more insane than some of the poor buggers in Bedlam, except he's clever with it, that's what is so frightening about him. He looks and acts quite normally, in fact appears to be a cultured gentleman, but he isn't normal in the head. At all. Money is what he was really after when he took me in Nice; it's all he raved on about, remember I told you? He wasn't seriously interested in Wellington or English military secrets, that was by the by, all he wants is money, just like his father when he took you prisoner. Except, unlike his father, I suspect that you, me, all of us, his father's mysterious death, have been a lifelong, deranged and now growing obsession, exacerbated since he discovered who I was and because I've now twice thwarted his nefarious money-making plans. Which is unfortunate in the extreme but couldn't be helped. I've racked my brains, Francis. My family's fortune is one thing, but I never knew anything about any golden hoard. I don't know where Bernheim's father got that from and there's no one around now who might have heard about it who would know or remember, all dead in the Revolution or from old age, no doubt. But the man's utterly consumed by it and it's inextricably mixed up in his mind with you, The Shadow."

"I've already doubled the security on all our houses, even Eddie's, though he doesn't know it, as I don't want to worry him and also, everyone is followed when they go out." Francis grinned a knowing smile. "THAT'S how I know what you and Bella were doing yesterday, You Dirty, Lecherous Bugger! Building repairs, my foot; what on earth did you need an entirely empty property for? No, don't tell me, my imagination has run riot enough as it is and I need to see Bella in a new light," he laughed, but he then turned deadly serious again. "I've had to do it, no one believes me nor takes any notice when I nag them always to take a groom or footman when they go out, not that half of them are really grooms, footmen or sundry retainers, they're all ex-military men out of the army. Well..." he shrugged at Nicky's widened eyes, "it gives them employment when they've finished their service; Heaven knows, there's not much work around for them, poor sods and some are very capable men."

"You should start some sort of security business," commented Nicky idly.

"I already have," joked Francis and laughed at Nicky's wide-eyed expression. "There's plenty of trouble brewing here in England with all the radicals and so much poverty around," he sighed. "Ever since Perceval got shot in the Houses of Parliament, people have suddenly become a lot more wary. Rich people, the well-to-do and aristocrats are frightened. Some, aristocrats especially, have long memories and remember Madame Guillotine and The Terror, the dead King and Queen and countless other headless nobility," he grimaced.

"You sly bastard," Nicky smiled, "but I'm glad you've done something. I don't know what all those ex-soldiers are going to do when this damn War is eventually over once and for all. There's enough of them in France too which is why they're all flocking to join Boney again. They don't know anything else other than how to fight. At least here, our factories and manufacturing are steaming ahead and the prospects for trade around the globe are opening up more and more; we seem to be building everywhere, so there will be work if you're willing to knuckle down. Navvy, shopkeeper, factory worker and the rest. But France is still in a mess, except perhaps Paris which Bonaparte has started to reorganise. But, unless they get a sensible Government over there, with or without a monarchy, I don't know how they'll get the country industrialised and back on its feet, embracing ALL the people, rich and poor, peasant and noble. As things are now, it's a recipe for further trouble, I'm sure of it."

Francis merely nodded in agreement and the pair of them sat quietly for a while before Nicky sighed. "Look Francis, I'm going to tell you, I've left instructions here with Carstairs that if anything untoward or strange, happens, or for some reason you're not around either, there's a letter in my desk to be opened in emergency and it's got Ashcroft's direction in it. He'll know what to do." He leaned forward, "I trust him and I think you should too, Francis."

Francis smiled at him. "You're getting more like me every day, Nicky, but I happen to think that's a wise decision. The man is devious and cunning and in some ways, I don't trust him an inch. But he has England's best interests at heart and in this case, ours too, I hope. I actually think perhaps you're right. I'll tell him." He took a deep breath, "Do you approve then?"

"You're asking my approval?" Nicky was stunned.

"Yes, I am. Bernheim wants me, as I am, or was, The Shadow and he also wants you. If he's half the menace you and Ashcroft believe he is, then it's more than my secret now. Cat killed his father and Bernheim suspects that, though of course we don't know for sure what he's found out, nor what he'll do," he sighed again. "For what it's worth, Eddie arrived at lunchtime and I had a quiet conversation with him about all this too, as you suggested, because he sees things from a different perspective sometimes. He agrees with you, so it's decided then. I'll tell Ashcroft when I next meet him. In any case, I should see if he's recovered from his introduction to the mad Granville household," he chuckled. "I dare say it'll make his day as he's been driving me mad for months, years even. I'm actually tired of playing cat and mouse with him."

"I'm glad. I think you've taken the right decision." Nicky felt relieved. "You will keep a close eye on Bella and Terrie when I'm away, won't you? And I mean a CLOSE eye," Nicky asked worriedly. "Bella's deeply involved now too. She suffered terribly at his hands, it was beyond shocking what she had to do to inveigle her way into his villa, once I finally wormed it out of her. Just because she's educated and has read so much and keeps herself informed on all sorts of matters, including somewhat inappropriate material for a well-bred Lady, not to mention running her gaming saloons and being more assertive and opinionated than a lot of her peers, she thinks she's a woman of the world now. But there are some things of which she had no knowledge or experience and being confronted with the reality of them took a terrible toll on her. I've tried to put it right, put everything into some sort of perspective, hopefully succeeded, but she still needs an eye kept on her."

"I rather suspected as much when you told me how you escaped; Cat and I knew something wasn't right with Bella when you all got home, but I hope she's over it now," said Francis softly. "Don't worry about her, Nicky, she's as good as another daughter to me, you know that and Cat has always tried to mother her as best she can after Carlotta died. The two are very close now, which is good for both of them, you know how they love to gossip together. If necessary, she and Terrie can come and live here again while you're away; whatever it takes."

"It's just, if he does catch me again, I don't know if I can hold out, not tell him anything." It was one of Nicky's deepest worries and he couldn't bear to keep it to himself any longer. "I'm sorry, Francis," he shook his head, "he nearly killed me before, the pain, you have no idea. If Bella and Jack hadn't come..." he left his words hanging in the air.

"Dear God," Francis was horrified. "Don't apologise for it, Man, I know what he did to you, you're only human and anyway, remember what his father did to me. Don't you think of all people in England I understand? I was in the same boat," he laughed strangely. "I actually told Dupont and Bernheim I was the rich Duke of Firle and my grand-mother would ransom me, pay them anything, I couldn't help myself; but they never believed me. The irony of it, all my fortune, the Shadow's was nothing." He shivered at the terrible memories and he shifted uncomfortably as he felt his burned and scarred back twinge, even after more than twenty years.

They talked on and eventually Francis went to collect his daughter from a relieved and exhausted nursemaid, together with her dolls and a box of strangely shaped jam tarts she insisted on taking home for her mother, him and Bubbles to eat. As he bade Francis farewell at the door of his coach, hustling in before him a chattering tot with a mouth full of jam tart and sticky hands, a sudden remembered thought occurred to Nicky. "Oh, Francis, by the way, Bella said to ask you if it was all right for her to tell me an old story about the Dowager? She said she thought I ought to know but I had to ask you first. Something about a picture?" He looked puzzled and then wide-eyed at Francis's odd expression. The man turned to him and stood, unheeding of the rain, looking enigmatic and thoughtful.

As they lingered there getting increasingly soaked, Nicky's curiosity grew. "You loved her very much, didn't you?" Francis said quietly. Not really a question, more a conclusion being formed.

Nicky nodded. "You know I did, as much as you, in my own way," he admitted quietly. "I still miss her terribly."

"She loved you too. She often told me it was like having a second grandson and she was so proud of you and terribly worried you were going to let Bella slip through your fingers." Francis continued to stand in the teeming rain, lost in thought. "You love Bella very much now, don't you?" he asked and Nicky nodded again, completely perplexed. "You finally understand what love is all about, how it can pull someone apart, change their life, for good or bad, how you could make a terribly wrong decision, like you so nearly did?" Again, Nicky nodded, thinking about how he'd almost lost Bella through his own stupid pride.

"I'd trust you with my life," Francis finally said. "You know about The Shadow, all my secrets, you're like a little brother to me, so close, so like me in a lot of ways I find quite eerie sometimes. There are only two other people in the world who know the story, Cat and Bella. I don't ever intend to tell the boys, they don't even know about The Shadow and that's how it will remain. My grandmother told Bella, literally hours before she died, leaving it to Bella to tell me. I never knew, not even Eddie knows and I'm not sure whether I'll tell him either, close as I am to him; he doesn't need to know, because it will never affect him." He looked at Nicky gravely for a further long, considering moment. Then, "Ask Bella to tell you, you deserve to know. You loved your Granny Granville and she loved you. You'll understand now about her Will, the letter..." and with that strange, choked speech he turned and got in the coach. Nicky stood in the downpour, watching it clatter away down the street. He hurried inside the house to find his wife, consumed with curiosity and rarely, if ever, having heard Francis talk like that.

Chapter Thirty-One

When Bella took him upstairs to the little locked attic room he'd always assumed was full of accumulated, unwanted household bits and pieces, old clothes and furniture, she did the same thing to him as she'd done to her uncle. She wouldn't let Nicky look at the painting of Francis's real grandfather until she'd related the Dowager's story of a love discovered and then lost, a fortune made, a life changed by one wrong decision and then full of bitter regrets to the very end. Nicky was completely dumbfounded and stared long and hard at the picture, realising the impact the truth about his real parentage must have had on Francis. He also realised why the Dowager had nagged him about Bella and left him her fortune. He was speechless and staggered and sat for a long time going over it all in his mind after Bella had crept from the room to leave him to his thoughts.

When he finally returned downstairs to find her, locking the door to the little room behind him, she was sitting quietly in her bedroom waiting for him. "I can't believe it," he whispered. "Dear God, if anybody knew or found out...it makes the story of The Shadow a nothing. Imagine the scandal? It would destroy him, the family..." He was still stunned and sank down on to her bed.

"No one will EVER find out that his real grandfather wasn't the old Duke," said Bella quietly. "Other than us, I gave my word to Great Aunt Elizabeth I'd tell Lizzie, when I deem her to be old enough, trustworthy, mature and sensible enough, to understand, though Heaven knows when that will be, the little baggage!" She held out her hand with the little gold signet ring on. "This is the ring he gave her; it's in my keeping for Lizzie, but Uncle Francis wanted me to have it until then. I still don't think he's come to terms with it, even now," She shook her head. "It shocked him to the core, more than me. He genuinely had no idea as she never told him anything. She was frightened he would run away to the Americas, like you threatened to do," she finally whispered as she took Nicky's hand. "Now do you understand why she did what she did, for you, for us?"

Bella continued to speak softly, "She truly believed you loved me even if you didn't realise it yourself at the time and of course, she knew how much I loved you. She also knew the only way to save you from yourself was to leave you her fortune and she told me never, ever, to give up on you, to follow you wherever you went. She was an amazing, lovely old woman and I'm beyond sad her life was so full of regrets and unhappiness that she lost the man she deeply and I suspect passionately, loved, much as I find it hard to picture her lost in the throes of lust and desire. But the man affected her so deeply, which explains why she was so full of regret, sorrow and bitterness for the rest of her life…and because I love you so much, I can in an odd way understand how she felt, as I would be the same if I lost you."

Tears started to run down Nicky's face. His emotions had been raw since the dawn hours and this was almost too much for him. Bella took him in her arms and kissed him. "That's partly why I followed you to France. I wasn't going to give up on you and I'll follow you wherever you go, My Love. I'm never going to lose you."

"Oh, Sooty," he choked, "I don't deserve you, any of you, what the family has done for me." Wracking sobs shook him as he wept. "After all, I was only an unintended acquisition, because I happened to be in Dupont's quarters and Madre refused to abandon me there to my fate. They didn't know who on earth I was, never expected to rescue anyone else, just Cat and Papa's family…but now, here I am."

"Hush now," she soothed him, wiping his cheeks. "Never say such a thing, it's complete twaddle. Mama took one look at you, and your fate was sealed. There was no way she would have ever left you behind, neither she, nor Auntie, nor Uncle Francis, nor the priest who helped them. Where's the Nicky I know? Come now, My Darling, you must know we all love you to bits and you gave the Dowager such pleasure over the years, I know you did, we all do. It's over and we're together now. She must be happily watching from Heaven with Mama and we can live happily ever after, with your little pride of Lions," she giggled. "Those wretched lions, it was all her fault taking you to The Tower to see them in the first place and putting that idea in your brain."

He laughed despite himself, wiping his eyes, slightly embarrassed to have broken down and sobbed in front of her. "Do you think so, Sooty? Did I make her happy?" He took a deep breath and pulled himself together. "I wish I wasn't going away, I love you so much I can't bear it and I loved her too as well as your Mama, my Madre; do you really think they're watching us from Heaven?"

Feeling emotional herself but relieved he was now more himself before she started crying with him, Bella chuckled. "You did make them both extremely happy and I'm sure they're watching over you. The Dowager will be a fearsome Guardian Angel, I'm quite sure," and despite himself, Nicky laughed at a sudden picture in his mind of the redoubtable old woman with cherubic wings. "Except," Bella gave him a wicked smile and poked him in the ribs, "I sincerely hope they were asleep last night and weren't watching, for they would have been completely scandalised, appalled and shocked!" making they both burst out laughing.

He kissed her then and looked down into her eyes, suddenly serious. "Are you all right, Sooty? Are YOU scandalised, appalled and shocked?" His eyes were now full of concern. "I never meant it to go so far, truly I didn't," he said softly. "I don't know quite what happened, all those things I made you do, what you did to me, where did they come from? And then, what I did to you at the end of it." He looked shamefaced. "I only meant us to have a bit of fun, to put your fears at rest and show you that what happened with Bernheim was wrong, so very wrong," he whispered, "and that when you love someone, it should just be love and pleasure and fun between the two of you, no matter what you do together," he sighed. "Because it's no one's affair except yours. Your Mama and Papa were like that, I'm sure they were and I know Francis and Cat are, you know how close they are and how devoted and happy. You had such a sheltered upbringing, despite all your books and reading, I just wanted to bring you out of yourself a bit, but when I'm with you, like when you were playing at being *Lionesse*, I... er... it all seems to get a bit carried away." He shook his head and pleaded, "Please, Sweetheart, tell me you don't mind and I promise I'll never do any of that to you again."

"Oh, stop looking like a worried hen who's lost a chick, You Moron," she sighed. "You know, Nicholas de Bresancourt, Ashcroft and I are absolutely right, you are completely brainless," Bella admonished slowly, shaking her head. "If I hadn't wanted to participate in your little 'games', I know, and you know," she poked him in the chest again and he looked startled, "there is no way I would have let you, or you would have made me; would you?"

She got up for a moment and started to prowl up and down in front of him. "I'm not talking about the whole Bernheim episode here, I'm talking about you and me," she said seriously, then suddenly she grinned. "Now you listen to me, You Idiot Man; I may have had a Lady's sheltered upbringing, but I am not a ninny like most of those silly women at Almack's. I do know babies don't appear under gooseberry bushes and most aristocratic marriages are some sort of arrangement rather than for romantic love, rarely for lust and passion. But for Heaven's sake, I did grow up a lot of the time in a house with Uncle Francis and Aunt Cat and I'm well aware their relationship is FAR from sedate; in fact I know it's positively scandalous, as I'm sure you're well aware too, seeing how thick you and Uncle Francis are. My dear parents had their moments too, little girl though I was before Mama died. Walls and doors are thin, you know, Mama was a trifle noisy in the bedroom and none of them were hugely discreet on occasion, even if I didn't totally understand what was going on behind the walls and doors at the time, especially when Mama moaned and screamed!"

Nicky looked aghast at her revelation which made her giggle. "But knowing about something and actually being confronted with it, let alone doing and experiencing it, are a whole other matter, especially for an inexperienced woman. I think that you do at least realise that." She paused for breath and then carried on, "And unlike you, I WAS terribly inhibited about it all. When it started, because you couldn't see me or watch me, that's when I started to lose my shyness. It was quite ironic and unintended of course, though Heaven knows why I was so shy when I grew up with a wretch like YOU, then my dreadful male Granville cousins who delighted in teasing me, running around naked and stroking themselves into an interesting condition when they KNEW I would see, filthy lot that they are, all encouraged by YOU I'm sure, without a self-conscious bone in your entire delicious body!" Nicky laughed at that, earning him a severe look. "But there you are. I needed you to force me to deal with my shyness after that first interlude at *Le Lion d'Or* and, well, you certainly did that," she finished. "Now, I'm just trying to come to terms with what I, me, myself, actually did. It's not so much what we did, shocking though that was at first. I knew about most of it and the rest of it, well I suppose people have been doing that for centuries and writing about it in books, but it's just that I, Bella, did it and I, um...quite enjoyed it and I just have to get my head around what I felt and why and, well you've obviously been doing all that with some Ladies of the Ton for years so why not me too?" she came to a sudden stop.

"Good God," gasped Nicky, "I thought it was just some slightly salacious sex I was worrying about! I didn't bank on philosophy and self-analysis." He smiled ruefully, "But all the same, Sweetheart, I do realise some of it was a bit much for someone not very experienced and whatever you may think, some of it did go WAY over most ordinary women's standards, I can assure you. Many men wouldn't approve either, believe me."

"Are you inferring I'm just an Ordinary Woman?" Bella looked affronted and started to tick items off on her fingers, "How many women do you know of my age who run two gambling houses, very successfully and profitably I might add; manage their own fortune and someone else's, I mean Lizzie's; can speak three languages fluently,

plus read Latin and Greek to the same standard; is a crack shot, virtually unbeatable at cards and chess – and is now a novice agent in Lord
Ashcroft's secret service?" she grinned. "And produces beautiful
golden haired children..." she added.

"Piffling," choked Nicky. "You can't sew a stitch, sing or play
music, you can't even draw a stick man, nor do you know one end of a
recipe from another; most 'Ordinary Women' can, as well as
procreate."

"What would you rather have then, Your Grace?" queried Bella
slyly. "An Ordinary Woman who sews samplers all day, does boring
needlepoint and sketches useless pictures or paints dull watercolours,
whilst singing to herself, who would faint away from shock at your
stripping act, or the sight of your ribbons and disgraceful silver chain,
or one who can't sing a note but can fuck you unconscious?" she
grinned triumphantly and laughed out loud at his expression at her
lewd speech.

"How am I ever going to cope with you?" he laughed. "You'd
terrify most men I know, no wonder Ashcroft is so smitten with you,
the old goat."

"Do I intimidate you?" Bella asked worriedly; she'd learned long
ago to keep her intelligence hidden from most men in Society. They
hated any woman with a brain or independent thought and ran a mile
from them, no matter how beautiful they were, unless they were men
like Ashcroft, or her Papa and Uncle Francis. Or Nicky.

"You're joking," Nicky laughed. "I know you far too well, and I
know just how to deal with a Brainy Bossy Boots."

"You do?" said Bella curiously. "How's that?"

"Come here and I'll show you," he grinned wickedly and pulled
her into his arms for a passionate kiss.

The family spent a happy evening at Firle House, all together, laughing
and joking as they always did, the men never revealing an inkling of
the quiet fears they'd discussed earlier between themselves.

Deliberately to irritate Francis, when they all sat down for dinner,

Nicky 'accidentally' let his shirt-cuffs fall back when he was sitting next to Cat and knew the minute she'd spotted his wrists. Her eyes widened, then narrowed slyly as she gazed from him to Bella who in turn looked up and choked on her soup, going beetroot red and coughing as she hastily pulled her fichu up round her neck and pulled her unusually half loose hair around it, then twiddled with the large, unusually ostentatious bracelets she was wearing on both wrists. Francis eyed Nicky venomously when Cat gave her husband a knowing, lecherous look, which made Nicky nearly fall off his chair in mirth and Eddie blithely carried on drinking his soup as if nothing else was going on at the table other than a mundane discussion about the terrible weather. Elise Montgomery, the new addition to the family and soon to be the new Baroness de Mornay, sat serene, impassive, silent and ladylike throughout, but Nicky could have sworn he saw her lips twitch. No wonder the Dowager had liked her so much, he thought to himself, she obviously missed nothing. Another quiet person with hidden depths he surmised, just like his step-father and he grinned in pleasure she was going to marry him.

That night, Nicky and Bella loved each other simply, quietly and intensely, in the peaceful darkness of his Hertford Street bedroom, a million miles from the torrid interlude of the previous night. In the morning Nicky left her, tears coursing down her face, bravely waving goodbye yet again, with all the family on the doorstep of the mansion in Berkeley Square, watching as his coach rolled away.

No one noticed the anonymous hackney carriage waiting quietly on the other side of the Square with the stony-faced man sitting inside, his obsidian eyes watching it all intently. He took particular note of the individuals standing there in front of the large mansion, all the players in the strands of a story he was finally pulling together as he continued to hatch his plan of misplaced entitlement, obsessive revenge and outright greed.

Chapter Thirty-Two

"So, Granville, who else knows?" Ashcroft finally asked. They were ensconced in Ashcroft's office a few days after Nicky had departed with Wellington. The ever-present Chalmers was now on the missing list and the outer office was deserted. Ashcroft had risen to lock the main door to the Department of Information as soon as Francis had started his story about The Shadow, along with all the other doors that led out of Chalmer's outer office. No one was going to come in and have an opportunity to eavesdrop. Nicky was right, Ashcroft was beyond wary.

"Oh, for God's sake, Ashcroft, call me Francis, this pantomime has gone on long enough," Francis smiled at Ashcroft.

"Then call me Miles, please," Ashcroft smiled back.

"No one other than those few people I've mentioned in my story...and now you," said Francis.

Ashcroft looked at the Duke thoughtfully. "I'm extremely flattered you've finally taken me into your confidence," he said quietly.

"Are you going to send me to Newgate or The Tower?" grinned Francis. "I would like to know so I can inform my butler if I'm to be home for dinner or not."

"I very probably should," responded Ashcroft icily, "not for being a smuggler, pirate, thief and murderer, or defrauding His Majesty's Government of much needed revenue...but you should definitely either swing or be transported for subjecting me to that 'interruption' in your house last week. Nelson and I still haven't recovered," his face was deadpan. "That hound of yours should be sent straight back to the Pyrenees."

"You know, Nicky said you were developing a sense of humour," responded Francis. "I should warn you that if you so much as lay a finger on Bubbles, my wife will run you through," he grinned again.

"I can well believe it. I'd already heard stories about her prowess with a rapier and also that she wears a nasty stiletto under her petticoats; you're all as peculiar as each other, you know," his face was still deadpan.

"Absolutely, I couldn't agree more," chuckled Francis. "You do realise if you continue to associate closely with us, you're likely to get contaminated with our disease. By the way, it's incurable. Consider yourself warned...imagine the Head of the Department of Information being considered deranged..."

"I'm immune," said Ashcroft disdainfully, but Francis suspected he saw a lip twitch.

"That's what you think..." and Francis chuckled. "Is there anything you don't know, Miles?" he then enquired.

"Not much," responded Ashcroft, now with a sly grin. "You know now how much I'd already discovered about you and your underhand activities, even it was twenty-five or thirty years ago."

Francis sighed. He'd been both astonished and horrified to realise how much Ashcroft knew about The Shadow from all sorts of sources in Normandy he wouldn't disclose. "What now then? What do you make of Bernheim's disappearance? I have to confess it disturbs me greatly; Nicky too."

"That facetious young pup?" but Ashcroft smiled. "I hope he's keeping his head down and out of the local ladies' petticoats," he tutted. "Wellington wanted someone to go undercover amongst the French forces and pick up any tidbits of gossip that might relate to strategy, troop movements, you know what I mean. He was the best man I have," he sighed. "It's hugely dangerous, but if anyone can do it,

I know he can. His methods are somewhat unorthodox at times, but he knows what he's up against and they seem to work…well they will, providing he doesn't need his boots mended this time," he tutted again.

"He's changed a lot y'know," said Francis thoughtfully, somewhat alarmed by Ashcroft's revelation of why Wellington really wanted Nicky. "That business in Nice I suspect…but he's grown up and come to his senses and has finally realised how much he loves Bella. I don't think you'll find him in anyone's petticoats except hers from now on, unless it's for your villainous purposes and he has no other option."

"Really? I'm glad to hear it, I happen to think very highly of your niece. She went through a great deal to save him from Bernheim down in Nice."

"Mmmm, I know," mused Francis. "But the question still remains, where is that bastard now?"

Ashcroft look very seriously at Francis. "I think he's here in London…" he said quietly.

Francis swore and sat forward in alarm. "What in Hell makes you think that?"

Ashcroft tapped his nose, "I'm reliably informed someone has been making enquiries about your family down in Sussex, near your local village."

"WHAAAT?" Francis was seriously alarmed and his face paled.

"Mmmm," said Ashcroft, "some of your new 'gardeners' know some of my itinerant 'gardeners' plus grooms, road sweepers, tinkers, beggars, vagrants…" he shrugged and smirked. "A couple of them happened to be in a quiet tavern having a drink a little way from Firle around two weeks ago. When your 'gardener' returned to your estate, mine was just finishing his ale when he overheard someone asking some very interesting questions about you and your various family members, including where they all lived in the locality. Could possibly have been French, my man wasn't sure. Anyway, to cut a long story short, he followed the fellow but lost him somewhere on the road back to London." He sighed, "It was pure chance my man happened to be in the tavern at the right time; piece of luck, really."

Francis swore again under his breath, "You've been watching my homes then?"

"Naturally, also those of your other family members connected to The Shadow. I'm glad to see you've enhanced your own security too," said Ashcroft, "not that I think it will do any good, personally," he mused. "Fine if all you want is to keep out burglars or protect yourselves from trouble-making radicals, especially when your family members go out and about; extremely wealthy and titled people can't be too careful these days, especially at night. But Bernheim is far too clever to try anything so obvious. Oh no..." he looked thoughtful, "I wouldn't if I was in his shoes."

Francis's face was now ashen and then his eyes narrowed, "What do YOU think he'll do?"

Ashcroft sat back in his chair and steepled his fingers under his chin. "I'm not sure," he mused slowly. "He's not his father and this country isn't as corrupt or dangerous as some parts of Normandy were when Edgar Bernheim was running the militia there, when he was Governor, hauling people off to that medieval fortress you destroyed, for his own personal gain under the guise of 'treason'. Frederick Bernheim has got to be much more careful and underhand over here, not drawing attention to himself in any way. One thing I am certain of, though," he paused, "he won't do anything while Nicky is out of the country. He wants you...or rather, The Shadow and his fortune, but he wants Nicky more, I'd stake my life on it. For personal revenge as well as his Valenciennes fortune, whether it exists or not. Bernheim won't make his move until he's back in England again. That's when we'll have to start worrying."

Francis looked at Ashcroft. "What do you suggest I do?" He was filled with anger and worry for his family, now hugely grateful to have the wily and able Ashcroft in his confidence and someone else he could talk to. He thanked God he'd listened to Eddie and especially Nicky and therefore confessed to the man. It was almost unknown for The Shadow to ask for anyone's help and guidance, but Francis was now older and wiser than he'd been twenty-five or thirty years before and it was a weight off his shoulders to have another outlet for his worries. Apart from Nicky, of course, who was now away again and the cerebral Eddie, whose opinion he'd always valued from the day he'd first met him and to whom he'd taken an instant and strange liking. Twenty-five or even more years before that, other than his grandmother, Uncle Gerard, Reynard, Benjy and Richard Ambrose, an old friend who knew nothing about his alter ego, he'd had no one particularly in his life who'd cared for him, or about whom he had cared to the extent he would rein back his dangerous lifestyle as The Shadow. Then he had met, fallen in love with and married Marie-Catherine de Mornay and his whole life had changed. Now, he was surrounded by an extended close family to whom he was devoted, who were his life and for whom he felt responsible. It made an enormous difference.

Ashcroft leaned forward and said softly, "Don't fret too much, Francis, at least for the time being. There's nothing you can do but I'm watching your back, you're not alone anymore." Francis's eyes widened. "I'm keeping my eyes and ears open and if we find him, we'll dispense with him quietly and no one will be any the wiser." He looked directly at Francis. "You may have been The Shadow, quite frankly I couldn't give a toss about that and besides, you know it will never go beyond these four walls. However, what you've done for your country and other people, then and since, is considerable and much appreciated in many quarters, so, believe it or not, I like and respect you very much. Therefore, the resources of this entire Department are on your side, not just me personally. That bastard killed a lot of my people too, very unpleasantly I might add. I take that extremely personally. I want him and I mean to get him. He's not making mischief in MY country and getting away with it, I can assure you."

Francis looked at the austere man across from him. He was shaken to his core. "I don't know what to say...except thank you, which doesn't begin to express my gratitude. It's not for me, it's my family, they were never part of all this and I couldn't face any of them getting hurt because of what I did all those years ago," he grimaced. "I never dreamed it would all come back to haunt me. Whoever would have believed Bernheim's son would be a threat after all this time? When Cat killed his father, we thought that would be an end to it all..." He banged a fist on the arm of his chair in frustration and swore to himself.

"Look, Francis, go home," said Ashcroft sympathetically, "and don't say anything to your family, even that clever brother-in-law of yours, not that I think you will, they'll only worry and there's nothing you can do for now. I have the resources to investigate and you don't, however much money you throw at it," he looked knowingly at Francis. "I know you'll realise I deliberately didn't tell Nicky all this. Heaven knows he's going to have enough on his plate over in Brussels with Wellington and he'll need to keep his wits about him without having to worry about what's going on here." He actually smiled at Francis, his expression reassuring as he leaned towards the other man. "I'll keep you informed if I hear anything...either here in London about Bernheim, or from Wellington's HQ about Nicky. I give you my word. That young scapegrace is one of my most resourceful men, apart from the fact I like him a good deal. But don't you EVER dare tell him I said either of those things," and Ashcroft actually winked at Francis

Francis sighed, "You're a good man, Miles, I'm so grateful now it's all out in the open between us and I can talk to you. Thank you for your help and I'm glad your people are watching out for us. I can't help but worry though. God knows how I'm going to sleep at night; I'll probably end up on midnight walks with Bubbles," he managed to laugh, brokenly.

"As long as you walk in a different place to me and Nelson, that will be all right," Ashcroft laughed. "Oh, talking of Nelson, that reminds me, I never did thank you for his collar; it completely slipped my mind last week, what with everything else."

Francis waved a hand in the air, "Piece of nonsense" he finally grinned.

"Diamonds, rubies and sapphires are a considerable piece of nonsense," said Ashcroft sarcastically.

"Not for England's greatest naval hero, surely? The Guardian of the Department of Information?" he looked down at the snoring, one-eyed dog sprawled in abandon in front of the fire.

Ashcroft chuckled. "But I couldn't let it go without getting you something in return," he said slyly and got up to retrieve a small square package from behind his desk which he handed over to Francis. "I dare say it's about time someone gave YOU a gift. It's for your mansion front gate in Berkeley Square, or your study door, whichever you feel is most appropriate," he said impassively. "Just a simple little gift I'm afraid, Government budgets, y'know; not quite up to bejewelled levels," he said, sighing.

Francis looked at the square package in curiosity and was about to open it when Ashcroft put a hand on his arm. "Oh no, not here, take it home and open it there. At the very least it might give Bernheim pause for thought, if he has any sense."

They spoke for a short while longer and then Francis took his leave. "Come to dinner, Miles, soon? I promise I'll tell Cat to keep her stiletto under her petticoats," he grinned. "I mean it, dinner that is."

Miles was touched, "I'd like that very much, Francis; thank you."

"My secretary will send you some dates. We're very informal as you've gathered, more interested in good company than making an impression; just bring your sense of humour now you seem to have developed one, with a spare pair of shoes, just in case..." and with a wicked wink, Francis sauntered out, leaving Ashcroft with his lips twitching.

Francis wandered around and around the Park on the way home, unaware of one of a squad of Ashcroft's men who now took it in turns to follow him everywhere, watching out for anyone who so much as looked at the Duke inappropriately, or appeared to also be watching his movements. He was lost in thought, deeply worried and frustrated. But he finally realised Ashcroft was right, there was little he could do except rely on the devious, all-seeing spymaster to keep his eyes and ears open and watch his back for him.

He got home and went into his study to pour himself a large brandy, then sat at his desk with the glass and his usual cheroot. He stared out of his window into the garden for a long time, lost in thought again as he sipped and smoked quietly. Eventually, he remembered the package and ripped open the paper covering and string.

It was just a small, plain brass plaque in a plain metal frame. Ready to be hung on an outside gate or a door, as Ashcroft had promised:

CAVE CANEM

THESE ARE <u>VERY DANGEROUS</u> PREMISES
DUE TO UNMANAGEABLE RESIDENTS.
ENTER AT YOUR PERIL

BY ORDER OF:
DEPARTMENT OF INFORMATION
His Majesty's Government

Francis's guffaws of laughter could be heard all the way down the corridor in the big mansion, bringing Browning to his study to enquire if there was anything amiss. Francis held out the plaque and told the bemused butler to hang it on the front gate, then burst out into further laughter at his affronted face. "Well, go along, Man, put it up," he chuckled, "PROMINENTLY, mind. The warning comes from the very highest echelons of Security in the whole bloody country...so who am I to ignore it?"

Chapter Thirty-Three

E aster was very late that year and as the end of April finally
approached, the spring weather had turned warmer. Cat had
gone down to Firle to prepare for the family gathering over
the forthcoming weekend, taking the two little girls with her for some
fresh country air and to vent their endless energy and mischief in the
estate gardens. A relieved peace reigned in the house in Berkeley
Square, but Francis secretly hated it and missed the constant chaotic
turmoil, usually caused by his noisy little daughter instead of his four
boisterous sons who were now grown up and away from home most
of the time, busy with their various interests or still at university. He
often called round to Hertford Street and, with his own key now,
would quietly go up to the attic room and sit there, deep in thought,
gazing at the picture of his grandfather, still amazed at his likeness to
the man his grandmother had loved, the whole sad episode and the
strangeness of fate. He was glad Bella had told Nicky the story so that
when the latter was home for good, Francis wouldn't have to explain
his odd comings and goings, even if Carstairs thought it all rather
strange.

One afternoon, he wandered downstairs and into Bella's little
sitting room. Jack had just arrived home from Eton for the Easter break

and was chattering to her with his news. Francis had grown very fond of the engaging young lad and had promised Nicky to take him under his wing while he was away. Bored by the peace in his own home, restless and privately fretting over the Bernheim issue, he was looking for a distraction and when he spied Jack, his eyes gleamed with relief and mischief.

Just before Francis and Nicky had taken him to Eton, the family had met to decide when Jack should have his birthday – he obviously needed one for his school application. He still had no idea how old he was, nor when he was born. After much debate and suggestion, Cat finally stood up and declared that since she had found Jack, she would decide. She said that because he was now a part of the wider Granville family, officially reborn as Jack Vallance, young Gentleman of leisure, his birthday should be on Easter Sunday as his former life was no more and he'd been resurrected from the Hell of The Dials to a fresh start in the Heaven that was Mayfair! Everyone groaned and rolled their eyes, but since nobody had a better idea and Jack was happy with it, she fetched a calendar and declared that the date of the following Easter Sunday would be his official birthday. As he was now a strapping young lad, they also all agreed with Bella that he seemed to be around sixteen. That was how it was decided and Jack would therefore turn seventeen at Easter.

So, Jack's birthday was upcoming and there would be a family party for him over the Easter weekend at Firle in a couple of weeks' time. Jack was still overwhelmed at how his fortunes had changed and was bemused by the prospect of having his first ever birthday party. He had matured over the past months at Eton and had fought every scrap of the way. Despite appearing with an escort of two Dukes, inevitably rumours arose about his background, servants' tittle tattle between aristocratic houses being what it was. He was accused of being everything from a Dials thief and murderer to a dirty, uncouth stable lackey, especially when it was discovered his sword-fighting ability was next to nothing and his education extremely patchy and lacking. As was typical in boys' public schools, bullying was rife and the worst offenders were cruel and heartless to those whom they believed didn't fit into their close-knit circle.

Jack was bullied, beaten and semi-tortured by his peers, but never once did he utter one single, betraying syllable of the gutter language of his birth, merely rising each time from the iniquities inflicted on him with a silent, disdainful aloofness. This of course confused his tormentors – he was always vague about his upbringing, merely saying he'd been abroad for years with an infirm, elderly relative who had died and that was how he'd been brought to live with the Duke of Valenciennes back in England, to whom he was distantly related. He generally kept to his silent self, most of the time, knowing the less he said the better, ignoring and simply rising above all the insinuations and questions. The alternative story about his Dials and stable background did the rounds, but it was his word against the gossips and he stuck to his story resolutely.

Francis and Nicky had been through the system and knew how it worked. Although they couldn't prevent the beatings and hardship, they could at least ensure other aspects of his life were apparently aristocratic. He'd been dressed to perfection by Benjy, the Duke of Firle's renowned valet and tailor, so was always immaculately and fashionably attired, in and out of his uniform, plus he had plenty of money to throw around for those who were impressed by such things. He modelled his perfect mannerisms on the two Dukes, both of whom he'd watched closely and charmed his teachers, absorbing his lessons like a sponge and working long into the night to catch up on his academic endeavours. Jack, however, could fight. Not as the other boys knew it, gentlemanly bouts of boxing were not for him. But gradually he learned to fight back against his tormentors and after he'd beaten several boys to a pulp, for which he was roundly caned by the teachers, most of his peers reluctantly came to accept him, even if many simply ignored him and the bullying lessened. A small group persisted in making his life a misery, but he could deal with that. He also learned to fight with a rapier, courtesy of Cat, Nicky and Francis and, since he practised incessantly, he was becoming quite a formidable fencer.

So Francis took Jack back to Berkeley Square with him, telling Bella he was going to continue with giving him a Gentleman's education in Nicky's absence until they went down to Firle. Bella merely grinned at this, suspicious as to quite what sort of 'education' her uncle had in mind, but keeping her amused thoughts to herself.

Francis talked to Jack in great detail about his earliest memories, privately agreeing with Bella there was definitely something aristocratic about his demeanour and physical characteristics. He had long, beautifully shaped hands which Bella had noticed from the first, but as he had grown even taller and his physique was starting to develop more, he was turning into a tall, lithely muscular and elegant young man with aristocratic high cheekbones, sparkling sherry eyes, thick glossy brown hair and a curling, sensual smile that he was learning how to use to advantage towards the young women he came across.

No matter how intensively Francis probed and Jack thought, he simply couldn't remember a single thing about his childhood except the grinding poverty and daily effort to keep alive in the fetid stews of The Seven Dials. He didn't know how he got his name, whether Vallance was his mother's name or his father's, or if they'd been married. He remembered little of his mother other than her name was Mary and that she'd died of a fever after virtually starving when she'd been unable to keep selling herself to keep her three children fed. Francis was shocked by the privations the boy had suffered to keep alive not only himself but his little half-sister and half-brother plus his adopted tribe of other children. After a particularly long afternoon of questions, Jack managed to remember a small necklet his mother had given him shortly before she'd died. He'd forgotten about it as he'd sold it almost immediately to buy food, no room for sentimentality when otherwise one starved; but under Francis's gentle probing, he said he thought the disc that hung from the chain had some sort of creature on it. He sat in Francis's study, gazing out through the window and thought long and hard, racking over long-ago memories and finally decided it was a dragon. Francis doodled images on a piece of paper for Jack to comment on and he eventually came to the conclusion it might have been some sort of Welsh dragon...but that was as far as it went. The image could have been a heraldic gryphon, or even some kind of medieval rampant lion design and Jack had no idea how his mother had come by the necklet. It could have been a gift from a customer, payment for her services in lieu of a coin, something she'd either found or stolen, he simply didn't know. When Francis asked if it could be an heirloom or clue to his parentage or identity, he'd shrugged his shoulders. His mother had never said, as far as he could remember and so the pair of them came to a dead end. Dragons didn't only relate to Wales and gryphons were everywhere, as were lions. Nicky could vouch for that as well as half the aristocracy and the royal family on their coats of arms!

In advance of his birthday, Francis took Jack to his personal little jeweller in Bond Street, the scene of his many crimes of unusual, comical and expensive gifts he had devised for his friends and family over the years, the last of which had been Nelson's collar. There, he collected a signet ring for him to wear on his little finger – the same as his own with the Firle crest and also like the one he'd bought Nicky on his seventeenth birthday so many years before with its lion coat of arms, about the only thing anyone had ever found in the ruins of the Valenciennes chateau that pertained to its former occupants. Jack's had a small fiery dragon on it with a ruby for its eye, just like the design Francis had drawn which pleased Jack inordinately. Francis didn't need the affectionate hug Jack gave him in the shop, his amazed and appreciative face said it all, apart from his endless words of thanks which he kept repeating as they made their way back down the street, the lad incessantly scratching his nose ostentatiously with his little finger, which entertained Francis no end.

The rest of the day they spent idling around Town and at Captain Carnie's fencing studio where Francis watched as the Captain himself, now well into his sixties but still a master, put Jack through his paces. He himself had a turn at fighting the lad while the Captain coached Jack from the sidelines. Jack was an adept pupil, taught and coached by Cat, Nicky and Francis over the previous months when the opportunity arose and was now quite a proficient fighter, certainly able to hold his own or sometimes surpass his peers at Eton and Francis was very pleased with his progress.

Finally, late that afternoon, they arrived at a discreet little establishment where Francis was greeted with screams of delight by its French proprietress who hadn't seen him for years, not since he'd taken Nicky there when he was Jack's age, more than ten years before. He had a quiet, humorous and unwanted financial interest in the business from a long ago favour he'd done the Madame, in return for a favour she'd done him in a roundabout way, and who insisted on sending him annual interest on her profits, which Francis always sent back, she returned, and then he sent anonymously to a charity for unmarried mothers. Their perennial game of bat and ball amused him and he'd told the Madame frequently to send the money direct to the charity, but she always insisted on sending it to him first...just so he would know how much interest he had earned from her splendidly profitable little business! Again, as he had with Nicky, Francis handed Jack over to her girls for a 'thorough furthering of his education' and with a broad wink, told him to stay there until he was worn out and that if he didn't see him in the meantime, he'd come and collect him when it was time to go down to Firle.

Over the next two weeks, during which time he never saw hide nor hair of the lad, to his comical entertainment, Francis devoted his time to investigating the boy's background. But no matter how far he searched – and he had one of his secretaries do nothing else as well – they could find no trace of any Welsh family with a crest like the dragon Jack had described, nor any aristocratic family at all with the name of Vallance. Francis also did what he could to trace any aristocratic French family with that name, though with the current situation in France, investigations over there were somewhat limited. Even his connections with the helpful French *émigré* community drew another blank. He'd been convinced Jack was a by-blow of some noble, but at the end of a fortnight of fruitless searching, he and his secretary faced one another across the desk in his study and concluded they had got absolutely nowhere.

"I just can't believe we've found nothing, Simpson," Francis sighed in frustration. "I'd stake a fortune he has noble blood in him somewhere. He is simply not from country or peasant stock, nor the offspring of some labourer; I mean, just look at his hands and those high cheekbones, for God's sake." Francis swore, "Dammit man, I refuse to give up on this!"

His secretary sighed also. "I know, Your Grace, but I've searched high and low. I've even had someone go over what records there are in

Paris, at least what's left of them with all the mess over there now, but I've heard nothing from them yet; bloody Frenchies," he swore under his breath. "Oh, begging your pardon, Your Grace."

Francis waved a hand dismissively. "I know," he sighed. "But even though we don't have a year for his birth, let alone a date, he would have been born long after the Revolution ended."

"Yes, Your Grace, but the country has been in chaos for years, what with Boney and the War and all, it's a real mess over there. But we could still put an advert in the paper like I suggested before?" Simpson offered.

"We can't risk that. If anyone saw it who knows him now, they'd soon find out at Eton and his whole cover in Polite Society would be blown. I'm not undoing all I'm sure he's gone through to do that to him, no matter how curious we are," and Simpson sighed in agreement.

"Vallance...Vallance," Francis muttered endlessly, as he drummed his fingers on the top of his desk, staring out through the study window.

"We could always try advertising in America or Canada?" suggested Simpson. "There's a lot of *émigrés* gone over there, if it is a French name, Vallance," he said it with a French accent. "It certainly seems more French than Welsh to me, despite that dragon necklet. Surely no one over there will associate it with a lad at Eton?"

"Mmmm..." said Francis thoughtfully, "that's an idea. Perhaps the French colonies in the West Indies, you could try there; didn't Bonaparte's first wife come from there? Get on with that, Man, everywhere in the Americas and Canada with a news sheet; good thinking," as he continued to drum his fingers. "Vallance, Vallance..." Simpson grinned, he knew once the Duke had a bee in his bonnet, it would plague him until he found a solution.

As they sat there pondering, there was a knock on the door and Bella poked her head round. "Are you busy or may I come in?" she enquired and strolled into the room.

"No, Puss, not at all; come in...that's all for now, Simpson," he sighed. "Keep digging."

"Yes, Your Grace." Simpson got up, bowed to Francis, then to Bella and hurried out. Bella took his place and looked at Francis, a big grin on her face. "I've had a letter from Nicky." She put a folded piece of paper on the desk in front of Francis.

Francis's big smile curled his mouth. "Well, well, that makes a change from his usual silence." He picked up the short missive and read it through, knowing what the man was really doing and how difficult it had been for him to communicate. He'd received a message from Ashcroft only the day before to say Nicky had been reconnoitring behind the French lines and had just returned safely to Brussels. He and Ashcroft had been hugely relieved.

"Mmmm, I know. It doesn't say much, full of his usual rubbish," she sighed, "but at least we know he's all right. Look at the date, it was only sent a few days ago; it came by a courier from the War Ministry, so he must have sent it in some sort of special delivery bag from Wellington's headquarters." She sighed again, "I suppose there are some consolations to being on his staff," and Francis grinned again.

"Can I keep this to show Cat, Eddie and Elise?" he asked. "They'll be thrilled, not to mention relieved, as am I," he looked at Bella, amusement still covering his face. Bella was looking like a cat with a bowl of cream in front of it; he knew the expression well.

"How are you feeling, Puss?" he queried nonchalantly. "I thought you looked a bit green about the gills when I called round yesterday?"

"I'm fine," Bella looked startled. "I just ate something that disagreed with me," she shrugged.

"Mmmm, of course," Francis smirked.

"Uncle?" Bella said thoughtfully, not taking in the amused expression opposite her. "I've been mulling it over. What do you think about opening up another saloon?"

"Whaaat?" Francis exclaimed. "What do you want another one for? Aren't two enough?" he was astonished.

"You see, they're doing so well, I was wondering about opening one somewhere else; where Society or other wealthy people gather...like Bath, or maybe Harrogate, but Bath I thought to start." She nibbled on a nail, "All those old biddies there and people with time on their hands with nothing to do but drink that vile water and go shopping."

Francis chuckled and Bella continued, "And of course if and I say IF, but I'm sure it will happen, Wellington gets rid of Bonaparte once and for all, sometime soon, I was wondering about opening one in Paris. There'll be so many people going there and the city has to get back to some semblance of normality eventually. I thought a lot about that when I was there last summer..." she sat back in her chair and looked at Francis thoughtfully, waiting for his advice.

"Paris?" Francis raised his eyebrows and laughed. "How can you open a gaming saloon in Paris? You can't go haring off there...or to Bath."

Bella looked irritated. "I don't see why not?" she reasoned.

"Tell me, Puss," Francis said with a straight face, "are you going to write and tell Nicky?"

"Tell Nicky? What? About opening a *Lion d'Or* in Bath or Paris? I'm not sure, do you think I should? I don't want to distract him and have him sending me all sorts of letters and orders when he should be keeping his mind on more important military things, let alone keeping himself safe," she stated baldly.

"No, I didn't mean about more gaming saloons," Francis said, his expression still deadpan.

"Whatever are you talking about then?" said Bella, puzzled.

"You know what I'm talking about," said Francis, "and it's definitely not more gaming saloons."

"I beg your pardon," said Bella. "What ARE you talking about, Uncle Francis?"

Francis gave up and chuckled. "Your condition."

"My condition?" Bella raised her eyebrows.

Francis sighed, "You're going to have another baby, aren't you? That's what I'm talking about."

Bella gasped. "How on earth did you know that? I barely knew myself until a very short while ago?"

"Bella, My Love, I've got five children and your Aunt Cat has been pregnant several times...including the other times she miscarried. You've got the same look on your face as she had. I know it well, a sort of secretive, self-satisfied look," he grinned.

"I have not!" Bella expostulated.

"You most certainly do. Besides which, ordering potatoes with jam on, which I overheard you telling your cook you wanted for lunch yesterday, is deuced odd, unless of course you are *enceinte*."

"You've got big ears," Bella giggled.

"So the answer to your question about more *Lion d'Or* saloons is rather out of the question, wouldn't you say?" he raised an eyebrow. "You can't go jaunting about the country, let alone over to Paris, in your condition."

"As I said, I really don't see why not; besides, I'm bored. Heaven knows how long Nicky will be away and the current saloons run themselves now with the sensible managers I put in. I just have to keep half an eye on them."

"Bella, be reasonable, Sweetheart; why on earth do you want more? You need to think about being a mother, not *Lionesse* any longer." he reasoned. "Nicky doesn't need the money now either, which is why you got involved in this whole project in the first place; in addition, I'm sure Nicky won't approve, now would he?"

"He might. I rather thought he could get involved and run them with me," Bella argued. "We could have a whole string of them."

"Well, you do have a point there, not that I think a lion mask is quite his thing...rawrrrrrr!" Francis joked, holding up his hands in claws with waggling fingers and making her laugh. "Oh, be reasonable, Bella," he sighed. "It's a sensible business decision, I agree, but for pity's sake, not now, there's too much else going on." Francis momentarily had horrors of Bella haring all over the place with Bernheim on the loose. "Why not wait until Nicky comes home and discuss it all with him, hmmm? It's his decision now, not mine you should be seeking, Puss."

"I know," she sighed brokenly, "but he's not here, is he?" and for no reason at all she suddenly burst into tears.

"Oh Lord, now I do know you're definitely expecting," Francis sighed. "Come here, You Silly Girl." He got up to come round the desk, pull her gently out of her chair and envelop her in a big comforting hug. He sat down and pulled her on to his lap. "Why don't you go down to Firle and talk to Cat? You need to tell her anyway, she'll soon find out and she'll be mad as Hell and upset, if she hears it first from

Clara or one of the other maids. You know what servants' gossip is like; I'm sure the whole of Hertford Street knows already, so your news will be here before you know it, then straight down to Firle; potatoes and jam indeed!" he chuckled.

"But I wanted to tell Nicky first," she sobbed irrationally, "that's another thing I came to tell you."

"You came to tell me you're writing him a letter to say he's going to be a father again?" Francis was bemused.

"No, Uncle, I'm going over to France to tell him. I want to be there when he hears. I want to tell him myself. He wasn't here before, so I want to tell him now. It'll give him something to look forward to."

"Whaaat?" Francis was alarmed, "You can't go haring off to France! Are you mad? They're at War there. I absolutely forbid it!" he thundered forcefully.

"I'm a big girl now, Uncle, you can't forbid me to do anything," Bella announced baldly, "and I want to see Nicky." She pulled a handkerchief from her sleeve, blew her nose loudly and wiped her face.

"I know you do, Puss, but I simply won't allow it. Nicky would never forgive me if I let you loose in Brussels, he'd have my gizzard, if not throttle me. It's chaos there, soldiers everywhere. Bella, be reasonable, we're at War again, you know that." he pleaded.

"But I'm not going to Brussels, I'm going to Valenciennes. It's not that far from Brussels and far enough away from any fighting. No one will disturb me there, they'll think I'm French anyway, besides, I'm a French Duchess."

"Oh, dear Lord," Francis sighed. "Bella, most French Duchesses had their heads chopped off and there are still a lot of people there who would like to cut off those that are left intact, not that there are that many. Why do you think Boney has come back and the Bourbons have run off? The place isn't safe, Sweetheart. Engage your brain, try to be sensible," he tutted.

"No, Uncle, I've made up my mind. I'm going to Valenciennes and I'll send a message to Nicky to come and visit. Surely he's entitled to a couple of days off? You know it's not far, a day's ride, if that, much less if he rides hard. I'll borrow your yacht; it can drop me off quietly on the coast and I'll make my way inland from there. No one will even notice me."

"But the French are all camped south of Brussels," Francis protested.

"Well he can ride round them, he's French after all, no one will take any notice of him either and anyway, he's not going to come in his army uniform, I'm quite sure," she got off his lap and started to patrol up and down the carpet. "I've thought it all out, it's quite straightforward and simple. I know he'll want to see me, he needs me now, Uncle, truly he does."

"Bella, Sweetheart, please be reasonable." Francis was at his wit's end. When Bella was determined on a course, there was no stopping her.

Bella came back over to him and plopped down in his lap. She leaned up and kissed his cheek and twirled her finger round in his hair, just like her daughter had done. "Peeease, Un-cul, let me take the yacht...peeeease? You don't want me to go on the packet from Calais, do you?" she grinned as she whispered loudly in his ear.

"Oh, dear God, not you too? Is that where those minxes got it from?" Francis sighed.

Bella grinned again. "Certainly not! I'm just copying them, it seems to work when they want something," she laughed. "Hoist on your own petard, Un-cul Fran-cissssss!"

"But I never taught them to do that, truly I didn't. Why the hell does everyone think I did it? It was Nicky, I'm sure of it," he laughed.

"He most certainly did not. I'd box his ears if he did. Anyway, Lizzie started doing it first at Christmas down at Firle and we were hardly there. Oh come now, Uncle, we all know it was you, we know what you're like, you're shockingly naughty."

"But truly, I DIDN'T!" laughed Francis.

"Oh, what a tarradiddle, no one believes you, I don't know why you bother to deny it. Anyway, I can take the yacht, can't I? I'll go after Easter, when we leave Firle, then I can go straight from there." She looked at him hopefully, "Peeeease, Un-cul Fran-cisssss, I won't be gone long," as she twirled his hair again and gave him another kiss.

"Oh, I give up," Francis sighed and groaned in despair, "but no more talk of gaming saloons, you hear me? That's for when Nicky comes back. Give me your word, Bella. Yes, you can have the yacht but you HAVE to take someone with you; no, several people in fact," he added as an afterthought. "There's NO way you're going ANYWHERE by yourself, especially not over to France!"

"Who's going over to France?" a curious voice entered the conversation as Jack appeared in the room.

"I am," announced Bella, turning to smile at him. "Just for a quick visit to Valenciennes. I'm going to send a message to Nicky to come and meet me there...and just where have YOU been, Young Man?" Bella got up from Francis's lap and grinned at Jack naughtily. "I haven't seen you for nearly a fortnight. What HAVE you been doing?" she gave him a piercing look.

"Shopping, fencing..." interrupted Francis before Jack could say anything. "You know, a bit of Town polish and all that, birthday treats, etcetera."

"I thought you'd come back home, at least for a day here and there," smirked Bella, "but you were obviously too BUSY." She looked him up and down and knew exactly where he'd been, so she hadn't been expecting to see him at all. He was now grinning all over his handsome young face. Servants' gossip was truly wonderful, but she could tell from his faraway look anyway. "Shopping, my foot," she giggled and turned to Francis. "YOU," she jabbed him in the chest, "are completely disgraceful. First the girls, now Jack. I should box YOUR ears!" she announced.

"How did you know?" sighed Francis, trying to look innocent but failing dismally.

"You told Benjy, Benjy told Clara, Clara told a housemaid, the housemaid told a kitchen maid, the kitchen maid told one of our kitchen maids and it came back up to me via a similar route until it got to my maid," she announced.

"I need a drink," announced Francis. "I can't compete, the whole world is against me," he sighed theatrically, making Bella and Jack laugh. "By the way, hello, Jack," he grinned. "Nice time shopping? Did you enjoy the Town while you were out and about?" he asked airily.

"Oh extremely. Thank you so much, Sir," he grinned slyly at Bella and scratched his nose, waggling his ring finger and Bella peered at his new accessory, smiling at him knowingly.

"Oh, for Heaven's sake, Jack, stop calling me 'Sir'. You're family now," sighed Francis with a smile. "I keep telling you to call me Francis, Uncle Francis for now, just Francis when you're a bit more mature. 'Sir' makes me feel like your bloody Headmaster," he chuckled and Jack saluted with a pleased grin.

"So," said Jack, wanting to avoid the topic of what he'd been up to while Bella was in the room, "you're going to France?" he look slightly perplexed. "Surely not? Not now with Boney on the loose again?"

Francis sighed again. "That's what I've been trying to tell her for the past half hour, perhaps you can knock some sense into her."

Jack shrugged and grinned at the pair of them. "Impossible," he announced. "I know what she's like," he said meaningfully. "When she wants to chase after Nicky, there's no stopping her."

"There you are," said Bella, "at least HE realises I know what I'm doing," she looked pointedly at Francis.

"I'm still not having you rushing off by yourself, you've got to have someone with you. I'm sending some men as well, just in case," he added.

Bella looked grumpy. "She's most certainly not going off anywhere by herself," announced Jack. "Certainly not to France, because I'M going with her."

"YOU?!" squawked Bella, "but you're going back to school after Easter."

"I most certainly am not, am I, Uncle Francis?" and he grinned slyly at the older man. "Besides, Nicky left me a note telling me to look after you, to keep a close eye on both you and Terrie, so that's precisely what I intend to do, school or no school," he huffed. "Eton can go hang as far as I'm concerned, your safety is far more important."

Francis was enormously pleased with Jack's pronouncement, knowing the resourceful young man was the ideal escort for Bella – hadn't he already proved that many times over? "But what about school?" asked Bella. "How can he be away for weeks?" Much as she'd enjoy his company, she didn't want him to fall behind at Eton because of her.

"Oh, Uncle Francis will sort it out," announced Jack loftily. "He can sort anything out, can't you, Sir, er, I mean Uncle," he grinned at the shaking head of Francis. "Estimable, highly regarded Peer of the Realm that he is."

Francis sighed. "All right, all right, I can handle the Headmaster, concoct some story or another, sudden illness or some such spurious excuse." Looking hale and hearty one minute, Jack suddenly bent over and starting sighing and coughing, much to Bella's amusement, but she swatted him around the head. "Don't think you're escaping your lessons, You Wretched Infant, you've got far too much to catch up on as it is. Anyway, I know far more than most of your teachers, don't I, Uncle?" she giggled slyly at Francis. "Mathematics, science, history, geography, classics, literature, languages," she ticked them off her fingers, "and I warn you, I'll cane you if you misbehave, You Horrible Boy," Bella waggled her finger at him. Jack fell about with laughter and Francis watched the pair of them fondly. They were like a bossy older sister and naughty little brother and he knew full well Bella would be a hard taskmistress with him and his lessons. He made a mental note to ask the Headmaster to send down the necessary books and set work for Jack when he wrote to the school.

"Right, that's all settled then," said Bella with asperity. "We'll set off in the next couple of weeks, after Easter." She immediately started muttering to herself, "Hmmm, I must make arrangements, go shopping, I'll need some new summer outfits, more clothes for Terrie..." Francis started rolling his eyes as she spoke to herself, aware of what Bella's usual shopping trips were like. She was completely incapable of buying solitary items, easy prey for an enthusiastic shop assistant and usually came home loaded down with packages. Visions of the mountain of parcels which had arrived periodically for his wife, sent over from Paris when Bella was there, came to mind and he smirked to himself when he thought of what had been in some of them. However, when she started to mutter about clothes for Terrie, he balked suddenly.

"Now look here, Bella, you going is one thing, but you can't think of taking Terrie. I just won't stand for it..." he tried to remonstrate.

"You mean you want TWO little anarchists inflicted on you for weeks?" she grinned. "Besides, Nicky will want to see her. Anyway," she smirked at Francis, "no one is likely to suspect a little family travelling around innocuously, as opposed to a single woman with an escort," she turned to look knowingly at Jack. "Isn't that right, 'Nephew'?"

Jack smiled back at her. "Oh absolutely, Auntie Dear."

"Oh very well," muttered Francis. He pointed a finger at Jack, "Don't you let the pair of them out of your sight, especially that little minx."

"Oh, you don't have to worry about THAT," laughed Bella. "She's quite besotted with Jack, more so than the cat," she giggled. "He's got endless patience with her, Lizzie too, heaven help him; quite the one for all the ladies now, Jack, eh?" she winked at him, knowingly. With that parting thrust, she turned and sashayed towards the door of her uncle's study with a wave at the two men. "I'll leave you to discuss Jack's shopping expedition. I'M off to do my own," and with a laugh, she left them to it.

Chapter Thirty-Four

The Easter weekend was a great success and the family showered Jack with birthday gifts, much to his embarrassment. They all watched in amusement as he blew out little candles on his first ever birthday cake, after which he promptly burst into tears, so overcome with everyone's care and generosity to him.

His main present had been his very own horse, chosen and bought by Nicky, with a saddle from Bella. The animal was a handsome and spirited young stallion which had been waiting in the stables at Firle for him. Jack had been very wary of going to the stables since his elevation to the family and had managed to avoid it up until now. Having had the horse presented to him at the front of the house so everyone could inspect and admire it, he led it back there himself with huge apprehension. However, he'd done himself an injustice. In the main, his former peers, the grooms and stableboys, coachmen and other lackeys, were pleased for his good fortune. He'd always been a kind and willing lad when he'd worked there with them and they knew what he'd done to care for his family and also his employers. Gossip being what it was among the servants, even if they didn't know the half of it, they had heard that he'd somehow saved Bella and

Nicky's lives, so they all wished him well and Jack returned to the house, relieved and happy.

He also slipped away over the weekend to visit his little siblings and the other children he'd taken under his wing in The Dials, now dispersed and being cared for by kindly families among the many Firle tenants or other local country folk. He showered them all with gifts of his own, for them and their families, bought with the allowance he now got from Nicky and later, returned to the big house, content that they too were now happy and thriving.

Bella had quietly told her aunt her good news when she, Jack and Francis had arrived at Firle on the day before Good Friday and Cat had been delighted as they sat in her bedroom for a private talk. However, she looked at Bella with an enormous smirk and Bella gasped. "No, Auntie? Surely not?" and she giggled. "Are you sure? Does Uncle Francis know?"

Cat laughed slyly at her niece. "Hah! That man thinks he knows everything, but I haven't told him yet," she grinned, still bemused at what had happened to her. "I wasn't sure myself, it's a bit early to tell, especially at my age. To be honest, that's why I came down here early, to get away so I'd know for sure," she sighed. "But all the signs are there, I ought to know by now after all my pregnancies, successful or not. I'm feeling slightly queasy at times so, that's it!" An enormous smile lit her face. "What do you think Francis will do when I produce another Lizzie?"

Bella shouted with laughter. "Australia? Shame he can't get to the moon," she fell about, well familiar with his comically endless threats to emigrate. "But Auntie, it could be a boy again or," she choked, literally doubling up with mirth, "you could have twins again...imagine...TWO Lizzies! Oh Auntie, he'll be suicidal with all the screaming."

Cat grimaced. "Oh, Bella, I despair of that child sometimes, I really do. I simply don't know what to do with her. I've been SO strict, I've lost count of the number of times I've paddled her backside. I've tried everything: coercion, threats, ignoring her, tempting her, but nothing works," she sighed. "Whatever am I going to do? I'm terrified she'll be completely uncontrollable when she grows up, an absolute nightmare." She looked at Bella's smiling face, "It's not funny, you know," she grumbled. "Terrie isn't half as bad when she's by herself, it's only when they get together the naughtiness gets worse and it's invariably Lizzie's doing. I've no idea where she gets it from." she sighed.

"With you and Uncle Francis for parents? You're asking me THAT?" Bella laughed again. "What a pair of reprobates you both are, it's no wonder she's like she is. Hah! I thought the boys were bad enough, horrible lot my cousins are," she teased, "but she's obviously inherited the wild and wicked side of both you and Uncle Francis. Besides, if like her namesake she's got any of Great Aunt Elizabeth's determination in her as well, or her brains..." she shrugged in huge amusement. "Mind you..." she mused thoughtfully, "she can be perfectly well-behaved when she wants to be, when she's with me, or we've been visiting some of my friends, providing no one annoys her, or she sees temptation beyond her control, like Bubbles and your hat," Bella grinned at Cat's grimace. "Then she's the perfect model of what every well-behaved little girl should be."

"Noooo," gasped Cat, "she never is with me."

"That's because she enjoys teasing you because you're so easy to wind up, Auntie and the servants are completely useless. That little madam knows exactly what she's doing, even if she is only three," she nodded her head sagely, "you'll see, I'm sure she won't be the night-mare you fear. Headstrong and a little wild, oh yes, but I'm sure she'll be just fine and she is such a loving little baggage, that's why we all can't resist her," she finally ended. She paused thoughtfully and sat back in her chair, hands protectively over her still flat belly. "Talking of Lizzie and Great Aunt Elizabeth, did Uncle Francis tell you, he gave me permission to tell Nicky the story before he left. I thought he needed to know, to help him finally understand the whole Will busi-ness...and everything..." she tailed off for a moment, "Also, the picture is in our house after all. Uncle Francis often just calls round to sit and look at it."

"Mmmm, so I gather. I'm glad Nicky knows. What did he make of the story?" she asked curiously.

"Overwhelmed," reflected Bella. "Completely overwhelmed. His rivers run very deep, Auntie," she said seriously, shaking her head. "It wasn't just the story or the inheritance or her letter, there was a whole lot more and it all just came out together," she sighed. "He got very emotional. I was stunned, I had no idea," she mused, almost to herself. "But it's all to the good now. Oh, he's so wonderful, Auntie, I love him so much and I'm so scared about the War starting up again, that's why I have to go and see him, tell him about the baby and watch his face when I do. He'll be so pleased, it's so important to him..." and once again she suddenly burst out crying for no reason.

"Oh, Bella, Darling, I understand completely," said Cat, patting Bella's hands and handing her a handkerchief. "He's such a lovely man now, though of course he'll always be a lovely boy to me, old crone that I am," she smiled. "But I'm sure he'll be thrilled whatever sex the child is, irrespective of the whole heir thing," she waved her hand in the air. "He loves you far too much now, we can all see it," she sighed. "Oh, Bella, the way he kissed you goodbye on the doorstep before he left, it was sooo romantic, if a bit shocking in public. But I nearly cried, it reminded me of Francis once, a long time ago..." and with that she herself burst into loud, boisterous tears.

Into this welter of sobbing erupted Francis. "What the Devil is the matter? I can hear your caterwauling all the way down the corridor," he looked between the two women, concern written all over his face.

Cat looked up at her husband tearfully. "Oh, go away, Francis...read another report," her usual comical remark to him. "Can't you see Bella is upset?" she pointedly tipped her head in the direction of the door he'd just come through with a meaningful look.

"If you're sure?" he queried. "Is it Nicky?"

"Of course it's Nicky, You Imbecile, just go away..." and she started to wail all the more.

Francis was just a man and couldn't deal with two tearful women, so he retreated rapidly back to his study and left them to it.

The two women finally recovered and resumed their chatter about babies. As Bella got up to go and change for dinner, Cat left her with a parting thought. "Watch your uncle's face at dinner," she smirked. "I'd better tell him before we come down as he'll start to suspect if I turn into a fountain like you. And another thing," she paused, regarding Bella with a slightly amused expression on her face. "You know, Darling," she mused, "I've had two sets of twins and you were one of a twin, the doctors told your dear mama so, but the other one died early they thought, that's why your birth was so...er...difficult and Charlie..." she couldn't bring herself to finish. "Anyway," she took a breath, "it all runs in the de Mornay family from my mother's side, they come out every so often down the generations, so you, being a de Mornay...you never know, you could have twins too," she winked. "You could have twin sons even, just like me. What do you think your rogue of a husband would make of that?"

"Two little Lions," Bella whispered and giggled to herself. "Oh, Auntie," she laughed, "that would be simply perfect," and now laughing, she went off to her own room.

After Bella left, Cat sat back on her bed in reflection. She herself was bemused and stunned by her condition and she laughed to herself as she anticipated what her husband would make of it all. She smiled like a cat...he'd be tickled pink, she knew...but it had all been sooo disgraceful and she actually blushed quietly at the memory...

A few days after Nicky had left, Francis had disappeared off on one of his myriad and neverending meetings. Cat never really bothered about who he met and where, she found most of it quite tedious. Her life, unlike many of her aristocratic peers, had been devoted to her children and she'd been a very involved, hands-on mother. She also bred her large, hairy dogs and then, as she had more time on her hands, became increasingly involved with her many charities of which she was a vigorous and tireless supporter, cajoling her and Francis's rich and powerful friends to dispense with their money and patronage to help the many thousands of poor and destitute with which London teemed. That was how she'd been so sympathetic when young Jack Vallance had tried to steal her reticule that fateful day in Bond Street and when she'd witnessed his tragic efforts to support his little tribe of children.

However, she'd been amused and taken note when Francis had idly mentioned he was going to see Lord Ashcroft to ensure he'd recovered from the chaotic fracas with Bubbles, her hat and the dolls' tea party. But when he'd returned later and for days after, despite their amusement over the notice that now hung prominently on their front gate, which had elicited no few curious remarks, Francis had been quiet and withdrawn, quite unlike his usual witty, insouciant self. He wouldn't talk about it, merely muttering about Nicky. At first, she'd supposed he was worried about the return of Bonaparte and Nicky's involvement in the War that was about to start up all over again – but she was sure there was more as she could sense his worry; it was most unlike him.

He didn't sleep well either. He had nightmares and would toss and turn restlessly...at one point she was sure he'd mentioned the name Bernheim over and over again, but she presumed it was the unwelcome return of the old nightmare he'd had constantly years previously, for ages after she'd rescued him from Rouen. He also got up in the early hours to disappear outside the house. She'd peered through the window several times and seen him strolling off with Bubbles, deep in thought, talking to the large, gormless, white fluffy dog, seemingly unconcerned about the dangers of walking the streets of London alone at such an hour.

She couldn't seem to bring him out of his distraction, so, in despair, she'd dragged him off to Firle the following weekend, thinking a change of scenery and some fresh air would cheer him up and some hard riding across country might help him sleep. She'd tried to talk to him about Nicky and after endless nagging and probing, he'd finally given in and told her a considerable amount about what the man was really going to be up to. Naturally, she'd then been as worried as he but she nonetheless suspected it wasn't all that was bothering Francis, but at least the pair of them were both now worrying about Nicky, so neither were sleeping well.

Discussing Nicky had reminded her of the business with the interesting marks on his wrists and neck the evening at dinner before he'd left. She knew full well what he'd been up to...and one look at Bella's face, especially after peering closely under the many bracelets she'd been wearing and seeing the tell-tale marks that were there as well, confirmed she'd been as involved as he, though Bella's were not so red and prominent. Cat had been slightly shocked by it all, as one is when confronted with something like that from someone she still thought of as an innocent little girl, Cat looking on her as almost another beloved daughter...but of course she wasn't a little girl any longer. The goings on three years before at *Le Lion d'Or* had shocked, fascinated and finally amused her enormously. She'd caught the look that had been exchanged between Nicky and Francis and realised her rogue of a husband knew all about what Nicky and Bella had been up to, so when Nicky had winked at her and then at Francis, it had all been too much and she'd felt herself flush at the salacious images that had popped into her head, coupled with a serious urge to box Nicky's ears, even at his age.

There was an old gamekeeper's cottage on the far edge of the Firle estate and over the years since they'd been married, Francis had used it as a bolthole when he wanted to escape the pressures of overseeing his vast estates and business interests. He would take her there for stolen weekends, just the pair of them, to make love, sleep and potter about doing nothing more than go for a walk if the weather was nice; or chop a bit of firewood, or simply sit in the garden with a glass of wine and a cheroot and gaze at the sky, or doze with his feet up...all without any servants or family to bother them. They hadn't been there for years and Cat thought, in desperation, she'd take them both to their little hideaway to see if they could shake off their troubles, talk out their worries and spend a bit of time in bed, with perhaps some frivolous naughtiness to take their minds off everything.

Francis Granville had been, still was, a very passionate, carnal, sensuous man, when he let go the exceedingly tight rein he kept on himself. He'd been a renowned and terrible rake in his youth and roistered around London with a small group of likeminded cronies. No attractive woman, married or unmarried, was safe from their licentious attentions. He'd finally tired of the meaningless existence, which he interspersed with his periodic disappearance to take up his alter ego and become The Shadow, so when his father had died unexpectedly early, after a mad period when he'd taken to piracy as well as the smuggling, Francis had finally taken up the reins of the Dukedom. He'd thrown himself into running the affairs of his estate and its wide-reaching business interests, supported and encouraged by his indomitable, fierce grandmother. He'd unexpectedly met, fallen head-long in love with and married his tempestuous, headstrong and passionate French wife, Marie Catherine de Mornay and in her, he had found a kindred spirit. She loved him equally desperately and argued and fought with him constantly, which had fascinated, irritated and enthralled him his entire life, never letting him gain the upper hand unless she chose to, rarely doing what she was told. Her uninhibited, passionate nature had soon revelled in all the licentious activities he'd previously enjoyed with other women, but which he'd since shared with her alone. Once married, he'd never looked at anyone else, something which had never failed to amaze him, whenever he'd reflected on it occasionally over the passing years.

Before all that, when he'd been The Shadow, he was a ruthless and feared smuggler along the Normandy coast and also a sometime, very successful pirate down the western coast of France and Spain as far as North Africa and the Canary Islands. He'd even crossed over to the West Indies a couple of times to explore opportunities for attacking treasure ships around the Caribbean. A big, tall and strong man, he'd learned early to keep himself fit and in excellent condition, able to fight, run, climb, jump and swim, when doing so could be the difference between life, death or capture if he hadn't been able to escape his enemies – whether other venal smugglers and pirates, or the Revenue, the Navy and other Authorities. Now approaching his mid-fifties, he still kept himself in peak condition, not that he'd fought anyone other than his wife, or the friends he laughingly fenced or occasionally boxed with, but the years of needing to keep his body fit and in trim were deeply inculcated in his psyche and way of life. It was something he'd taught Nicky when the latter had joined the army, particularly when he'd started to get involved in his undercover activities. That his fitness and strength had kept Francis alive when captured by Edgar Bernheim and his barbaric lieutenant, Pierre Dupont, years previously in Rouen, he'd never doubted. Nicky had believed the same about himself when it had happened to him, and he'd regularly thanked Francis as well as the Heavens, for the advice he'd impressed upon him.

Francis was therefore a man who looked and acted far younger than his years and peers. Cat, too, was fit and young for her age. Despite three full-term pregnancies and several miscarriages, she was

still tall, beautiful and voluptuous. She rode, regularly and energeti-
cally walked her dogs and still practiced fencing to keep herself fit and
her figure in trim...something she did partly to irritate Francis so she
could fight him herself around the gardens at Firle, which they occasionally did over the years when they'd had yet another of their arguments, but also for her own self-satisfaction. Moreover, she wanted to
reassure herself she could fight off any miscreants who might try to
attack her when she went out anonymously into the fetid stews of
London to do her charitable works among the starving poor.

So, amid much grumbling and reluctance, Cat had finally enticed
Francis down to their cottage and as they sat and sipped chilled wine
and desultorily picked from a delicious cold buffet assortment that had
been left there for them in picnic hampers, Francis had looked over at
her. "I know you mean well, Sweetheart, also what you've no doubt
got in mind," he sighed, not even smiling, "but I'm really not in the
mood for any of it. I know I've been out of sorts, but I've just got a lot
on my mind," he shrugged and quaffed back the remains of his glass
before refilling it.

"Oh, Francis," pleaded Cat, "I wish you'd tell me what's bothering
you. I know you're worried about Nicky, so am I, but I know you,
there's something else. You're not sleeping, or eating properly, you've
got bags under your eyes, no appetite and you're miles away most of
the time," she looked at his virtually untouched plate. "I just wanted to
take your mind off it all, whatever it is. I don't know what else to
suggest." She looked at him with love in her eyes, "That's all; I'm at
my wit's end because you won't talk to me about it," she shrugged in
that Gallic way of hers.

Francis looked back at her and gradually drank his full glass
before answering. "It's all so complicated," he shook his head. "I
don't know what to do," he half muttered to himself. "I can't think
straight anymore." He looked haunted and he got up and retrieved a
bottle of brandy from the hamper, filling up his wine glass with the
tawny liquid. No stranger to the brandy bottle over the years either,
Cat simply held out her glass and Francis filled hers the same,
without any query, almost unknown for him to do without some facetious comment. For the next while they simply sat and talked about

nothing in particular and worked their way down the bottle of wine, interspersed with the brandy. Francis periodically got up and wandered about, lost in thought, smoking a cheroot, his face unemotional, his eyes distant. Cat just sat drinking quietly, watching him and looking into the small fire that was burning in the hearth. She periodically wondered what Nicky was doing, imagined visions of him dead in a trench somewhere or being shot as a spy going round and round in her head. Another vision of him as a little boy when she'd found him in the Rouen Fortress also threaded through her thoughts and she was distraught. When a second bottle of wine and the bottle of brandy was finished, Francis opened another couple and they started to work their way down those until both were nearly empty.

Finally, he sat down and looked at her. "I'm dead drunk," he announced baldly, "but it doesn't help. Th' worry won't go 'way." he whispered.

Cat looked back at him. "Mine neith'r," she shook her head which was starting to swim but her terrible thoughts WERE actually starting to drift away on a sea of alcohol. "You jus' need a bi' more..." she suggested pointing at a new bottle, squinting as she tried to make out what was in it, but she didn't care. So they sat and drank some more, just gazing at each other, electricity starting to crackle between them as it always had. She suddenly leaned back in her chair and grinned at him. "Ai'm VAIRY drunk!" she announced, pronouncing her words slowly, waving her glass in the air. "'Ow'bout you?" she looked at him expectantly. "Sh'll I cha'nge YEW to a du-el?" she wafted her hand in the air as if it contained a rapier.

Francis looked at her, his terrible worried thoughts finally faded and then he too grinned, but his lips curled salaciously. "I got a betta 'dea," the alcohol had finally taken over and he was more drunk than he'd been in years, not that he was capable of remembering anything by that point.

"Oho..." she grinned back at him idiotically. "Wassat?"

"Come t'bed an' I'll show ya..." he grinned lopsidedly.

"I wan' more b'andy...or wine, don't care...'nd I c'n still beat you 'n a du-el," she giggled like a teenager.

Another lurid grin. "I'll give ya somethin' else ta think 'bout, You French Baggage."

"Who you callin' a French Baggage?" she tapped herself on the chest. "AI'M th' Dutch-ess of Fairle," and she giggled again.

"But I'M a pie-rat," he chuckled tapping himself on the chest, "an' I'M goin' t' carry ya off. I'll ransom ya ter yer rich Dook."

"Oooooooh! Ai'm t'rrified. Ai t'ink one's goin' t'faint..." she put her hand to her forehead.

"Not bloody likely, Baggage... not 'til I've carried ya off 'n' 'ad my wicked way with ya," his laugh was comically evil.

"You're too old, past-it, you c'n't carry *moi* 'nywhere..." another giggle as odd words of French started to percolate her language.

"Wanna bet?" he laughed evilly again. "I'm gonna carry ya off ter me ship, tie ya up an'... an'...."

"*Et quoi?*" she giggled, "You's too drunk!"

"I'M Th' Shad-dow!" he threw his head back and laughed, suddenly feeling carefree and twenty years younger than he was. "I tol' Miles."

""Ooo's Miles?"

Francis looked at his wife idiotically and paused, wrinkling his forehead and looking perplexed. "I've f'gotten," he announced. "Neva mine", then he grinned, "but I AM The Shad-dow. I'm neva too drunk t'carry off Laydees an' do wick'd thin's to 'em..." and with that, he tried unsuccessfully to undo his cravat and shirt but gave up when his fingers wouldn't work properly, so he picked Cat up as if she was just a bag of feathers, carried her across the room, weaving and stumbling as he went, tossed her down on the bed, tripped over the edge of the bedside rug and fell down across her making her double up in drunken mirth.

"The Shaddoo?" She shook her head, trying to sit up and pushing his big body off her. "*Qui est-il?* Neva 'eard of 'im...ooooh," she giggled, "is 'e an eevil villen? Ooooooh er... 'ave mer-sea on me sole..."

"No mer-sea," he chuckled, "'m a roooth-less smuggla. Acshally, nah, forgot, I'm reeeeally a pie-rat," he winked rather lopsidedly.

"Oh noooo, what you gonna do t'*moi*? I don't wanna walk th' plank," a thought struck, "my dress'll get wet."

"'S'no problem. Tekit off!" He reared up over her, grabbed the material and ruthlessly ripped it from bodice to hem. "Nah then…" his eyes sparkled as they roved lecherously down her partly naked torso, "where's me rope?"

"You 'aven't got 'ny," she cackled, "*quel* sorta smuggla *ou* pie-rat *es tu*?" she tickled him ruthlessly and he burst out laughing, rolling around on the bed in mirth. "*Voilà!* Yoos-less.. can't cope wi' a mere woman!" she crowed.

"'ll impro-vise," and he finally pulled his part-undone cravat from around his neck.

"Tut tut. Benjy'll complain," Cat laughed.

"Fuck Benjy," was his response and his eyes started to glitter drunkenly down into hers.

"I'd rather you fucked *moi*" she giggled, letting her hand wander down his body.

"Such choice lang-widge…Granny 'ranville'd turn in 'er grave t'ear that… but… *Ma Chère Duchesse*….a fuck c'n be 'rranged. C'm 'ere you……"

And that was how it began. Desperate to drive the world and its reality from their thoughts, they never sobered up the entire weekend and once they'd started, it was like a floodgate had opened. Every single depraved and licentious thing Francis had ever done in his life, which was considerable, happened over the next few days and what-ever he did to her, she did to him in return, in spades. He'd never, ever, been submissive and only very occasionally had he let Cat loose on his body, but that weekend he was too drunk to care or stop her. Laughing uproariously, they left scrawled, almost illegible notes in the hampers outside their front door for more food and copious bottles of brandy, wine and Champagne. They hardly slept and what the 'gardeners' pruning trees and scything grass in the distance, keeping a wary eye on the cottage day and night, made of the occasional cries and tormented screams of passion, not to mention the language that emanated from the little cottage window, they never knew. When

Ashcroft read the reports afterwards, his eyes almost came out on stalks and he threw the papers straight into the fireplace, watching in stunned silence as they were consumed in the flames.

They finally emerged, horrendously hungover, exhausted, with red marks all over themselves: teeth marks, scratches, bruises, wrist and ankle burns. It was beyond appalling. Cat couldn't remember half of what they'd done, she'd been so drunk; as he sat at his desk over the next few weeks, Francis kept getting flashbacks of it all that made even him blanche as he put his head in his hands and frequently groaned. They never discussed it and only the occasional speaking look they exchanged over sedate dinners with the great and the good of Society, was the reference to what had happened.

Cat went hot and cold with embarrassment when Francis looked at her and grinned salaciously across the table or silently toasted her with a glass of wine or brandy.

That was how the Duchess of Firle, so late in life and much to her astonishment, became pregnant for the final time.

Chapter Thirty-Five

Bella studied her uncle's face the minute the family gathered in the drawing room before dinner. He looked absolutely stunned, bemused, but hugely pleased with himself and there was an evil glint in his eye that she couldn't quite fathom. Bella almost choked over her sherry when her aunt caught her eye and winked.

It was a small, intimate family dinner before the rest of the Granville sons arrived home from university or further studies and travels abroad, with their usual retinue of lively friends. With the War finally over, as everyone had foreseen and their time at university ended, the older set of Granville twins had been despatched across to the Netherlands to stay with friends of their father for a few months. It was partly a holiday but afterwards they were to travel around the Low Countries and beyond to Prussia and other German states, to see how other landed estates in that part of the world, not too affected by the War, were run. It was one aspect of their preparation before they became directly involved in the running of the vast Firle family estates and business empire. However, they had been hastily summoned back by their worried father and were soon to take up permanent residence at home once more, until Europe was once again safe and at peace. So, with just six of them around the dining table and when the servants had departed, Bella took the opportunity to announce she was going to have another child and her father and Elise got up to hug her in delight. Jack looked slightly stunned and, much to Francis's amusement, puffed his chest out importantly and started to fuss over her excessively as he realised his newly added responsibility in looking after Bella on their trip, at least until Nicky came home again.

Much to the complete amazement of Eddie, Elise and Jack, but obviously not to Bella and Francis who now grinned at each other, they looked stunned when Cat calmly announced she was going to produce another Granville and told everyone to pray the child wasn't going to be a second Lizzie or to buy ear muffs just in case, whereupon everyone laughed and Francis groaned theatrically.

While Bella, Jack and an excited Terrie quietly made their way across the Channel on the Duke's sleek yacht, Society in London smirked at the gossip that the Duchess of Firle was expecting again. Very little could be kept secret in that cauldron of tittle tattle. Some Matrons of the Ton tutted and pronounced it disgraceful behaviour, whilst others looked at the still tall, handsome and vigorous Duke over their fans and sighed with envy.

There was also another small complication. Despite Eddie's best efforts to prevent such an occurrence until they were married, much to the surprise and pleasure of both, Elise Montgomery had discovered she too was pregnant. Their original plan had been for her and Eddie to marry quietly in the little church at Firle over Easter with just the family in attendance, but they'd decided to postpone the wedding when Nicky had gone away unexpectedly with Wellington, as Eddie was adamant he wanted him there and would wait for him to come back. However, all those plans had been put in disarray with Elise's scandalous announcement and the ceremony was therefore hastily and very quietly reconvened before Bella left with Jack. Privately, Francis and Cat were both extremely entertained that the very organised, knowledgeable and careful Eddie had been caught out, but were pleased as punch for them both. Bella, at first rather taken aback, was now enthusiastically looking forward to having a third pregnant lady in the family.

Elise looked serenely beautiful as Francis escorted her down the aisle of the little village church. Bella's young brother, Charlie, a studious, quiet, fair-haired boy in his early teens, now growing into the spitting image of his late grandfather, stood proudly next to his father as they watched her approach the altar. Cat and Bella kept all their fingers and toes crossed as their two little daughters, in matching dresses and wearing flower garlands in their hair, marched importantly behind the bride, holding up her short train. They plopped down on the floor, cross legged, behind Elise while the ceremony proceeded, but started to get bored when the Vicar droned on. Their mothers looked on in despair when Lizzie started to fiddle with the decorative bows on her cousin's dress, much to that little girl's annoyance so she started to do the same thing back and they began to squabble quietly, pulling up their dresses and petticoats over their heads. Francis merely grinned in amusement, earning him a sharp dig in the ribs from his furious wife and the reprehensible Granville sons snorted and guffawed silently from their pews. Fortunately, a sternly quelling look from Jack, of all people, made the little girls sit back up properly from where they'd almost been wrestling on the floor and the rest of the ceremony went off without any further distraction.

Bella, Jack and Terrie made their way as fast as their wagon would go from the quiet, small coastal port of *Boulogne-Sur-Mer* where they'd been dropped off from Francis's yacht. They were dressed simply and looked like ordinary country folk. If they were stopped on the road, or anyone spoke to them, Bella did all the talking as she spoke French like a native and she'd instructed Jack to play dumb and stupid and not say anything. She'd laughed as he pulled a gormless face at her, but they knew it was a serious game they were playing. Terrie already had a few words of French amongst her rapidly expanding vocabulary, but Bella was taking no chances and had given the little girl a tot of brandy in some warm milk before they'd left the harbour. She snored like a trooper on Jack's lap for most of the way and they stopped only to rest and stretch their legs, away from the country lanes they were following, well hidden from view of anyone else heading in the same direction.

Ahead of them, a little way further down the road, a farm cart was rolling along, driven by two yokels – who appeared even more gormless than Jack – and a little way behind was another cart which looked merely to be carrying local produce to market. The driver seemed to be half asleep over the reins of his nag and his assistant was snoring in the back with a hat over his face. Francis's 'bodyguards' for Bella were watching the wagon from front and rear and had been loaned to him by Ashcroft as the four men all spoke fluent French. Francis had no idea where they'd come from, but he trusted Ashcroft who had sent them round to Berkeley Square with his blessing when Francis had told him what Bella was going to do. Francis knew he was now in Ashcroft's debt, but he didn't mind, he'd pay anything or more probably, do anything for the man, so long as he was reassured of Bella's safety.

They'd frequently passed bands of French soldiers on the way, en route to join Bonaparte or simply scouting the countryside, but, as Bella had predicted, no one was interested in a little family returning to their village from a trip to see an aged, sick relative. When she'd offered some of the soldiers a few morsels of simple food and drink from her wagon and expressed her support for Bonaparte's return, they'd merely smiled at her and left her to continue her journey without a word. Nevertheless, though she didn't express her concern to Jack, she was anxious at the number of French military they came across and began to wonder if she hadn't made a big mistake in going to Valenciennes. Perhaps she should have gone to the old de Mornay house instead, which was further west in Normandy and therefore away from the French borders and likely battlegrounds.

However, they all arrived at the estate safely and took up residence in the partly refurbished chateau, which was still not finished as work there had been abandoned for the time being. The workmen had vanished and the Estate Manager too, so there was no one to continue to design, order and supervise the repairs and rebuilding. The only people left in residence were the housekeeper and a couple of old retainers who pottered around the home farm and the grounds. The surprised housekeeper recognised Bella from her visit the previous summer and the old woman cooed over Terrie, hauling the sleepy child off to her kitchen to cosset and fuss over her while Bella and Jack settled themselves in. The four men took off to the stables and there was always one or another to be seen around the grounds, apparently working, but keeping an eye out in case any French soldiers decided to pay a visit.

Bella worried if the housekeeper and retainers were trustworthy, at one point even feeling the back of her neck as she gazed at them but was reassured after the old lady spent a happy hour gossiping in her kitchen with Bella over how wonderful the young *Duc* had been to all the old tenants of the Estate he'd found the year before, giving them money to repair and refurbish their homes and cottages, replant their fields and buy new stock. She told Bella he'd done all he could to rebuild the little local community that used to comprise part of the Valenciennes holdings and that he was so different from Antoine de Bresancourt, the previous icy *Duc*, his father. Bella had raised her eyebrows when the old woman spat after mentioning his name. It was therefore obvious that Nicky had charmed everyone and they now seemed quite devoted to him, even if he'd suddenly disappeared as mysteriously as he'd suddenly re-appeared in their midst. They'd apparently been promised he would return at some point to continue the restoration and they hadn't been abandoned or forgotten again and the money had continued to arrive to cover their wages, plus any other 'essentials'. Then the woman swore to Bella that she and the two old retainers would keep them all safe from Bonaparte's soldiers. The old housekeeper had no truck with them, saying soldiers were soldiers whoever they fought for and had spat again.

Bella was slightly bemused and taken aback at her vehemence and spitting every time she mentioned a name she disliked, but so long as she was on their side, she was relieved. Nevertheless, everyone was extremely wary and on their guard. The four bodyguards didn't hesitate to remonstrate with Bella that in their opinion this was definitely not a safe place to be and to leave while they could. But Bella was adamant; she was there now and there she intended to stay until Nicky either turned up or she received a message to say he couldn't come.

Bella had written a private note which she'd sealed up and handed over to her uncle who had promised it would be delivered by the fastest method possible to Brussels and the army HQ. That was via Ashcroft once again, another favour for Francis who was beginning to realise Ashcroft had a soft spot for Bella – nothing was any trouble when he mentioned her name, much to his private bemusement. Obviously not quite the reputed cold fish after all, Francis thought. The note went via special courier and ship, along with Ashcroft's own security communications, direct to Wellington's headquarters and then onward for personal delivery to Nicky.

In the meantime, Bella waited and hoped he would come. Francis had told Bella Nicky may well not be in Brussels and she might have to wait a while, or Nicky might not be able come at all, but she still insisted on making her trip. She just hoped Nicky would get the message and find a way to come to see them for a day or two. Now she'd understood how many French soldiers were roaming around, Bella was slightly concerned, but for a man who had spent the past few years working undercover and assimilating himself into the local population, either in Spain or in France, she didn't think Nicky would find it too difficult to make the sixty or so mile trip to Valenciennes, even if it meant going a longer way around to keep his distance from the French military.

They whiled away their days very quietly, with Bella strictly supervising Jack's lessons and Terrie running about the little home farm that was on the estate: chasing chickens, collecting their eggs, watching in fascination at the cow being milked, feeding the ducks on the pond and also a couple of fat pigs. *Madame* Foubert, the housekeeper, was besotted with the little girl and was happy to keep her occupied in the kitchen for hours on end or let her follow her round the farmyard while the little girl chattered merrily to the animals in her rapidly-improving, childish French, tutored by the housekeeper. The men made themselves useful as well and set to continuing to repair some of the outbuildings in the grounds to pass the time, between visits to one or two local hamlets and taverns to keep their eye on what the military were doing and to ensure anonymity. The *chateau* and estate were located to the north-west of Valenciennes itself, deep in the remote, rural countryside, surrounded in part by extensive woodland, so they kept well away from the city and its environs. It was a quiet, bucolic, if somewhat stressful existence at the isolated and secluded estate, given their proximity to Bonaparte's army. Bella fretted for hours as she gazed constantly out of the first floor windows in her bedroom, looking and listening for the sound of hoofbeats up the drive.

When it was quiet and there were no soldiers around on the wooded roads and lanes nearby, Bella wandered around the *chateau* grounds, familiarising herself with them. One sunny afternoon, she eventually ended up in a small grove at the edge of their land, near the local hamlet. It was railed off and a little ruined chapel stood there surrounded by faded, toppled and desecrated gravestones and the ruins of ancient, ornamental mausoleums. As she scrubbed away at old lichen, she read the names of long dead de Bresancourts and the dates ran back hundreds of years from what she could make out in the weather-beaten stone. Her hand ran over her belly and she prayed she was carrying the son Nicky wanted, so the old family line would continue for him.

She finally came across a small stone plaque on the wall of the ruined chapel. It was new and there were no graves underneath and when she looked closely and saw the dates, she realised it was a simple memorial to Nicky's dead parents. All the dead de Bresancourts were now remembered in the old family graveyard. She wandered in and out of the ruined mausoleums, images and effigies of lions every-where. The graves were badly desecrated, even though it looked like someone had tried to erase the worst of the vile and obscene messages and carvings, done presumably during the Revolution by people wanting to wreak vengeance on the hated aristocrats. A chill ran down her spine as she thought of the terrible events that had taken place in France in the few years just after she was born. She realised if it hadn't been for the perseverance of her father and aunt in rescuing her late grandfather and the rest of her relations, aided by her Uncle Francis, then coming to England instead of staying in France and possibly ending up on the guillotine, the de Mornay family might well have been wiped out and she would never have been born. It was a horrible thought and Nicky would no doubt also be dead. She shivered as she stood in the still afternoon sunshine and reflected on the strangeness of fate.

Bella continued to wander idly through the graveyard and came across what had once been a fine mausoleum, the stone crumbled and part ruined. Two enormous, black stone lions sat at either end of the top of the crumbling brickwork and as she poked her head inside the dark interior, from the rays of sunshine pouring through the broken stone blocks, she could see the tombs had been desecrated and smashed, the tops of the sarcophagi pushed off and the interiors contained merely a few skeletal bones, no skulls, with a few bits of rotting clothing. Bella couldn't help shuddering slightly.

The doors had long disappeared and as she looked around, she saw a plaque on the wall. As she worked out the dates, she realised these must have been the tombs of Nicky's grandmother, Mathilde de Bresancourt, *Duchesse de Valenciennes* and his grandfather Philippe, the *Duc*, who she vaguely remembered Nicky telling her had died long before his grandmother who had passed away shortly before his birth. He was the man who apparently just about remembered the glory days of Louis XIV and his Court at Versailles which he'd attended as a teenager. She wondered if he had looked like Nicky, trying to picture a man who resembled her husband but dressed in the satins and lace of the early decades of the previous century, complete with a big long wig; for a moment, she giggled.

But then she shivered again as she gazed around the dank little vaulted edifice and the markings on the stone floor, which she couldn't make out. The whole place was eerie and with another shudder she returned with relief into the sunshine. She strolled around for a while longer and then, with a final look at the black lions on his grandmother's tomb, she walked slowly back to the house. As she meandered, she thought about the people in that little cemetery, wondering what they had been like, what they had done in their lives, their thoughts and experiences at the famous Court in Versailles. She considered whether further back, a de Bresancourt had been present at the famous meeting with the English Henry VIII at his Field of the Cloth of Gold in the 1500's, perhaps even earlier during the Hundred Years War or had known Joan of Arc. That was another vague memory Nicky had, something about how the Dukedom had been earned, but it had all been so long ago, when he was a child of three or four, so it was all very vague and now no one knew the true facts. She gusted out a big sigh of regret and decided she would pick up her diary again, Sooty's Secrets, to record every thought and happening she knew about her family and events that were not already written up. Maybe, some day in the future, someone would know about her life and what she had experienced in what she realised with her knowledge of history, were epic times in Europe.

Chapter Thirty-Six

Nicky was exhausted and his nerves worn to a frazzle. When he'd finally arrived in Brussels with Wellington, the place was in a fever.

News of Bonaparte's reappearance in France had galvanised the arguing delegations at the Congress in Vienna. Even before he'd reached Paris on 20th March they'd declared him an outlaw and the four major Powers of the Seventh Coalition – Austria, Prussia, Russia and the British – had bound themselves each to supply an army of men with the aim of, once and for all, ending Napoleon's renewed threat to the peace and stability of Europe. Plans were now in progress to deal with the resurgent French army and Wellington had been put in command of the Anglo-Allied forces, supported in the main by the Prussians under Field Marshal Blücher, who were already trying to prepare themselves near the French border with the Low Countries. Wellington had, as expected, headquartered himself in Brussels with his camp south-west of the city. Blücher was based a bit further away in Namur, to the south-east.

However, the Coalition members were still bickering amongst themselves, politics being what it was, with a never-ending stream of plans and strategies constantly discussed by the generals of differing nations, in readiness for a forthcoming battle most thought was now inevitable. The main decision seemed to be where and when to attack France and while Wellington and Blücher were readying themselves, the rest of the Coalition were still busy mustering their forces and either preparing to march to support Wellington or Blücher, defend their own borders or align themselves on another front. To all intents and purposes, France would eventually be surrounded by Coalition forces by land and sea and a date of 1st July was eventually agreed for a concerted attack.

In the meantime, Wellington desperately needed information on what Bonaparte's forces were doing, so Nicky was sent off to infiltrate the various camps of *L'Armée du Nord*, the Army of the North, which Napoleon himself was leading, to pick up what information he could. It was hair-raising work and he knew if he was caught he would inevitably be summarily shot or tortured for information first if they found out his connection with Wellington.

He had acquired a French officer's uniform, middle ranking enough to enable him not to be questioned by any marauding troopers or small camps he passed through, as well as the main French lines, not senior enough to raise eyebrows. With all the veterans continuing to pour in to sign up to serve again, there was such confusion that no one took much notice of an unfamiliar junior officer asking to find his way around. As a cover, in case he was questioned, which he often was, leading to many close calls and hasty escapes, he'd also purloined some dispatches from a military courier he'd come across on the road one day. Like Francis, Nicky was no cold-blooded killer and would have been content merely to leave the man uninjured and horseless on the roadway, having found what he wanted. But the French courier had come after Nicky with a murderous venom as he'd turned to mount his horse and they'd fought viciously. When pushed, again like Francis, Nicky was completely ruthless and the man was now lying in a ditch with his throat cut; he'd been in the wrong place at the wrong time and picked the wrong man for a fight.

Nicky spent time surreptitiously moving around the many camps setting up daily as more veteran French troops arrived to join their former General and Emperor. He also frequented the taverns nearby to pick up information there from off-duty men who had had one too many glasses of ale or wine. Rumour and gossip abounded – plans and troop movements seemed to change almost daily – but he passed all the information he gleaned back to Wellington's HQ and left others based there to make of it what they could.

One late May morning, he rode back into Brussels, slid wearily off his horse and made his way to Wellington's camp. He looked tired, haggard and dishevelled and strode wearily to Wellington's private quarters. After waiting around for what seemed like hours, he was finally shown into his presence.

Wellington always spoke to Nicky alone, wishing as few people as possible to know what he was actually doing, which was just fine from Nicky's perspective. Wellington took one look at his bedraggled clothes, dirty, unshaven face with its hollow cheeks, bloodshot eyes with heavy black circles underneath and long, unruly hair and waved him to a seat. "You look appalling, de Bresancourt; when did you last wash?"

Nicky shrugged. "The bathing facilities where I was weren't quite up to my exacting standards," he sighed. "Absolutely shocking; no warm towels."

"How distressing, most uncivilised," opined Wellington, his tone arctic, sighing at the accustomed facetious answers he always got from this man, but he was one of his best undercover agents and he was worried at how bad he looked. "You look terrible, when did you last eat, or sleep?"

Nicky answered truthfully for once. "A few days ago, for a few hours in some woods somewhere. I can't seem to sleep properly when I'm surrounded by the French army..."

"Quite so," the older man commented, "and it shows. Look here, de Bresancourt, you're no good to me or yourself if you fall asleep on your horse, you need to have some rest. When did you last have a break from all this?"

Nicky shrugged. "Not since we arrived, Sir, it has been rather busy round here lately."

"Well, much as it pains me to suggest it, matters coming to a head as they are, I don't think you should go out again for a while. For

Heaven's sake, Man, go and find a quiet corner and get some decent rest and a square meal. Then a bath perhaps? You are a trifle... ah...fragrant."

"That would be appreciated, thank you, Sir; at least then I won't have to worry if I sing an English ditty in my sleep," he grinned.

"Oh, goodness sake," muttered Wellington, "you're getting worse, if that's possible. Now then, to important matters, what have you got for me this time?"

For the next half an hour, Nicky briefed Wellington on the information he had acquired from his latest foray into Bonaparte's camps and when he'd finished, Wellington sat back with a pleased smile. "Hmmm, that's very interesting," he said thoughtfully, tapping his steepled fingers together on his chin. "Have you given those mapped out troop movements and deployments to my ADC?"

"Yes, Sir, everything I could find."

"Capital, capital. I wonder what my commanders will make of them?" he murmured to himself.

"Bonaparte's whole northern army is coming together as we speak," said Nicky. "He's in personal charge, so far as I can make out. He's left Rapp in charge of the Fifth Corps over in Strasbourg and Suchet is down in Lyon with the Seventh. They're the nearest to us. The others are dotted around elsewhere to deal with other potential Allied threats, it's all in my notes. So the whole focus is his *Armée du Nord* and he's going to strike very soon, I'm sure of it, not wait for us to attack. He'll be a formidable opponent to overcome, Sir."

"I'm sure you're quite right," Wellington nodded "it's what I would do, if I were in his shoes, for a number of reasons. It's going to take an almighty effort to deal with him, but deal with him we must. We simply HAVE to prevail and I refuse to let that Corsican upstart better me. He's no more an Emperor than I am!"

The two men looked at each other for a couple of silent moments, both aware of what the Allied forces were up against.

"Look, you go and find food, a bath and a bed and come back in a day or so. We'll decide where you should go and poke your nose in next. Let someone know where you are, just in case I need to speak to you in the meantime." He rose to his feet and Nicky rose too. "Damn glad you came with us, de Bresancourt," he said, clapping Nicky on the shoulder, "damn glad," and having been suitably praised, thanked and dismissed, Nicky wearily took his leave, following Wellington's instructions.

On his way back to where he'd been quartered on the outskirts of the town, Nicky bumped into another of Wellington's ADCs. "Hello, de Bresancourt," he looked slightly askance at Nicky's grimy, scruffy appearance. "Rough ride, eh?" He assumed Nicky had been carrying messages back and forth between the Allied commanders – his cover story.

Nicky sighed, "You could say that," he laughed tiredly.

"Going to get some shut-eye, eh? You need a wash…" he sniffed politely and Nicky grimaced. He hated being so dirty, especially while he'd been with Wellington. "I think someone said there were a couple of letters for you; not sure where they are, though; tell you what, you go and get cleaned up and have a nap, then come and find me later, I'll get them for you," and with that, he wandered off.

Nicky was tempted to go with him to get the letters, but assumed they were more rambling missives from Cat and Bella. He enjoyed reading them, full as they were of Society gossip and general prattle about what the little girls had been up to, but he was dead on his feet. He therefore decided to find some hot water and a quiet corner, catch up on his sleep and then read them while he found some food and a drink. So, with that intention he ambled off, but when he got to his quarters, he was so tired he simply fell down on his narrow cot and went out like a light. However, worn out though he was, his nerves were in shreds and every slightest noise from the constant to-ing and fro-ing outside woke him up with a start. Fed up with tossing and turning, he eventually gave up and went to find somewhere to wash, shave and get something to eat. On his way out, he happened to pass the same ADC again who'd just come off duty. "Ah, there you are, just a jiffy," and he pulled a small wad of letters from the inside of his uniform jacket, handing them over to Nicky with a smile. "Happy reading," and with a nod, he hurried off.

Everywhere he went, the place was teeming with men and Nicky began to fantasise about his peaceful dressing room in Hertford Street, lounging in a deep, hot, fragrant bath, a glass of fine brandy in one hand and a cheroot in the other, doing nothing except soaking and dreaming of making love to Bella when he got out, then falling bliss-fully asleep, undisturbed all night. He decided to leave the busy encampment and locate an inn or hotel in Brussels where he could find some peace and hot water. As he walked past the mess tent, he was suddenly assailed by the smell of hot food and his stomach rumbled. He wandered in and sat down with a platter but the letters were burning a hole in his pocket, so as he ate the warm, plain and unap-petising meal, he began to open them one by one and read.

The first was from Cat and had been written soon after his depar-ture. It was loving and motherly and written in French as she often tended to do with Nicky, rambling on with anecdotes about Francis and Lizzie. She'd finished with a promise to box Nicky's ears severely, like she had when he was a boy and he'd been naughty, for his disgraceful behaviour at dinner the night before he left. Since he was now a respectable married man and a father, he should know better than to misbehave with her niece and he was lucky she hadn't run him through with her rapier in a very delicate place...and P.S., she hoped his wrists were better!

Nicky chuckled as he read it and then moved on to the next. It was from his step-father and had been sent shortly before Easter. He wrote more succinctly with news about Charlie and life at Arlington in general, then apologised profusely but said that his postponed wedding would now be going ahead after all. He explained he had so wanted Nicky to be there to stand up next to him as his Best Man, as his eldest son should, at which Nicky was supremely touched, but unfortunately, Elise had found herself to be in a rather delicate condi-tion, so matters would have to be hastily reversed and the ceremony would now take place at Firle, just after Easter. He promised they would toast him in his absence and that he would be sorely missed. Nicky smiled at the news. He was delighted for Eddie, who everyone believed to be so quiet and unassuming, Elise too, and laughed again to himself as he remembered his conclusion that the self-effacing pair both had hidden depths.

He looked at the remaining four missives. He recognised Francis's writing on a small thin one, he wasn't sure about the next but thought he recognised Jack's scrawl. The other two were from Bella. One thick and the other obviously just a short note.

He quaffed down some ale and opened the one from Francis first. He, too, had written a few days after Nicky had left. It was a strange note, a letter in two halves. The first told him he'd been to visit The Man and The Man now 'knew everything'. Nicky sighed and was pleased Francis had taken Ashcroft into his confidence and then he read on to the expected amusing part. The gentleman had recovered from the trauma of his visit to Firle House but was still threatening to exterminate Bubbles, send him to The Tower or exile him back to the Pyrenees. He had been warned Cat would challenge him to a duel and kill him if he so much as touched the dog. As for Francis, he couldn't cope with the thought of Bubbles pining in the Tower of London, as no doubt he would be called upon to help effect a rescue from another fortress, yet again. It was all too much for him. He was emigrating. His amusing rubbish finished with the news that his house now had an Official Government Plaque outside which was deterring all comers. He had copied out the wording but underneath had written that the author, The Man referred to above, had got his Latin wrong and instead of *Cave Canem* the words should instead read *Cave Filiam*. After Nicky stopped laughing at the refence to the naughty little girl, he read the final paragraph, which was forthright, again brutal and to the point albeit written in couched terms for obvious reasons, as had his references been to The Shadow and Ashcroft. Francis was always careful. Nicky read:

I am Taking Care of Everyone here. I know what You are up to. Remember what I said before - don't be in the Wrong Place at the Wrong Time. Head Down. We do NOT want a Dead Hero in the Family and I HATE funerals. We all Love You Very Much. F

Yet again Nicky was overwhelmed by the expression of care from Francis and was deeply touched. With a sigh he looked at the two missives from Bella and the one from Jack. He decided to open the thicker one from Bella first. It contained a funny picture of what he presumed was him and Duchess, not that he could really tell from the scribbled image and he grinned. It had Terrie's name underneath and *"I love you Papa and I miss you"* scrawled in very babyish letters with a big X at the end.

Like her aunt's, Bella's letter was long and rambling and full of expressions of love and how much she and Terrie missed him already. It had been written a week or so before Easter and she told him Jack had come home and been 'taken under Uncle Francis's wing to be 'polished" and she'd hadn't seen hide nor hair of him for days, but she KNEW what he was up to and she was going to have strong words with her uncle for such a disgraceful birthday present. Nicky also knew full well what Francis had done as he'd told Nicky briefly when they'd discussed it just before he left, along with arrangements for Jack's new horse. For a short while he remembered back to his self-same birthday and chuckled. Francis was indeed a disgraceful rogue and age didn't seem to deter him for a moment. As he read Bella's letter and thought about the one from Francis himself, he reflected on the many facets of the complex man and acknowledged he loved and admired him more than ever.

He opened Jack's next. It had been written at the end of the week after Easter and contained a droll recounting of Eddie and Elise's wedding, the misbehaving bridal attendants, how the Granville boys had all got seriously drunk at the Reception and sundry other laddish anecdotes. He talked about school, his signet ring from the Duke, his other birthday presents and contained effusive thanks for his horse, for which he was still trying to think of a name. He said he'd had an 'interesting' time in Town before Easter, thanks to the Duke and he would tell Nicky more when they next met. He would be delighted to compare notes and pick up any tips Nicky could offer him. Nicky shouted with laughter at this. What a shocker he was going to turn out to be, in precisely the same mould as himself and Francis. He grinned, exceedingly entertained.

Finally, he picked up the last missive from Bella. Unlike the other letters, which had either come in the mail or via one of Francis's many couriers, this one had no date and was addressed to him purely care of Wellington's Headquarters. He turned it over curiously and slit open the seal. The contents sent him ashen and his tankard fell to the floor.

At Valenciennes.

There is a terrible crisis - a matter of life and death.

Come at once, if you possibly can.

I will always love you more than life itself....

B

The writing wasn't her usual beautiful script but scrawled and blotched, as if it had been written in a panic or hurry. All sorts of terrible images raced through his mind: illness, Terrie...Bernheim.

Nicky didn't stop to think. Grabbing his letters and stuffing them inside his shirt, he ran back to Wellington's headquarters and burst into his outer offices, brushing past the astonished ADCs beavering outside. As luck would have it, the Duke was just on his way out. He looked Nicky up and down. "Good God, what on earth are you doing here? You look even worse than you did a few hours ago! Haven't you washed or slept yet?"

Nicky took a deep breath and thought quickly. "I'm not feeling too well, Sir, not at all. I'm hot," he wiped his face and then shivered, "I couldn't sleep. I was wondering if you would grant me a few days off? I hope I haven't picked up something from one of those French camps, they're so filthy..." he let the suggestive remark hang in the air.

Wellington took a step back. "Dammit Man, what the Devil are you doing here then? Be off with you, you'll infect us all!" He looked horrified, as did the men around him. "Go and find a doctor, this minute!"

Nicky bowed. "I just wanted to ask, Sir, you said to let you know what I was doing. I'm sure it's nothing but best to be on the safe side. I'll disappear off for a few days to make sure, if that meets with your approval, Your Grace?" he bowed again and shivered theatrically.

"Of course, of course, be off with you, but come back as soon as you can, we need you." He looked concerned as he dismissed Nicky and the latter wasn't sure if it was because he was supposed to be ill or if Wellington was just annoyed he'd be out of action for a few days. He grimaced, feeling like a naughty schoolboy playing truant, but if he'd just asked for some leave, he doubted Wellington would have granted it. He had to get to Valenciennes. Besides, he reasoned with himself, he'd be passing right through the enemy lines to get there and back, so he could no doubt pick up more information for Wellington as he travelled...and it would only be a few days...he hoped.

Tiredness forgotten, he ran to the stables, collected his horse again and set off, fear of the unknown that was waiting for him at Valenciennes racing through his mind. What was Bella doing there anyway, so near the French military? How long had she been there? Was Terrie there? When had the note arrived? He'd been in such a panic he'd not thought to go and find Harrison, the ADC who'd given him the letters, to enquire if he knew when the last one had arrived.

Horse and rider raced through the gathering dusk and then on through the night. Nicky knew the way but was also wary of the French, so inevitably had to circle round some of the main roads. He was wearing simple clothes when he left Brussels, but as he approached enemy territory over the border in France, he stopped to pick up his disguise and stolen dispatches hidden in the countryside outside the city. A random thought ran through his mind as his horse pounded along, to remember to hijack another courier soon to ensure the papers he carried were reasonably up to date. In the meantime he could always say if stopped he'd been delayed as he'd been attacked on the way; his strange humour made him laugh out loud.

As he approached Valenciennes, he was alarmed to see the increasing number of French regiments quartered in the area, even more than he'd expected and wondered what on earth Bella was doing there. That terrified him even more.

Both he and his horse were exhausted but he pushed on, going slower now as he cantered through the thick woodland surrounding the estate, perfect territory to be attacked. His nerves were at fever pitch as he made his way under the trees, every twittering bird and rustling branch making him jump.

He'd ridden through the night and it was only moonlight that had directed his path. As the early morning sun rose, he finally saw the new roof of his old family home shining in the distance and he slowed the horse to a quiet walk. He still had no idea of what had caused that desperate message and, ever wary, he slid off the horse's back and crept along with it following silently, so he could have a quiet look around before approaching. There was a slight rise in the woodland as he neared the estate boundary on one side, and tying his horse to a bush, he swung up into a likely tree to get a view of the chateau and surrounding gardens. He pulled a small eyeglass out of an inner pocket and surveyed the grounds but all seemed quiet and peaceful. A couple of gardeners were scything the grass and Madame Foubert appeared to be hanging out some washing in the early sunshine, near the back door to the kitchen, scullery and laundry room, singing to herself. Surely she wouldn't be doing that if there was trouble? Nevertheless, his mind went immediately to Bernheim...could he be inside? He watched for a while as the housekeeper went to and fro, carrying out her domestic chores. She fetched some fresh bread, cheese and ale for the gardeners and chatted to them for a few moments before returning to the back door, disappearing into the scullery. It all seemed so normal and Nicky was confused. However, he was still worried and slowly dropped back and remounted his horse. He pulled the message out of his shirt once more and re-read it.

"I will always love you more than life itself...."

The words tore at his heart, it sounded like something terrible was going to happen to her, as if she was ill or had to go away somewhere. Suddenly terrified, Nicky kicked the horse and set off at a gallop, unreasoning fear overwhelming him and within a few minutes the horse was swerving past the giant rampant stone lions which guarded the entry gates and pounding up the drive, flanks heaving, froth spewing from its mouth. He raced past the startled gardeners who took one look at his uniform and started to chase after him. Bella, Jack and Terrie were having breakfast in the kitchen when they heard the hoofbeats and as she raced to a hall window overlooking the drive and saw an approaching horseman, blonde hair flying behind him, Bella shrieked with pleasure and ran back to Jack. "HE'S COME, HE'S COME...!" she cried, face alive with joy.

Chapter Thirty-Seven

Having no concept of exactly what he'd been through for nearly the past two months, Bella and Jack had innocently wanted to surprise Nicky so, as per their plan, Madame Foubert scooped up the bewildered little girl and carried her off with a promise to go and look at the new kittens down in the stables. Jack ran to the front of the house to greet Nicky and Bella raced upstairs. She hurried over to her bedroom window and watched as Nicky slid off his heaving horse and ran up the steps to the front door. Jack came out to greet him and waved away the two panting gardeners who were looking askance at Nicky's French uniform.

"JACK!" Nicky's face registered shock. "What the Devil are you doing here? What's happened? Where's Bella?"

Jack pulled Nicky into a hug and grimaced, "Oh Nicky, I'm so glad you've come," his face was a tormented picture, "it's Bella...inside...upstairs..." he said no more, put his face in his hands and turned away. Nicky tore into the house, so didn't see Jack was covering his face to stop the paroxysms of laughter now seizing him. Oh, truly, he and Bella were wicked, he thought, as he turned to hurry down to the stables with the exhausted horse and to find Terrie; but serve Nicky right, he was always playing practical jokes on them!

Nicky ran up the grand staircase as if the hounds of Hell were after him, along the deserted corridors and into the bedroom suite of the Duchesses of Valenciennes. It had been completely replastered, repainted and refurbished, despite his terrible anger the previous year when he'd started his restoration project. For reasons then he wouldn't admit to himself, he'd lavished as much care and attention on those rooms as he had on his own Ducal suite. But as he burst through the repaired and newly painted double doors and into the light and airy sitting room, all was deserted and still. He rushed through to the bedroom and stood on the threshold and stared at the bed. A solitary candle was burning next to it and the covers were drawn back in a suggestively eerie fashion. The curtains were half-drawn and the whole room seemed sombre despite the sunshine outside. Horror-struck, he approached the bed and so never heard the figure creeping up behind him. Two hands went round his eyes and a loud shout of "BOOOO!" gave him such a fright he nearly passed out.

He spun around, his hands shaking as he rubbed his bloodshot eyes and looked at her. "What the fuck...?" she looked the picture of health and he literally staggered.

Bella collapsed in fits of laughter. "Ooooh, language! But serves you right," she cackled as he tottered over to the bed and sat down, looking white and shellshocked while she blew out the candle and drew back the curtains, letting the sun stream in once more.

"Sooty? You're not ill?" he stuttered. "You look fine..." a thought struck, "Terrie? Oh my God..."

"She's running around the stables with Jack and Madame Foubert; there's kittens there," she chuckled.

"But...but...you said there was a crisis? It was a matter of life and death...?" he started to gather his wits. "Jesus, I've just nearly killed myself to get here."

"There is a crisis," Bella said softly. "I'm having a crisis."

"You are? What crisis?" he was bewildered.

"I haven't seen you for three months; that's a major crisis!"

Nicky was beginning to realise he'd been had. "And the life or death?" he sighed.

"I can't live for a moment more without a cuddle," she held out her arms, "and I'll simply die if you don't kiss me this minute," looking his uniform up and down, "you horribly, dirty Frenchman!" as she crowed with laughter.

Nicky didn't know whether to laugh or cry, kiss her or paddle her backside, he was simply overwhelmed. When he didn't move, Bella just threw herself on his lap, hugged him fiercely and then kissed him hungrily. His arms snaked around her and they fell back on the bed together kissing passionately.

He pulled up and away from her, "Oh, Sweetheart, I could murder you, but it's so good to see you," he whispered and grinned, then swore as he realised he'd made her dress grubby from his mud and dirt spattered clothes and there was a splotch of mud on her cheek. "Ah, I'm so dirty. I'm sorry, look at your dress," he sat up and sighed.

"Who cares? I don't," she chuckled. "But you are a trifle… er…bedraggled and," she sniffed, "'aromatic,' and wherever did you get that uniform? I thought you were fighting FOR Wellington, not AGAINST him?" she laughed.

Nicky sighed. "Long story," he murmured.

Bella sat up and took a good look at him. "You look absolutely shocking," she said quietly. "What have you been doing?" She picked up his hands in concern.

"Not having a regular bath," he grinned, "and you're the second person to tell me how terrible I look – and smell – in the last twenty-four hours, it's getting quite tedious."

"Who else said it?" she asked curiously.

"Wellington," he grinned.

"Well, it's nice to know our estimable General and I are of the same opinion," she sniffed, "but seriously, Nicky, don't jest, you really do look done in. I've never seen you in such a state, even when I pushed you in the duck pond at Firle," she grinned, "and what's happened to your hair?" she tutted and peered more closely at the dark shadows under his eyes and a belligerent light lit hers, "and when did you last sleep properly, or eat a decent meal?"

"Are you trying to mother me?" he chuckled. "Anyway, it's your fault…'come at once, it's a matter of life of death'" he put on an affected voice. "Do you know what I had to do to get here, You

Baggage, or how tired I am? You bloody frightened the life out of me. I could have been tucked up in bed in Brussels now if it wasn't for you and your 'crisis'."

Bella laughed slyly. "Well, yes, but of course now you can be tucked up in bed with me in Valenciennes instead. Isn't that better?"

Nicky laughed, "It would be if I wasn't too bloody tired to do anything about it," he grimaced. "Seriously, Sooty, I haven't slept properly for weeks and then only patchily. I can't remember when I last washed and I haven't had a proper dinner since who knows when. Army food leaves a lot to be desired, compared to our cook in Hertford Street."

"Good God," tutted Bella, shocked. "Right, well we'll soon remedy that. Bath first I think, then you can sleep as long as you like and Madame Foubert will make you a wonderful dinner. How's that?"

"It sounds perfect, Sweetheart." He held out his arms to her again, "Can you bear to give me another kiss? It's so good to be home again."

Bella plopped herself down in his lap and looked at him. "Do you feel this is really your home, Nicky?" she asked quietly. "Here in France, not Hertford Street, or with the family in Berkeley Square or Firle or Arlington?"

Nicky kissed her again and responded with a sigh. "Sweetheart, my home is wherever you and Terrie are. Will that do? I just want to be with you."

"Perfectly," she sighed and kissed him again. "How long have we got you for?" she asked softly.

"Only a few days," he sighed. "I shouldn't be here at all. Wellington would have me shot for desertion if he knew. There's a few French soldiers out there, in case you haven't noticed. There'll be a battle shortly, it's inevitable, there are quite a number of skirmishes going on already." He looked at her worriedly, "What on earth made you come here? It's bloody dangerous. I'll have Francis's guts when I get back for letting you escape from London."

"Don't blame Uncle Francis, he was powerless to resist me. He put up a terrible fight."

"He did?"

"Mmmm," giggled Bella. "I've been taking lessons from experts," and she repeated the trick she'd copied from Terrie and Lizzie. "Ooooh, peeeease, Un-cul Fran-cisssss. Mwah, mwah," she giggled again as she placed two slobbery kisses on both his cheeks. Nicky chuckled. "Do you want to see the latest trick? He swears it wasn't him and it was you. I hope it wasn't or I'll box your ears, it's disgraceful," she scolded, "but of course it was him, we saw it at Easter. You should have seen Papa's face when they did it to him," and she giggled before leaning over to blow softly in his ear and then run her tongue lightly round its edge.

"What the hell? Lizzie did that? And Terrie? I'll kill him!" Nicky couldn't help himself, he burst out laughing.

"Are you sure it wasn't you?" Bella asked suspiciously. "I wouldn't put it past you, it's got your signature all over it."

Nicky held up his hands. "Completely innocent; besides, I was hundreds of miles away from the scene of the crime so how could I have done it?"

"Oh, I don't know, you could have taught them before you left, just to get your own back on Uncle Francis and simply told them to do it at Easter," she suggested.

"They're three, well Terrie isn't quite, even though she seems very advanced for her age, but that's a bit much of a subterfuge even for them," he laughed. "No, it was definitely Francis, he just gets worse as he gets older; dirty bugger," he muttered.

"AHA!" cried Bella, poking him in the chest. "So that's where THAT came from," she grumbled wrathfully. "You're both as bad as each other. Have you any idea how many people they've said that to over the past few weeks? I've never been so embarrassed in my life."

Nicky tried to look innocent. "It was an accident, truly, I was tired and forgot they were there," but he failed miserably and laughed again.

"It's NOT funny. Really, Nicky, you should have more sense than to say ANYTHING in front of them, they're worse than parrots. I've given up on Uncle Francis, he's a lost cause, a complete scoundrel," she started to mutter on about him.

"What's he done now?" joked Nicky.

Bella smirked. "Auntie is going to have another baby."

"Noooo!" Nicky gaped, and then a wicked look stole over his face. "The dirty, depraved, licentious old bugger," he murmured to himself and doubled over with laughter.

"Well really! Is that all you've got to say on the matter?" Bella huffed. "Aren't you pleased?"

Nicky pulled himself together. "Of course I'm pleased. What a carry on," he chuckled.

Bella hastily changed the subject before he started asking her too many questions as she didn't want to tell him her news just yet. "So, what's a few days? I need to know. Are we talking two, three, four?" she looked hopeful.

Nicky sighed. "Two, maybe three. Remember, I've got to get back to Brussels, that'll take best part of a day."

Bella looked mournful. "Only two or three? Still, that's better than nothing I suppose," she grumbled.

"There is a War on, y'know. I can't just disappear for some romantic interlude because you're having a crisis. Consider yourself lucky I'm here at all. Now then," he pushed her off his lap, "how about that bath?"

"Oh, very well," she sighed, then grinned at him, "do you want me to scrub your back?"

"You can scrub me all over, You Witch. Just go and find me some hot water and a lot of soap," he ordered.

"Yes, Sir," Bella saluted and hurried off.

Nicky lay back in the scented water, sipping a glass of brandy and smoking a cheroot after Bella had washed and trimmed his hair, sighing with pleasure each time he dipped down in the big tub in his dressing room and immersed himself in the steamy heat. He reappeared in his bedroom, freshly shaven with a towel round his waist and Bella watched as he flexed his back and arms with a groan and sank down onto his big bed. He lolled back and rolled on to his stomach with a tired sigh. She wandered over and silently started to massage his back and arms and then, pulling off the towel, down his thighs and the back of his legs, looking at the little lion birthmark, desire starting to curl through her as she ran her hands over his body and he sighed with pleasure. She was just considering crawling into bed next to him when a loud snore reached her ears and she realised he was fast asleep. So, quietly and reluctantly, she pulled the covers over him, kissed him lovingly on the back, drew the curtains and crept out the now darkened room.

He slept all day. Bella periodically sat and watched him in the candlelight and soothingly kissed and caressed him as he occasionally started to mutter in his sleep, tossing and turning. He always responded with a deep sigh and settled back to slumber on.

Bella, Jack and Terrie were all sitting in the kitchen again as darkness fell and Nicky strolled in, his mouth watering at the smell of Madame Foubert's roasted chickens.

Jack grinned at him and winked. "I'll deal with you later, Young Man, you and your theatrics, just you wait," Nicky grinned back and then held out his arms as Terrie screeched and ran into them. He scooped her up and hugged her as she placed big slobbery kisses all over his face. "'Lo Papa, where's you bin? Has you seed th' duckies an' pigglywigglies? An' there's kitties in th' staybul."

Nicky chuckled "No, not yet You Little Minx, you can show me tomorrow. I can see your vocabulary has extended… fascinating!"

"But I wanna go NOW! Now Papa…" and she tugged on the collar of his shirt.

"No, it's too late now, it's dark; I can't see pigglywigglies in the dark. Tomorrow," he smiled and kissed her on her little pert nose

"Oh, peeease, Papa," and before he knew it a little puff of warm breath wafted into his ear as Terrie reached round and licked it, then kissed him on both cheeks and twirled her finger in his hair.

Jack laughed and Bella grinned at the expression on Nicky's face. "Told you so," she smirked.

Nicky was momentarily shocked. "That's appalling," he chuckled. "I'm going to have a serious conversation with Francis. God knows what he'll teach them next."

"I's gonna be a poozzy cat whens I's a big girl, Papa" a little voice announced. "I've 'cided."

Jack laughed. "I thought you wanted to be a chicken? You were clucking enough to drive us all mad last week."

"No, I's notta chickin 'ny more, 'an I's a girl, so I can'ts be a big fooffy lion like Papa an' go rawrrrrrr," she growled and shook her head, her golden curls bouncing around her face, her hair-ribbon, as ever, askew, and Nicky felt his heart turn over with love for her. He hugged her tight as her innocuous comment stabbed him somewhere deep in his gut, "so I's a fooffy lickle poozzy cat an' go meeeeeeee-owww," Terrie chattered innocently on and meowed.

"Why can't you be a chicken? They've got lots of fooffy feathers?" asked Jack

"'Cos I don't wanna be your dindins, Silly!" and as they all burst out laughing, Nicky sat down at the table and knew in his heart he had come home. It was all he'd ever wanted and dreamed of – to be at Valenciennes again, with a loving family around him.

As he looked over at his laughing wife, Terrie's lion comment struck again and a momentary pang of jealousy stabbed through him as he thought about Francis, Eddie and their pregnant wives and their sons who would inherit. He wondered why it had happened to them but not him and he silently sighed to himself. What was the point of refurbishing Valenciennes and claiming back the lands if there would be no one to come after him? He still had no idea if Terrie's descendants, if she had sons, could inherit, being in the direct line, but that was something lawyers would no doubt have to investigate and argue about, if it was even possible. He'd thought the same last year when he'd had the little plaque mounted on the wall of the ruined chapel in the cemetery. That was just after Ashcroft's visit and he'd gone chasing off after Bernheim. Now he wondered idly, yet again, if he would be the last of the de Bresancourts with his own little plaque on the chapel wall and no grave underneath, as the looming and dangerous battle with Bonaparte grew more imminent. He kept being assaulted by premonitions that something terrible was going to happen to him, or that he was going to die in the battle. Thoughts of Francis's letter returned to his mind and his words ran round Nicky's brain....'*don't be in the wrong place at the wrong time....don't be a dead hero...keep your head down...*" but he simply laughed and smiled and joined in the chatter and kept his stark, fearful and sad thoughts to himself.

After dinner, while Bella bathed and put an overtired Terrie to bed, Nicky spent an amusing hour with Jack, wending their way through a bottle of brandy and hearing about his birthday treats from Francis, including his experiences in the exclusive whorehouse where'd he'd had such an enjoyable and educational time. Nicky shouted with laughter when he was informed Jack now looked on him and Francis as his mentors and he was determined to out-rake the pair of them. He also showed Nicky his new signet ring and explained how Francis had chosen the motif and thanked Nicky effusively for his new horse. He told Nicky he'd decided to call him Janus, after the Roman god who had two faces, one looking forward and one looking back. He said it was because he was looking forward to his new life, but would always look back, never forget his roots and where he'd come from. Nicky was bemused and touched at the mature thought that had gone into the choice of name and simply swatted the lad's head affectionately, calling him a rogue, before making his way up to bed.

He took Bella to bed that night and loved her repeatedly and intensely, until he was drained and finally fell into exhausted slumber again. Bella lay awake for a while, watching him sleep, knowing something was bothering him but merely assumed it was worry over the forthcoming battle. Frightened as she herself was, especially as she'd seen him surprisingly turn up in a French officer's uniform, she merely let him be. She finally fell asleep herself but woke up a few hours later to watch him, staring into the darkness outside the bedroom window, lost in thought. She crept out of bed to stand behind him, wrapping her arms around his waist and leaning her head into his muscled back. But despite her quiet query as to the cause of his insomnia, he merely picked her up, carried her back to bed and made love to her fiercely again until they both fell asleep in each other's arms.

Chapter Thirty-Eight

T he following day was spent in the sunny gardens, picnicking under the spreading branches of a large tree. Francis's guards were no more immune to Terrie's innocent charms than the housekeeper and one of them had made her a small swing. Nicky, Jack and Bella lazed around on the grass, consuming bread, cheese, pate and local wine, watching the little girl sway back and forth, demanding Jack to push her which he happily did. Terrie had also dragged an amused Nicky around the farmyard, showing him the ducks and their ducklings, the chickens and pigs and then the kittens in the stables. He shouted with laughter at her rendition of the various animal noises and no more so than when she'd finally demonstrated her prowess at milking the cow, which despite her frantic pulls on the animal's udder, produced no more than a solitary drip. It was like a day out of time, peaceful and happy without any intrusions of the War that loomed so closely on their very doorstep.

He had another uproarious drinking session with Jack that evening before sending the inebriated youth staggering unsteadily up to bed. He went up to his own suite of rooms where he found Bella in her bedroom, waiting for him, staring out of the window. He pounced on her before she had a chance to speak and tossed her on the bed, pushing up her dress and driving into her like a man possessed, leaving her breathless and stunned at his ardour. She dozed off as he rolled over, exhausted and slightly overwhelmed, waking an hour or two later to find him, yet again, still dressed, sitting in a chair, staring sightlessly into the empty fireplace, a glass of brandy and a cheroot in hand.

What IS it, Nicky?" she asked softly "What's worrying you, My Love?"

He turned and smiled at her where she lay on the bed. "Oh, you know, Wellington, Bonaparte, the battle that's coming..." he shrugged.

"Are you sure?" she asked, not convinced he was being totally truthful.

"Of course, *Chérie,*" he smiled, "what else would there be? Isn't that enough?"

Bella sighed "I know. Dear God, I wish Wellington had never crossed our threshold that day."

"What will be, will be," he replied enigmatically.

Bella looked at him, lost in thought herself and got up to pour herself a drink, sipping it slowly while deciding what to do. She'd had a lot of time to think over the past three months since he'd been away. About Nicky, his history and his memories, her relationship with him, what had transpired that torrid day and night at *Le Lion d'Or*, what she'd discovered about herself and what Nicky had said to her. She'd gone over it all in her mind in enormous detail, trying to analyse what she'd done and felt. She'd found a sympathetic listener in her Aunt Cat and they'd had several deep, frank and mature discussions about what it was like being married to men like Francis and Nicky. Cat, being French and quite forthright, had given her a lot of wise counsel once she'd got over her own hurdle of trying to talk about sex to someone who was like a second daughter to her.

Not long after, one afternoon, Cat had introduced Bella to an entertaining Frenchwoman with a shock of white hair standing out amid the grey, who apparently owned one of the most infamous, if discreet and exclusive whorehouses in London. With an enigmatic smile, Cat had left them to their own discussions and Bella had met the woman several times in the weeks that had followed, over tea in her own house in Hertford Street.

Bella was no fool. Despite Nicky's endless protestations of love and commitment, she was still worried that his lengthy time absent from her would offer temptation he either couldn't or wouldn't resist. That he loved her, she had no doubt, but he was a man: a carnal, passionate, uninhibited, very experienced, very sensual and sometimes demanding man, who enjoyed fornication in all its forms, just like her uncle, according to her aunt; and regularly, not just now and again when the fancy took him, so she worried about keeping his interest. She enjoyed everything he did, as did he and just as enthusiastically, like her aunt did with her uncle. That wise woman had advised her that particular aspect was important as they were matched and there was nothing worse than a reluctant partner. So that wasn't her problem. It was just that the thought of him with another woman, even if only for Ashcroft's shady purposes, had her seething with jealousy.

She'd been to see Ashcroft too. She'd turned up in his office, totally out of the blue, one dull afternoon and challenged him to another game of chess. They'd battled constantly over a couple of days, during which she'd plied him with questions about what Nicky was doing in Belgium and France. Ashcroft had told her truthfully he was working for Wellington, undercover, to glean information about Bonaparte's intentions and troop movements and that it had no connection to what Bernheim was doing. Their game had ended eventually in a stalemate and she'd sauntered out of his office with a smiling toss of her head, information found, telling him she would return soon for a rematch and promising to beat him next time.

In his late fifties, Miles Ashcroft was not much older than Francis Granville, although to look at him one would never know. Francis looked so much younger than his age whereas Ashcroft was grey-faced, ascetic, balding and carried the stresses and strains of his occupation hard. The man had silently watched her go with an impassive smile, more in love with her than he'd been before.

So Bella sat and watched the man she loved and reached a decision. She disappeared into her dressing room, reappearing quite a long while later, covered in a wrap. Nicky looked up at her, hardly registering she'd been, gone and returned. "I'm sorry, *Chérie*, if I disturbed you?" he said with a smile, shaking his head as if trying to dismiss his thoughts.

"You didn't really, it's not that late and I'm not tired, or ready to sleep yet," Bella smiled at him enigmatically. She pulled up a chair across from him and sat down. "Do you want to come back to bed?" she raised an eyebrow at him.

He smiled at her, electricity again arcing between them. "Of course, *Chérie*, you don't have to ask...if you're awake?"

"Oh, I'm awake," she smiled. "Do you want to play a game, or are you tired?"

Nicky looked over at her and shook his head, his dark thoughts suddenly forgotten, eyes alight with mischief "And what sort of game would that be?"

"Oh, I don't know, I'll think of something. Have another brandy, I'll be back shortly and stop thinking... unless it's about me!" She gave him a saucy look as she got up, bent to kiss him quickly before disappearing again into her dressing room.

She sauntered back into the bedroom and Nicky looked up and gawped, his glass in mid-air, his drink forgotten. Her hair was down but teased into a black, waving froth, with red bows here and there. Her face was painted like a harlot, her eyes enhanced with green and black, highlighting their colour as they glinted at him, her lashes heavily sooted. Her lips were painted bright red and she had a couple of beauty spots, one on her cheek and another above her mouth. She put a small casket down on the table next to him and retreated backwards, grinning lecherously. His lips curled into a smile.

"Are you ready?" she purred quietly and started to peel off her wrap. The covering slid to the floor and underneath she was wearing just a simple, thin silk shift; very short, barely reaching her thighs. But it was very damp and clung to her, revealing her torso underneath. Nicky looked her up and down. Her voluptuous breasts had been rouged heavily, the wet silk clinging to them enticingly, her nipples taut and reddened. He could just see her little lion charm on its chain around her neck, glimmering through the material. His eyes glittered as they traversed downwards and her hairless lower body showed through the thin material. Black silken stockings ended above her knees, held up by a froth of red lace garters. He grinned. She looked outrageous, like some low-class prostitute vying for business in a tawdry brothel. However, few low-class prostitutes looked as beautiful as she did.

Her eyes glittered across from him as she swivelled her hips, her hand caressing her body and he watched in fascination as she pranced and twirled in front of him, continuing to fondle herself suggestively, moaning slightly and tossing her head back as she did so. She turned her back on him and continued her performance, bending forwards and wriggling her behind invitingly, scything her hand between her legs.

Lust roared through his veins even as he chuckled and he felt his body's hardening response. She turned back to face him and smiled naughtily as he crooked a finger at her. But she stood where she was, unmoving, hand on hip and writhed again. Slowly, she crooked a finger at him and pointed to the floor in front of her. They looked at each other, the endless challenge between them as alive as ever.

He crooked his finger at her once more and she crooked hers again, pointing to the floor at her feet. He threw back his head and laughed as he slowly rose from his chair, putting down his forgotten glass and tossing his cheroot into the empty fireplace. He prowled across to her, a lecherous, laughing expression on his face. "I always knew you were a trollop at heart," he smirked, "my personal trollop." He stood, looking down into her narrowed, painted green eyes. "So, what now, *Madame*?" his lips curled in a salacious smile.

Bella looked him up and down, "I'm a fierce and dangerous lioness," she purred, "on the prowl..." she licked her lips suggestively, "vairrrry dangerous," she took hold of his loose shirt and ripped it open, "and extremely hungry," and she leaned forward to lick his chest, biting his nipples, hard, making him cry out softly.

"No one can capture me," she purred again, "no one can tame me... grrrrrrr," she growled at him. "Are you man enough to try?" She curled a hand into a claw and scratched her nails, quite viciously, down his chest from his throat to his abdomen, leaving a trail of red marks in their wake.

Nicky chuckled at her and fast as lightning he curled a fist into her hair, pulling her head back to laugh down into her face. "You Little Witch," he grinned, "don't you know I'm a famous lion tamer? You've met your match in me..." and he kissed her hard and hungrily as she writhed and tried to pull away from him.

When he raised his head again, wiping the back of his hand across his mouth to remove the red paint he suspected was there from her lips, she smirked at him mockingly and danced away, lifting a small chain from over her head and sucking the small key dangling from it, before waving it in front of him. "Don't be too sure," she laughed as he grabbed the chain.

"Now what do we have here?" he asked curiously, eyeing her before turning to the small casket on the table. He sauntered over to it, unlocked and opened the little chest and lifted the lid curiously. A pile of ribbons lay inside and the small silver chain with its charms lay twinkling in the candlelight on top. His eyes lit up and he glanced back at her, lasciviously. "Oho..." he chuckled lecherously "Lioness taming equipment!"

Bella grinned back at him. "If you can catch me," she challenged.

Completely captivated, Nicky picked up a long length of ribbon and pulled it through his fingers and then looked over at her. "No problem whatsoever. No Lioness has ever escaped ME," he warned softly, turning to face her across the room. They looked at each other momentarily and then with a saucy grin, Bella turned tail and fled. He chased her through to his room, down the corridor outside, around the vast deserted house and then back into his room again, around the furniture before he finally cornered her, breasts heaving in the wet silk, back in her own room. He grabbed her and tossed her on the bed where they battled and wrestled before he tied her wrists behind her. She panted up at him and laughed.

"I've got you now," he chuckled.

"Oh, no, you haven't," she cackled and growled at him, writhing and trying to escape. "Rawrrrrrr... don't you know how dangerous a lioness is when captured?"

"Is that so?" and he dragged her over to the casket. "Now then..." he pondered, looking down into the contents, "how to tame a very

Unladylike Lioness?" he mused, looking at the chain and then back at Bella.

For a moment his face went serious. "Are you sure, Sweetheart? It was only supposed to be a one-off demonstration. I never meant to repeat it, it's too much, not really appropriate for nice women, no matter how close or intimate they are with their husbands. It's more the territory of whorehouses and courtesans or torrid affairs, to be honest. I wouldn't dream of doing it again unless you were quite positive you both liked and wanted it, in which case that's a different matter."

Bella looked at him, face serious as well, "I was thinking... after you left..."

He groaned. "You think and read far too much for your own good," he muttered.

Bella ignored him. "I thought about it a lot...what you did, I did, what we did together at *Le Lion d'Or*, ALL of it. And what I felt about it."

Nicky looked at her curiously. "I was shocked at first, you know I was, despite all my reading," she said softly. "But then, afterwards, when I thought about it in the cold light of day, sober as a judge," she smiled at him wickedly, "it was just a game, wasn't it? Not serious, no harm done, no one knew or saw, just us, so although it was very bad, quite perverted actually, I... I... admitted to myself I rather enjoyed it," she whispered and slowly, she smiled salaciously up at him under her lashes, "it's far more distracting than shopping, so do your worst, Lion Tamer," and she winked at him.

Nicky's eyes widened. "You're absolutely sure?" She smiled and nodded.

"Only if you enjoy it too," she added softly. "Do you, Nicky?"

"What? Getting the better of you, BossyBoots?" he chuckled. "Always." He pulled her into his arms and kissed her, their mutual lust and hot desire bursting into flames between them.

"Right," he said, "prepared to be tamed, You Baggage," dangling the chain in front of her.

"Oh, no, you won't," she challenged, smiling.

"Oh, yes, I will," he laughed and chased after her as she danced away from him again.

He caught her easily and pulled her back to the casket where he repeated the exercise from *Le Lion d'Or* and pulled her shoulders and upper arms taut behind her, binding them tightly, more so than before, now she knew what he was up to. He looked at her lecherously as he slowly ripped open the damp shift, exposing her jutting breasts with their rouged nipples.

"You're glorious," he whispered to himself as he bent to kiss her breasts and fasten on the chain, watching her jerk momentarily and cry out as the clamps bit in to her reddened nipples. "Surely you weren't so voluptuous before?" He shook his head in momentary confusion and wonder. "I never realised. Talk about not paying attention..."

Bella smiled secretly to herself. Her breasts had swollen already in her pregnant state and she'd wondered how she would react to the clamps, if it would be too much...but the temporary pain diminished and the feeling was even more intense than before; she writhed in plea-surable torment as her over-sensitive nipples reacted to their gentle torture and she felt herself start to burn inside as the wetness increased between her legs.

He pulled her gently into her dressing room by the chain. "You never saw before, look at yourself," he ordered in a whisper, "look at what I see," and Bella gasped as she gazed at herself in the looking glass, more heat shooting through her body at the erotic image in front of her. "One day I'll make love to you and you can watch yourself in a mirror," Nicky continued to whisper behind her, smiling wickedly as she gasped again.

"Oh nooo, that's shocking," she said softly. "I read about it, but still..."

"You'll see," he merely said enigmatically, shaking his head at her admission. "You'll be amazed, you won't be able to tear your eyes away..."

Bella tossed her head and retreated from the arousing images in front of her and in her mind, dancing away from him again, the charms tinkling as she moved and backed into her bedroom, laughing at him, tempting him. "You won't tame me this time," she cackled, "I know what's going to happen now, I'll just lie back and enjoy it!"

"Really?" he said sarcastically "How much will you bet me?"

"Five guineas," she chuckled, "the going rate."

"Done," he grinned at her, "cheap at half the price," and he laughed a terribly wicked laugh.

They dodged each other around the furniture and he laughed at her again, "You're like a skittish young horse; you know I'll master you in the end."

"No, you won't." It was just like when they were children, teasing each other.

Nicky went over to the casket, rummaged around and pulled out the length of black silk.

"Ooooh noooo," Bella gasped playfully.

"Ooooh yessss," he smirked. "It's how to tame horses, it'll do just as well on you." He crooked his finger, "Come here, You Dangerous Lioness."

Bella shook her head but it made no difference, he soon captured her, waving the long length of dark material in front of her teasingly, laughing as he tied it round her eyes and twirled her around. She was lost and the feeling of helplessness and overwhelming arousal crept over her again. She decided she was beyond a wanton but didn't care, which shocked her even more. Once again, everything she'd read and discussed with her aunt, and Marguerite Beaumont, the whorehouse owner, compared to the reality, were entirely different things.

"Now then," Nicky teased, "I've got you now," and he kissed her mercilessly, ripping the shift off her completely, letting his hands rove all over her body, tantalising every crevice, making her gasp and writhe as his knowing hands felt the wetness between her legs.

"How much will you bet me now?" he chuckled.

"You won't win," she gasped. "I'll never let you win."

"You'll see," he whispered, "well maybe you won't, but I'll win, I can feel your five guineas in my pocket already."

"I'll always be dangerous," she laughed. "You may be a famous lion-tamer, but you won't tame me, not this time."

Nicky picked up her wriggling and resisting body and carried her through into his bedroom, draping her over a small desk in a window alcove. He licked and tormented her body, driving her wild with want and then for the next half hour, proceeded to do the same around their suite. At one point he carried her out into the deserted house, ignoring her horrified protestations. He'd poked his head around Jack's door and knew the lad was snoring the sleep of the dead after his copious amounts of wine and brandy earlier, so the house was deserted, the housekeeper, the few servants and guards either in the outbuildings or patrolling the grounds. Finally, he brought her back into her bedroom.

"Are you still a hungry lioness?" he chuckled. "You know what I want, would you like a taste of human flesh?" he asked lewdly.

Bella panted, "And you trust me not to bite you?" she breathed. "Foolish man!" She laughed but sank to her knees and licked her lips. "I dare you…" she smirked seductively in a hoarse voice.

Nicky looked at her, not quite sure she wouldn't do as she'd threatened, then bent and kissed her. "Don't you even consider it…" he chuckled.

"Well, well…" Bella suddenly asked. "Now how much do you trust ME?" and she cocked her head to one side, teasingly.

Silence hung in the room for moments as he took a deep breath. "Always," he whispered, and let her take him in her mouth.

As he felt her mouth and tongue work its magic on him, he let his head fall back at the intense feelings she was creating, wondering if it was his imagination or was she doing all sorts of little things she hadn't done before? He could feel the tingle, his release rising, but suddenly, amongst all the humour, playfulness and erotic pleasure they were enjoying, a terrible image of the cemetery entered his mind and he pulled back. He didn't want to waste an opportunity to lose himself in her, plant his seed where it counted, so much to Bella's surprise, he unexpectedly withdrew from her with a strange laugh and pulled her to her feet, wondering at this obsession which was overwhelming him.

"Tut, tut," he chuckled. "That wasn't up to your usual standard," he complained as he tried to refocus his mind away from his heaving, unsatisfied body. "You'll need to be punished and I can see you'll need some extra private lessons." He looked down on her, his eyes now glittering with unsatisfied lust as she merely laughed at him in confusion.

He tossed her on the bed and started to tease her again in earnest, bringing her easily to the point of climax several times before withdrawing until she was screeching at him in frustration, also sucking and nibbling on her breasts and nipples and tightening the clamps even more to torment her still further until she was jerking, moaning and swearing at him.

He pulled her over onto his lap and slapped her bottom hard. "That's for coming over to France instead of staying safe at home with your uncle," he breathed as she yelled at him. He slapped her again, harder, "That's for sending me that dreadful, lying message," he continued. Another hefty smack, "And that's for making me nearly drop dead on the spot and frightening the life out of me when I arrived here and came into your bedroom." He was pulling on the chain as he spanked her, knowing full well how much he was tormenting her breasts. Bella was so incoherent she couldn't speak for the feelings he was creating. She felt his hand creep beneath her and she was so wet, she could feel the moisture seep out of her and run down her legs. "Do you give in, have I tamed you yet?" he whispered. "Christ, how aroused are you?" he muttered to himself.

She shook her head. He spanked her again, several times, hard. This time, she felt his fingers delve deep inside her, knowingly and teasingly, her legs drumming up and down as she screeched unheedingly at him. "You need more lessons before you take me in your mouth again, shocking performance, what a hopeless, ugly trollop you are," he was trying not to laugh now, unsure how long he could hold out. "I won't stop until you admit you've challenged the wrong Liontamer. How much more can you take? I'll drive you mad," he threatened. "I'll torture you all night, I'll tie you in some terrible positions and I won't let you climax," he whispered as he tweaked the chain again.

Bella had never known such torment. her body was on fire, far worse than before. "All right," she sobbed brokenly, "you win, you win. Please," she moaned, "please, please...fuck me...now...hurry...hurry... I want it hard, fast...be quick about it..."

"Really? Should I?" he teased, tweaking the chain and Bella thought she would explode at him.

"NICKYYYYYY!" she shrieked "I'll KILL you!"

He gave in. He tossed her over and thrust inside her. When he gently pulled off the clamps Bella yelled her head off and then her body exploded as he started to move and thrust inside her in earnest, doing as she'd begged. "You owe me five guineas, My Beloved Trollop," he panted brokenly and felt himself spend deep within her belly like an erupting volcano, "and give me a son, *Chérie*," he pleaded almost incoherently to himself, lost in the epic feelings he was experiencing as he felt her climax around him.

For the rest of her life Bella swore she would never experience such an intense orgasm again as he gave her that night. Her tormented breasts were on fire and her belly and whole body contorted with such contractions that momentarily she feared for the burgeoning life within her. A random thought wondered if the intense feelings were because she was expecting and also hadn't had him for three long months, but she had no idea and promptly forgot about it. "I can, I will, you'll see..." she screamed. The climax went on and on until she saw stars and blacked out.

She came to and found herself released and nestled in his arms in the bed. She looked up into his grinning and loving face. "I refuse to pay you," she whispered. "You're a useless lover. I didn't feel a single thing," and promptly closed her eyes and went out like a light, completely overcome. Nicky kissed her gently, feeling overwhelmed with love for her and fell into his own exhausted slumber. The games they played simply bewildered him. He'd never dreamed in a thousand years he'd ever experience anything like this in a marriage, but then he'd never dreamed he'd marry a woman like Bella.

He woke up with a start hours later, heart thumping and sweating. He'd had a terrible nightmare where he'd been blown to pieces on the battlefield, surrounded by mangled bodies and seeing his own plaque in the cemetery. Bella was snoring gently by his side, body sprawled out on her back in complete abandon, remnants of her rouged breasts and painted face still evident in the early dawn light. He pulled the covers over her and staggered out of bed, shaking, to sit on the chair, tipping the remains of his abandoned glass of brandy down his throat.

He pulled a coverlet off the bed, wrapped it around himself to stop his shivers and poured some more brandy into his glass. He put his head in his hands and felt tears on his face.

Bella rolled over and sought the comforting warmth of his body, but there was nothing except cold bed. She opened her eyes and saw him across the room, hunched over in the heavy bed cover, drinking brandy. Alarmed, she got out of bed and went over to sit on his lap, putting her arms around him. "What IS it Nicky? There's something really wrong, isn't there?" she asked softly.

He looked up at her, a haunted expression on his face. "I had a nightmare," he whispered. "I dreamed I was dead on a battlefield, shot to pieces. I keep getting these premonitions I'm going to die."

"Hush now, don't talk like that." Bella lived with that constant fear too, she'd often had the same nightmares. "But there's more, something else?" she whispered knowingly.

He sat sombrely for a long while and then it all burst out of him. "It's been almost two years. I know I've been away a lot, but I've still made love to you in between, even when I was angry," he shook his head, "and we still only have Terrie," he agonised brokenly. "Why can Francis and Papa manage to have boys and not me?" He waved his hand in the air, "All this, it's all pointless..." and he put his head in his hands.

"Ah," whispered Bella, finally realising what was eating at him as she kissed him gently and his words as he'd climaxed, slowly came back to her. "Look at me, Nicky," she said softly. "I have something to tell you."

He looked up at her again sadly and she smiled at him. "I know I keep telling you how useless you are," she whispered with a small chuckle, "but you're not really. Well, only sometimes," and she grinned triumphantly. "I AM going to have another child. That's one of the main reasons I wanted to come here to see you." she paused. "I wanted to tell you to your face," and she watched with enormous pleasure as her words registered and his face lit up.

His arms came around her and he hugged her tightly. "Really, Sooty? Are you sure?" she nodded and his smile broadened like the sun coming out. "You BAGGAGE! Why didn't you tell me before now?" he shook his head, bemused, "I can't believe it," he looked at her again, "you're really sure?"

Bella nodded, suffused with pleasure at his reaction and so pleased she'd come to France to tell him. "I just wanted to wait until the right moment. You see there really was a crisis, I was telling the truth in my note."

Nicky looked confused. "There was?"

"I kept wanting jam on my potatoes and the housekeeper ran out of jam..." and Nicky threw back his head and crowed with laughter.

He thought for a moment, "So that was why Jack gave you such a funny look over dinner last night when you were eating your potatoes? He knows then?" he laughed.

Bella nodded. "He's been like a mother hen, fussing over me every minute, driving me completely mad. Uncle Francis gave him strict instructions before we left not to take his eyes off me or let me do anything. It's all I can do to lift a cup and saucer," she sighed forlornly. "The pair of them think I need mollycoddling to the Nth degree."

Nicky chuckled, "Quite right too," he muttered, grinning hugely. Then his expression suddenly looked appalled. "My God, Bella. What we've just done, are you mad?" his face was a picture. "The baby? Are you all right? Is it all right?"

It was Bella's turn to laugh. "Oh, don't you start, I don't need you fussing as well, that WILL drive me mad for sure. Of course I'm all right." She poked him in the chest, "You may think you know everything about ladies, You Terrible Lothario, but obviously not expectant ones. YOU'VE got a lot to learn," she giggled.

"Not at all, for a start you certainly shouldn't be running around with nothing on in the middle of the night." Nicky looked at her in alarm, "You could catch a chill!" He stood up suddenly, holding Bella in his arms tenderly and carrying her back to bed, putting her down carefully and pulling the covers over her. She lay there laughing at him, "Oh Lord, have I got to put up with this for the next six months?" she muttered.

He looked down at her sternly, "Absolutely. No arguments. From now on, you'll do exactly as you're told, You Baggage. You're not going to pick up anything more than a reticule, if that. Certainly, there'll be no more games for you," he waggled his finger at her. "You're shocking, completely irresponsible and disgraceful. That's my son you're carrying," and he tutted, "what must he think?"

Bella was in fits of laughter. "How do you know it's going to be a boy?" she asked, "it could be another girl."

"No, it's not. I won't allow it," he declared.

"What will you do," she chortled, "send it back?"

"We've already got a daughter, so it must be a son this time."

"Not at all. The odds are fifty – fifty. I run two gaming saloons, I understand the odds very well," she chuckled.

Nicky got back into bed beside her and took her gently in his arms, his hand lying on her flat stomach. He still looked worried, "Bella, what we did, are you sure?"

"You ARE an idiot, of course I'm sure. You're not going to stop making love to me just because I'm going to have a child," she grinned. "If everyone did that, the world would go quite mad, I'm sure."

"But what we did, that was... er... beyond making love, it was very perverted," he muttered and then a thought struck. "Your breasts, I thought they were larger than I remembered!" He glared at her, "Why didn't you say?" He looked angry and then suddenly stricken with guilt, "Oh my God, I tightened those clamps. THEY are getting thrown out first thing tomorrow morning," he announced, "everything else too," and Bella laughed.

He lay back on the pillows, obviously struggling to take it all in. "I still don't understand," he grumbled. "Why did it take so long? I thought there was something the matter with me."

Bella merely smiled like a cat. "Simple," she grinned. "It just needed my secret formula. I TOLD you," she said knowingly.

"You did?" he looked puzzled.

"Don't tell me you've forgotten already?" and she fished out the black silk from under a pillow, waved it at him and burst out laughing again.

"Sootyyyy," he laughed "you are completely impossible."

"Well at least you know what we've got to do now when you want your next little lion cub," she giggled.

He looked at her sombrely, "If I'm still here," he sighed. "I'm going to have to leave shortly, Sooty. Who knows if I'll ever see you again?" he whispered.

Bella flinched, but resolutely wouldn't think about such a terrible prospect. "Don't start all that again," she muttered. "Come here, you fool. I need a cuddle."

"When is it due?" he asked, pulling her into his arms and tugging the covers over them both.

"Christmas, I think, perhaps just before, maybe the end of November. I'm not sure but it can be your present," she grinned. "The next little Granville is due around then too, so you and Uncle Francis can emigrate together when the pair of them yell the house down," and with that she snuggled up next to him, chuckling to herself as she went back to sleep.

Nicky lay awake for a long while as he continued to absorb it all. He was thrilled and relieved and he smiled to himself like a village idiot. But the niggling premonition was still there at the back of his mind and he was also beyond cross with Bella about what they'd done that evening. He wanted to have a serious talk to her, about that and other things before he returned to Brussels. However, the worry about the Ducal succession had lessened as he convinced himself Bella was carrying his son, so he eventually fell asleep dreaming of a little boy with golden hair; the next Lion of Valenciennes.

The following day they spent as the previous one, but when Terrie for her nap, Nicky disappeared in the early afternoon and Bella finally tracked him down to the cemetery. He was leaning against a tree, chewing on a long piece of grass and staring at his grandmother's ruined mausoleum, sombre-faced. She went up behind him and put a hand on his shoulder, "Are you still troubled, My Love?" she asked softly.

He turned to her, a hard expression on his face and his answer was biting, "Of course I am, there's going to be a battle. A really big confrontation between two really big armies. Tens of thousands of men on both sides, if you can picture that. So face the reality, Bella. I have a very large chance of being wounded, seriously, or probably dying." His eyes glittered into hers. "This isn't going to be a mere skirmish, this is going to be a major, bloody, desperate fight. So much is at stake, the future of France, Europe as well if that megalomaniac wins, perish the thought. It's been a long time coming and thousands and thousands of men, English, French and our Allies, will be cut to death or literally blown to pieces. You have no idea of the carnage of the battlefield, your history books never cover the real details." Then, to her horror he gripped her by both shoulders, "Frankly, My Dear," he said cuttingly, "I'm amazed I'm still alive as it is. Have you any idea what I've been doing since I've been away?"

Bella shook her head, eyes wide at his tone. "You mean you haven't managed to worm it out of Ashcroft or your uncle yet?" he said sarcastically. "Dear me, you're letting your considerable charms slip." Bella gasped at his sarcasm. He pushed her up against the tree trunk and glared down into her face. "I'm a spy," and she gasped. "Yes, that's right, not just an agent for Ashcroft's machinations any more, I'm finally a fully-fledged spy and I report direct to Wellington himself. I've spent the past three months, not fornicating and debauching with women like you obviously assumed, but creeping in and out of various French military camps, picking up gossip, stealing plans, papers and information where I could, wondering every single second if I'd been discovered and was about to be dragged off, tortured and summarily executed." His hands dug into her flesh, "To be honest, my nerves were so shot to pieces, I doubted I could get it up, let alone fornicate with anyone," his words were lewd and brutal and Bella looked on him with dawning horror. "And then what happens?" he asked, almost conversationally. "I finally make it back to Brussels in one piece, so tired I couldn't think or even walk straight, amazed I was still alive, but what was there waiting for me?" He shook her and Bella finally realised he was deeply and coldly angry and she had never, ever, seen him quite like this. Hot, passionate, even frightening anger, yes, but this…this cold, icily cutting man was something else and she didn't recognise him. Yet another facet of his complex character.

"What was waiting for me, Bella?" he shook her again as he answered his own question. "Your little message, that's what. All about a matter of life and death. Do you have the slightest inkling what that did to me? But in the state I was in, I STILL got on my horse and risked my life, yet again, to cross enemy lines to get to Valenciennes, not knowing what was waiting for me. When I finally get here, what do I find? Why, my delightful wife wanting to play perverted bedroom games because she said she's missed me...."

One hand now left her shoulder to wrap itself in her loosely tied-up hair, pulling her head back ruthlessly so Nicky could stare angrily down into her face. "Then, to top it all, she finally deigns to tell me she's expecting another child. A child she knows I want desperately, given the chance it could be the son who is needed to continue the line for sure..." and he paused to take a deep breath.

"Well, what do you make of that, Your Grace?" He didn't give a speechless Bella the chance to say a word. "Have you any idea what I could have done to you last night, You Wanton Bitch? You and your tempting games? You think you know, but you DON'T KNOW what you're playing at. That was the tip of the iceberg of those very particular sexual aberrations and what those inclined to enjoy them actually do. If you witnessed some of it, you wouldn't believe it, I promise you. You could have put our child at risk and for what? Your perverted pleasure? Mine? Is that what you think I like or want?" Anger spewed out of him like a torrent now and Bella could feel the tears rising inside as his words dropped like shards of ice over her. "You have no idea what I like, DO YOU?" as he pulled her hair more forcefully. "It might occur to you to ask me one day now you are so forward. Also, you really don't know what I'm capable of, in and out of the bedroom; DO YOU? You have no experience of men, or what can happen when you wind them up and tempt them too much, push them over the edge; you only know me... and HIM. Didn't your lesson from Bernheim teach you anything?" He took a deep breath. "Why did you do it, Arabella? Really. Tell me why, because I want to understand?"

Finally she got some words out. "I'm... I'm sorry... I'm sorry..."

"Is that all you can say? 'I'm sorry'? Why don't you stop thinking for once and just use your common sense?" he rasped.

"You don't understand," Bella cried brokenly.

"No, I don't," he bit out.

"I'm so sorry. I had no idea what you were doing over here. If I'd been told, I would never have sent a message like that, you have to believe me. You know it was a joke, but it all went wrong." Tears started to roll down her face. "Is it so terrible to want to see someone because you love them so much and you're so frightened about what might happen to them?" she begged.

"You could have come to Brussels, seen me there. It's quite civilised. It's what other wives have done, if they feel THAT impelled to do so. Or perhaps it's only you who can't keep away? Don't you think other wives care very much for their husbands, miss them in their beds, or are frightened for them? It's a good job they all don't want to descend on Brussels or northern France," he said sarcastically. "The whole place would be overrun with them, English, French, Allies alike."

"But I wanted to tell you about the baby," Bella whispered.

"You could have done that easily in Brussels, not here in the middle of the French rear lines. So why didn't you? And why wait? Last evening, were you so desperate for a night like that you couldn't tell me something that was crucially important to me, to us, as soon as I arrived? But then, of course, you wouldn't have got your dirty thrills last night, would you? And we can't have the Duchess of Valenciennes do without all this new perverted, erotic pleasure she's just discovered, oh dear me no..." She could see what they'd done was eating at him and felt him pull her head back further.

"I didn't understand," Bella sobbed. "I wanted to give you something to remember, make me different from other women, stop you going with someone else; it was just a game."

"For God's sake, Arabella," his icy frustration was frightening. "Grow up. I could have hurt you, or the child."

"No, you wouldn't. I know you would never hurt me, I trust you," she cried.

"You stupid, STUPID woman! You've been with Bernheim, seen how he nearly strangled you in his pleasure. Haven't you been listening to me at all? I've just TOLD you, you have absolutely no idea how you can drive a man wild with those sorts of games, what I could have made you do, if I'd got carried away, especially knowing you'd asked for it." He swore then, venomously. "Heaven help me, I can't resist you now, Bella and I'm no angel, as you now realise. But you are

ENCEINTE. For God's sake, what were you THINKING?!" and for the first time in his entire life he premeditatedly slapped a woman, coldly and unemotionally. Bella's mouth dropped open in complete shock as she put a hand to her cheek.

"Now, you listen to me and you listen hard." His face was mere inches from hers as his hand tightened its grip on her hair even more, making her mewl. "This is the last time I am EVER going to tell you. I have NO interest now in going with any other woman. What I did before was another lifetime and I have no intention of playing Ashcroft's games again either. When I tell you to trust me, you trust me. DO. YOU. UNDERSTAND?"

Bella couldn't nod as he had her head in such a tight vice so she whispered, "Yes, Nicky."

"You are NEVER, EVER, going to put at risk any child of ours like you did last night, no matter whether you think the idea is preposterous or not. Do you understand that?"

"Yes," another whispered response.

"When I go back to Brussels, you are going to pack up and return to Francis, Cat, your father and Elise, so they can all look after you, Terrie and the baby you carry. STRAIGHT AWAY. Do you understand me?"

"Yes."

"And finally, understand this as well. That was the first and the very last time I will ever raise my hand to you like that. It disgusts me that I even had to contemplate doing it, but I think it is the only way I will ever get through to you." He breathed deeply again, "Arabella, you will NEVER, EVER get the better of me, order me around, or lie and send me letters or messages like that again. You might think you can now seduce me with your beautiful face, your charming wiles and everything else you've obviously been learning to do from God knows what salacious and depraved sources…with a body that drives me almost beyond reason, but only because I. LET.YOU. Do you understand? Do you now finally see the man I am inside, what I have become? I AM NOT YOUR BIG STEP-BROTHER, the joking fool, or the womanising charmer, unless that is what I want people to see or believe. I am my father's son. I am the Duke, the Lion of Valenciennes."

Bella was stunned, shocked and virtually speechless. She looked up at him, her mouth gaping open. She couldn't believe this was Nicky talking to her like this and she looked at him finally as if she was seeing him for the first time. It was like her Uncle Francis at his most serious and most frightening, something she had rarely, if ever truly seen.

She realised he'd let go of her hair and her shoulder but she was rooted to the spot, still stupefied by everything he had said to her – and how he'd said it..

She stared up into his face, putting her hand to his cheek as he stood there looking down at her impassively. Big, commanding, proud, golden... and ice cold. "You do still love me, don't you?" the uncertainty was there in her voice, "and you do know that everything I do is because I love you, so much, more than anything and everything?"

"Yes, I know that and yes, I do love you, more than I thought I was ever capable of loving anyone. It quite frightens me at times, the feelings you incite in me, but that doesn't change a word of what I've just said," he responded, very slowly and without emotion.

She nodded, a new respect for him dawning in her. "I'm so very, very sorry," she spoke seriously and sank to her knees in front of him, taking one of his hands in hers, kissing it submissively. "Will you forgive me?"

"Get up, Arabella, this minute," he ordered quietly. "I don't want a subservient wife, any more than I want a foolish one either. I just want you to be sensible. We're living in unbelievably strange times with Bonaparte, as well as our own problems with Bernheim. All I'm asking is for you to show some common sense from now on. Do you really understand what I've been trying to say?"

Bella nodded and cringed, shamefaced.

"Very well. Now come, give me a kiss and then go and see what Terrie is up to, then tell Madame Foubert to make some tea. I'll be along shortly."

Bella gave him a hesitant kiss and walked away quietly, leaving him once again leaning against the tree, deep in thought.

Putting aside the interlude with Bella which had distressed him more than she would ever know, but which Nicky knew was necessary if their future relationship was ever to have a sensible foundation, his mind returned again to contemplating his grandparent's mausoleum.

He'd thought about it on and off since he'd returned to Valenciennes the previous year and started the renovations, his mind rolling back to his father's final words to him that last time he'd seen him in the fortress at Rouen when he was a little boy of four. "*Go and see your grandmother in her little house...*" Any other father would surely have hugged and kissed their only child, but seemingly not his, the aloof, icy and proud *Duc de Valenciennes*. Nicky had slowly reached the conclusion the man had been as obsessed with keeping his fortune as Edgar Bernheim had been at stealing it from him. The pair had been both more concerned with money than people. The image of his father standing impassively, watching his wife and child being abused had haunted his mind more and more. He simply couldn't begin to understand the man.

His father's words had taunted and haunted him all his life and as he sauntered over to the little ruined edifice, he thought of them again. He was convinced the *Duc* had been talking about the mausoleum and Nicky was sure some or all of the Valenciennes treasure had been concealed in his grandmother's coffin or sarcophagus. It would have been a good hiding place and surely his father couldn't have foreseen the terrible scenes that would unfold a year or two later on other estates around France, where the homes and anything connected with the hated aristocrats were ransacked, destroyed or confiscated. Nicky stood in the dimness gazing at the open tomb and skeletal remains and wondered if their entirety had somehow covered the fabled gold or treasure from the desperate and vitriolic peasants who had devastated and looted the chateau and its grounds, leaving just a few bones behind and the remains of once rich clothing to rot.

His boots idly kicked the stone flags as he pondered and, like Bella had done a week or so previously, he glanced momentarily at the marks on them, noting how worn and lichened they were. With a final sigh, he turned to stroll out of the cemetery, taking a final look at the snarling black stone lions on the top of the mausoleum before heading back to the house.

Chapter Thirty-Nine

He'd been away three days and Nicky knew he would need to return shortly. Full of his own premonitions, he'd decided to head west and circle around the French lines before going back to Brussels, instead of cutting straight through in the more direct route. He was sick of the work he'd been doing and the few days' respite at Valenciennes had made him realise how exhausted he'd been, both mentally and physically. However, he'd committed himself to Wellington, so would see things through…but, he decided, without putting himself at risk any more than necessary. Therefore, he would set off late the following day and once again travel through the night until he reached the safety of the Allied lines.

It was their last night together and Bella was subdued as she sat and waited in her bed for Nicky. He'd gone to look in on Terrie and, as she knew, was always fascinated with watching the little girl sleep, so presumed he had stayed in her room for a while. Finally, wondering where he'd got to and fearful of the odd mood he'd been in since the afternoon, Bella put on a robe and wandered out, down the long first floor corridor. As she approached Terrie's room, she heard the soft sounds of singing and silently crept up to peer round the slightly open door. Nicky was sitting in an armchair by the window, Terrie dozing in his lap, thumb in her mouth, while he sang to her and stroked her hair. Bella listened to his soft, lilting tenor and her mind instantly went back to Paris the previous summer when she'd first heard him sing; she felt her heart turn over in her chest. He was crooning to the little girl with the same emotion and love as he'd sung in the tavern, lost in the words of the song. Bella suddenly felt a tightness in her throat and tears welled in her eyes. It was too much for her and she couldn't bear to stand there a moment longer, watching and listening to him. Silently, she crept back down the corridor and took herself to bed, the tears now rolling down her face.

He came through to her bedroom and as she stared at him, full of remorse, the air crackled between them. After everything he'd said to her that afternoon, Bella wasn't even sure he would make love to her and she felt heartsick, knowing it was his last night. But silently he stripped off his clothes and got into the bed next to her. "Take off your nightrail, Sooty," Nicky said softly, "you won't need that tonight."

Bella looked at him, apprehension written all over her face, "But...but...you said," she stuttered, "I shouldn't risk the baby."

He looked at her, "I want to make love to you, not fuck you; there is a difference," he said quietly as slowly, he pulled up the thin, plain voile material over her head. She sat like a statue, looking at him, long black hair curling over her shoulders and down her back. Slowly, his eyes feasted down her body, looking at her creamy skin glowing in the candlelight and he leaned forward to gently kiss her neck, his mouth roaming down towards her lush breasts. Her head fell back as the touch of his lips sent tingles down her spine and a soft, incoherent moan drifted from her. He lifted his head from licking and sucking her nipples until they were taut and throbbing, and looked intently into her passion-drugged face. His golden eyes glittered into hers. "I love you, Sooty; never, ever doubt me," and he kissed her. It was a kiss full of desire, passion and deep love. Bella's world tilted off its axis as she was lost in the welter of feelings he always created inside her.

He worshipped her body, loving every inch of it, gently and passionately, until she was mindless and, as she finally climaxed in his arms, weeping quietly with the emotion of it all, he whispered, "THIS is what I want, Sooty; forever, with you. Games are all very well and I can take them or leave them, just as I could fuck anyone, if I had a mind to, which I haven't. Because with you it's different. I love you, that is the difference so I just want to love you and be loved in return. Nothing else."

Carried away on a tide of love, Bella rolled over on top of him and kissed him passionately. "I've always loved you, I always will. I am your Eurydice, except nothing and no-one will keep me from you," she looked into his eyes. "The same goes for the family. You are one of us and we'll never abandon you, no matter where you roam or where your missions take you." She started to sob, "Love me, Nicky. I need you. I need you so much, you're my everything, my master and my Lion," and she wrapped her arms around him as if she would never, ever let him go.

Nicky's arms stole around her, moved by her words. "You heard me sing to Terrie?" he asked softly. "Oh Sooty, My Love, I can't bear the thought of losing you; you'd never abandon me, would you?" He momentarily thought of his father and cursed him to oblivion, with his destructive coldness and obsessional, aristocratic pride.

"Never," she breathed. "I swear, I told you long ago, I'll never let you go," and then he kissed her, a kiss of such longing she started weeping again. "I'm like a watering pot at the moment," she sobbed. "Oh, Nicky," she couldn't speak for emotion, the frightening thought she might never feel him in her arms again after that night overwhelming her.

And so he loved her all night with a sweet, gentle passion that stole her breath away and they finally fell asleep in the breaking dawn, wrapped in each other's arms.

Jack had woken early, his head throbbing from the excesses of the previous evening and had gone in search of some water and some coffee. He spotted and scooped up the little wandering tot as she wended her way down the hallway to find her parents. "Oh no you don't, You Fooffy Little Poozzy Cat," he chuckled as he gathered her in his arms. "I'm sure your Mama and Papa will be sleeping late this morning," he sighed, smiling sadly, aware Nicky was departing later that day and not wanting to disturb their time together. He'd decided to be mature and take charge of the little girl, knowing she was always awake early and he felt pleased, responsible and grown up. But even as he cuddled Terrie in his arms and hurried quietly downstairs to the kitchens to find Madame Foubert and some coffee, he smiled like a naughty schoolboy and whispered conspiratorially in her ear, "Come along with your Uncle Jack, Miss Pickle. I've got another little trick to teach you today, Lizzie too when you next see her. Your Uncle Francis and your Papa are just going to love it and your Mamas won't," he chuckled. "Another secret between just you, Lizzie and me," he whispered and winked at the little girl. "Right?"

Terrie giggled naughtily. "S'right, Un-cul Jack, our speshul sea-crit," and she tapped a little chubby finger on the side of her nose and tried to wink back. "You show me an' I show Lizzie. Ooooh, what we gonna do now? Then Papa an' Un-cul Fran-cissss'll give us ev-ri-fin!" As she cackled in glee, Jack hauled her off to her breakfast, his eyes alight with wickedness.

Bella ran Nicky to earth again that afternoon. He was in the cemetery once more. It was an hour before he was going to leave, Terrie was napping and she was wound up like a spring. "What IS your compulsion with this place?" she asked quietly. "It's so melancholy and some of those tombs are really creepy, especially your grandmother's with just the few bones left in it," she grimaced.

He turned to her, "I don't know. History, destiny, fate...what happened to them all..." he shrugged and looked at her with a glittering light in his eyes. "This is it, Sooty," he spoke slowly. "I'm off shortly. I wonder what MY destiny, my fate, will be?" His eyes turned towards the plaque on the chapel wall.

"NO! You WILL come back to me," Bella exclaimed forcefully.

His head swivelled back to her. "Will I?" A haunted look took over his face. He took her in his arms then, giving her a passionate kiss and suddenly, without a word he pulled her down onto the soft grass under the tree and tossed up her skirts. He ripped open the front of his pantaloons and drove into her hard and obsessively, eyes still glittering into hers, making her cry out, but then he stilled and moved more slowly, each exquisite, searing thrust sliding into her deeply, as far as he could go. He paused each time, lingering, as if he was trying to reach her very soul, his hands gripping hers fiercely. Bella lay beneath him, eyes wide, this final, silent, dramatic episode the culmination of his time with her over the past few days.

It was if he didn't want it to ever end, but finally, a tearing sob was wrung out of her as Bella climaxed and with a heart-wrenching, tormented cry, Nicky lost himself in her for what he truly believed was going to be the last time ever.

Words were beyond them both as they lay there, hearts pounding with the force of their passion until eventually, Nicky pulled himself out of her and stood up, straightening his clothes. He helped her up and silently they made their way back to the house.

They all stood around the front steps of the chateau as Nicky came down to leave, clutching Terrie in his arms. The four guards stood, impassive and silent, peasant caps in their hands. Madame Foubert was quietly weeping into her white apron and Jack was holding his horse ready. With a final tight hug, he kissed his little girl goodbye and with a fond peck on the housekeeper's cheek, he handed Terrie over to her. He turned to Bella who was looking ashen, like a statue.

Bella had often heard the family story of how her Uncle Francis had kissed her Aunt Cat goodbye in the middle of the grand ballroom in St James's Palace, in front of the Royal family and the cream of Society and the Government, before he'd gone off to France for his final confrontation with Edgar Bernheim. The scandal was still tutted over in some quarters, even after twenty-five years, by those with long memories. As Nicky took her in his arms for his final farewell, she wondered if history was repeating itself.

Jack, the housekeeper and the four guards watched in stunned silence. He kissed her as if the world was ending. Deeply, passionately, endlessly, a torrid act of love and despair on the steps of his ancient family home, seeming as though he was eating her alive and her body was a part of his. Finally, breathing raggedly, he dragged himself away as Bella stood with a stunned expression, tottered slightly and went even paler than she had been before.

He strode to his horse and paused in front of Jack who stood, gripping the reins so tightly in an effort to contain himself and not cry, his hands were white. "Take care of her for me, always," Nicky quietly instructed the emotional youth, then kissed him on both cheeks and hugged him.

"I'm a Gentleman now, I would lay down my life for her and for you. I'm your man, always. I will be there for you and your family, no matter what the circumstances. I give you my word, as a Gentleman, and as Jack Vallance, formerly of The Dials, both are my bond." Jack whispered proudly and Nicky smiled at him sadly, patting him on the shoulder. With a final nod and salute at the four guards, who he now knew were ex-soldiers, he leaped on his horse and galloped down the drive.

Jack got to Bella just in time as she swayed momentarily, eyes glazing over, then, for the first time in her life, exactly as her aunt had twenty-five years before, she keeled over in a dead faint.

To Be Continued...

Read on to the fourth part of the story:
FIGHTING LION

As the shadow of war looms once more, the scene is set for a final confrontation between the Duke of Wellington and Napoleon Bonaparte. England vs France, yet again, with the future of Europe at stake.

Nicky is back in the British army, at the heart of things, and an epic battle is inevitable, with all its terrible repercussions for the men who fight. As Francis so sagely warned him, 'keep your head down and don't be in the wrong place at the wrong time...' but will that be possible? A battlefield is a dangerous place...

Read on for a taste of what is coming next:

FIGHTING LION

PREVIEW

Chapter One
WATERLOO – SUMMER 1815

F rancis hadn't been settled since Bella had left for France and he was also deeply concerned about Nicky, worrying in case he was captured by the French. He talked to Ashcroft, seeking some sort of reassurance, but instead, their conversations made him even more twitched; in the end he gave up and decided to go over to Brussels and see what was transpiring there for himself. He also decided he'd haul Bella back to London while he was about it, whether she'd seen Nicky and whether she liked it or not. He was now in no mood for further arguments.

When he told his wife, Cat naturally insisted on going with him; she took no notice whatsoever of his objections, temper tantrums, shouting, pleas, and everything else he threw at her, concerned not only for her safety but also her delicate condition and susceptibility to miscarriage. He gave up eventually, knowing full well if he went without her, she'd only follow him and there was no talking to her when she'd made up her mind about something important.

When Eddie found out, already concerned that his daughter was over on the other side of the Channel with a major conflict looming, in addition to his own concern for Nicky, he announced he was going as well, saying he was still the only one in the family with any sense, in case one or more of them got into trouble, which wouldn't surprise him in the least. Elise said her new husband wasn't going anywhere without her, so all four set off. After considerable difficulty, but not an insurmountable problem for a man with Francis's wealth and influence, they found themselves residing in temporary and somewhat cramped accommodation in Brussels.

A message had been sent to Valenciennes summoning Bella to Brussels and so it was that all the family finally met up early in the second week of June – Bella, Jack and Terrie having travelled with their guards by a circuitous route north and then east along the French coast, away from the military comings and goings, until they had crossed the border into Allied territory.

Brussels was a hive of rumour and activity with diplomats and the Allied military scurrying like ants everywhere, and while Francis and Eddie socialised in those circles and sought word of Bonaparte's movements and Nicky, Bella was welcomed with open arms by her aunt and new stepmother and gave herself up to their loving care. Jack, somewhat at a loose end, helped entertain Terrie during the day as Lizzie had been left in London, and at night investigated the seamier side of the city for his own amusement.

Nicky had been continuing his nefarious activities in and out of the various French encampments and finally galloped back to Wellington's headquarters at the end of the second week of June. A battle was imminent and more serious skirmishes were already taking place. Blücher and his Prussian army were squaring up for a potential engagement against Bonaparte, somewhere south of Brussels. Wellington was concerned that Bonaparte's intention was to attack him from the southwest or west and cut off his supply lines from the Channel coast, but when Nicky was shown into his presence, grubby and dishevelled as ever, he had a different opinion.

"I think it's a feint, false information," he told Wellington baldly. "I know that's what all the intelligence is showing, but I don't like it or agree." He got up to prowl around the small room they were in, "Just call it my weird intuition and some odd comments I overheard... but it's all too pat and Bonaparte, whatever the rumours that he's not quite the man he was, is still a crafty bastard."

Wellington humphed and leaned back in his chair. "Do sit down, for heaven's sake; you're making me worn out watching you patrol up and down like that," he tutted. "So, you're expecting me to accept that you alone disagree with all the other intelligence reports we have that Bonaparte will come at us from the south-west and cut our supply lines...." and as usual he steepled his hands under his chin and regarded Nicky intently.

"That's about it," Nicky sighed. "But you can expect and accept what you like, Your Grace. I can only tell you what I've picked up, surmised and concluded for myself... and what you and your advisors decide with all the other intelligence," he shrugged, "well, it's up to you, and of course it also depends on what Blücher does..."

Wellington sat for a long while, seeming lost in thought while Nicky sat and fidgeted. "You've served me well, de Bresancourt, over the past few months, and I'm not unaware of the considerable risks you've exposed yourself to in bringing intelligence to me, and the game is now afoot, finally." For a moment his eyes gleamed with the challenge, "You've served me and Britain, above and beyond, and you have my grateful thanks; but I want you to stay with me from now on, act as an ADC on my staff. I'll need men to liaise with the other commanders over the next week or two as the fighting heats up until it comes down to him and me, which it will, mark my words," he sat forwards now, "so go and get yourself cleaned up and report back tomorrow first thing. I'm going to discuss our strategy and what Bonaparte's up to with the other commanders and then we'll see."

Nicky stood up and bowed. "Oh, by the way, de Bresancourt," Wellington added as he dismissed the younger man, "I gather some of your family may be here in Brussels. Someone told me they'd bumped into the Duke of Firle a few days ago, asking about you." His smile was slight, "There's a Ball coming up in town in a few days, the Duchess of Richmond y'know. Come along with me as a member of my staff and I'm demmed sure the Duke will have wangled an invitation. You can spend a few hours enjoying yourself there with him and his wife, if he doesn't run you to earth beforehand."

Nicky saluted, smiling as he turned to leave, "He does tend to pop up in the most unexpected places," he sighed, "and we are a close family; thank you, Sir."

"Not at all, he is the damnedest fellow, the Duke," Wellington mused. "Hovering in the background most of the time, like a shadow, but always in the know, a finger in all sorts of things," he shook his head momentarily and therefore missed Nicky's smirk at his unknowing reference to a shadow. "Besides, you deserve a few hours socialising, and it'll put the wind up the French if nothing else, to see us all dancing and enjoying ourselves as if nothing is bothering us at all..." he smiled again to himself, conspiratorially, and nodded as Nicky exited his office.

Nicky went and found himself a quiet corner, wrapped himself in a blanket, and with the knowledge he wouldn't have to go out spying anymore, fell into an exhausted, relieved sleep, despite the to-ing and fro-ing in the camp around him.

By the time he'd got himself cleaned up, back in his proper uniform, and had eaten, he was summoned back on duty but, by dint of asking enough people, he tracked down where the Duke of Firle was staying and sent a message to say he was safely back in Brussels and, assuming it would be just him and Cat, would see them at the Duchess of Richmond's Ball as he would be on duty with Wellington as one of his ADC's.

His note caused consternation in the temporary accommodation of the Duke of Firle. Francis was dispatched instantly to get an invitation as in fact he had not been invited, purely because space was limited, and Charlotte Lennox had not known he was in Brussels. Francis knew Charlotte, the Duchess, well, and it was no difficulty for him to charm her into inviting his family to call in to the Ball, especially when Francis turned his soulful blue eyes on the lady and gave her his most seductive smile as he kissed her hand, explaining his nephew was in Brussels on Wellington's staff and they had come to the city expressly to see him. The woman was complete putty in his hands, and he returned to Cat and the others with a satisfied smirk on his face at the success of his mission.

The three ladies spent the day of the Ball in a panic of preparation, especially Bella who had not brought a ball gown with her. Eddie and

Francis decided to keep well away, but when they all gathered to leave, no one would have known of the frantic activity that had taken place that afternoon and the group of five, Jack deemed not quite old enough to attend, left for the rented house taken by the Duke and Duchess of Richmond. Charles Lennox, the Duke, was in command of a reserve force in Brussels which was protecting the city in case Bonaparte invaded, and the Ball was being held in a converted carriage house at the back of their rented building.

Virtually every senior officer in Wellington's army was there, together with a host of foreign diplomats and dignitaries. There was even a troop of Gordon Highlanders who played the bagpipes and danced reels for the entertainment of the guests. It was a sparkling affair, the pending battle giving the atmosphere a frisson of apprehension and excitement, and the small group waited for Wellington to appear.

Marie-Catherine Granville was still a stunning woman, even as she approached her fifties, with her cat-like green eyes and an abundance of toffee-coloured hair and she looked nothing like her real age. While Francis conversed with diplomats and royalty, Cat was surrounded by a circle of middle-aged gentlemen and officers, keen to engage her in conversation or dance. Eddie and Elise watched quietly from the sidelines, amusing themselves with their overview of the assembled multitude and keeping a watchful eye on Bella. Beautiful as ever with her mother's Spanish looks, she was surrounded by a bevy of young officers but was only watching for one man.

Finally, Wellington arrived. Elegant, calm, impassive, a slight smile on his hawk-like face as he greeted his hosts. His small retinue of staff arrived with him and then Bella spotted Nicky. Lounging nonchalantly against a pillar, obviously looking out for Francis's tall, striking form. Excusing herself from her little court, she crept up behind him and he started as a pair of soft hands crept around his eyes. "Boo! I hope you're going to spare me a dance?"

He knew who it was in an instant; the familiar perfume overwhelming his senses and giving her away, and he turned in amazement and starting anger, "I thought I told you to go home?" he shook his head, torn between delight at seeing her and irritation that she wasn't back in London.

"Ah, but I'm doing exactly what you told me, My Love. I'm safe back in the care of Uncle Francis and Aunt Cat, and Papa and Elise are here too, and I'll go back to London when they do," she smiled satisfactorily at him. "Don't I even get a kiss,

He bowed low over her hand and kissed it, before turning it over to kiss her palm, then her wrist, and several more nibbles up her arm. Bella shivered in reaction as he looked up, "I can't win, can I?" he grinned at her. "Where are they all? I thought it was just Francis here, and possibly Cat?"

Bella laughed. "Well, Uncle Francis got a touch of the 'Bella's', came over to ensure I was all right and duly haul me back, and also to come to Brussels while he was about it and see what you were up to. Auntie did a Ruth and Naomi act, and I gather there were a few china missiles involved in the hostilities at one point, as she insisted on accompanying him. He lost, needless to say." She giggled yet again at the images conjured up of the arguments that apparently went on in Firle House for days. "Papa demanded to come too, to stop anyone doing anything harebrained, so he said, and Elise wouldn't let him go alone, another Ruth scenario, *et voila*," she shrugged Gallicly, like her Aunt, "here we all are, come for an inspection and no doubt Auntie will give Wellington a piece of her mind and threaten to run him through if she thinks he's been mistreating you."

Nicky laughed and hauled her off to waltz round the small dance floor. "I can't believe you're all here," he sighed, "and I hardly ever get a chance to dance with you," he smiled his charming smile, "we really ought to do this more often..."

"Does this mean you're actually going to venture through the hallowed doors of Almack's?" Bella grinned. "My, my, you have reformed if you're happy to settle for such a sedate evening?"

Nicky sighed. "I'm a very respectable, boring married man now," his expression was deadpan but Bella could see his eyes were twinkling, "disreputable thoughts never even cross my mind, so what better place than to spend my evenings? I might even get to like musical soirees too, there's nothing like the sound of a screeching soprano or a violin to pass the time."

"You? Boring?" her eyebrows raised. "You, My Lord Duke, will be exceedingly disreputable til your dying day," laughed Bella, "and when I find you listening to the violin, I'll call in the men from the asylum to carry you off, as I'll know for sure you will have most definitely lost the plot... unless you've gone deaf, of course!"

They danced around the floor for a while longer, jesting and bantering with each other, the air crackling between them until the music finished and they made their way back to Eddie and Elise. Nicky had only just extricated himself from his step-father's embrace when he was grabbed by Cat who, ignoring the proprieties, hauled him into a hug and a torrent of voluble French, asking if he was all right. He laughed, "Oh, hush, Cat," he put a finger across her lips with a smile. "French is a bit sensitive around here at the moment, and I'm just fine," he twirled around, "can't you see, all in one piece, all limbs present and correct and not a mark on them," he grinned, waved his wrists in front of her and winked broadly and she swatted him round the head with her fan as she chuckled.

Francis appeared and slapped him on the back. "Boney's hordes not caught you yet then?" and he smirked. "Thank God for that. I thought I might have to lay out at least ten guineas to ransom you back from their clutches, or come and effect a daring rescue, easier than getting Bubbles out of The Tower... what an exhausting thought." he sighed theatrically.

"So sorry to disappoint you, Francis, I'll try a bit harder next time," he grinned at the older man then looked at them all. "What on earth are you all doing here?" he looked bemused. "I can hardly believe it."

"Well, there was nothing happening in London," drawled Francis. "Lizzie's been consigned to Newgate, Bubbles is in a decline, there's no mice or rats left in Mayfair for Duchess to catch, there was nothing going on socially, the weather was intolerable... so we thought we'd come over to the Continent and annoy you... and Bonaparte of course."

They all burst out laughing at his droll humour and chatted amicably for a while. Francis tugged Cat off to the dance floor and Nicky stood closely behind Bella as they watched them. "They're still a stunning couple, aren't they?" he mused. "You can almost feel the *frisson* between them from here." He could see Francis looking down into Cat's eyes before he leaned in close to whisper something in her ear, making her throw back her head, throaty laughter spilling from her lips as she smiled wickedly back at him.

"Do you think we'll be like that when we're their age?" Bella replied, sighing.

Finally, the unspoken worry surfaced. "Well, you will, Sweetheart. Whether it'll be me smiling down into your eyes is another matter."

Bella swung round to face him. "I don't want to hear another word like that, do you hear me?" she waggled her fan at him. "I had quite enough at Valenciennes, thank you. You're coming back to London when Wellington's done for Boney, and that is final," she huffed.

"Ah, Bossyboots is back, I see," he chuckled. "Well, it's in the lap of the Gods," he sighed, "or as Francis says, not being in the wrong place at the wrong time."

"Then make sure you're not, Nicholas Antoine de Bresancourt, or I'll be exceedingly cross with you!"

"Oh, come and dance with me again, Bossyboots," Nicky chuckled, "let's give the Duke and Duchess of Firle a run for their money and show them what the Duke and Duchess of Valenciennes can manage," and with that he twirled her off to the dancefloor, bowing at Francis and Cat facetiously as they glided and spun past them.

Wellington and the invited guests had gone in for supper, but the little Firle group stayed in the ballroom, and Nicky and Francis took it in turns to dance with Elise de Mornay. Elise had got to know Francis quite well since Cat had turned up in her drawing room one day shortly after the Dowager's funeral and carried her off for tea and to meet her brother. Initially overwhelmed by Francis's reputation and charm when she met him, it didn't take her long to realise his droll wit and dry, occasionally cutting humour hid a clever brain alongside a ruthless determination to succeed in whatever he set out to do, and that he loved Cat and his somewhat wilful and eccentric family to bits. Once they were married, Eddie had sat her down one evening and related to her the whole history of The Shadow and the family secrets, knowing he could trust her never to speak about any of it outside their close circle. Having come to her own opinion about Francis Granville, hearing about his youthful exploits and the family adventures hadn't surprised Elise in the least, and she'd merely burst out into fits of mirth over most of it, especially the story of how he had courted Cat.

However, when Eddie told her about what Bernheim and Dupont had done to him, Francis, and his family, and that his son was now a threat to Nicky and continuing the feud, she fell into a shocked silence. Nicky, however, was something of an unknown quantity to her. She'd heard endless stories about him from the Dowager over the years, and that he was another charming rogue with a facetious sense of humour she had already surmised. However, like Francis, she soon concluded there was a hidden, ruthless and determined part of him as well, and she was looking forward to getting to know better the man her husband had adopted, loved, and cared for, for most of his life, as if he'd been his own flesh and blood.

And so the group amused themselves and they were all laughing over Terrie's latest little outrageous mannerism, with Francis and Nicky accusing each other of being responsible and the ladies tutting over how disgraceful it was all getting, when a sudden hush overran the room and news spread like wildfire that a courier had just arrived for Wellington with urgent and disturbing information.

Nicky hurried into the dining room and returned shortly, his face sombre. "It's started in earnest," he announced to five anxious faces. "Bonaparte's crossed the border at Charleroi. We've just had a message from the Prince of Orange… Ney is attacking us at Quatre Bras and Boney himself is moving against the Prussians over at Ligny," he sighed. "I warned Wellington he was being humbugged," and he shook his head, "but never mind that, we'll all be off shortly…"

The three women gasped and Francis and Eddie looked at each other in consternation. Nicky looked at Francis, "What are you going to do? Stay in Brussels or make for the coast? Calais is nearest, is that where your yacht is? Then head back to Sussex? Just in case…" he tailed off.

"I don't know," said Francis, "it's all a bit sudden." His mind was turning, "But one of the reasons I'm here is I want you to come back with us after it's over. You've done more than enough, so just resign and be done with it, once and for all," he gave Nicky a knowing look. "And, if it was just me, well you know the answer, I don't run from anyone," then he sighed, "but there's the women to consider, and Terrie and Jack, and Benjy insisted on coming as well, you know what a fusspot he is, and Cat and Elise's maids." He paused, tapping his finger to his lips, and looked at Eddie and then back at Nicky, "You don't SERIOUSLY think Wellington will be defeated, do you?" For once Francis looked slightly aghast as he considered the possibility.

"No, I actually think he's capable of taking Bonaparte... and in my opinion, he's the only one amongst the Coalition military commanders who can actually match him... but so many of our veterans are still in America or Canada compared to the French, we need to rely on the Allies, especially the Prussians, so anything could happen," sighed Nicky.

Eddie looked horrified, "No, Nicky, surely not?" he murmured.

"He was defeated in the Peninsula before he finally got a grip. Ney and the other generals are no pussy cats," said Nicky, "it's going to be carnage whatever happens and any mistakes on either side could prove fatal."

"Dear God," this was Elise. "How reliable are the Prussians and the rest of the Allies?"

"They've been fighting Boney for years, off and on," shrugged Nicky, "so they know what they're up against, but most of them are no match for Boney's Marshals, take it from me." He looked at Elise, "I've just spent the past three months in and out of his camps, spying, talking to his officers and men," and everyone except Francis and Bella gasped, "so I know better than most what we're up against," he looked grim, "and believe me when I say I, personally, think it could go either way."

He looked directly again at a grim-faced Francis. "Valenciennes isn't far, you could all go and wait there and then decide. It's far enough away from the town, as you know, deep in the countryside." He then looked round at all the other worried faces, "You're all either French or speak it like natives," he raised a querying eyebrow at Elise, and Eddie spoke for her, "it's not up to Francis's or Bella's standard, but it's coming on, and besides, any sign of trouble and I'm taking her, and Bella, Terrie, and Jack, straight to the coast, or we could go on towards Rouen and my old de Mornay home, and then head off to England from Dieppe; at least the English and the Navy still control the Channel. Francis and Cat can come with, or wait for you, it's their decision, although personally, I think we should all stick together and get as far away from any fighting as possible…"

Nicky looked directly at his step-father and Francis and then his gaze swept all of his family once more, and he spoke in a matter of fact tone. "You've also all got to accept I might not make it through the battle, in which case I have to ask you…" he looked again at Francis and Eddie, "to look after Bella and sort out my Estate, and dispose of Valenciennes if Bella doesn't bear a son this time… you know," he looked meaningfully at both of them and nodded slightly, "we have discussed it before. I've still no idea what the direct line of succession actually means, but it could take lawyers forever to argue once Terrie grows up and marries and has children of her own, and given French politics, who knows what the law will say at the time about aristocratic titles; however, all that aside, this battle will kill thousands on both sides, it's going to be an epic confrontation," he shrugged, "so my life will be in God's hands and that of Fate."

All five people in front of him went ashen and as one, all gasped, "NO!" together.

Bella had already been here and she spoke for them all. "Stop this, Nicky, it's becoming almost wish fulfilment and I WON'T have it!" She stomped her foot, "You ARE coming back, and I am not going anywhere until you do."

Nicky was about to reply when another officer came up and touched him on the shoulder and whispered in his ear. He turned to his family, "I have to go, Wellington needs his staff."

They all looked at him, and then around them, suddenly becoming aware of what was happening. The ballroom was in disarray, women starting to weep, sombre conversations between military men, people in shock, officers packing up, making their farewells to family and loved ones. There were a few people dancing desultorily but a pall hung over the entire proceedings as they almost lurched to a standstill.

Nicky looked at them all in despair. "Here we are again, more farewells..." he held out his arms, "we should be used to this by now," he smiled at them all sadly, "so who's first?"

Elise stepped forward. "I want to get to know you better, so you come home, you hear me? Your FATHER," she emphasised the word, "needs and loves you, and I want to get to love you too, just as the Dowager did. She talked about you to me constantly, so come home, My Dear... and bugger Boney!" she grinned at him and pulled him into a big hug.

Nicky hugged her back and kissed her on both cheeks. "You look after my Papa," he said to her quietly, "he is the best father in the world, you are so blessed to have him, and look after yourself and the new babe."

Eddie stepped forward and hugged him next. "We've been through this before, *Mon Fils*, as you say," he was so choked he could barely speak properly, "just keep your head down and come home, you know how much you mean to me," and a tear plopped on to his scarred cheek.

"Oh, Papa," Nicky looked stricken and wiped the tear away with his finger. "I love you so dearly, you have been the best father I, or anyone, could have wished for, and if I haven't told you that more often, I should have. Take care of yourself, and Charlie, my Bella and your grandchildren," and he kissed him on both cheeks and hugged him back.

Cat was next, mopping her eyes already. She let loose a torrent of passionate, emotional French and kissed him frantically all over his face as he hugged her tight. "If anything happens to you," she threatened, "I'll kill Boney myself, I swear it; but I won't accept you're not coming back to us, I simply won't," and she stamped her foot just as Bella had and burst into a torrent of weeping and Elise put her arms around her as Francis stepped forward and the two big men looked at each other wordlessly for a moment. "They've said everything for me, Little Brother," he whispered, hugging Nicky tight. "Be careful, for God's sake, don't be a dead hero..." and then more loudly, "besides someone has to come back and take responsibility for the disgraceful behaviour of those little girls, and IT IS NOT MY FAULT!" he grinned. "So, just think of me and my poor nerves, I simply will NOT be abandoned to cope with it all by myself." Despite the humour Nicky saw the glisten of tears in his eyes and hugged Francis back and kissed him on both cheeks.

"Don't you accuse me, You Dastardly Smuggler," he grinned back, "I know it was you," and as he kissed him on the cheek one final time he whispered, "I love you, Francis. You are simply the best, my hero and mentor, look after them all for me." And then finally, he turned to Bella.

"You just want me to kiss you again, don't you?" he joked as she stood there looking lost and frightened and trembling from head to foot. "Come here, Sooty," he whispered and held out his arms. "Pray for me, My Love," he murmured as he folded her in a tight embrace and bent his head to kiss her. It was almost painful to watch for the other four, each one of them weeping, even Francis wiped away a surreptitious tear. The kiss was so loving: hungry, soulful and despairing. It went on endlessly and Cat turned into Francis's shirtfront and sobbed copiously as she couldn't watch the heart-rending display in front of her any further.

Nicky finally pulled back, an unreadable expression on his face as he gently pushed Bella into the comforting arms of her father. He addressed them, "Think of me, and pray hard for us all," and with that he turned and strode away, his own eyes full of tears.

It was a sombre, quiet group of five who went back to their lodgings. They found Jack there waiting for them. News of what had happened had percolated to the little select establishment he was enjoying himself in as it was also frequented by a number of the military, and when they had hurriedly left, Jack had done so as well. They sat down disconsolately and, as one, all looked towards Francis who looked back at them and sighed. "I don't like it any more than you," he said, holding out his hands to them, feeling unaccustomedly helpless, "but I think Nicky is right, and Eddie, and I'm not about to risk any of you ladies. We'll pack up and make our way to Calais, then I will come back here and wait for Nicky."

Bella stood up and confronted her Uncle. "Absolutely NOT!" she bit out belligerently. "I quite agree you should all go to safety, but I am not going anywhere. I will wait here in Brussels until I know he's all right."

"NO!" said Francis forcefully. "I expressly forbid it. I promised Nicky I would look after you and I'm damned if you're going to disobey me now."

"Well, that's unfortunate," responded Bella equally determined. "You have NO control over me, I am of age and my own woman. A married woman and a Duchess. He is my husband and I'm waiting here and there is NOTHING you can do about it. And," she pointed a finger at him, "if you try and take me forcefully, I can promise you at the first opportunity I will simply turn tail and come back here... and... I will never forgive you or speak to you again. Are you going to be responsible for splintering our family which is what that means?"

Francis looked furious, Eddie bemused, Jack taken aback and the two other women smirked at the confrontation; the immovable object versus the unstoppable force. Cat knew the situation well, she'd been there enough times herself with Francis so watched with interest.

"I will not have you refuse me, Arabella, nor is it necessary to upset your father and aunt," Francis was now at his most forbidding and forceful self. The great and the good from Government ministers and capable men of business, to villains and pirates, all had quailed before him in this mode, but Bella simply stood her ground and stared back at him.

"I AM refusing you, Uncle, so just accept it," and with that Bella sat herself back down again and started inspecting her nails.

"Bellaaaa..." Francis ground out and Cat tittered behind her fan, making her husband throw her a killing look which only made her smirk more.

"Yes, Uncle?" Bella was all sweetness.

Francis swore venomously and obscenely, not that anyone took the slightest notice, even Elise. "Oh, I give up, and it's no good expecting your father to get any further with you," and he gave Eddie a murderous look which that man simply ignored as he was as entertained as the rest, knowing how obstinate his daughter could be, not that he didn't agree wholeheartedly with Francis. "Is this what Nicky has to put up with?" Francis continued to rage, "He has my sympathies," he muttered direly and gave Bella a look which would wither most people but which only made her laugh out loud. "I should simply drag you off and lock you up somewhere, and ignore your idiotic threats, but some horrible maggot in my brain tells me MY WIFE would simply come after me and rescue you, so I simply am not going to bother..." Cat sat and looked heavenward with an innocent expression on her face which made Bella giggle and her father smirk.

Elise suddenly spoke and everyone turned to look at her in slight astonishment. "If I may make a comment and perhaps a suggestion?" she smiled serenely, calmness itself. "Bella, My Dear, much as I understand your reluctance to leave Brussels, I really don't think Terrie should wait here, for all sorts of reasons," she merely raised an eyebrow, the unspoken message obvious, and then carried on, "so how about we take her and the servants and head over to Valenciennes, as Nicky also suggested, and you can wait here with Francis and continue your congenial discussions." This raised another titter from Cat.

"Oh Elise, that would be the best idea," exclaimed Bella, "you are sooo sensible! All the military are going to be occupied with the battle, so no one is going to bother about us at Valenciennes. It's not far, and way out in the countryside anyway."

Jack piped up next. "Just so you all know, I am NOT going back to Valenciennes," he announced mutinously. "I gave my solemn word to Nicky I would protect Bella, always, and that means if she is staying here in Brussels, so am I. I never break my word, never."

"If my husband thinks he's staying here in Brussels without me to look after him, he's even more delusional than usual," said Cat sarcastically.

Eddie spoke quietly. "I KNEW I did the right thing in insisting I come over here. You definitely need a voice of sanity to keep you all from doing something stupid; so Francis, I've never left you to face an enemy by yourself since I met you, and I'm certainly not going to start now, especially as my daughter is here too, carrying my grandchild."

Francis looked ready to explode. "What have I EVER done to deserve a family like this?" he gritted out, looking as if smoke was about to come out of his ears. "Apart from the fact I feel completely redundant, with a randy schoolboy thinking he can protect my niece better than I, I mean who am I? A mere ineffectual, brainless weakling?" and Cat choked on this comment, trying to keep a straight face, "and YOU!" he turned to Cat, "Assuming, as ever, that I am COMPLETELY incapable of looking after myself..." he was lost for words.

"What does that make me then?" enquired Eddie drolly.

"Away with the fairies," said Francis icily. "You are not the sane one round here, you are completely and utterly unhinged; since when do I need a nursemaid?" Eddie merely gave him a beatific grin in return. Francis almost growled.

"Well, Francis," said Elise sweetly, "it appears you and I are indeed the only sane people here. So, that being the case, I will leave you to be nannied by your family, and I will take Terrie, the maids and Benjy, and your guards, and head over to Valenciennes and make everything ready for you all to join us there when this little... er... fracas... is over."

"Welcome to the family, Elise," smiled Cat. "A little fracas, eh?" she laughed, "I think you fit in perfectly; yes, definitely, you and Francis are a fine pair... and of course he needs nannying, he's a man, isn't he?" and with that, she burst out laughing.

It somehow broke the sombre cloud that had been hanging over everyone and they all burst out laughing with her, except Francis who continued to look at them all venomously, even more so as Jack made some comical side comment to Eddie about his nursemaiding skills, which Francis overheard. "YOU! You Randy Little Bugger, I'll put you over my knee and thrash the living daylights out of you if I hear another comment like that."

"Oh, I don't think so," grinned Jack, now realising the fearsome Duke was, in reality, no such thing as far as his family was concerned.

"WHAAAT?" yelled Francis, now almost beside himself with angry frustration. "Come here, You Cheeky Sod," and he spun round in an instant as his hand shot out to grab Jack.

But the latter was a child of The Dials, and danced away, suddenly producing a dagger which in a flash Francis found at his throat, making him look at Jack in astonishment as the latter whispered in his ear, "Not so much of a schoolboy now, eh, 'Un-cul Fran-sisss'?"

"GOOD GOD!" exclaimed Eddie, flabbergasted at anyone who bested Francis and who was not familiar with some of Jack's unadvertised skills, as Elise's eyes also widened, and Cat and Bella looked at each other and giggled.

"Right. That's it," announced Francis with a theatrically loud and very grumpy sigh. "I know when I'm beaten and should retire." He looked at Cat. "We're off to Bath," he announced. "You can take the waters and get a stick and wear a frilly lace cap, or a hideous turban like those old biddies at Almack's, and I'm going to seek out some pretty young thing to push me around in one of those wheeled chairs with a blanket over my knees."

Cat raised her eyebrow at Francis as Jack pulled back, put his dagger away, and leaned nonchalantly back against the wall with a big smirk on his face. "Oho, and what are you going to do with your chair and a pretty young thing, may I ask?"

Francis gave a wicked laugh, "I said I was going to retire, I didn't say I was past it, My Dear," and he looked speakingly at her slightly swollen belly.

Cat looked back at him her eyes narrowing crossly. "Francis Granville! Behave yourself!" she exclaimed. "I swear you really are getting worse and I absolutely forbid you to teach those girls ANYTHING else, that latest trick of Terrie's is beyond decent," she tutted.

"But I never taught her anything," Francis protested, finally laughing. "I keep telling you, it's Nicky. For heaven's sake, she spent a few days with him a couple of weeks ago, so how could it have anything to do with me?"

"Because we KNOW you," laughed Bella, "and we've been here quite long enough for you to misbehave, you really are shocking, Uncle. I paddled her bottom when I caught her doing it to Papa and asking for a lollipop. I know she's a bit forward for her age but whoever heard of a tot of not even three French kissing a gentleman's palm," she tutted, "and when Lizzie learns it there'll be no stopping her."

Jack was creased up with laughter at all this family banter, but no one thought he was grinning at anything other than the jokes, and he immediately began planning what he would teach the incorrigible little girls next.

"Right, enough of all this," eventually Francis got everyone's attention again as they all calmed down. "Since everyone seems completely disinterested in the monumental battle that is about to take place, and whatever the outcome, it appears we are not to be moving from here, therefore we need to get ourselves organised…"

Chapter Two

And so it was the following morning, as Bonaparte attacked the Prussians at Ligny, Elise set off to Valenciennes with Terrie, accompanied by Benjy, Clara, Cat's long-serving maid, her own maid, and the four guards who had accompanied Bella to France.

The remaining five sat around in their lodgings and waited for news. Bella sat down and started a game of chess with her father, Jack and Francis played cards, and Cat tried to read, but soon gave up and sat and watched her husband being summarily thrashed by Jack, much to her amusement.

The day dragged on and eventually, Francis and Eddie ventured out in search of news. They came back late, sombre-faced. "It's not good. The Prussians have been defeated and Wellington has pulled back his forces, the last I heard he was making for a small hamlet called Waterloo..." he looked at them all, worry etched on his features. "I suggest we all say our prayers before we go to bed..."

The following day was another fraught one and no one could settle. A messenger brought news that everyone had arrived safely at Valenciennes, so all they could do was sit and wait. Again, Francis went out in the early evening in search of news, alone this time, and returned very late, soaking wet. "Wellington has dug himself in at Waterloo," he produced a small map from his pocket which he put on a table so everyone could see. "Other Allied forces are here and here and here, and the French are here and here," his finger moved over the map, "and the Prussians are re-grouping here, around Wavre, as I understand it."

"How did you find all this out," asked Bella and Francis merely tapped his nose and her father just raised an eyebrow.

"However, the weather is simply shocking, it's raining in torrents so the ground will be a quagmire in the morning. I'm not sure what difference that will make, but it will do. We'll just have to wait and see," he sighed. "It will all happen tomorrow," he finally announced, looking at everyone with anxiety written over his face. "This is finally it. It's Wellington versus Bonaparte at long last. Heaven help us all, I just hope Wellington is up to it."

"I want to go to church," announced Bella quietly. "I want to light some candles for Mama and Great Aunt Elizabeth, and ask them to look after Nicky."

None of the family were particularly religious or devout, and Eddie raised an eyebrow at Bella's unexpected announcement. "I'll take her," said Jack softly, "this is a special and strange time. I think we all need to pray for him."

They made their way to St Michael and St Gudula, the City's old cathedral. While Jack sat quietly in a pew, saying his own prayers, Bella did as she'd intended and lit her candles, standing for a long while looking up at the saintly statue above them. She then knelt in prayer in her own pew and when she'd done, they left quietly and made their way back to the lodgings. On the threshold, Jack took her hand in his and gripped it tightly. "He'll come through it," he kissed the hand, "he'll be careful, I'm sure he will, and they will watch over him, your mother and great aunt."

"Oh, but Jack, he had a terrible premonition when he was at Valenciennes, he was convinced he was going to die. You saw him when he left us there, you heard what he said to us the other night..." she gripped Jack's hand and turned to him. "I can't bear it. If he doesn't come back, what shall I do?"

"He WILL come back," Jack muttered. "He has to, pleeease, God," he gazed up at the moonlit sky for a moment, "so don't even think about anything else. Come now, you and the little one need to sleep," he put his arm around her and led her indoors.

The next day was a nightmare for them all. They could hear the guns in the distance, endlessly pounding. Francis and Eddie wandered in and out, seeking news from the battlefield and the whole city was on edge as rumour and news flew around. The Allies were winning, the French were winning, no one seemed to know what was happening. The battle was still raging as dusk fell and there seemed no conclusion. Francis disappeared and left Eddie in charge of the rest of them, just in case. Rumour was now rife that the French had been unable to break through the British defence, the Prussians had re-grouped and after a monumental march from Wavre, had attacked Bonaparte again in the late afternoon, but no one was sure, and gradually, as the hours passed, hope rose that the tide had turned. Finally, very late in the evening, nearing midnight, Francis erupted into the small sitting room. "By God and all that's holy, he's actually done it! The news is that Wellington has won the day!" he exclaimed. "Bonaparte is on the run and his army in retreat," and everyone cheered and hugged each other.

"Nicky?" Bella asked the question they all wanted to.

Francis went over to her, "I don't know, Sweetheart, it's chaos everywhere," he took her by both shoulders and looked into her eyes, "we'll wait til morning, and hopefully he'll send a message."

Later, after they'd all gone to bed, Francis pulled Cat to him, his arms around her, his hands on her belly, like a pair of spoons. Cat put her hands over his and in the darkness asked quietly, "Do you think Nicky is all right, Francis? Please tell me. What do you know that you didn't tell the others?"

Francis sighed. "It's been utter carnage, thousands are dead and wounded, thousands," he shuddered. "French and English and the Allies. I couldn't face telling Bella, it doesn't bear thinking about," he shuddered again, "shocking. I can't even contemplate what it must be like on the battlefield."

Cat turned in his arms, "Oh Francis, do you think he survived?" she cried softly.

"I really don't know," he sighed. "I'm worried sick, but couldn't do anything more tonight, it's dark and chaos and confusion everywhere. I'm off again at first light, I won't sleep anyway. Look, Sweetheart, he was on Wellington's staff, I'll make enquiries there and see what anyone has heard. Please God, he'll send us a message and put our minds at rest," he leaned down to kiss her and her arms stole around him, both needing reassurance from each other.

"You're such a good man," Cat whispered. "Come, let's try and sleep. I pray to God Nicky is sleeping peacefully tonight as well…"

If you want to find out what happens, get your copy of Fighting Lion here and if you've been enjoying the rest of the story, I'd love for you to leave a review for the books and tell others about them.

The Pride of Lions is the second set in the whole **Granville Legacy** series, lots more to come, and don't forget, if you're interested in joining my little group and getting advance reader copies of the books to review as they come out, or to hear about special offers, or read my occasional blog, or get a monthly newsletter, go to my website https://antoinettegeorge.com/ and join my lists. You'll find out about all the rest of the **Granville Legacy** series there, especially the contemporary stories which are being published next, in Spring 2022, starting with *Soldier Banker*, all about Francis Granville's direct descendant,

Marcus Forsyth, and after that is the tale of Nicky's descendant, a Scottish Earl no less....

Thank you so much and... keeeeeep reading!

This is
THE GRANVILLE LEGACY

Coming soon, the full series of The Granville Legacy

18th and 19th century

The life and times of Francis Granville and his friends

Behind The Shadow

Pride of Lions

Publish And Be Damned

To Catch a Thief

21st century

The adventures of Marcus Forsyth, Francis Granville's direct descendant, and his close friends and family.

Soldier Banker

Lions and Feathers

Matilda's Diamonds

Never Left Behind

The Chameleon and The Swan

The Cat's Whiskers

Pins and Noodles

Acknowledgments

Barbara – thank you for your continued enthusiasm and support, endless useful comments on everything, and of course, the editing.

Zivan – thank you for your graphics and covers and grappling with a coat of arms!

Clare – thank you for the formatting and pulling all the content into shape.

www.ingramcontent.com/pod-product-compliance
Lightning Source LLC
Chambersburg PA
CBHW051310250626
47155CB00014B/75